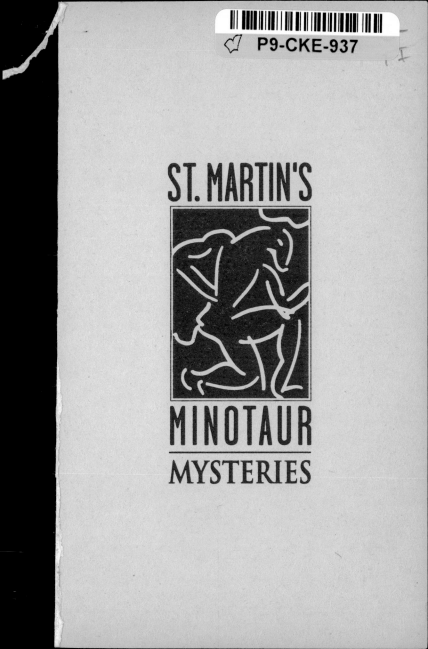

ST. MARTIN'S

MINOTAUR

MYSTERIES

DON'T MISS THESE MYSTERIES IN
STEVEN SAYLOR'S ROMA SUB ROSA SERIES

Catilina's Riddle

Last Seen in Massilia

Roman Blood

Arms of Nemesis

The House of the Vestals

The Venus Throw

A Murder on the Appian Way

Rubicon

AVAILABLE FROM
ST. MARTIN'S/MINOTAUR PAPERBACKS

A MIST OF
PROPHECIES

STEVEN SAYLOR

St. Martin's Paperbacks

A MIST OF PROPHECIES

Copyright © 2002 by Steven Saylor.

Cover art © Scala / Art Resource, NY.

The epigraph on page xiii is from *Aeschylus I: Oresteia*, translated by Richmond Lattimore and published by the University of Chicago Press, copyright ©1953 by the University of Chicago.

Library of Congress Catalog Card Number: 2001058901

ISBN: 0-312-98377-8

Printed in the United States of America

St. Martin's Press hardcover edition / May 2002
St. Martin's Paperbacks edition / May 2003

St. Martin's Paperbacks are published by St. Martin's Press, 175 Fifth Avenue, New York, NY 10010.

10 9 8 7 6 5 4 3 2 1

To Rick Lovin

THE ROMAN MONTHS

Januarius (January, 29 days)
Februarius (February, 28 days)
Martius (March, 31 days)
Aprilis (April, 29 days)
Maius (May, 31 days)
Junius (June, 29 days)
Quinctilis (July, 31 days)
Sextilis (August, 29 days)
September (29 days)
October (31 days)
November (29 days)
December (29 days)

Kalends: the first day of the month
Nones: the fifth or seventh day
Ides: the thirteenth or fifteenth day

CHRONOLOGY

THE STORY OPENS ON 9 AUGUST 48 B.C.
SOME DATES CITED BELOW ARE CONJECTURAL. THE
ENTRIES THAT MENTION CASSANDRA ARE FICTIONAL.

B.C. 82–80   Sulla rules Rome as dictator.

73   The Vestal Fabia is tried for breaking her vow of chastity with Catilina. Spartacus begins the great slave revolt, suppressed the next year.

63   Cicero serves as consul; he suppresses Catilina's conspiracy.

56   April: Marcus Caelius is tried for murder with Cicero defending; Clodia is behind the prosecution.

55   18 November: Milo and Fausta are married.

52   18 January: Clodius is murdered.

April: Milo is tried for the murder of Clodius with Cicero defending, Marc Antony prosecuting; he is convicted and flees to Massilia.

49   11 or 10 January: Caesar crosses the Rubicon.

17 March: Pompey flees across the Adriatic Sea to Greece.

19 May: Cicero's daughter, Tullia, gives birth to a baby, who dies shortly thereafter.

7 June: Cicero leaves Italy to join Pompey in Greece.

2 August: Pompey's forces in Spain surrender to Caesar.

October: Massilia surrenders to Caesar, who pardons all the Roman exiles there except Milo. Caesar returns to Rome to accept the dictatorship for eleven days, expressly to conduct elections; Caelius elected praetor.

November: News of Curio's death in Africa reaches Caesar in Rome.

48   5 January: Caesar crosses the Adriatic Sea.

Late February: Caelius erects his tribunal next to Trebonius and sets off a riot.

Late March: Antony crosses the Adriatic Sea to join Caesar. Caelius sets off a second riot.

April: Pompey and Caesar begin military operations at Dyrrachium. The Senate invokes the Ultimate Decree against Caelius. Milo escapes from Massilia to return to Italy.

17 July: Pompey nearly overruns Caesar's forces at Dyrrachium. Caesar decides to withdraw. The theater of battle moves inland to Thessaly.

5 August (the Nones of Sextilis): Cassandra is murdered.

9 August: Cassandra is buried. Caesar and Pompey engage in battle near the town of Pharsalus in Thessaly.

Cassandra:
Apollo, Apollo!
Lord of the ways, my ruin
You have undone me once again, and utterly.

❦

Chorus:
After the darkness of her speech
I go bewildered in a mist of prophecies.

—Aeschylus, *Agamemnon* 1080–82; 1112–13

I

The last time I saw Cassandra . . .

I was about to say: the last time I saw Cassandra was on the day of her death. But that would be untrue. The last time I saw her—gazed upon her face, ran my fingers over her golden hair, dared to touch her cold cheek—was on her funeral day.

It was I who made all the arrangements. There was no one else to do it. No one else came forward to claim her body.

I call her Cassandra, but that was not her real name, of course. No parents would ever give a child such an accursed name, any more than they would name a baby Medea or Medusa or Cyclops. Nor would any master give such an ill-omened name to a slave. Others called her Cassandra because of the special gift they believed her to possess. Like the original Cassandra, the doomed princess of ancient Troy, it seemed that our Cassandra could foretell the future. Little good that accursed gift did either of the women who bore that name.

She called herself what others called her, Cassandra, saying she could no longer remember her real name or who her parents were or where she came from. Some thought the gods had given her glimpses of the future to compensate for robbing her of the past.

Someone else robbed her of the present. Someone snuffed out the flame that burned inside her and lit her with an inner glow such as I have seen in no other mortal. Someone murdered Cassandra.

As I said, it fell to me to make the funeral arrangements. No outraged friend or lover, no grieving parent or sibling came forward to claim her. The young man who had been her sole companion, the mute she called Rupa—bodyguard, servant, relative, lover?—vanished when she was murdered.

For three days her body rested on a bier in the foyer of my house on the Palatine Hill. The embalmers clothed her in white and surrounded her with pine branches to scent the air. Her killer had done nothing to destroy Cassandra's beauty; it was poison that killed her. Drained of color, Cassandra's smooth cheeks and tender lips took on a waxen, opalescent quality, as if she were carved from translucent white marble. The hair that framed her face looked like hammered gold, cold and hard to the touch.

By day, illuminated by sunbeams that poured through the atrium skylight, she looked no more alive than a white marble statue. But each night, while the rest of the household slept, I stole from my wife's bed and crept to the foyer to gaze at Cassandra's body. There were times—strange moments such as occur only in the middle of the night, when the mind is weary and flickering lamplight plays tricks on an old man's eyes—when it seemed hardly possible that the body on the bier could be truly dead. The lamplight infused Cassandra's face with a warm glow. Her hair shimmered with highlights of red and yellow. It seemed that at any moment she might open her eyes and part her lips to draw a quickening breath. Once I even dared to touch my lips to hers, but I drew back with a shudder, for they were as cold and unresponsive as the lips of a statue.

I placed a black wreath on my door. Such wreaths are a warning in one sense, alerting others to the presence of death in the household, but in another sense they issue an invitation: come, pay your final respects. But not a single visitor came to view Cassandra's body. Not even one of those compulsive gossips came to pester us, the type who make the rounds of the city looking for wreaths and knocking on doors of people they've never met, just to have a look at the latest corpse so they can deliver an opinion on the embalmers' handiwork. I alone mourned Cassandra.

Perhaps, I thought, death and funerals had become too commonplace in Rome for the passing of a single woman of unknown family, commonly thought to be as mad as—well, as mad as Cassandra—to excite any interest. The whole world was swept up in a civil war that dwarfed all other conflicts in the history of the world. Warriors were dying by the hundreds and thousands on land and on sea. Despairing wives were wasting into oblivion. Ruined debtors were found hanging from rafters. Greedy speculators were stabbed in their sleep. All was ruin, and the future promised only more death and suffering on a scale never known before by humankind. Beautiful Cassandra, who'd haunted the streets of Rome uttering shrill, crazy prophecies, was dead—and no one cared enough to come and see her body.

And yet, someone had cared enough to murder her.

When the period of mourning was done, I summoned the strongest of my household slaves to lift the bier onto their shoulders. The members of my household formed the funeral cortege, except for my three-year-old grandson, Aulus, and my wife, Bethesda, who had been ill for quite some time and was not well enough to go out that day. In her place my daughter, Diana, walked beside me, and beside her walked her husband, Davus. Behind us walked my son Eco and his wife, Menenia, and their golden-headed twins, now old enough, at eleven, to understand the somber nature of the occasion. Hieronymus the Massilian, who had been residing in my house since his arrival in Rome the previous year, also came; he had suffered much in his life and had known the pain of being outcast, so I think he felt a natural bond of sympathy with Cassandra. My household slaves, few in number, followed, among them the brothers Androcles and Mopsus, who were not quite as old as Eco's children. For once, sensing the gravity of the occasion, they behaved themselves.

So that all would be done fittingly, I hired three musicians to lead the procession. They played a mournful dirge, one blowing a horn and another a flute, while the third shook a bronze rattle. My neighbors in their stately houses on the Palatine heard them coming from a distance and either closed their shutters, irritated at the noise, or opened them, curious to have a look at the funeral party.

After the musicians came the hired mourners. I settled for four, the most I could afford considering the state of my finances, even though they worked cheaply. I suppose there was no shortage of women in Rome who could draw upon their own tragedies to produce tears for a woman they had never known. These four had worked together on previous occasions and performed with admirable professionalism. They shivered and wept, shuffled and staggered but never collided, pulled at their tangled hair, and took turns chanting the refrain of the playwright Naevius's famous epitaph: " 'If the death of any mortal saddens hearts immortal, the gods above must weep at this woman's death. . . .' "

Next came the mime. I had debated whether to hire one, but in the end it seemed proper. I had been told he came from Alexandria and was the best man in Rome for this sort of thing. He wore a mask with feminine features, a blond wig, and a blue tunica such as Cassandra wore. I myself had coached him on mimicking Cassandra's gait and mannerisms. For the most part his gestures were too broad and generic, but every so often, whether by accident or design, he struck an attitude that epitomized Cassandra to an uncanny degree and sent a shiver through me.

Funeral mimes are usually allowed a great deal of latitude to caricature and gently lampoon their subject, but I had forbidden this; it is one thing to sketch a loving parody of a deceased patriarch or a public figure, but too little was known about Cassandra's life to offer fodder for humor. Still, the mime could not offer a portrait of her without imitating the one thing that everyone would recall about her: her fits of prophecy. Every so often, he suddenly convulsed and spun about, then threw back his head and let out a strange, unnerving ululation. It was not an exact imitation of the real thing, only a suggestion—not even remotely as frightening or un-

canny as the real Cassandra's episodes of possession by the
god—but it was close enough to cause any bystanders who
had ever seen Cassandra prophesy in the Forum or in a public
market to nod and say to themselves, *So* that's *who's lying
upon that funeral bier*. Directly after the mime came Cassandra herself, carried aloft and ensconced amid fresh flowers and
evergreen boughs, her arms crossed over her chest and her
eyes closed as if she slept. After Cassandra came the members
of my household, marching in solemn procession for a woman
none of them but myself had actually known.

We strode slowly past the great houses on the Palatine and
then down into the region of the Subura, where the narrow
streets teemed with life. Even in these impious days, when
men scorn the gods and the gods scorn us in return, people
pay their respects when a funeral passes by. They stopped
squabbling or gossiping or bargaining, shut their mouths, and
stood aside to let the dead and the mourning pass.

Often, as a funeral cortege makes its way through Rome,
others join the retinue, inspired to pay their respects by following along behind the family and adding to the train. This
invariably happens with the funerals of the famous and powerful, and often even with those of the humble, if they were
well-known and well liked in the community. But on that day,
no one joined us. Whenever I looked over my shoulder, I saw
only a gap behind the last of our retinue, and then the crowd
closing ranks behind us, turning their attention away from the
passing spectacle and getting back to their business.

And yet, we were observed, and we were followed—as I
soon would discover.

At length, we came to the Esquiline Gate. Passing through
its portals, we stepped from the city of the living into the city
of the dead. Sprawling over the gently sloping hillsides, as far
as the eye could see, was the public necropolis of Rome. Here
the unmarked graves of slaves and the modest tombs of common citizens were crowded close together. Ours was not the
only funeral that day. Here and there, plumes of smoke from
funeral pyres rose into the air, scenting the necropolis with the
smells of burning wood and flesh.

A little way off the road, atop a small hill, the pyre for Cassandra had already been prepared. While her bier was being laid upon it and the keepers of the flame set about stoking the fire, I stepped into the Temple of Venus Libitina, where the registry of deaths is kept.

The clerk who attended me was officious and sullen from the moment he slammed his record book onto the counter that separated us. I told him I wanted to register a death. He opened the hinged wooden diptych with its inlaid wax tablets and took up his stylus.

"Citizen, slave, or foreigner?" he asked curtly.

"I'm not sure."

"Not sure?" He looked at me as if I had entered the temple with the specific intention of wasting his time.

"I didn't really know her. No one seems to have known her."

"Not part of your household?"

"No. I'm only attending to her funeral because—"

"A foreigner then, visiting the city?"

"I'm not sure."

He slammed shut his record book and brandished his stylus at me. "Then go away and don't come back until you *are* sure."

I reached across the counter and grabbed the front of his tunic in my fist. "She died four days ago, here in Rome, and you *will* enter her death into the registry."

The clerk blanched. "Certainly," he squeaked.

It was only as I gradually released him that I realized how hard I had been clutching his tunic. His face was red, and it took him a moment to catch his breath. He made a show of reasserting his dignity, straightening his tunic, and slicking back his hair. With great punctiliousness, he opened his register and pressed his stylus to the wax. "Name of the deceased?" he asked, his voice breaking. He coughed to clear his throat.

"I'm not sure," I said.

His mouth twitched. He bit his tongue. He kept his eyes on

the register. "Nevertheless, I have to put down something for a name."

"Put down Cassandra, then."

"Very well." He pressed the letters crisply into the hard wax. "Her place of origin?"

"I told you, I don't know."

He clicked his tongue. "But I have to put *something*. If she was a Roman citizen, I have to know her family name; and if she was married, her husband's name. If she was a foreigner, I have to know where she came from. If she was a slave—"

"Then write, 'Origin unknown.'"

He opened his mouth to speak then thought better of it. "Highly irregular," he muttered, as he wrote what I told him. "I don't suppose you know the date of her birth?"

I glowered at him.

"I see. 'Birthdate unknown,' then. And the date of her death? Four days ago, you said?"

"Yes. She died on the Nones of Sextilis."

"And the cause of her death?"

"Poison," I said, through gritted teeth. "She was poisoned."

"I see," he said, showing no emotion and hurriedly scribbling. "With a name like Cassandra," he said under his breath, "you might think she'd have seen it coming. And what is *your* name? I have to have it to complete the record."

I felt another impulse to strike him, but resisted. "Gordianus, called the Finder."

"Very well, then. There, I've written the entry just as you wished. 'Name of deceased: Cassandra. Family and status unknown. Birthdate unknown. Death by poison on the Nones of Sextilis, Year of Rome 706. Reported by Gordianus, called the Finder.' Does that satisfy you, citizen?"

I said nothing and walked away, toward the pillars that flanked the entrance. Behind me I heard him mutter, "Finder, eh? Perhaps he should find out who poisoned her. . . ."

I walked down the temple steps and back toward the funeral pyre, staring at the ground, seeing nothing. I felt the heat of the fire as I drew closer; and when I finally lifted my eyes, I beheld Cassandra amid the flames. Her bier had been tilted upright so that the funeral party could view the final moments of her physical existence. The musicians quickened their tempo from a mournful dirge to a shrill lament. The hired mourners dropped to their knees, pounded their fists against the earth, screamed and wailed.

A gust of wind suddenly whipped the flames higher. The roar of the fire was punctuated with loud cracking and popping and sizzling noises. While I watched, the flames gradually consumed her, frizzling her hair, withering and charring her flesh, turning everything black, destroying her beauty forever. The wind blew smoke in my eyes, stinging them, filling them with tears. I tried to look away—I wanted to look away—but I couldn't. Even this awful spectacle constituted one more moment, one final chance to look upon Cassandra.

I reached into my toga and pulled out a short baton made of leather. It had belonged to Cassandra; it was the only one of her possessions that still existed. I clutched it in my fist for a moment, then hurled it into the flames.

I felt Diana's presence beside me, then the touch of her hand on my arm. "Papa, look."

I finally tore my eyes from the funeral pyre. I looked blankly at my daughter's face. Her eyes—so beloved, so vibrantly alive—met mine, then turned elsewhere. I followed her gaze. We were no longer alone. Others had come to witness Cassandra's end. They must have arrived while I was in the temple or staring at the flames. The separate groups stood well away from the fire, scattered in a semicircle behind us. There were seven entourages in all. I looked at each in turn, hardly able to believe what I was seeing.

Seven of the wealthiest, most powerful, most remarkable women in Rome had come to the necropolis to see Cassandra burn. They had not joined in the public funeral procession, yet here they were, each woman seated in a litter surrounded by her own retinue of relatives, bodyguards, and litter bearers, not one of them acknowledging the presence of any of the others, all keeping their distance from ourselves and from each other, each gazing steadily straight ahead at the funeral pyre.

I took stock of them, looking from left to right.

First, there was Terentia, the pious, always proper wife of Cicero. With her husband off in Greece to side with Pompey in the civil war, Terentia was said to be hard-pressed to make ends meet, and in fact her litter was the most modest. The draperies that surrounded the box were no longer white but shabby gray, with tatters here and there. But her litter was also the largest, and squinting, I made out two other women in the litter with her. One was her daughter, Tullia, the apple of Cicero's eye. The other was farther back in the shadows, but from her distinctive clothing and headdress, I saw she was a Vestal Virgin. No doubt it was Fabia, Terentia's sister, who in younger days had very nearly met her end for breaking her sacred vow of chastity.

In the next litter I saw Antonia, the cousin and wife of Marc Antony, Caesar's right-hand man. While Caesar had been off fighting his enemies in Spain, Antony had been left in charge of Italy. Now both men had departed for northern Greece to do battle with Pompey. Antonia was said to be a very attractive woman. I had never formally met her and might not have recognized her except for the bronze lions' heads that surmounted the upright supports at each corner of her litter. The lion's head was Antony's symbol.

Her presence was all the more remarkable because of the woman whose litter was next in the semicircle. Anyone in Rome would have recognized that gaudy green box decorated with pink-and-gold tassels, for Cytheris, the actress, always made a show of her comings and goings. She was Antony's lover, and he had made no secret of that fact while he ruled Rome in Caesar's absence, traveling all over Italy with her. People called her his understudy-wife. Cytheris was famous for her beauty, though I myself had never seen her close enough to get a good look. Those who had seen her perform in mime shows for her former master, Volumnius the banker, said she was talented as well, able by the subtlest gestures and expressions to evoke a whole range of responses in her audience—lust not least among them. She and Antonia cast not a single glance in each other's direction, apparently oblivious of one another.

I looked to the next litter, which was draped in shades of deepest blue and black suitable for mourning, and recognized Fulvia, the twice-widowed. She had been married first to Clodius, the radical politician and rabble-rouser. After his murder four years ago on the Appian Way and the chaos that followed—the beginning of the end of the Republic, it seemed in retrospect—Fulvia had eventually remarried, joining her fortunes to Caesar's beloved young lieutenant, Gaius Curio. Only a few months ago, word had arrived from Africa of Curio's disastrous end; his head had become a trophy for King Juba. Some called Fulvia the unluckiest woman in Rome, but having met her, I knew her to possess an indomitable spirit. Seated with her in her litter was her mother, Sempronia, from whom Fulvia had inherited that spirit.

As I moved my eyes to the occupant of the next litter, the incongruities multiplied. There, reclining amid mounds of cushions in a typically voluptuous pose, was Fausta, the notoriously promiscuous daughter of the dictator Sulla. Thirty years after his death, the dictator's brief, blood-soaked reign still haunted Rome. (Some predicted that whoever triumphed in the current struggle, Caesar or Pompey, would follow Sulla's merciless example and line the Forum with the heads of his enemies.) Sulla's ghost haunted the Forum, but Sulla's daughter was said to haunt the more dissolute gatherings in the city. Fausta was still married, though in name only, to the banished gang leader Milo, the one political exile whom Caesar had pointedly excluded from the generous pardons he'd issued before leaving Rome. Milo's unforgivable crime had been the murder four years ago of his hated rival Clodius on the Appian Way. According to the court, it was Fausta's husband who had made a widow (for the first time) of Fulvia. Were the two women aware of one another's presence? If they were, they gave no more indication of it than did Antonia and Cytheris. At that moment Milo was very much on everyone's mind, for he had escaped from exile and was said to be raising an insurrection in the countryside. What did Fausta know about that? Why was she here at Cassandra's funeral?

Next to Fausta's litter, surrounded by the largest retinue of bodyguards, was a resplendent canopy with ivory poles and white draperies that shimmered with golden threads, hemmed with a purple stripe. It was the litter of great Caesar's wife, Calpurnia. Now that Marc Antony had left Rome to fight alongside Caesar, many thought it was Calpurnia who functioned as the eyes and ears of her husband in his absence. Caesar had married her ten years ago, purely for political advantage some said, because in Calpurnia he had found a woman to match his own ambition. She was said to be an uncommonly hardheaded woman with no time for superstition. Why had she come to witness the funeral of a mad seeress?

One litter remained, a little farther off than all the others. When my eyes fell on it, my heart skipped a beat. Its occupant couldn't be seen, except for a finger that parted the closed drapes just enough for her to see out. But I knew that litter, with its red-and-white stripes, all too well. Eight years ago its occupant had been one of the most public women in Rome, notorious for her flamboyance and high spirits. Then she had dragged her estranged young lover into the courts and made the grave mistake of crossing Cicero. The result had been a disastrous public humiliation from which she had never recovered. Then her brother (some said lover) Clodius met his end on the Appian Way, and her spirit seemed to have been snuffed out altogether. She had retreated into a seclusion so complete that some thought she must be dead. She was the one woman in Rome—before Cassandra—who had threatened to break my heart. What was Clodia—beautiful, enigmatic Clodia, once the most dangerous woman in Rome, now all but forgotten—doing there that day, lurking incognito amid the litters of the other women?

I gazed from litter to litter, my head spinning. To see these particular women all gathered in one place at one time was more than remarkable; it was astounding. And yet, there they all were, their various litters scattered before the burning pyre like the pavilions of contending armies arrayed on a field of battle. Terentia, Antonia, Cytheris, Fulvia, Fausta, Calpurnia, and Clodia—the funeral of Cassandra had brought them all together. Why had they come? To mourn Cassandra? To curse her? To gloat? The distance made it impossible to read the expressions on their faces.

Beside me, Diana crossed her arms and took on the hard, shrewd look so familiar to me from her mother. "It must have been one of them," she said. "You know it must have been one of those women who murdered her."

I felt a chill, despite the heat of the flames. I blinked at a sudden swirl of smoke and cinders and turned to look again at the burning pyre. The fire had consumed yet more of Cassandra, had taken another portion of her away from me, and I had missed it. I opened my eyes wide despite the burning smoke. I stared at the blackened remains upon the upright bier reduced now to a bed of glowing coals. The musicians played their shrill lament. The mourners raised their cry to heaven.

How long I stared at the flames, I don't know. But when I finally turned to look behind me again, all seven of the women with their litters and their entourages had vanished as if they had never been there.

II

The last time I saw Cassandra—truly saw her, looked into her eyes and beheld not just her mortal shell but the spirit that dwelled within—was on the day of her death.

It was shortly after noon on the Nones of Sextilis, a market day, or what passed for a market day in Rome in those times of shortage and mad inflation. Bethesda felt well enough to go out that day. I went along as well, as did Diana. My son-in-law, Davus, accompanied us. In those uncertain days, it was always wise to bring along a big, hulking fellow like Davus to play bodyguard.

We were on a quest for radishes. Bethesda, who had been ill for some time, had decided that radishes, and radishes only, would cure her.

We made our way from my house on the Palatine down to the market on the far side of the Capitoline, not far from the Tiber. We walked from vendor to vendor, searching in vain for a radish that would satisfy Bethesda's discriminating gaze. This one was pitted with black spots. That one was too elongated and soft. Another had a face on it (leaves for hair, straggling roots for a beard) that looked like a dishonest cobbler with whom Bethesda had once had a row. To be sure, none of these radishes looked particularly appetizing to me, either. Despite the best efforts of the magistrates put in place by Caesar before his departure, the economy was in constant turmoil, with no end in sight. I make no claim to understand the intricacies of the Roman economy—production of food, transport to market, borrowing against future crops, the care and feeding of slaves and the cost of replacing runaways (a particular problem these days), the constant, grinding tug of war between creditors and debtors—but I do know this much: A war that splits the whole world in two results in a paucity of radishes fit to eat.

I suggested that Bethesda might look for carrots instead— I had seen one or two of those that looked edible—but she insisted that the soup she had in mind would allow no substitutions. Since this was a medicinal soup, meant more for her recovery than for my nourishment, I kept my mouth shut. A vague, lingering malady had been plaguing Bethesda for months. While I doubted that any soup would rid her of it, I had no better cure to suggest.

So the four of us strolled from vendor to vendor, searching for radishes. It was just as well that we weren't looking for olives, since the only ones to be had were selling for the price of pearls. Moldy bread was easier to find, but not much cheaper.

Behind me I heard Davus's stomach growl. He was a big fellow. He required more food than any two normal men to fill his belly, and in recent days he hadn't been getting it. His face had grown lean, and his waist was like a boy's. Diana made a fuss over him and fretted that he would dry up and blow away, but I suggested we needn't worry about that as long as Davus still had legs like tree trunks and shoulders like the arch of an aqueduct.

"Eureka!" Bethesda suddenly cried, echoing the famous exclamation of the mathematician Archimedes, although I doubt she had ever heard of him. I hurried to her side. Sure enough, she held in her hands a truly admirable bunch of radishes— firm and red, with crisp, green leaves and long, trailing roots. "How much?" she cried, startling the vendor with her vehemence.

He quickly recovered himself and smiled broadly, sensing a motivated buyer. The price he named was astronomical.

"That's robbery!" I snapped.

"But look how fine they are," he insisted, reaching out to caress the radishes in Bethesda's hands as if they were made of solid gold. "You can still see the good Etruscan earth on them. And smell them! That's the smell of hot Etruscan sunshine."

"They're just radishes," I protested.

"*Just* radishes? I challenge you, citizen, to find another bunch of radishes in all this market to match them. Go ahead! Go and look. I'll wait." He snatched the radishes back from Bethesda.

"I can't afford it," I said. "I won't pay it."

"Then someone else will," said the vendor, enjoying his advantage. "I'm not budging on the price. These are the finest radishes you'll find anywhere in Rome, and you'll pay what I ask or do without."

"Perhaps," said Bethesda, her dark brows drawn together, "perhaps I could manage with just two radishes. Or perhaps only one. Yes, one would do, I'm sure. I imagine we can afford one, can't we, Husband?"

I looked into her brown eyes and felt a pang of guilt. Bethesda had been my wife for more than twenty years. Before that she had been my concubine; she was practically a child when I acquired her in Alexandria, back in the days of my footloose youth. Her beauty and her aloofness—oh yes, she had been very aloof, despite the fact that she was a slave—had driven me wild with passion. Later she bore my daughter, the only child of my loins, Diana; that was when I manumitted and married her, and Bethesda settled into the role of a Roman matriarch. That role had not always been a comfortable fit—a slave born in Alexandria to an Egyptian mother and a Jewish father did not easily take to Roman ways—but she had never embarrassed me, never betrayed me, never given me cause for regret. We had stood beside one another through many hardships and some very real dangers, and through times of ease and joy as well. If we had become a little estranged in recent months, I told myself it was merely due to the strain of the times. The whole world was coming apart at the seams. In some families a son had taken up arms against his own father, or a wife had left her husband to side with her brothers. If in our household the silences between Bethesda and me had grown longer, or the occasional petty arguments sharper, what of it? In a world where a man could no longer afford a radish, tempers grew short.

It didn't help, of course, that we were constantly confronted with the contrasting example of our daughter and her muscle-bound husband. They, too, had begun life in unequal stations—Diana born free, Davus a slave—and the gulf between Diana's sharp wits and Davus's simplicity had struck me from the first as unbridgeable. But the two of them were inseparable, constantly touching, forever cooing endearments to each other, even as they approached the fourth year of their marriage. Nor was their attraction purely physical. Often, when I came upon the two of them in my house, I found them deep in earnest conversation. What did they find to talk about? Probably the state of her parents' marriage, I thought. . . .

But the guilt I felt came from more than long silences and petty squabbles. It came from more than the very major row we had had after my return to Rome from Massilia the previous autumn, bringing a new mouth to feed—my friend Hieronymus—and the news that I had disowned my adopted son Meto. That announcement very nearly tore the whole household apart, but over time the shock and grief had lessened. No, the guilt I felt had nothing to do with household matters or family relations. I felt guilty because of Cassandra, of course.

And now Bethesda, who complained of feeling unwell every day, who seemed to be in the grip of some malady no doctor could diagnose, had taken it into her head that she must have radishes—and her wretched husband was trapped between a greedy vendor and his own guilty conscience.

"I shall buy you more than one radish, Wife," I said quietly. "I shall buy you the whole bunch of them. Davus, you're carrying the moneybag. Hand it to Diana so that she can pay the man."

Diana took the bag from Davus, loosened the drawstrings,

and slowly reached inside, frowning. "Papa, are you sure? It's so much."

"Of course I'm sure. Pay the scoundrel!"

The vendor was ecstatic as Diana counted the coins and dropped them into his hand. He relinquished the radishes. Bethesda, clutching them to her breast, gave me a look to melt my heart. The smile on her face, such a rare sight in recent days, made her look twenty years younger—no, younger than that, like a gratified and trusting child. Then a shadow crossed her face, the smile faded, and I knew that she suddenly felt unwell.

I touched her arm and spoke into her ear. "Shall we go home now, Wife?"

Just then, there was a commotion from another part of the market—the clanging of metal on metal, the rattle of objects spilled onto paving stones, the crash of pottery breaking. A man yelled. A woman shrieked, "It's her! The madwoman!"

I turned about to see Cassandra staggering toward me. Her blue tunica was torn at the neck and pulled awry. Her golden hair was wild and unkempt. There was a crazed expression on her face. That was how she often looked, especially during a fit of prophecy—but when her eyes met mine, I saw in them a look of utter panic, and my blood turned cold.

She ran to me, her arms reaching forward, her gait uneven. "Gordianus, help me!" she cried. Her voice was hoarse and strained. She fell into my arms. Beside me, Bethesda gave a start and dropped her radishes. Cassandra fell to her knees, pulling me down with her.

"Cassandra!" I gasped. I lowered my voice to a whisper. "If this is some pretense—"

She clutched my arms and cried out. Her body convulsed.

Diana knelt beside me. "Papa, what's wrong with her?"

"I don't know."

"It's the god in her," said Bethesda from above and behind me, her voice tinged with awe. "The same god that compels her prophecies must be tearing her apart inside."

A crowd gathered around us, pressing in from all sides. "Draw back, all of you!" I shouted. Cassandra clutched at me

again, but her grip was weakening. Her eyelids flickered and
drooped. She moved her lips, but no sound came out.

"Cassandra, what's wrong? What's happened?" I whispered.

"Poison," she said. Her voice was failing. I could barely
hear her above the hubbub of the crowd. "She's poisoned me!"

"Who? What did she give you?" Our faces were so close
that I felt her shallow breath on my lips. Her eyes seemed
huge, her blue irises eclipsed by the enormous blackness of
her pupils.

"Something—in the drink . . ." she said. I could barely hear
her.

She convulsed again, then was still. I felt a last, long exhalation against my lips, strangely cold. The fingers clutching
my arms relaxed. Her eyes remained open, but the life went
out of them.

The crowd pressed in. Diana was knocked against me and
gave a squeal. Davus bellowed at the onlookers to back away,
brandishing his fists at those who didn't move quickly. As they
dispersed, I heard snatches of excited conversation:

"Did you see that? She died in the old man's arms!"

"Cassandra—that's what people called her."

"I heard she was a war widow. Went crazy with grief."

"No, no, no! She was a Briton, from way up north. They're
all crazy. Paint themselves blue."

"She didn't look blue to me! Rather beautiful, in fact . . ."

"I heard she was a Vestal who broke her vows and got
herself buried alive. Managed to claw her way out of the grave
but ended up raving mad."

"Nonsense! You'll believe anything."

"All I know is, she could see the future."

"Could she? I wonder if she saw *that* coming?"

I swallowed hard. I wanted to press my lips against Cassandra's, but I felt the eyes of my wife and daughter on me.
I turned to Diana, kneeling beside me. What must my face
have looked like for my daughter to gaze back at me with
such pity and puzzlement? I peered up at Bethesda. For a long

moment, she registered no emotion—then suddenly raised her eyebrows in alarm.

"The radishes!" she cried, slapping her hands to her face. In all the commotion, someone had stolen them.

III

The first time I saw Cassandra was in the Forum. It was a day in mid-Januarius. When I count the months on my fingers, I realize that from the first day I saw her to the last, not quite seven months passed. So brief a period! Yet in some ways it seems I knew her for a lifetime.

I can place the date precisely, because that was the day word reached Rome that Caesar had successfully crossed the Adriatic Sea from Brundisium to the coast of northern Greece. For days, all Rome had been holding its breath to learn the outcome of that bold gambit. The gray-bearded, self-styled sages who passed their days gossiping and arguing in the Forum all agreed, whether they favored Caesar or Pompey, that Caesar was mad to attempt a naval crossing in winter, and madder still to attempt such a thing when everyone knew that Pompey had the superior fleet and ruled the Adriatic. A sudden storm could send Caesar and all his soldiers to the bottom of the sea in a matter of minutes. Or, in clear weather, Caesar's fleet was likely to be outmaneuvered by Pompey's and destroyed before they could reach the other side. Yet Caesar, having settled affairs in Rome to his liking, was determined to carry the battle to Pompey, and to do that he had to convey his troops across the water.

All through the previous year, from the day he crossed the Rubicon and drove Pompey in a panic out of Italy, Caesar had campaigned to secure his mastery of the West—mustering troops from his stronghold in Gaul; destroying the Pompeian forces in Spain; laying siege to the seaport of Massilia, whose inhabitants had sided with Pompey; and arranging to have himself declared temporary dictator so as to set up magistrates of his choosing in Rome. Meanwhile, Pompey, driven in confusion and disarray from Rome, had been biding his time across the water in Greece, insisting that he and his fellow exiles constituted the true government of Rome, compelling Eastern potentates to send him massive contributions of money and vast numbers of troops, and building up a huge navy that he stationed in the Adriatic with the express purpose of keeping Caesar in Italy until Pompey was ready to face him.

At the outset of that fateful year, which of these rivals found himself in the stronger position? That question was argued endlessly by those of us who frequented the Forum in those uncertain days. We sat under the weak winter sun on the steps of the treasury (plundered by Caesar to pay for his troops) or, as on that particular day, we found a spot outside the wind near the Temple of Vesta and discussed the issues of the day. I suppose I must say "us" and "we," including myself in that group of tireless chinwaggers, although I opened my mouth less frequently than most. Mostly I listened, and thought what a useless lot of know-nothings we all were, too old or frail or crippled to have been compelled to take up arms by either side, and not rich enough to have been extorted by either side to hand over gold or gladiators to their cause. Overlooked by the warlords, we spent our days idling in the Forum, expounding our opinions on the latest rumors, arguing and insulting one another, gnashing our teeth while we helplessly waited for the world we had known all our lives to come to an end.

"What does it matter if Caesar's won the West, when all the wealth of Asia and the grain of Egypt are at Pompey's disposal?" This came from a mild-mannered fellow called Manlius, who seemed equally distressed at the impending destruction of either side in the conflict. Manlius hated violence. "I don't see why Caesar's so eager to make the crossing. He'll only be stepping into the trap Pompey's laid for him. The slaughter will be horrific!"

"Why is Caesar eager to cross? That's plain enough. Once it comes to a head-on confrontation, sword against sword, Caesar's got the clear advantage." So declared one-armed Canininus who, if his tales of combat were true, had more fighting experience than the rest of us combined; he had lost his right arm fighting for Caesar in Gaul and had received a generous retirement from his grateful imperator. "Caesar's men are battle-hardened from constant fighting. Years and years spent conquering the Gauls, then the march on Rome, then the mad chase down to Brundisium—Pompey barely slipped out of that noose!—and most recently, that little foray in Spain to put an end to Caesar's enemies there."

"And don't forget the siege of Massilia!" This came from my friend Hieronymus, a Massilian of Greek descent and the only one of the group who was not a Roman citizen. The others suffered his presence partly because I was his patron, but also because they were a little in awe of him. A cruel fate had led to his selection by the priests of Massilia to serve as the city's scapegoat during the siege by Caesar. It had been his role to take on the sins of the whole city, and at some critical juncture, by his death, to save the city from destruction. Massilia had indeed been spared from destruction, but a strange twist of fortune had spared Hieronymus from his fate, and he had ended up in Rome living in my house. Hieronymus was tall and physically striking, with a curious demeanor. Having begun life as the heir of one of Massilia's more powerful families, but having spent most of his life as a beggar, he combined the haughtiness of a fallen aristocrat with the crafty pragmatism of a streetwise survivor. He often played referee in our little group, since he favored neither Caesar nor Pompey.

Caninius snorted. "The siege of Massilia! I'd already forgotten about it. Massilia was nothing more than a pimple on Gaul's butt! Caesar simply dispatched Trebonius to pop it open before it could fester."

Hieronymus raised an eyebrow. How he had despised his

native city while he lived and very nearly died there! Since he had left Massilia, I never once heard him express a sentimental longing for the place. Still, it rankled him to hear a Roman express contempt for the city of his Greek forefathers.

"If 'squeezing the pimple' of Massilia, as you put it, was such a smallish thing," he said dryly, in slightly stilted Latin, "then why did Caesar reward Trebonius by making him city praetor for the year and charge him with enforcing Caesar's own plan to shore up the Roman economy? Such an important task is handed by a man like Caesar only to one who has shown his true mettle. I think that Caesar must have rated the taking of Massilia a far more important achievement than you do, my friend."

"In the first place," snapped Canininus, "Caesar didn't 'make' Trebonius city praetor, the voters did."

This met with catcalls from the Pompeians in the group. "Nonsense!" said the most vocal of them, Volcatius, who had a surprisingly strong voice for such an old man. "The only voters left in Rome are the common rabble, who'll cast their lots however Caesar tells them to. Pompey and all the Best People ran for their lives when Caesar crossed the Rubicon— except for those who couldn't bear the journey, like myself. How can any so-called election held under such circumstances constitute a true vote of the people? The last elections were a farce and a scandal, a mime show put on for the sole purpose of putting Caesar's handpicked men in office. The whole process was an illegal and illegitimate—"

"Oh, please, Volcatius, not all this again!" groaned Canininus. "You'll still be whining about the last elections when it comes time to hold the next."

"If the next round is as corrupt and meaningless as the last, I won't keep silent!"

"Corrupt, maybe"—Canininus shrugged and smirked— "but hardly meaningless. The fact of the matter is that Rome has a government in place, and that government is running the city, whether you like it or not. Get used to it and move on!" Canininus laughed spitefully, along with some of the more vehement of the Caesarian faction. "But back to the point I was trying to make before we became distracted by politics: Caesar holds the military advantage because his men are primed and ready to fight."

Mild-mannered Manlius, who had started the whole exchange, objected. "You say Caesar's men are battle-hardened, but aren't they battle-weary as well? Some of them staged a revolt while Caesar was on the way back from Spain—"

"Yes, and Caesar promptly put the ringleaders to death and rallied the rest to his side," said Canininus. "He knows how to handle a mutiny; he's a born leader of men. You, Manlius, never having been a soldier, wouldn't understand such things."

"But Pompey's had almost a year to catch his breath and gather his forces," observed Manlius, ignoring Canininus's insults. "They'll be fresh and unscathed. There must be some advantage in that."

"They'll be soft from all that idle waiting, if you ask me," said Canininus.

"But what about Pompey's superior numbers?" said Manlius. "Above and beyond his Roman legions, they say Pompey's gathered hundreds of archers from Crete and Syria, slingers from Thessaly, thousands of cavalrymen from Alexandria—"

"We know about Pompey's forces only from rumors. People always inflate the actual numbers," said Canininus.

"But Pompey's fleet isn't a rumor," observed Hieronymus. "Surely that's real. People have seen galleys sailing into the Adriatic Sea for months, hundreds of them arriving from all over the eastern Mediterranean. Battle-hardened or battle-weary makes no difference if Caesar can't get his men across to the other side."

"His timing could hardly be worse," observed Volcatius the Pompeian, smiling grimly. "Winter's arrived. Boreas can blow a storm from the north and whip the Adriatic into a seething caldron before a ship's captain has time to utter a prayer to Neptune. They say Caesar consulted the auguries before he left Rome, and all signs boded against him. Birds were seen flying north instead of south, and a sparrow attacked a vulture—bad omens! But Caesar hushed up the augurs before his troops could hear about them and raise another mutiny."

"That's a lie," said Caninius, "a blasphemous lie!" He lurched toward Volcatius, but some of the others held him back. Hieronymus raised an eyebrow at the spectacle of a truculent, one-armed Roman attempting to physically attack the oldest graybeard in the group.

All this time I said nothing. In the contest between Pompey and Caesar, I had so far managed to keep myself neutral—more or less. Like virtually every other Roman citizen, especially those who played any part whatsoever in the city's public life, I had strong ties to both sides. If anything, my loyalties and animosities were more conflicted and tortuously intertwined than most because of the sort of work I had done all my life—playing the hound for advocates like Cicero, digging up the truth about powerful and not-so-powerful men accused of everything from deflowering a Vestal Virgin to murdering their own fathers. I had met and had dealings with both Pompey and Caesar, as well as many of their confederates. I had seen them at their best and their worst. The idea that Rome's fate must inevitably fall into the hands of one or the other—that either Caesar or Pompey would ultimately become a king or something very close to it—filled me with dread. I attached no sentimentality to the old way of doing things, to the doddering, mean-spirited, greedy, frequently stupid maneuverings of the Roman Senate and the unruly republic over which they presided. But of one thing I was certain: Roman citizens were not born to serve a king—at least, not Roman citizens of my generation. The men of the younger generation seemed to have other ideas. . . .

My thoughts had led me, as they often did in those days, to Meto.

It was for Meto that I had gone to Massilia the previous year, seeking news of my adopted son's fate; an anonymous message had informed me of his death in that city while spying for Caesar. How Meto loved Caesar, whom he had served for many years in Gaul! Having been born a slave, Meto could never become an officer like Caesar's other lieutenants, but he had become indispensable to his imperator nonetheless, serving him as a private secretary, transcribing his memoirs, sharing his quarters—sharing his bed, some said. In Massilia, I had found Meto alive, after all; but the play of events had so disgusted me that I turned my back on Meto, and on Caesar. I had spoken words that could never be taken back. I had publicly disowned Meto and declared that he was no longer my son.

Where was Meto now? Since that fateful parting in Massilia, I had heard no news of him. I assumed that he remained by Caesar's side, that he had returned with him to Rome, then followed him to Brundisium for the attempted crossing of the Adriatic. Where was Meto at that very moment? For all I knew, he might be at the bottom of the sea along with Caesar himself. As a boy, when I first met him in the coastal town of Baiae, Meto couldn't swim. At some point he must have learned—to please Caesar?—because swimming had saved his life in Massilia. But not even the strongest swimmer could hope to survive if his ship foundered in the middle of the Adriatic. I imagined Meto in the water, wounded, frightened, bravely attempting to stay afloat even while the waves closed over his head and cold, salty water filled his lungs. . . .

Hieronymus gave me a nudge. I looked past the skirmish between Caninius and Volcatius and saw two of my slaves on the far side of the Forum, heading our way. Little Androcles was in the lead, but his older brother, Mopsus, was running to catch up with him. From the heated competition between them, I knew they must be on a mission of some importance. I felt a tremor of intuition. A god must have whispered in my ear, as the poet says, for I knew they must be bringing news of that which was uppermost in my thoughts.

Caninius and Volcatius, abruptly separated, each went about reasserting his dignity. Like mirror images, they straightened their tunics and threw back their chins. The gap between them afforded a space for Mopsus, now in the lead, to enter the group, followed by Androcles. Everyone knew the boys, for they frequently tagged along with me when I visited the Forum. Everyone liked them. Volcatius patted Androcles on the head. Caninius made a mock salute to Mopsus. Slightly out of breath from running, Mopsus struck his chest and saluted back.

"What brings you here, boys?" I said, trying to ignore the sudden fluttering in my chest.

"News of Caesar!" said Mopsus. His eyes lit up when he spoke the imperator's name. Recently, Mopsus had decided that Caesar was his hero. His little brother, to be contrary, had become a confirmed Pompeian. Caninius and Volcatius aligned with them accordingly, playfully treating each boys as either an ally or a foe.

"What news?" I said.

"He's made the crossing! He reached the other side safely, along with almost all his men!" said Mopsus.

"But not *all* of them! There was *trouble*," said Androcles darkly.

I drew a breath. "Mopsus, where did you hear this news?"

"A messenger arrived at the Capena Gate an hour ago. I spotted him right away, and I remembered he was one of Calpurnia's slaves."

"And Calpurnia is Caesar's wife!" added Androcles needlessly.

"And I decided to follow him—"

"*We* decided!" insisted Androcles.

"And sure enough, he headed straight to Caesar's house. We stayed out of sight and watched him knock on the door. The slave who answered made a great show of patting her bosom and almost fainting, and she said, 'Tell me straight out, before we bother the mistress, have you come with good news or bad?' And the messenger said, 'Good news! Caesar made the crossing, and he's safe on the other side!' "

I let out a sigh of relief and blinked away sudden tears. The surge of emotion caught me by surprise. I coughed and managed to speak despite the catch in my throat. "But, Androcles, you said something about trouble?"

"And there was!" He addressed himself as much to Volcatius as to me, drawn by the glimmer of hope in his fellow Pompeian's rheumy eyes. "When Caesar reached the other side, it was the middle of the night; and right away he un-loaded his troops and sent the ships back to Brundisium to pick up the rest of his men, including the cavalry. But some of those ships were waylaid and separated from the rest by some of Pompey's ships, and Pompey's men set fire to them and burned them right there on the water, with the captains and the crews still on board! They were burned alive; or if they managed to jump off, Pompey's men killed them in the water, spearing them like fish."

"Burned alive at sea!" gasped Manlius. "A horrible fate!"

"How many?" asked Volcatius eagerly. The news of Caesar's successful crossing had visibly shaken him, but now he rallied at the prospect of a setback to Caesar.

"Thirty! Thirty ships were captured by the Pompeians and burned," said Androcles proudly.

"Only thirty!" scoffed his older brother. "Hardly any considering the size of Caesar's fleet. His cavalry still managed to make it across. They just had to crowd more men and horses onto each ship, and some of the men had to sit on horseback the whole way. A good thing they had clear weather—that's what the messenger said."

"Thirty ships lost," I muttered, imagining the agony of those thirty captains and thirty crews. Could Meto possibly have been among them? Surely not. He was a soldier, not a sailor. He would have been by Caesar's side, safe on the farther shore. In any case, of what concern was Meto's fate to me?

Suddenly, all around us in the Forum, there was a sense of movement and occasion. I caught glimpses of messengers running across nearby squares. In the distance I saw a group of men gather before the steps leading up to the Temple of Castor and Pollux to listen to an elderly senator in a toga who had something to tell them—from such a distance, I could hear only a vague echo of his voice. From a house somewhere up on the Palatine—probably not far from my own house, from the sound—I heard a loud cheer and the banging of cymbals. A moment later a citizen came running by, shouting, "Have you heard? Caesar's landed! He made the crossing! Pompey's done for now!" The news was spreading across the city as rapidly as voices could carry it.

Then I heard another sound, jarringly out of place amid the swelling hubbub of excited male voices in the Forum. It came from nearby, from the little open square in front of the Temple of Vesta. It was a woman, wailing and shrieking.

From the sounds she made, I thought she was being attacked. I stepped away from the group and circled around the temple until I saw her, kneeling on the paving stones at the foot of the temple steps. The others followed me.

When he saw her, Caninius sneered. "Oh, it's only *her!*"

I stared at the woman in wonder. There was something unnatural about the way she rolled her shoulders and swung her head in a circle. She held her arms aloft, her palms raised to heaven. Her eyes were rolled upward. The wailing I had heard was actually a sort of incantation. As I listened, I began to hear words amid the grunts and shrieks.

"Caesar—Pompey—it comes to this!" she cried. And then, after a long keening moan: "Like vultures they circle over the carcass of Rome—eager to pick the bones clean—wheeling and wheeling until they collide!"

"Who is she, Caninius?" I said.

"How in Hades should I know?" he snapped. "I only know she's been haunting the Forum for the last few days, begging for alms. She seems normal enough, but every now and then, this happens—she goes into a sort of trance and shouts nonsense."

"But who is she? Where did she come from?"

I looked at the others. Manlius shrugged. Volcatius raised a bristling white eyebrow. "I haven't a clue—but she's certainly a tasty-looking morsel!"

I looked back at the woman. She had risen to her feet, but her blue tunica had become tangled at her knees, pulling down the neckline to reveal the cleavage of her breasts. No woman in her right mind would display herself so immodestly in the Forum, and certainly not before the Temple of Vesta. She shook her head back and forth, whipping the air with her unpinned blond tresses.

"She's called Cassandra," said Mopsus.

Why had I even bothered to ask the other graybeards, when Mopsus was present? "Is there anything that goes on in Rome that you *don't* know, young man?"

He crossed his arms and grinned. "Not much. Cassandra— that's what they call her on account of the way she can see the future. I heard some slaves at the butcher's market talking about her just this morning."

"And what else do you know about her?"

"Well . . ." He was momentarily stumped, then brightened. "She's very pretty."

"And if she's Roman, she must not be married, or else she'd be wearing a stola instead of a tunica," observed Androcles. His older brother looked chagrined at having missed this deduction.

As we watched, the woman suddenly went limp and collapsed. I was on the verge of going to help her when I saw a figure descending the steps of the temple. It was one of the Vestals, dressed in the traditional costume of the sisterhood that tends the sacred hearth fire of the Roman state. She wore a plain white stola and a white linen mantle about her shoulders. Her hair was cut short, and around her forehead she wore a white band decorated with ribbons. I caught a glimpse of her face and recognized Fabia, the sister-in-law of Cicero. She was quickly followed by two younger Vestals.

The three of them gathered around the prostrate form of the woman called Cassandra. They put their heads together and conferred in low voices. Cassandra stirred and rose to her knees, using her arms to steady herself. She looked dazed. She seemed hardly to notice the Vestals as the three of them helped her to her feet. I could see that Fabia was speaking to her, apparently asking her questions, but Cassandra made no reply. She blinked like a woman waking from a deep slumber and seemed finally to register the presence of the three women surrounding her. She straightened her tunica and her disarrayed hair with awkward, halting movements.

Taking her by the elbows and gently guiding her, talking

to her in low voices, the three Vestals led her up the steps and into the Temple of Vesta.

"Well!" said Canininus. "What do you make of that?"

"Perhaps the old virgin wants to ask the young madwoman what it's like to take a man," said Volcatius, leering. "I'll bet that one's had more than her share of men between her legs!"

"Who knows what women talk about when there aren't any men around?" said Manlius.

"Who cares?" said Canininus. "Now that Caesar's about to give Pompey a good thrashing . . ."

And with that, the conversation turned away from the madwoman, for now, at last, there was the fresh news of Caesar's crossing to give us men something to talk about.

ॐ

Later that day, at the evening meal, I happened to mention the incident of the madwoman. The family was gathered in the dining room. Shutters were drawn to keep out the cold air from the garden at the center of the house, and a brazier had been lit to heat the room. Bethesda and I shared a couch. Davus and Diana, having already put little Aulus to bed, shared the one to our left. Hieronymus reclined alone on the couch to our right.

"Yes, yes, the woman called Cassandra," said Bethesda, putting down her bowl of chickpea soup and nodding. This was before her malady set in, when her appetite was still strong. The soup smelled strongly of black pepper. "I've seen her down in the marketplace."

"Have you? How long has she been about?"

Bethesda shrugged. "Not long. Perhaps a month."

"Have you seen her experience one of these fits?"

"Oh, yes. A bit unnerving the first time you see it. After it passes, she doesn't seem to know what's happened. She gradually comes to her senses and carries on with whatever she was doing before. Begging for alms, usually."

"No one helps her?"

"What's to be done? Some people are frightened by her

and move away. Others want to hear what she says and move closer. They say she utters prophecies when she's like that, but I can't make sense of the noises she makes."

"Why didn't you ever mention her to me?"

"What possible interest could you have in such a wretched woman, Husband?" asked Bethesda, lifting her bowl of soup to take another sip.

"But where does she come from? Has she no family? How long has she been experiencing these spells?"

"If you were to ask after every odd character who wanders about the markets nowadays begging for scraps, you should find yourself very busy indeed, Husband. These are hard times. Maimed soldiers, widows, farmers, and shopkeepers who've lost everything to greedy creditors—there's no end to the beggars and vagrants. Cassandra's just one more."

"Mother's right," said Diana. "Sometimes you see whole families wandering about with no place to go, especially down by the river. You feel sorry for them, of course, but what can anyone do? And some of them are dangerous. They *look* dangerous, anyway. That's why I always take Davus along when we go to the markets."

"Victims of the war," I said, shaking my head. "It was the same when I was your age, Diana, during the first civil war. Refugees from the countryside, runaway slaves, orphans running wild in the streets. Of course, things got even worse *after* the war." I was remembering Sulla's bloody dictatorship and the heads of his enemies mounted on spikes all over the Forum. "Who named this woman Cassandra, anyway?" I asked, wanting to change the subject.

"Some wag in the market, I imagine," said Bethesda.

"People give nicknames to the more colorful characters," noted Davus. "There's one they call Cerberus because he barks like a dog; a fellow they call Cyclops because he's got only one eye; and a woman they called the Gorgon because she's so ugly."

"She's not *that* ugly," objected Diana.

"Oh, yes she is," insisted Davus. "She's as ugly as Cassandra is beautiful."

"And there are even those," said Diana, raising an eyebrow but snuggling closer to him, "who call a certain fellow 'mighty Hercules' behind his back."

"No!" said Davus.

"Oh, yes, Husband. I've heard them: admiring women; envious men." She smiled and reached up to squeeze one of his bulging biceps. Davus blushed and assumed a particularly stupid expression.

I cleared my throat. "The original Cassandra was a Trojan princess, as I recall."

"Indeed she was," said Hieronymus, ready to assert his authority on the subject. As a boy he had received a fine Greek education at one of the renowned academies for which Massilia was famous. He could recite long passages from the *Iliad* and knew many of the Greek tragedies by heart.

"Cassandra was the fairest daughter of King Priam and Queen Hecuba," he said, "and she was the sister of Paris, the prince who started all the trouble by stealing Helen and carrying her back to Troy. Cassandra could foretell the future. That was her terrible curse."

"But why call it a curse?" asked Diana. "I should think that knowing the future would be rather useful. I could tell whether or not I'd be able to find anything decent to buy at the markets, instead of trekking down there only to come back empty-handed."

"Ah, but you see, there's the rub," said Hieronymus. "Knowing the future doesn't mean that you can alter it. Suppose in the morning you had a vision of yourself down at the markets later that afternoon finding not a thing to buy. You'd still be destined to make that trip down to the market, only now you'd know ahead of time that you were doomed to accomplish nothing."

"And that would be doubly frustrating," acknowledged Diana.

Hieronymus nodded. "Foreknowledge is a curse. Imagine knowing the circumstances of your own death, as Cassandra did, and being able to do nothing about it."

Davus frowned. "Imagine knowing ahead of time your

greatest joys as well. Wouldn't that spoil them? Everyone loves a good surprise, even small surprises. When someone tells you a story, you don't want to guess the ending beforehand. You want to be surprised." Every now and then Davus said something to make me seriously doubt that he was as simple as he looked. "But how did the Trojan Cassandra come to have this gift, or curse?" he said. "Was she born with it?"

"No, but she had it from a very early age," said Hieronymus. "When she was only a small child, her parents left her alone in the sanctuary of Apollo at a place called Thymbra, near Troy. When Priam and Hecuba returned, they found Cassandra entwined by two serpents flicking their tongues in the child's ears. Afterward, Cassandra was able to understand the divine sounds of nature, especially the voices of birds, which told her of the future. But the child kept this gift to herself, not trusting it and uncertain of how to use it. When she grew older, she returned on her own to Thymbra and spent a night alone in the sanctuary, hoping for guidance from Apollo.

"The god appeared to her in human form. Cassandra was beautiful. Apollo wanted her. He made a deal with her: in return for his instruction, Cassandra would allow him to make love to her, and she would bear him a child. Cassandra agreed. Apollo was as good as his word. That night he initiated her into the arts of prophecy. But afterward, when he moved to touch her, she resisted. When he embraced her, she struggled and fought against him. Who knows why? Perhaps he overawed her. Perhaps she feared the agony of giving birth to a demigod. Apollo was insulted. He grew furious. Cassandra was afraid he would strip her of the gift of prophecy, but he did something far worse: he ordained that no one should ever believe her prophecies.

"Poor Cassandra! As one calamity after another befell Troy, she saw them all coming and tried to warn her loved ones, but no one would listen to her. King Priam thought she was mad and locked her away. Perhaps in the end she truly was mad, tormented to distraction by the curse Apollo had put upon her.

"Of course, everyone knows about the end of Troy—by the

stratagem of hiding in a giant horse the Greeks gained access to the city and then torched it, killing the men and taking the women into slavery. During the sack of the city, Cassandra fled to the sanctuary of Athena and embraced the statue of the goddess as a suppliant. Little good that did her; Athena had no sympathy for any Trojan. Ajax broke into the temple and dragged Cassandra from the statue, tearing her fingers from the cold marble. He raped her there in the sanctuary.

"But it was Agamemnon, asserting his privilege as leader of the Greeks, who claimed Cassandra as his booty. Mad or not, she was the most beautiful of Priam's daughters, and Agamemnon wanted her. He had the audacity to bring her home with him and flaunt her in the face of his wife, Clytaemnestra, who was outraged. While Agamemnon and Cassandra slept, Clytaemnestra stabbed them both.

"Cassandra foresaw her own death, of course, but she was powerless to do anything about it. Or perhaps, by that point in her miserable life, she welcomed her end and did nothing to stop Clytaemnestra. Ultimately, it was the god she blamed for her woes. In his play about Agamemnon, Aeschylus gives us Cassandra's lament: 'Apollo, Apollo, Lord of the ways, my ruin.' "

Poor Cassandra, I thought, first punished for preserving her chastity from a god, then made the concubine of the man who killed her family. Was the Cassandra I had seen that day yet another woman victimized by men's war and gods' cruelty? What misfortune had driven her mad? Or was she not mad at all, but cursed, like the original Cassandra, and truly able to perceive the future?

If I were to ask her, what could she tell me about my fate and the fates of those I loved? And if I were to hear her answers, would I regret having asked?

IV

The day after Cassandra's funeral, I spent the morning alone in the garden. The day was hot and the sky cloudless. I sat on a folding chair, wearing a broad-brimmed hat and watching my shadow recede until the sun was directly overhead.

Bethesda felt unwell and was spending the morning in bed. Every now and again I heard the sound of her gentle snoring from the unshuttered bedroom window that opened onto the garden. Diana and Davus had gone out to do the day's marketing. They had given up on finding radishes and were in search of fennel, which Bethesda was now certain would cure her. Hieronymus had gone down to the Tiber to fish, taking Mopsus and Androcles with him. No one had asked if I wanted to go along with them; they all sensed that I wished to be left alone.

At length I heard Diana's voice. She and Davus were back. I saw her hurry along the portico to the back of the house and step into the bedroom to look in on her mother. A little later she came to the garden and sat beside me.

"Mother's asleep. We should keep our voices low. I couldn't find any fennel, but can you believe it—there were radishes everywhere! So many they were practically giving them away. By Juno, it's hot out here! Papa, you shouldn't be sitting in the sunlight."

"Why not? I'm wearing a hat."

"Has it kept that brain of yours from overheating?"

"What do you mean by that?"

She paused and assumed an expression she had inherited from her mother, a look at once pitying and presumptuous. She might as well have said aloud: *I know exactly how your sluggish, tortuous thought processes play out, dear Papa. I'm well ahead of you, but I'm resolved to be patient. I shall wait for you to catch up to your own inevitable decision.*

Instead, she said, "You've been thinking about her all morning, haven't you?"

I sighed and readjusted my bottom on the folding chair, which was suddenly uncomfortable. "Your mother isn't well. Of course she's in my thoughts—"

"Don't be coy, Papa." My daughter's voice assumed a stern edge. "You know what I meant. You've been thinking about *her*. About that woman, Cassandra."

I took a deep breath. I stared at a sunflower across the way. "Perhaps."

"You're brooding."

"Yes."

"You must stop it. We need you, Papa. It's getting harder every day just to get by, and Mother's ill, and Davus does all he can to help, but still, sometimes I don't know what we're going to do. . . ." Her voice became grave, but there was no self-pity in it. Always hardheaded, always practical and forward thinking and resourceful, never despairing, that was Diana. She was truly our child, the inheritor of what was best in both Bethesda and myself.

"What are you saying to me, Daughter?"

"I'm saying that you must leave her behind. She's dead now. You must stop thinking about her. It's your family who need you now." Her tone was not reproachful, merely matter-of-fact. How much, exactly, did she know about Cassandra and me? What did she know for a fact, and how much had she guessed, rightly or wrongly?

"Leave her behind, you say. Supposing that you're right, that I'm sitting here brooding about . . . that woman . . . how do you suggest I stop brooding, Daughter?"

"You know the answer to that, Papa! There's only one way. You must find out who killed her."

I gazed long and hard at the sunflower. "What good will that do?"

"Oh, Papa, you sound so hopeless. I hate to see you like this. It's bad enough that Mother's ill, but for you to be sick as well—sick at heart, I mean—and you've been this way ever since you came back from Massilia. We all know why. It's because of what happened between you and—"

I raised my hand to silence her. As a Roman paterfamilias, with the legal power of life and death over every member of my household, I was usually quite lax, allowing them all to speak their minds and do as they wished. But on this one subject, my break with Meto, I would allow no discourse.

"Very well, Papa, I won't speak of that. Still, I hate to see you this way. You're like a man who thinks the gods have turned against him."

And haven't they? I wanted to say, but such an expression of self-pity would have contrasted too glaringly with my daughter's stoicism, and not to my credit. Besides, I had no reason to believe the gods had singled me out to vent their displeasure. It seemed to me lately that the gods had turned against all mankind. Or perhaps they had simply turned their backs on us, allowing the most ruthless among us, like Caesar and Pompey, to wreak unchecked havoc on the rest.

"Hundreds, thousands, tens of thousands of men—and women—will die before this war is over, Diana. Not one of those restless lemures of the dead is likely to find anything resembling justice in this world or the next. If Cassandra was murdered—"

"You know she was, Papa. She was poisoned. She told you so."

"If she was murdered, what good will it do to find out who killed her? No Roman court—presuming the courts ever return to normal—would be interested in prosecuting such a crime, perpetrated on a woman nobody knew or cared about."

"You cared enough to give her a decent funeral."

"That's beside the point."

"And some of the most powerful women in Rome cared enough to come to her funeral. You saw them, skulking on the periphery, staying well away from the pyre as if the flames might scorch them—or show the guilt on their faces. It was one of them who killed her, wasn't it?"

"It might have been." Before her death, Cassandra had been courted by the highest circles of Roman society, summoned to the houses of the rich and powerful who had learned about her gift. Had she known the danger she might face by consorting with such women? What uncovered secrets from the past—or from the future—might have led one of those women to silence Cassandra forever?

"Shall I do it for you, Papa?"

"Do what?"

"Shall I do it in your stead—uncover the truth about her death?"

"What a ridiculous idea!"

"It's not so ridiculous. I know how you work. I've watched you since I was a child. I've listened to all your stories about snooping for Cicero, and uncovering chariot races that were fixed, and going off to Spain or Syracuse to look for a murderer at some rich man's behest. Do you think I'd be incapable of doing the same thing myself?"

"You make it sound like baking a batch of flat bread, Diana. Mix this list of ingredients, bake for a certain length of time—"

"Baking is harder than you make it sound, Papa. It takes skill and experience."

"Exactly. And you have neither when it comes to—well, to the sort of work you're talking about."

"It's because I'm a woman, isn't it? You don't think I could do it because I'm a woman. Do you really think I'm not as clever as a man?"

"Cleverness has nothing to do with it. You have a three-year-old son to raise! Besides that, there are places a woman can't go. There are questions a woman can't ask. And don't forget the danger, Diana."

"But I'd have Davus for all that! He's big and strong. He

can go anywhere. He could twist arms or break down doors—"

"Diana, don't be absurd!" I took off my hat and fanned myself with it, squinting at the bright sunlight. "You've done some thinking about this, haven't you?"

"Perhaps."

"Well, stop any such thoughts at once, and abandon any ambitions you may have in such a direction—'Diana the Finder,' indeed!"

"No—Diana and Davus the Finders, plural."

"Double absurdity! I absolutely forbid it. You'll follow the example of your mother. She began with every disadvantage, yet look at her now—she's made herself into the very model of a Roman matron: modest, respectable, responsible, running a household, raising a family—"

"Is that how you'd describe those model Roman matrons who showed up at Cassandra's funeral?"

I thought of some of those women and the scandals that attended them, and I had to cede the point to Diana. In such times, did any real standard of Roman womanhood exist any longer? It was the same for men and women alike—virtues had turned to vices and vices to virtues.

I put on my hat and stood, listening to my knees crack as they straightened. "If your intention was to incite me to action, Diana, then you've succeeded. Fetch Davus for me, would you? I shall take him along with me—in case I have to break down some doors or twist some arms. And you, meanwhile, will stay home and tend to your ailing mother. I expect to smell radish soup bubbling on the hearth when I come home!"

ᗡᗜ

The easiest place to begin was also the closest—at the house of Cicero, just down the street from my own.

With the assistance of Mopsus and Androcles, Davus and I put on our best togas. The two of us left the house and walked along the rim road that skirted the crest of the Palatine Hill, with a view of the Forum below and the Capitoline Hill surmounted by the Temple of Jupiter in the distance. It was a beautiful summer day.

At Cicero's house, Davus knocked politely on the door with his foot. An eye peered at us through a peephole in the door. I stated my name and asked to see the mistress of the house. The peephole slid shut. A few moments later the door opened.

I had visited the house of Cicero many times over the years. At the zenith of his fortunes, in the year he served as consul and quashed the so-called conspiracy of Catilina, this house had arguably been the very center of the Roman world, the site of the most important political meetings as well as the most dazzling cultural gatherings. Men of letters and men of affairs had passed through its portals; they had sipped wine and listened to one another's poems and monographs in its gardens; they had shaped the future course of the Republic in Cicero's study.

At the nadir of Cicero's fortunes, the house had been burned to the ground by Clodius and his gang, and its master had been sent into exile. But Cicero had eventually returned to Rome, regained his rights of citizenship and his place in the Senate, and rebuilt his house on the Palatine.

Now the master of this house was again in a kind of exile, far away in Greece with Pompey. For months after Caesar crossed the Rubicon, Cicero had procrastinated and vacillated, agonizing over his choices. Both sides had wooed him, not for his military skills, but for the political weight he carried; Cicero's endorsement of either side would do much to sway the sentiments of those who considered themselves steadfast upholders of the Republic. On principle, Cicero sided with Pompey from the start, seeing him as the only possible protector of the status quo; but for as long as he could, Cicero hedged his bets, sending letters back and forth to both Pompey and Caesar, desperately trying to hew a middle course. But there was no middle course, and finally, when exaggerated news of a temporary setback to Caesar's fortunes in Spain reached Rome in the month of Junius of the previous year, Cicero took the great leap and with his son Marcus, who was barely old enough to wear a manly toga, left Italy to join Pompey. A year had passed since then. I had to wonder if Cicero was now regretting his decision.

I had known Cicero for over thirty years. My assistance in the murder trial that made his early reputation had done much to further my own fortunes. It was not long after I first met him that he married. His wife, Terentia, ten years his junior, had come from a family of considerable social standing and brought with her a substantial dowry. She was said to be an excellent household manager and devoutly religious. Unlike the wives of many powerful men, she took no interest in legal matters or affairs of state. While the fortunes of the Republic ebbed and flowed within the walls of Cicero's house, and the fates of the accused men he represented hung in the balance, she went about her duties of honoring family ancestors, making sacrifices to household gods, and furthering the social advancement of their two children.

In all the times I had visited Cicero, I had exchanged only a few words with Terentia. On the rare occasions when circumstances obliged her to speak to me, she had been polite but haughty, projecting the unmistakable message that my social standing was too insignificant to warrant more than the bare minimum of conversation. I think she found it unfortunate that her husband had to deal with a character as unsavory as myself.

The last time I had been in the house, Caesar had just crossed the Rubicon, and Cicero and Terentia had been frantically preparing to leave Rome, ordering secretaries to pack up scrolls in the library and issuing last-minute instructions to the slaves who would look after the house in their absence. On this day the house was almost ominously quiet and still.

Davus and I waited in the foyer only a short time before Terentia herself appeared. She wore a simple yellow stola and no jewelry. Her gray hair was pulled back in a tight bun, a severe style that suited her austerely handsome face.

"Gordianus," she said, giving me a curt nod of recognition. "Isn't this your son-in-law?"

"Yes, this is Davus," I said.

Terentia appraised him coolly. She herself had so far been

notoriously unlucky with sons-in-law. Her daughter, Tullia, still in her twenties, had already been once widowed and once divorced and was now on her third marriage, to a dissolute but dashing young aristocrat named Dolabella. The betrothal had taken place while Cicero was off governing a province and without his approval. Dolabella had apparently swept both mother and daughter off their feet. As I watched Terentia's eyes linger on my brawny son-in-law a little longer than necessary, I gathered that she was not immune to male charms. Cicero himself was said to have been heartbroken by the marriage, having once defended Dolabella on a murder charge and knowing what a vicious character the fellow was. To compound Cicero's embarrassment, Dolabella had since taken up arms for Caesar; he had been put in charge of Caesar's fleet in the Adriatic, where he had consistently been outmaneuvered and outnumbered by Pompey's navy. Like so many families of the ruling class, Cicero's had been split down the middle by the civil war. And if that were not enough, rumor had it that Dolabella had been utterly faithless as a husband, carrying on a dalliance with Marc Antony's wife, Antonia.

"You haven't come to talk about this business with Milo and Caelius, I hope?" She referred to the insurrection rumored to be developing in the countryside south of Rome led by two of Cicero's old associates, Marcus Caelius and Titus Annius Milo.

"As a matter of fact, no."

"Good! Because everyone thinks I should have an opinion about it, and I refuse to give one. Both of those fellows have brought my husband nothing but grief over the years, but at the same time, who can blame them for reaching the end of their patience? Of course they shall both get themselves killed, poor fools. . . ." She shook her head. "Then I suppose you've come about Cassandra," she said, forestalling any apprehensions I might have had about coming directly to the point. Unlike her husband, who could speak for hours and say nothing, Terentia was not a woman to mince words.

When I nodded, she indicated with a gesture that we should follow. She took us to the same room to which Cicero had shown me on my last visit, a secluded little chamber off the central garden. But the room seemed different and strangely empty. What was it Cicero had told me? *"This was one of the first rooms Terentia decorated when we came back and rebuilt after Clodius and his gang burned down the house and sent me into exile. . . ."*

Cicero had been quite proud of this room and its exquisite furnishings, but where were those objects now? I vaguely recalled a sumptuous carpet with a geometrical Greek design; now there was only cold stone underfoot. There had been several fine chairs carved from terebinth with inlays of ivory; now there were only a couple of folding chairs of the simplest sort. There had been a finely wrought bronze brazier with griffin heads; that, too, was gone. The only decorations that remained were the ones that couldn't be removed, the pastoral landscapes painted on the walls that depicted herdsmen dozing amid sheep and satyrs peeking from behind little roadside shrines.

Terentia sighed. "Ah, how Marcus loved this room! This was where he entertained his most important visitors—senators and magistrates and suitors for Tullia's hand. My husband brought *you* to this room the last time you called on him, did he not? His study was too crowded, as I recall—all those secretaries running about in a panic, packing up his confidential papers." There was a note of disapproval in her voice that implied the room was really too good for the likes of me and, at the same time, a note of resignation. Now that the room had been stripped of its exquisite furnishings and reduced to a shadow of its former luxury, why not meet with me here?

The portable furnishings were gone, and Terentia wore no jewelry. Was she really in such dire straits that she was having to sell her personal possessions? I myself had fallen into debt thanks to the hardships of recent months, but it was a shock to think of a woman like Terentia facing the same hard choices.

"Was she a kinswoman?" she said.

"I beg your pardon?"

"The woman called Cassandra. Was she kin to you?"

"No."

"Yet you conducted her funeral. There must have been some . . . relationship . . . between you."

I made no reply. Terentia shrugged knowingly. The presumptuous gesture reminded me of her husband, and I felt a pang of resentment that she should assume she understood my connection to Cassandra, even if she was correct.

"You must have known her as well," I said. "Why else did you come to see her funeral pyre?"

"Yes, I did have a slight acquaintance with her. I asked about *your* connection to her only because I wanted to thank you for conducting her funeral. It's good that someone took the time and went to the expense of giving her a fitting ceremony. And you showed good taste. Not too many musicians and mourners. It's unseemly when they outnumber the real friends and family."

"I could hardly afford the few I did hire."

"Ah, money . . ." She nodded understandingly. "And no long-winded speech before the funeral pyre. I always think that's rather pretentious when it's a woman, don't you? It's fitting to list the accomplishments of a man of the world, but if a woman's lived a proper life, what is there to say about her, really, at the end? And if she's led an improper life, the less said the better."

I cleared my throat. "If you came to her funeral, Cassandra must have been more than a passing acquaintance. How did you meet her?"

Terentia pulled back her shoulders and lifted her chin. She was not used to being questioned. In the courts her husband had become famous for his penetrating interrogation of witnesses; even the strongest men quailed before the fierce onslaught of Cicero's questioning. But in the daily course of married life, when Cicero had cause to question his wife and she had cause to remain silent—when the battering ram met the iron wall—which of them usually won that test of wills? Looking at that immovable jaw, I suspected it was Terentia.

Her demeanor gradually shifted. Her shoulders relaxed. She lowered her head. She had decided to answer me.

"If you know anything at all about Cassandra, you know that in the last few months she became something of a celebrity in society. I used the word 'society' loosely, since no such thing exists at the moment—we are all adrift, waiting for tomorrow. It was my sister Fabia who—for lack of a better word—'discovered' her. Cassandra appeared one day in front of the Temple of Vesta. Fabia was the senior Vestal on duty that day, tending to the divine flame. She heard a woman wailing outside. She went to see what was happening. These days, who knows? A woman might be raped or murdered in broad daylight on the temple steps. That was how Fabia came upon Cassandra, who was in the throes of one of her prophetic spells."

"Yes, I know."

Terentia gave me a curious look.

"Purely by cioncidence," I said, "I happened to be in the vicinity of the Temple of Vesta that day. I, too, heard Cassandra. I had never seen her before. I wasn't sure how to react. While I hesitated, I saw Fabia emerge from the temple with two other Vestals. I saw them take Cassandra inside. What happened next?"

Terentia gave me a long, hard look. "My husband calls you an honest man, Gordianus, 'the last honest man in Rome,' in fact."

"Cicero honors me."

"And don't think, just because I never had occasion to formally thank you, that I've ever forgotten the great favor you did for my sister all those years ago when you sniffed out the truth when some of the Vestals were accused of breaking their vows. Fabia would have been buried alive if her accusers had succeeded in convincing the court that she conducted an improper liaison with Catilina. Buried alive! It still pains my heart, just to think of it. My darling half-sister was so young back then. So beautiful. There were those who actually believed she might have committed such a foul crime, but you saved her life. Cicero called on you to investigate the matter, and you proved that Fabia was innocent."

This was not quite how I remembered the affair. At the

time, it had seemed to me that Catilina—a dissolute and charming upstart not unlike Terentia's son-in-law Dolabella—might or might not have managed to seduce the tremulous young virgin Fabia within the very confines of the House of the Vestals. But that was twenty-five years ago, and a great deal had happened since; and if Terentia remembered one reality while I remembered another, only the gods—or Fabia herself—could have said which of us remembered the truth.

Terentia gave me a long, appraising look, then seemed to come to some decision. She clapped her hands. A slave came running. Terentia gave the girl a whispered instruction, and the slave ran off. A few moments later I heard the rustling sound made by the folds of a voluminous stola, and a moment later Fabia herself appeared in the doorway.

She was magnificently attired in the full costume of a Vestal. Her hair, shot through with gray now, was cut quite short. Around her forehead she wore a broad white band, like a diadem, decorated with ribbons. Her stola was white and plain, but cut to hang from her body with many folds. About her shoulders she wore the white linen mantle of a Vestal.

"Sister, I think you may recall Gordianus," said Terentia.

Fabia had grown older, but she was a striking woman. What had changed most was her manner. I had met her at a time of crisis, when she was young and confused and in terrible danger—and quite possibly guilty of the unspeakable crime of which she had been accused. She had survived that episode, and the travail had made her stronger. Presumably she had maintained her vow of chastity, whether she had briefly interrupted it with Catilina or not; and that sort of discipline, year in and year out, and the state of childlessness it ensured, was said to give a woman a special kind of strength. Fabia certainly looked imposing enough, standing there in the doorway, taking stock of her sister's two visitors. Her eyes swept over Davus with hardly a pause and settled on me. In her steady gaze I saw little to remind me of the frail girl I had once assisted at Cicero's behest.

"I remember you, Gordianus," she said, without emotion.

"Gordianus is here to ask questions about Cassandra," said Terentia.

"Why?" said Fabia.

"I believe she was murdered," I said.

Fabia drew in a breath. "We thought—because her mind was frail—that perhaps her body was frail as well. We thought perhaps she died of some . . . natural cause."

"She was poisoned," I said, trying to make my face as rigid as Fabia's to hide the pain the words caused me.

"Poisoned," whispered Fabia. "I see. But why have you come here? What do you want from me?"

"You were one of the first women in Rome to befriend her," I said.

"Befriend? Not exactly. I saw a woman in distress. When I approached her, when I heard the nature of her ranting, I sensed the truth—that she was a woman possessed of the gift of prophecy. I took her into the Temple of Vesta, where the goddess could keep her safe while the gift possessed her. I acted as a priestess, not a friend. I acted out of piety, not pity."

"Who was she? Where did she come from?"

"Of her earthly origins, I know nothing. She herself had forgotten."

"But how could you tell that she possessed this gift you speak of? How could you tell that she wasn't simply mad?"

Fabia smiled faintly. "You may be wise in the ways of the world, Gordianus, especially in the ways of men. But this was a divine matter—and a matter for women."

"Are you saying that men have no access to divine knowledge? The augurs—"

"Yes, the College of Augurs is made up of men, and for centuries they've passed down their own methods for reading omens—studying the flights of birds, listening to thunder, watching the play of lightning across the heavens. The sky is Jupiter's realm, and such signs come directly from the King of Gods himself. And the men elected to the College of Fifteen likewise look for signs of the future by consulting the oracles in the ancient Sibylline Books. But there are other, more subtle ways in which the gods make their will known to us, and by which they show us the paths to the future. Many of those methods fall outside the ken of men. Only women know. Only women understand."

"And it was your understanding that Cassandra possessed a true gift of prophecy?"

"When she was possessed, she saw beyond this world."

"The Trojan Cassandra heard messages from the other world."

"Our Cassandra's gift came to her mostly in the form of visions. What she saw, she didn't always understand and couldn't always put into words. She herself made no interpretation of her visions; she only related them as they occurred. Often she had no recollection of them afterward."

"I should think such a gift would be rather unreliable, producing more riddles than answers."

"Her visions required interpretation, if that's what you mean. Not a suitable job for your College of Augurs! But if a person listened to her closely, and if that person already possessed a genuine sympathy for the divine world—"

"A person like yourself," I said.

"Yes, I was able to make sense of Cassandra's visions. That was why I arranged for her to come here, to Terentia's house, on more than one occasion."

"And did she always prophesy?"

"Almost always. There was a method that helped to induce her visions."

"What was that?"

"If she sat in a still, dark room and gazed at a flame, almost always the visions would come to her."

"And before or after, you would give her food and drink?"

"Of course we would," said Terentia. "She was treated as kindly in my house as any other guest."

"Even though you had no idea of who she really was or where she came from?"

"It was her gift that interested us," said Fabia, "not her family history or the name she was born with."

"And when Cassandra delivered these prophecies, what did you make of them?"

The two sisters exchanged a searching look, silently debating how much they should tell me.

Fabia finally spoke. "Cassandra had many visions, but there was one in particular—a recurring vision of two lions battling one another over the carcass of a she-wolf."

"How did you interpret this vision?"

"The she-wolf was Rome, of course. The lions were Pompey and Caesar."

"And which of them killed the other and ate the carcass?"

"Neither."

"I don't understand. Did they split the she-wolf between them?" I imagined the Roman world split permanently between two factions, Caesar ruling the West, Pompey ruling the East. "One world split between two Roman empires—could such an arrangement ever last?"

"No, no, no!" said Terentia. "You misunderstand. Tell him, Fabia!"

"The vision ended with a miracle," said Fabia. "The she-wolf sprang back to life, and grew until she towered over the lions, who gave up fighting and meekly lay down together, licking at each other's wounds."

"What did the vision mean?"

Fabia began to speak, but Terentia was too excited to remain silent. "Don't you see? It's the best possible outcome! Everyone assumes that Caesar and Pompey must come to blows, that one of them must destroy the other, with Rome as the prize. But there's another possibility—that both sides will come to their senses before it's too late. It's one thing for Romans to shed the blood of Gauls or Parthians, but for Romans to kill Romans—it's unthinkable. Such madness offends the gods themselves. Cicero knows that. It's what he's been trying to tell both sides all along. They must find a way to settle their differences and make peace! That's what Cassandra's vision foretold. For the moment Rome appears paralyzed and helpless; but the she-wolf only sleeps, and when she wakes she'll show herself greater than either Caesar or Pompey. They shall be awed by her shadow, and there shall be a reconciliation between the two factions." Terentia smiled. "It's my belief that Cicero himself will broker the reconciliation. It's the real reason the gods guided his footsteps to Pompey's camp. Not to fight—we all know my husband is no warrior—but to be on hand when the two sides finally do meet, and to make them see the madness of their ways. There shall be peace, not war. Every day I look for a messenger to arrive with a letter from my husband bringing the glorious news."

Fabia walked to her side and laid her hand on Terentia's shoulder. The look on both their faces was transcendent.

I took a deep breath. "How did you learn of Cassandra's death?"

"She died in the marketplace, didn't she?" said Fabia. "People saw. People recognized her. News travels fast in the city."

"Yet neither of you came to my house to pay your respects."

They both averted their eyes. "Well," said Terentia, "she was hardly of our . . . I mean, as you yourself pointed out, we didn't even know her true name, much less her family."

"Yet you came to see her burn."

"An act of piety," said Fabia. "The burning of the body is a holy rite. We came to witness that."

I lowered my eyes, then looked up at the sound of another voice from the doorway.

"Aunt Fabia! I was wondering where you'd gone. Oh—I didn't realize you had company, Mother."

Cicero's daughter, Tullia, had suffered the misfortune of inheriting her father's looks rather than her mother's, and had grown from a spindly girl into a rather plain young woman. The last time I had seen her had been at her parents' house down in Formiae the previous year, while Cicero was still trying to decide which way to jump. She had been pregnant then and just beginning to show. The child had been born prematurely and had lived only a short while. A year later Tullia appeared to be in good health, despite her slender arms and wan complexion.

Unlike her mother, Tullia wore several pieces of costly-looking jewelry, including gold bracelets and a silver filigree necklace decorated with lapis baubles. Despite the drastic economies the war had imposed on the household, I suspected that young Tullia would be the last member of the family called upon to make personal sacrifices. Cicero and Terentia had spoiled both their children, but Tullia especially.

"Actually," said Terentia, "my visitors were just leaving. Why don't you escort your aunt back to the sewing room, Tullia, while I show them out?"

"Certainly, Mother." Tullia took her aunt's hand and led her from the room. Over her shoulder Fabia gave me a long, parting glance in lieu of a farewell. Tullia's parting glance was at Davus, who reacted by shuffling his feet and clearing his throat.

I began to move toward the door, but Terentia restrained me with a hand on my forearm.

"Send your son-in-law on to the foyer," she said in a low voice, "but stay here a moment longer, Gordianus. There's something I want to show you, in private."

I did as she asked and waited alone in the room, gazing at the pastoral landscapes on the wall. A moment later she returned, carrying a scrap of parchment. She pressed it into my hand.

"Read that," she said. "Tell me what you make of it."

It was a letter from Cicero, dated from the month of Junius and headed *From Pompey's Camp in Epirus*:

IF YOU ARE WELL, I AM GLAD. I AM WELL. DO YOUR BEST TO RECOVER. AS FAR AS TIME AND CIRCUMSTANCES PERMIT, PROVIDE FOR AND CONDUCT ALL NECESSARY BUSINESS, AND AS OFTEN AS POSSIBLE WRITE TO ME ON ALL POINTS. GOOD-BYE.

I turned the scrap of parchment over, but that was all there was to it.

I shrugged, not knowing what she wanted from me. "He advises you to recover. I take it you were unwell?"

"A trifle—a fever that came and went," she said. "You'll notice he doesn't even wish me a speedy recovery or the favor

of the gods or any such thing. Merely, 'Do your best to recover.' As if reminding me of a duty!"

"And he charges you with conducting necessary business—"

"Ha! He expects me to run a household—two households,
my own and Tullia's—on a budget of thin air! Just to make
ends meet, I'm selling off the best furniture and the finest
pieces of jewelry handed down from my mother—"

"I don't understand why you showed me this letter, Terentia."

"Because you know my husband, Gordianus. You've
known him from the bottom up. You have no illusions about
him. I'm not sure you like him—I'm not even sure if you
respect him—but you *know* him. Do you detect in that letter
one shred of love or affection or even goodwill?"

Perhaps it's written in code, I wanted to say, knowing from
experience that Cicero was prone to such tricks in his correspondence. But Terentia was in no mood for jokes. If she had
mustered the courage to bare her soul to me of all people, I
knew she must be in genuine distress. "I hardly think it's for
me to say what Cicero felt when he wrote this letter."

She took the letter from me and turned away, hiding her
face. "The tensions in this household—you can't imagine! For
months on end; for years, really. Fighting over what's to be
done with young Marcus—his father insists he's to be a
scholar, in spite of the fact that all his tutors say he's hopeless.
And now the boy's off to fight, though he's barely old enough
to wear a toga. And Dolabella, choosing to side with Caesar
and carrying on with Antonia behind our backs—my husband
could hardly stand the mention of his name even before this
trouble began. How he hated the marriage! And when Tullia
lost the baby, the pain we all felt was unbearable. But I could
tolerate anything, stand any trial, if only I knew that Marcus
still—" Her voice caught in her throat, and she shook her head.
"The hard fact of the matter is, Marcus no longer loves me.
He didn't love me when we married—no woman expects that
at the outset of an arranged marriage—but he came to love
me, and that love grew and lasted for years. But now . . . now

I don't know what's become of it. I don't know where it went or how to get it back. Too much squabbling over money, too many fights about the children, the bitterness of the times we live in . . ."

"Terentia, why are you telling me this?"

"Because you knew *her* as well, didn't you? Better than you let on. You must have, if you made the arrangements for her funeral."

"Yes, I knew Cassandra."

"The prophecy Fabia mentioned—there was more to it . . . of a personal nature. Cassandra saw her vision of the she-wolf and the lions doubled, reflected in miniature, she said, as if in a distant mirror. It was my household she saw in that mirror—a reflection of the world at large. The she-wolf was our family, the thing that's nurtured and sustained us through even the hardest times. And the beasts were Marcus and myself, drawing blood from each other and fighting over the carcass of our own marriage. But just as Rome is greater than those who squabble over her, this family is greater than its parts. We shall make a reconciliation. Marcus . . . will love me again. Cassandra said as much!"

"Did she?"

"That was Fabia's interpretation."

"Fabia knows far more about such things than I."

"Yes, but *you* knew Cassandra. Was she genuine, Gordianus? Was she what she seemed to be? Can I trust the visions she saw in the throes of her gift?"

The interview had been reversed. Now it was Terentia seeking knowledge of Cassandra from me.

"I don't know," I said, and spoke the truth.

V

As I can place the first time I saw Cassandra, because on that day word reached Rome of Caesar's successful sea crossing, so I can place the second time I saw her and the first time I actually spoke to her, because of something significant that occurred on the same day. It was on the morning in late Februarius that Marcus Caelius set up a tribunal next to that of the city praetor Trebonius and commenced his campaign to flout Caesar's will and become the radical champion of Rome's downtrodden.

Before he left Rome, Caesar, by proclaiming edicts and bending the will of the Senate, had set in place a program to shore up the faltering Roman economy. The problems were many and daunting. With the commencement of the war, money had grown increasingly scarce even while prices soared. The treasury of Rome had been emptied to pay for Caesar's military campaigns. No taxes were flowing in. Pompey had cut off all revenues from the East as well as vital grain shipments from Egypt. Commerce was at a standstill; ships, horses, and even handcarts had been commandeered for the war effort. Tradesmen were in distress because no money was in circulation. Free laborers were unable to find employment. Hungry slaves were growing restive. Shopkeepers and tenants were unable to pay their rents. Families whose heads of household had fled Italy or joined Caesar's legions were being cheated by the bailiffs left to mind their masters' prop-

erty. Bankers were demanding payment of old loans and refusing to make new ones. Unscrupulous profiteers were
squeezing all they could from the anxious people of Rome.

I myself had gone increasingly into debt for the first time
in my life. It seemed that only a handful of people had money,
and that they had a great deal of it, and that the rest of us had
to go to them begging for loans at whatever terms they demanded. Simply to pay for the daily expenses of life, I found
myself indebted to the wealthy banker Volumnius to such an
extent that I despaired of ever being able to repay him.

To address these problems, Caesar had ordered that all
property values and rents should be rolled back to prewar
prices. Debtors were allowed to deduct all interest paid from
the principal they owed. Arbitrators were appointed to settle
disputes over valuations and bankruptcies. An antihoarding
law decreed that no one could keep more than sixty thousand
sesterces of gold or silver out of circulation.

Caesar's efforts had been moderate and were moderately
successful. Money began to circulate. Shops reopened, and
vendors reappeared in the markets. The growing sense of panic
among the general population began to subside and gave way
to a grinding, day-to-day scrabble for sustenance.

There were those—some because they truly despised the
status quo and wanted to see it overturned, and some because
they themselves were hopelessly in debt and were desperate
for a way out—who had hoped Caesar would enact a far more
radical program. They wanted him to abolish all debts, refund
rents, perhaps even confiscate the property of the wealthy and
redistribute it to the poor. These people were bitterly disappointed.

The man whom Caesar had appointed to administer his eco-
nomic program was Gaius Trebonius. I had met Trebonius the
previous year in the Roman encampment outside Massilia,
where he was the commanding officer in charge of the siege.
He was a thoroughly competent and resourceful military man
with a good head for figures and an intuitive sense of how the
world works. Trebonius could look at a catapult and tell you
why it wasn't working properly, calculate the load and trajec-

tory, then watch the men loading it and pick the one best suited to give orders to the others. He had conducted an efficient and successful siege, and Massilia had been subdued at very little cost to Caesar's legions. In recognition of his competence, Trebonius was the man Caesar put in place to run the city of Rome in his absence.

Some called Trebonius's magistracy a reward for services rendered, but it was not a job I would have wanted. No doubt Trebonius was able to profit immensely by accepting bribes from the disputants who came before him, but I found it mind-numbing to imagine the endless caseload of property valuations and bankruptcy negotiations over which Trebonius had to preside.

Trebonius conducted this tedious business from a tribunal, a raised platform, in the Forum. He sat on his official chair of state, a particularly ornate specimen in the traditional shape of a folding camp stool but heavily decorated with ivory and gold, with four elephant tusks for legs. Secretaries and clerks hovered about him, fetching documents, consulting ledgers, and taking notes. On most days a long line of litigants awaiting their interview with Trebonius wound snakelike through the Forum. Among the contesting parties, tempers were short, and stakes were high. Not infrequently, fights broke out up and down the line. Armed guards would rush to quell these disturbances before they could expand into a full-scale riot.

It was on a morning in late Februarius that another magistrate, Marcus Caelius, strode into the Forum, carrying his own chair of state and attended by his own retinue of secretaries and clerks, who quickly erected a raised platform only a short distance away from that of Trebonius. Caelius mounted the tribunal and, with a flourish, unfolded his chair of state, which was a notably simpler affair than that of Trebonius—the ivory decorations were less ornate and without gold accents, and the legs were not of ivory but merely of wood carved in the shape of elephant tusks. By the example of his chair of state, Caelius was already proclaiming himself the standard-bearer of austere Roman virtue and the champion of the downtrodden.

Still in his thirties, slender as a youth, and as handsome
and charming as ever, Marcus Caelius already had a long and
checkered career in public life. I remembered him best as Cicero's unruly young protégé, learning the arts of rhetoric at the
feet of his prim and proper master by day, carousing and carrying on a debauched social life by night—much to the chagrin
of all concerned, especially when Caelius found himself
dragged into the courts by his ex-lover Clodia, who accused
him of the murder-for-hire of a visiting Alexandrian philosopher. Cicero rushed to his protégé's defense. The trial degen-
erated into a squalid exchange of name-calling, and ultimately
Cicero managed to turn the tables on Clodia by picturing her
as a wanton, incestuous whore out to ruin an innocent young
man. Acquitted, Caelius had turned his back on the alluring
Clodia, her rabble-rousing brother Clodius, and the rest of their
radical clique and had committed himself wholeheartedly to
the cause of the so-called Best People, like Cicero and Pompey, until—tugged back and forth like all the other bright,
ambitious young men of Rome—he finally cast his lot with
Caesar. On the eve of Caesar's decision to cross the Rubicon
and commit himself to civil war, Caelius had ridden out of
Rome to join him—leaving Cicero once again much chagrined.

Caelius became one of Caesar's lieutenants and served him
well in the Spanish campaign. Returning to Rome saddled with
debts, he had hoped to be installed in the lucrative post of city
praetor, and made no secret of his bitter disappointment when
that magistracy had gone instead to Gaius Trebonius. Caelius
had been stuck with a lesser praetorship, which put him in
charge of adjudicating the affairs of foreign residents in the
city. Perhaps Caesar thought it wise to tuck an ambitious fellow of shifting loyalties like Caelius in a safe niche, giving
him a job of minimal importance with not much to do—but
Caesar should have known that Caelius, with time on his
hands, was a dangerous man.

I happened to be in the Forum along with Hieronymus and
the usual chin-waggers when Caelius set up his mock tribunal

next to that of Trebonius. I also happened to see the look of consternation on Trebonius's face.

What was Caelius up to? I stepped closer to his tribunal. The chin-waggers followed along. Caelius sat in his chair of state, slowly turning his head to take in the long line of litigants waiting to see Trebonius and the curious crowd that had begun to gather before his own tribunal. For a moment his eyes fell on me. Our paths had crossed many times in the past. He gave me a nod of recognition and flashed his dazzling smile—the smile that had once melted Clodia's heart and gotten him into endless other mischief over the years. Our eyes met for only a moment, but I had a premonition of all the trouble he was about to hatch for himself and so many others.

Caelius stood up from his chair of state. A hush fell over the line of litigants waiting to see Trebonius and the crowd that had gathered.

"Citizens of Rome!" cried Caelius. He had one of the best orator's voices in Rome, able to reach great distances with trumpetlike clarity. "Why do you stand there, lined up like obedient sheep in a fold awaiting your turn to be sheared? The magistrate from whom you are seeking redress can do absolutely nothing to help you. His hands are tied. The law as it stands gives him no power to do anything but inflict more damage. All the city praetor can do is look at the numbers you put in front of him, shift them around a bit—like one of those confidence tricksters who haunt the markets, shifting the cup that hides the nut—and then send you home with less than you had when you arrived here. The government of Rome should be able to do better than that for its hardworking, long-suffering citizens! Do you not agree?"

At this there were scattered cries from those in the line— some mocking and jeering at Caelius, but others raising voices in agreement. A few men at the back of the line, unable to hear, gave up their places to come see what was going on. Word quickly spread that Caelius was staging some sort of political demonstration, and the crowd rapidly grew as men arrived from all over the Forum. Trebonius, meanwhile, went on about his business, pretending to ignore Caelius.

"Citizens of Rome," Caelius continued, "think back and remember the situation just a little over a year ago, when Caesar crossed the Rubicon and drove out the smug, self-satisfied scoundrels who were running the state for their own advancement. Did you not feel, as I did, a rush of excitement, a thrill of anticipation when we were suddenly confronted by all the glorious possibilities of a bright future—possibilities that had been unthinkable only a day, even an hour before Caesar took that first step across the Rubicon? All at once, in the blink of an eye, *anything could happen!* How often in the course of a man's lifetime does such a prospect of boundless hope open before him? The world would be remade! Rome would be reborn! Honest men would finally triumph, and the scoundrels among us would be sent scampering off, their tails between their legs.

"Instead—well, you know the bitter truth as well as I do, or else you wouldn't be here today, begging for crumbs from the magistrate in charge of the city. Nothing has changed—except for the worse. The scoundrels have triumphed once again! Is this what men fought and died for—the rights of rich landlords and moneylenders to grind the rest of us beneath their heels? Why has Caesar not put a stop to this shameless situation? Citizens, think of your own circumstances exactly a year ago and tell me: are you better off today? If your answer is yes, then you must be a landlord or a banker, because everyone else is worse off, far worse! Our wrists have been slashed, and the blood drinkers are sucking us dry—and though I hate to say it, it was Caesar himself who put the knives in their hands!"

A few men in the crowd, most of them conspicuously wealthy, booed and jeered along with their entourages of secretaries and bodyguards. But these catcalls were drowned out by angry shouts of agreement that rose up from others. Some of those supporting Caelius may have been hirelings—seeding a crowd with vocal supporters was one of the first lessons he'd learned from Cicero—but the discontent he was tapping into ran deep, and the majority of the listeners were with him.

Trebonius was still ignoring the situation, trying to carry

on his business, but even the litigants with whom he was dealing were giving him only one ear as they bent the other to hear what Caelius was saying.

"Citizens of Rome, Caesar did us all a great service when he crossed the Rubicon. By that bold action, he set in motion a revolution that will remake the state. I myself proudly joined the cause. I did my part on the battlefield, fighting with Caesar in Spain. Now the military struggle continues in a new arena where we have every expectation of success. But while we wait for news of the final victory, we cannot remain idle. We must continue to move ahead here in Rome. We must accomplish in his absence what Caesar, for whatever reasons, failed to accomplish while he was here. We must enact new legislation that will give genuine relief to those who truly need it!"

There was a fresh outburst from the crowd. "It's already been done! Shut up and go home!" shouted one of Caelius's critics. "Hooray! Hooray for Caelius!" shouted a rough fellow who had the look of an agitator-for-hire. The crowd grew so noisy that even Caelius had a hard time speaking above the hubbub. Trebonius gave up on trying to counsel the two litigants before him and sat back in his ornate chair of state, his arms tightly crossed, a scowl on his face.

"Toward that end," Caelius shouted, raising his voice to clarion pitch to make himself heard, "toward that end, I shall begin by proposing a new law to stop all debt payments for a period of no less than *six years*. I repeat, I will ask the Senate to impose a *six-year* moratorium on all existing debts, with no interest to be accrued in the meantime! Those who have been crushed to their knees by debt will finally be given a chance to get back on their feet. And if the wealthy moneylenders complain that they'll starve, then let them eat the wax tablets on which those loans were recorded!"

There was a huge response from the crowd. Caelius, his face flushed with excitement—for I think the crowd had grown even larger and more enthusiastic than he'd expected—managed to make himself heard above the roar. "In anticipation of the passage of this law, I have set up my tribunal here today. I shall take up my post in my chair of state, and my clerks shall record the names and circumstances of all citizens who are currently in debt, so that their relief can be expedited immediately when the law goes into effect. Please form a line beginning on my right." And with that he sat down on his chair of state, looking quite pleased with himself.

The line of litigants waiting to see Trebonius evaporated in the rush to join the line to see Caelius. Why should any debtor waste his time haggling with the city praetor, when Caelius's legislation, if enacted, would supersede whatever settlement Trebonius decreed?

"What a pack of fools," grumbled one-armed Canininus in my ear. "There's not a chance in Hades the Senate will pass Caelius's legislation. If Caesar had wanted such a thing, he'd have enacted it himself. And if Caesar doesn't want it, the Senate won't even consider it. Caelius is just stirring up trouble."

"But why?" I said. "What's the point of setting off a riot?" For in fact a near riot had ensued. Angry cries and insults filled the air. Shoving matches and fistfights broke out. Snarling bodyguards formed cordons around their wealthy patrons, who rushed to escape the rabble. At a sign from Trebonius, glowering down at the chaotic scene from his chair of state, armed guards set about trying to restore order, though it was hard to know where to begin. The crowd was like a boiling caldron, bubbling over everywhere at once.

What *was* Caelius up to? Canininus was right; as long as the Senate was in the palm of Caesar's hand, Caelius had no hopes of enacting his own radical programs. Nor, as the praetor overseeing foreign residents, did he have any legitimate business to involve himself with debt settlements. Was he simply trying to make Trebonius's job harder, out of spite? Or did Caelius have a definite agenda in mind and a goal toward which he was moving?

Hieronymus and I, fearing the madness of the mob, made our way to the edge of the crowd. I acquired a couple of bruises from flying elbows, but otherwise emerged unscathed. At last we found a quiet place to catch our breaths, beside the

Temple of Castor and Pollux. That was when I saw Cassandra for the second time.

The narrow platform that projected perpendicularly from the porch of the temple, flanking the steps, was just above our heads. I happened to look up, and saw her standing alone on the platform. She was watching the seething crowd beyond us and took no notice of the two of us below her.

Hieronymus saw the expression on my face and followed my gaze. "Beautiful!" he whispered. The word escaped from his lips as involuntarily as a breath.

And she was beautiful, especially when seen from that low angle—the vantage point of a suppliant looking up at a goddess on a high pedestal. To be sure, there was nothing remotely divine or regal about her threadbare blue tunica or her unkempt hair, but in her bearing there was a certain rare dignity that would command the immediate attention and respect of any man. In me it commanded more than that. I gazed up at her and felt my heart skip a beat. A vaguely remembered sensation from my youth, at once thrilling and painful, shot through me, and I suddenly felt like a man a third my age. I rebuked myself for such foolishness. I was an old, married man. She was a beggar, and a madwoman to boot.

She happened to look down and saw us staring up at her. That was the first time I looked into her eyes and saw that they were blue. Her face was blank, without expression—the face of Athena as molded by the Greek sculptors, I thought—and that in itself seemed odd, considering that she was watching a riot. I thought of a bird watching the activities of humans below her, apathetic to their violence against one another.

She gave a jerk. I thought that we had frightened her somehow, and that she was about to bolt. Instead, her eyes rolled back, and her knees buckled under her. She swayed, lost her footing, and tumbled forward.

To say that Cassandra quite literally fell into my arms would be true but misleading, lending the moment a romantic flair in no way evident at the time. In fact, when I saw that she was about to fall, I felt a quiver of panic—not for her, but for myself. When a man of my years sees a woman falling toward him from a considerable height, he thinks not of heroism but of his own frail bones. Still, I suspect that the instinct to catch a falling woman is strong in any man, no matter what his years. Hieronymus reacted just as I did, and it was into both our arms that she tumbled.

The moment was painfully awkward. Hieronymus and I essentially collided, and an instant later Cassandra fell onto us, and all three of us very nearly collapsed to the ground in a heap. If we had been actors in a comedy by Plautus, the staging could not have been more hilarious. By some miracle of balance and counterbalance, Hieronymus and I both stayed on our feet. Together we managed to lower our dazed cargo to her own unsteady feet, supporting her arms to keep her upright.

The breath was knocked out of me. A sharp pain shot up my spine. Spots swam before my eyes. None of this mattered when Cassandra fell swooning against me, one hand across her face and the other across her bosom.

To observe the form of a beautiful woman at a distance is one thing. To abruptly feel a warm, solid, breathing body enclosed within your arms is another thing altogether. It was precisely for this, to experience such moments of human contact, that the gods made us. That was what I felt in that instant, even if I did not consciously realize it.

Cassandra gradually came to her senses and drew back from me, but only slightly, still remaining in my embrace. Over her shoulder I saw Hieronymus looking rather envious of me. I looked in Cassandra's eyes and saw again that they were blue, but not quite the shade I had thought. There was a bit of green in them, or was that only a momentary trick of the light? Her eyes fascinated me.

"Was I . . . did I . . . fall?" she asked. It seemed to me that her Latin carried a slight accent, but I couldn't place it.

"You did. From up there." I nodded toward the platform.

"And . . . you caught me?"

"*We* caught you," said Hieronymus, crossing his arms petulantly. Cassandra glanced at him over her shoulder. She gently pulled herself from my embrace.

"Are you all right?" I said. "Can you stand?"

"Of course."

"What happened? Did you faint?"

"I'm perfectly all right now. I should go." She turned away.

"Go where?" I reached for her arm, then stopped myself. Where she went was none of my business. Perhaps she thought so too, for she made no answer. Yet it seemed to me that there must be more to say. "What's your name?"

"They call me Cassandra." She looked back at me. Her expression, briefly animated after she recovered from her daze, had become remote again—goddesslike, birdlike, or simply the affectless face of a madwoman?

"But that can't be your real name," I said. "You must have another."

"Must I?" She looked confused for a moment, then turned and walked away with a slow, imperturbable stride, her head and shoulders erect, seemingly oblivious of the men who occasionally ran across her path in flight from the continuing melee before the tribunals of the rival magistrates.

"What an extraordinary woman," said Hieronymus.

I merely nodded.

VI

My interview with Terentia and the Vestal Fabia had yielded some new information about Cassandra, if not much. I decided next to consult Fulvia the twice-widowed; I had rendered her a service in the past by investigating the murder of her husband, Clodius—as partial payment she had given me Mopsus and Androcles—and I could expect at least a cordial welcome at her door. And so, after leaving Cicero's house and returning to my own for a frugal midday meal and a fitful nap during the hottest part of the day, I set out as the sun was lowering to the house of Rome's most famous widow.

As before, I took Davus with me for protection. As we walked down the familiar streets of the Palatine, I was reminded of the days when Davus first entered my household as a slave, only shortly after I first met Fulvia as a stunned and grieving widow. It seemed a memory from another age. Could it actually have been only four years ago that Clodius was murdered on the Appian Way? Rome had been wracked with riots. Clodius's radical supporters had burned the Senate House. Pompey had been called upon to restore order and given almost dictatorial powers; he had exploited the situation to engineer a series of trials that banished many of his enemies from Rome, upsetting once and for all the precarious constitutional balance between his interests and those of Caesar. In retrospect, the murder of Clodius had been the temporal fulcrum between the moment when civil war seemed unthinkable and the moment when it became inevitable. The murder of Fulvia's first husband had been the beginning of the end of our tattered Republic.

Her grief for Clodius had been deep and genuine. They had been true lovers, I think, as well as partners in a broader sense; for Fulvia, as a politician's wife, had always been the exact opposite of Cicero's Terentia. She was a woman with opinions, plans, projects, allies, and enemies. She plotted and schemed alongside her husband and served as his closest advisor. His death had robbed her not only of a husband and a father to their two children; it had robbed her of her role in the political sphere. Women can play no part in the Senate or the magistracies. Women cannot vote. By law they cannot even own property in their own names, although clever women find ways around such technicalities, just as women who care about the course of worldly events find ways to wield their influence, usually through their husbands. While Clodius lived, Fulvia had been one of the most powerful people in Rome, male or female. When he died, she was like a strong man suddenly paralyzed and stricken mute.

But a woman as intelligent, wealthy, and ambitious as Fulvia—who was also a striking woman, if not beautiful—did not have to endure the helplessness of widowhood for long. To a certain kind of man, her combination of qualities must have been almost maddeningly attractive. When she consented to marry Gaius Curio, many people thought that she had found the perfect match. He had been a part of her circle for many years, one of that coterie of ambitious, bright young men with voracious appetites and endless schemes to remake the world in their own image, men like Dolabella, Clodius, Caelius, and Marc Antony. Some said that Fulvia actually would have preferred Antony, had he been available and not already married to his cousin Antonia, and that Fulvia had settled on Antony's boyhood friend (some said lover) Curio as the next best thing; but most agreed that Curio was in fact the better choice because he was more malleable and less inclined to debauchery than Antony.

Like Antony, Curio early on allied himself with Caesar and

never wavered in his devotion or relented in proselytizing on Caesar's behalf. Indeed, it was largely Curio's influence that had brought Marcus Caelius into the fold. On the eve of the war, Caelius and Curio had ridden out together to be by Caesar's side when he crossed the Rubicon. But while Caelius had ultimately been relegated to a minor praetorship in Rome, Curio had been given command of four legions. When Caesar headed for Spain, he dispatched Curio to take on the Pompeian forces led by Cato in Sicily. Cato, disorganized and unready like the rest of the Pompeians, abandoned the island without a fight. Curio, flush from an easy conquest, left two of his legions in Sicily and with his other two pressed on to Africa— and that was where Curio's troubles began.

Some said his conquest of Sicily had been too easy, that it led to overconfidence and rash judgment. Some said it was Curio's youth and lack of military experience that led him into King Juba's trap. Others said it was simply bad luck.

Curio's African campaign began well enough. First, he set about taking the rich seaport of Utica, which was held by the Pompeian commander Varus. A small band of Numidian soldiers dispatched by King Juba attempted to come to the city's aid, but Curio drove them off. He baited Varus to meet in battle outside the city. There Curio made his first mistake, which only by a stroke of good luck proved not to be fatal. He sent his foot soldiers into a steep ravine where they might easily have been ambushed; but in the meantime his cavalry managed to sweep away the enemy's left wing, and Varus's men—sent fleeing back to the city—missed an easy opportunity to destroy their enemy. Such a near miss might have given Curio pause, but instead it emboldened him. He prepared to lay siege to Utica.

In the meantime, King Juba had mustered his army and was marching to relieve Utica. Juba had close ties to Pompey, having been a patron of Pompey's father. And he had cause to hate Curio, who in recent years had proposed that Rome should annex Numidia by force.

Curio received news of Juba's approach. Alarmed, he sent to Sicily for his other two legions. But deserters from Juba's army told him that only a small body of Numidians were advancing. Curio sent out his cavalry, who skirmished with Juba's vanguard. From the intelligence he received, Curio thought that this vanguard was the whole Numidian force. Thinking to destroy it so that he could get on with the siege, he hurried out with his legions to do battle. The season was blisteringly hot; the march over burning sands. The Romans blundered into the entire Numidian army. They were surrounded and slaughtered.

A handful of Curio's men managed to escape. Curio, too, might have fled and saved himself, but he refused to desert his men. A survivor, bringing news of the disaster to Caesar shortly after Caesar's return from Spain, reported Curio's last words: "I've lost the army Caesar entrusted to me. How could I face him?"

Curio fought until the Numidians killed him. They cut off his head and sent the trophy to King Juba. Fulvia was once again a widow.

Pondering her situation, imagining her mood, I felt some hesitation as I approached her house. The structure itself presented a daunting aspect—the giant, fortresslike monstrosity that Clodius had erected on the Palatine, the opulent headquarters from which he had directed the street gangs under his command. Steep terraces overgrown with roses and glimmering with many-colored marble veneers flanked the huge forecourt that had served as a rallying place for Clodius to address his supporters. The iron gate stood open, and as Davus and I strode across the forecourt, gravel crunching under our feet, I gazed ahead at the flight of steps leading up to the broad porch and saw a black wreath upon the massive bronze door. Nine months into her widowhood, Fulvia was still in mourning for Curio.

We mounted the steps. A huge bronze ring on the door served as a knocker. Davus lifted it and let it fall, delivering a dull, reverberating clang. We waited. So far as I could see, no peephole opened in the door, but I had the uncanny sensation of being observed. Clodius's passion for installing secret passages, concealed doors, and hidden spy holes had been notorious.

Eventually I heard the sound of a bar being thrown back on the other side of the door, and then it slowly opened, creaking slightly on its hinges. An athletic-looking slave ushered us inside, then quickly closed the door and let the heavy wooden beam fall back into place, barring it securely.

I had been in this foyer before, in the hours and days that followed the murder of Clodius. It appeared that Curio, in becoming the new master of the house, had made no changes. The floors and walls were of highly polished marble. Red draperies shot with gold threads framed the passageway that led to the atrium, where the ceiling, supported on soaring black marble columns, rose to the height of three stories. In the center of the atrium, a shallow pool was decorated with shimmering mosaic tiles of blue-black and silver, picturing the night sky and the constellations. The actual sky, visible through an opening far above, was just beginning to deepen to the rich blue of twilight.

I turned to the slave who had admitted us. "Tell your mistress that Gordianus—"

"The mistress knows who you are and why you've come," he said, with a sardonic smile. "Follow me."

He led us through halls and galleries decorated with wall paintings and statues. Slaves moved quietly about, lighting braziers and lamps set in sconces on the walls. I was fairly certain that I had traversed the same passageways before, but the house was so sprawling that I couldn't be sure. Eventually we mounted a flight of steps and were shown into a room with large windows, their shutters thrown open to admit the last of the day's light. The walls were stained green and decorated with blue-and-white borders in a geometrical Greek design. Through the windows I saw the golden light of the lowering sun glinting across Palatine rooftops and lending a warm glow to the west-facing temples atop the distant Capitoline Hill. The reflected glow flooded the room, giving it a cozy feeling despite its lofty ceiling and spectacular view.

Fulvia and her mother, Sempronia, sat before one of the

long windows, dressed in stolas of darkest blue. A tiny child—Curio's son—was attempting to walk on a blanket at the women's feet. Fulvia's other children, her son and daughter by Clodius, were not in the room.

"Your visitors, mistress," said the slave.

"Thank you, Thraso. You may go." As Fulvia turned her gaze to me, she lifted a stylus from the wax tablet upon which she had been writing and laid the stylus and tablet aside. There was a popular catchphrase regarding Fulvia and her ambition: "She was not born to spin." Indeed, it was hard to imagine walking into her presence and finding her in the midst of some common female occupation. Instead, like a man of affairs with numerous ideas and projects to keep track of, she kept a wax tablet and stylus about her.

Her mother, Sempronia, despite her hard features, seemed the more maternal of the two. She ignored Davus and me while she clucked and cooed and reached out to the little boy on the blanket, encouraging him to rise to his feet and attempt another faltering step.

"Thank you for seeing me, Fulvia. But I'm curious—how did you know it was me, when I never announced myself?"

She glanced at her son, who managed to stand upright for a moment before tumbling forward onto his hands and knees, then she turned her gaze back to me. "There's a hidden peephole at one end of the porch. Thraso took a good look at you, then ran to give me your description. It could only have been you, Gordianus. 'Nose like a boxer's; a full head of iron gray hair shot with silver, but eyes that sparkle like those of a man half his age; a beard trimmed by a wife to suit herself.' "

"Actually, my daughter, Diana, trims my beard these days. But I feared you might have forgotten me, Fulvia."

"I never forget a man who might be useful to me." She turned her gaze to Davus. "But I don't think I've met this other fellow. 'Shoulders like a Titan's,' said Thraso, 'but a face like Narcissus.' "

"This is Davus, my son-in-law. Thraso also told me that you know why I've come. Surprising, since I'm not sure of that myself."

She smiled. "Aren't you? I saw you at the funeral; you must have seen me. I've been half-expecting you to call on me. This *is* about Cassandra, I presume?"

Sempronia abruptly clapped her hands. A slave girl came running. Sempronia planted a kiss on her grandchild's forehead, then told the girl to take him from the room. As he was carried out, the boy began to cry. His wails echoed and receded down the hallway. Sempronia bit her forefinger and fidgeted, but Fulvia showed no reaction.

"I hope you didn't send the boy away on my account," I said.

"Of course not," said Sempronia, finally looking at me and raising an eyebrow at the notion that I could consider myself important enough to merit any action regarding her grandson. Since I had last seen her, one of her eyes had become cloudy white; if anything, it seemed to fix on me more penetratingly than the other. Under her gaze, I quailed a bit. Strange, that a woman who could be so tender to a child could be so intimidating to a grown man. "If we're going to talk about the witch, it isn't fitting for a man-child to be present," she said.

"Is *that* what Cassandra was? A witch?"

"Of course," said Sempronia. "Did you think she was a mere mortal woman?"

"She was most certainly . . . mortal," I said quietly.

"She was murdered, wasn't she?" said Fulvia. With both of them now looking at me, I realized that the daughter's gaze was no less piercing than her mother's, yet somehow it gave me no displeasure to be looked at so openly by Fulvia. Sempronia's gaze was caustic; it stripped a man naked. Fulvia's gaze seemed cleansing, as if its purpose was to strip away whatever veils of confusion or misunderstanding might intervene between us. Her eyes were intelligent, lively, inviting. No wonder she had secured two of Rome's best and brightest, if unluckiest, to become her husbands.

"Why do you think Cassandra was murdered?" I asked.

"Because I know the curious circumstances of her death. How she died suddenly . . . in the marketplace . . . in your arms. Was it poison, Gordianus? They say she was wracked with convulsions."

"They?"

"My eyes and ears."

"Your spies?"

Fulvia shrugged. "There's very little that happens in Rome that doesn't reach me."

"What else do you know about her murder?"

"If you're asking me who might have done such a thing or how or why, I can't tell you. I don't know. But a woman like Cassandra might have been dangerous to any number of people. She couldn't just see the future, you know; she had visions of faraway events."

"*Could* she see the future?"

"She was a witch," said Sempronia, interrupting. Her tone implied that I had already received my answer and should pay closer attention.

"A witch, you say? Did she cast spells, place curses, heal the sick?"

"She did none of those things in this household," said Sempronia, "but who can say what powers she possessed? She most certainly was able to see beyond the present moment and the four walls surrounding her."

"How do you know that?"

Sempronia opened her mouth to answer, but Fulvia raised a hand to silence her. "Let me tell him, Mother."

Sempronia huffed. "Why should we tell this fellow anything?"

"Have you forgotten, Mother? When Clodius was murdered, Gordianus was among the first to come to this house to pay his respects. He cared enough to seek out the truth."

"But he's an old lackey of Cicero's!" Sempronia spat the name.

Fulvia's eyes narrowed. She and Cicero were old and very bitter enemies. "It's true that you made your reputation working for Cicero, isn't it, Gordianus?"

"I wouldn't say that. I would say, rather, that Cicero made *his* reputation while *I* was working for *him*. I was never his lackey. Over the course of many years, we've had our ups and downs. Of late, I've lost touch with him completely. I haven't heard from him in months."

"Yet you visited his house only today," noted Fulvia. I raised an eyebrow. "I told you, Gordianus, there's little that happens in Rome that I don't know about."

"Yes—your eyes and ears. Yet you don't know who killed Cassandra?"

Fulvia smiled ruefully. "I'm not omniscient. I do have . . . blind spots."

I nodded. "Yes, I went to Cicero's house this morning to see Terentia for the same reason I've come to see you. You made an appearance at Cassandra's funeral, which suggests that you must have known her in more than a casual way. Who was she? Where did she come from?"

I addressed Fulvia, but her mother answered. "She was an Egyptian witch! It stands to reason. All the most powerful witches come from Egypt these days. They carry Greek blood in their veins—which explains Cassandra's blond hair and blue eyes—but unlike the modern-day Greeks, they haven't forgotten the old magic. The traditions are still kept alive in Egypt—the making of amulets, the memorizing of curses, the arts of fortune-telling. Cassandra was an Egyptian witch."

"We don't know that for a fact, Mother," objected Fulvia. "It's only a supposition."

"Your eyes and ears never told you where Cassandra came from?" I asked.

"Where she was concerned, I was strangely deaf and blind," admitted Fulvia. "It was as if Cassandra dropped to earth on a comet—and for all I know, she did."

"When did you first encounter her?"

"Many months ago."

"How many?"

"It was in November of last year."

If that were so, Fulvia had encountered Cassandra even before the day in Januarius when I saw the Vestal Fabia take her into the temple. "Are you sure?"

"Of course I am! How could I forget that bitter day?" Her

face darkened. "Just how much shall I tell you, Gordianus? Everything? Yes, why not?" She raised a hand to silence her mother, who seemed poised to object. "Caesar was still here in Rome, flush from his triumphs in Spain and Massilia. Word from the Adriatic Sea was not so good; Dolabella was powerless against Pompey's fleet. But from Sicily . . ." She sighed and closed her eyes for a moment. "From Sicily there had come the excellent news of my husband's conquest of the island, followed by the even more promising news that Gaius had pressed on . . . to Africa." She lowered her eyes and cleared her throat.

"Every day, here in this house, we waited for word of his progress. A messenger arrived with the news that he had taken Utica. We rejoiced. Then a second report arrived that contradicted the first, saying that Utica was still under siege but would fall into Gaius's hands at any moment. The mood in this house was one of joyful restraint. We lived in anticipation of great and glorious news. My mother made a joke, that soon . . ." Her voice broke. "Soon Gaius would have a new honorific to append to his name, and we would thereafter be the family of Gaius Scribonius Curio *Africanus*—conqueror of Africa!" Fulvia shook her head. "It's bitter to be left behind. A woman should be allowed to follow her husband onto the field of battle."

I raised an eyebrow. "Pompey's wife went with him when he fled from Rome. I understand she's with him even now."

"I don't mean that—to follow along like baggage! In a better world I should have been allowed to go along with Gaius, not merely as his wife, but as his co-commander! Yes, I know, the notion is absurd; no centurion would ever take commands from a woman. But I should have been there—to counsel Gaius, to help him weigh the advice of his subordinates, to evaluate intelligence from the field, to plot strategy. If I had been there . . ."

Sempronia touched her arm to comfort her. Fulvia gripped her mother's hand and went on. "Instead of going with him, I waited here in Rome. Is there any torture worse than waiting and not knowing? Some days I felt as if I were riding a storm-tossed ship, pitched between hope and despair until I thought I'd go mad. Other days were so still and quiet it was like being trapped on a ship in flat water—hours passing without a word, without a sign, only endless waiting and watching and wondering. Until . . ."

She drew a deep breath. "As I said, it was on a day last November. I had been to the house of one of Gaius's relatives to see if they had had any news of him, but they knew no more than I did. I was on my way home, passing through the Forum in my litter. The curtains were drawn. No one could see in, but because it was a bright day and the curtains are not entirely opaque, I could see out, at least well enough to tell that we were passing by the Temple of Castor and Pollux. I was thinking about Gaius, of course. Then I heard a voice.

"It was a woman's voice. It came from outside the litter. But the quality of that voice was so strange . . . and because of the words it spoke . . . it seemed almost to come from inside my head. The voice said: *He's dead now. He died fighting. It was a brave death.*

"Those words sent such a chill through me that I thought I might faint. It suddenly seemed dark inside the litter, as if a cloud had swallowed the sun. I called on the litter bearers to halt. My voice must have been very nearly a scream. The litter stopped so abruptly that I was pitched forward. Thraso stuck his head through the curtains, looking alarmed. He asked me what was wrong.

" 'Did you not hear it?' I asked. He looked at me blankly. 'A woman's voice,' I said. 'She spoke to me as we passed the temple.'

"Thraso looked back, toward the way we had come. 'There's no one there,' he said, 'except a crazy woman muttering to herself and pacing the temple steps.'

" 'Bring her!' I told him. He went to fetch her. A few moments later he pulled back the curtains of the litter, and I first saw Cassandra.

"She was dressed in a filthy tunica. She looked frightened and confused. Thraso had to hold onto her tightly, or else she would have fled. 'You spoke to me just now,' I said, 'as my litter passed the steps.' She shook her head and looked at me as if I were the mad one. 'You spoke!' I insisted. 'Say it again. Say the words you said before!'

"The voice that emerged from her was so otherworldly that even Thraso quailed a bit. It didn't match her body, you see. The voice was too old for such a young woman. It didn't quite seem to come from her open lips, yet there was nowhere else for it to have come from. It was uncanny, unnerving. 'He's dead now,' she said. 'He died fighting. It was a brave death.'

"The words were even more disturbing the second time I heard them. They shattered me. I began to shiver and weep. I ordered Thraso to take me home as quickly as possible. 'What shall I do with this one?' he asked. I could see he wanted nothing to do with the woman, but I told him to bring her along with us. He made a face, but he tightened his grip on the woman's arm. He let the curtains drop and ordered the bearers to hurry homeward.

"When we arrived, I told Thraso to bring the woman here, to this room. She was even dirtier than I had realized. Her clothes were ragged and worn. She had a distinct odor, as if she hadn't been to the public baths in days. In a voice as normal as anyone else's, she told me she was hungry. There was nothing menacing or uncanny or even odd about her. She seemed intimidated at being in such a grand house, and rather pathetic. I told Thraso to fetch some food and drink for her. Then I asked her what she had meant by what she said."

"And what did she tell you?"

"She said she couldn't remember saying anything at all. I was already shaken. I became angry . . . confused . . . I pressed her. She cowered and wept. Suddenly she began to quiver and twitch. Her eyes rolled back. She spoke again in that strange, hollow voice that seemed to come from the ether. She described to me a desert plain, blinding sunlight, a hot wind. She heard men shouting, saw flashing swords, heard the sizzle of blood spattered on hot sand. She saw Gaius—it could only have been Gaius, for she described him to me perfectly: his curling black hair, his glittering blue eyes, his defiant jaw, the half smile that would light his face when prospects were grim.

She saw him clothed in shimmering armor, though his head was bare, for he had lost his helmet. He was alone, cut off from his men, surrounded, slashing his sword through the air, until finally . . . he fell. They swarmed over him. And then—"

"Fulvia, no!" Her mother gripped her arm with white knuckles, but Fulvia pressed on.

"And then . . . she saw Gaius's face rise up again, as if by some miracle he had gotten to his feet, even amid all that murderous swarm. Not only that, but he was . . . smiling. Grinning like a boy, she said. But then . . . then she saw the vision more clearly and realized . . . there was no body below his neck, which was severed and dripping with blood. His head was being held aloft by the Numidian who had beheaded him. He only seemed to smile because . . . because the fist clenching his black curls pulled taut the muscles of his face, opening his mouth, baring his teeth . . ."

Throughout this long recitation, Fulvia kept her eyes on mine as if daring me to look away. At last I did, unable to bear the pain I saw there. It was not the glimmer of eyes brimming with hot tears, but a hard, dry grief, tearless and cold.

Fulvia drew a deep breath. "As abruptly as it began, the spell ended. She was simply a meek beggar again, dazed, hungry, with no recollection of what she had just said. I was stunned, shocked, speechless. Food was brought. I watched her eat. She was like a beast, with no manners at all. Her odor offended me, so I sent her to be bathed. I ordered that her old rags should be burned and told one of my slaves to find a proper tunica for her. The slave found an old blue one that suited her. When I saw her cleaned and properly dressed, I realized how beautiful she was. I told Thraso that she should be given a place to sleep, and that he should keep watch on her.

"At dawn Thraso came to me and told me that the woman had slept the night through, quite soundly. I myself had slept not at all. I told Thraso to keep the woman in the house, to offer her whatever food and drink she wanted, to lock her in her room if he had to. But I was the one who behaved like a prisoner. I shut myself in this room. I saw no one, spoke to no one, not even my mother. I simply waited, sick with dread. From these windows I watched the sun rise and fall over the city. I passed another night without sleep.

"It was on the next day—two days after the woman related her vision to me—that Caesar summoned his inner circle and told them that he had just received word from Africa. Marc Antony came at once to give me the bad news. I received him in this room, my heart beating so hard that I could barely hear him. He knew I would demand to know every detail. He carefully recited everything the messenger had told Caesar. The battle in the desert, the stifling heat, Gaius's last stand, even the fact that he had lost his helmet before the enemy swarmed over him—every detail matched what the woman had told me. Strangest of all, the messenger reported a rumor that King Juba had laughed when he received Gaius's head, not out of spite, but because Gaius appeared to be grinning at him. Do you understand, Gordianus? The woman had seen everything—*everything*—as clearly as if she had been there.

"I contained my emotions as best I could—after all, I was prepared for the worst even before he arrived—but still I wept. Antony did his best to comfort me. In the end I think it was I who comforted him; he and Gaius had been close ever since they were boys, as close as two men can be, even closer in some ways perhaps than Gaius and myself.

"Eventually I told Antony about the woman in my house, and the fact that she had already delivered the news to me two days before. Antony said that was impossible—word had only just reached Caesar, and Caesar would tell Antony before anyone else. I tried to tell him how precisely the woman had seen the details of Gaius's death, but Antony wouldn't listen. We had drunk quite a bit of wine by then, and his senses were muddled. He wasn't in a listening mood. I put him to bed in the guest quarters, then went to find the woman.

"But she was gone. She had vanished somehow, even with Thraso watching her. I realized that I knew nothing about her, not even her name or where she lived, if indeed she had a fixed abode. I thought of sending Thraso to search for her, but at that moment I saw no point. She had told me what I wanted to know, and the knowledge had only served to make me wretched for two sleepless nights before the news arrived from a more trustworthy source. And also . . . also I was a little frightened of her. She was a witch of some sort. If she could see events in Africa, who knew what other powers she might possess? She herself seemed not to understand her gifts and how to use them. She might be dangerous. I didn't *want* her in my house."

I nodded, taking in all that Fulvia had told me. "That was the last you saw of her, then?"

Something in her eyes changed, as if a door that had been open was abruptly shut. She seemed evasive. "Thraso reported to me later that she had become something of a fixture in the Forum and the markets, and that people had given her a name: Cassandra. I asked him to find out more about her, but there was very little he could discover, except that others in the city besides myself were availing themselves of Cassandra's gifts."

"Others?"

"You saw them—the women who appeared at her funeral. If you want to find out what they knew about Cassandra, ask them yourself. If you do discover something of interest about her—if you do find out who killed her—come tell me, Gordianus. I'll pay you well for the information. I'd like to know, simply out of curiosity. I've been entirely open with you, after all." As if to contradict her words, the faint smile that had been absent from her face since she began the tale of how she met Cassandra returned, and I had the feeling that she was holding something back from me.

"You never saw her again, face-to-face?"

She shrugged. "Perhaps, briefly. But that meeting was of no particular consequence. There's nothing more of any significance I can tell you." She sighed. "I'm tired now. I think I shall rest a bit before taking dinner. I'm afraid I must say farewell, Gordianus, to you and to your taciturn but very ornamental young son-in-law. Thraso will show the two of you out." She turned her gaze from me to the window. After a moment, her mother did likewise. Together they stared at the framed image of a distant cloud lit by the twilight's last blush of lurid pink against a backdrop of lapis lazuli. A scattering of faint, early stars twinkled in the darkening firmament.

The slave showed us down the stairs and through the long hallways. We had reached the soaring atrium when another slave, running at a trot, caught up with us and told us to wait. Thraso raised an eyebrow, then saw the reason we were being detained. At the far end of the hallway we had just traversed, coming toward us at a surprisingly fast clip for a woman her age, was Sempronia. As she drew closer, her gaze fixed on me as if I were a rabbit and she a descending hawk.

With a curt wave she dismissed the slaves. We stood at the base of one of the immense black marble columns that supported the skylight far above our heads. Sempronia drew close to me, speaking in a hoarse whisper. The vast space swallowed up her voice without giving back an echo.

"My daughter was not entirely forthcoming with you, Gordianus."

I raised an eyebrow, afraid that any comment might put her off. For some reason, despite her earlier suspicion, she had decided to trust me. What did she want to tell me?

Sempronia frowned. "My daughter has endured a great deal of suffering in her life. It's because she's so ambitious, of course; even more ambitious than I was at her age." She flashed a thin smile that contained no warmth. "I sometimes think: *If only she'd been born a boy.* But of course, if that were the case, she'd probably have gotten herself killed already—like Clodius, like Curio—or perhaps not. Fulvia is smarter than either of those fellows were. That's a curse for a woman, to be smarter than her husband. Fulvia's carried that curse twice in a row. Clodius and Curio—at least their ambitions and their dreams matched hers, if not their wits." She shook her head. "Now she's a widow again, with children from both her marriages, children who must be given the best possible chance in the world that's about to be created on some battlefield far from Rome."

"What if Pompey wins that battle?" I said.

She drew a sharp breath through her nostrils. "Such a disaster doesn't bear considering. No, Caesar will win. I'm sure of it."

"Because Cassandra said so?"

Sempronia gave me another chilly smile. "Perhaps."

"And if Caesar does triumph, what then?"

"My daughter will need another husband of course. And this time she must choose the *right* one, a man as shrewd and ruthless as she is, a man who knows how to seize an opportunity, a survivor! A man who can give my grandchildren their rightful place in the new world about to be born."

I nodded. "Fulvia saw Cassandra a second time, didn't she?"

"Yes."

"Because Cassandra could give her a glimpse of the future."

"Exactly! The witch could see across time as well as space. But it wasn't Fulvia who brought Cassandra here the second time. *I* sought her out. Fulvia didn't want her here. She was afraid to know her future, afraid it would match the misery of her past. But I told her that a woman must use whatever tools she can to make her way in the world. If the witch could give us even a faint glimpse of what lay in store, then we must seize that knowledge and use it!"

"When did you bring her here?"

"A little less than a month ago."

"And what did Cassandra foresee for Fulvia?"

"Glory! Power! Riches! My daughter shall rise to the first place among all the women of Rome."

"Even ahead of Calpurnia?"

"Caesar will triumph, but he can't live forever. He must have a successor."

I frowned. "You mean to say that Caesar will be a king and pass his crown to another? That was what Cassandra foresaw?"

"Nothing that specific. When her visions came, she didn't always see them clearly or understand what she saw. She couldn't even recall them afterward; she could only describe them as they came to her."

"And when you brought her here the second time, what did she see?"

A look close to rapture crossed Sempronia's face. Rather than softening her features, it made them even more severe and intimidating. "She saw Fulvia in a stola of purest purple, striped with gold, with a golden diadem on her head. Beside Fulvia, but in her shadow, stood a man—a great brawny beast of a man dressed in battle armor spattered with blood and holding a bloody sword. He, too, wore a diadem on his head. The witch was unable to see his face clearly, but she saw the image on his breastplate and on his shield—the head of a lion."

"Marc Antony," I whispered.

"Who else? It's their destiny to marry. I could have told Fulvia that myself without the witch's help." The fact that Antony was already married seemed to be of no consequence to her.

"What else did Cassandra see?"

The look in Sempronia's eyes made my blood run cold. "Like Antony, Fulvia was holding a bloody sword in one hand."

"And in the other?"

Sempronia bared her teeth. "A head, severed at the neck!"

"As Curio's head was severed?" I whispered.

"Yes, but this was the head of another, the head of the man my daughter hates most in all the world."

Was she speaking of Milo, who had been exiled for the murder of Clodius, and who at that moment was said to be raising a revolt in the south with Marcus Caelius? Or King Juba, who had laughed when he received Curio's head? I whispered their names, but Sempronia shook her head and looked at me scornfully.

"The witch described him clearly enough. Not as a portrait painter or a sculptor might, but in symbols. Lips dripping with honey, she said; a tongue like a snake's, eyes like a ferret's, a nose with a cleft like a chickpea——"

"Cicero," I whispered. His name was taken from the word for chickpea.

"Yes! It was Cicero's head that Fulvia held aloft!"

Caesar triumphant but dead, Marc Antony a king and Fulvia his queen, and Cicero beheaded—was that to be the future of Rome? My heart sank. I suddenly realized why Sempronia had confided in me. It was not that I had somehow won her trust. She still suspected me of being Cicero's lackey, perhaps his spy. In the next moment she made her desire explicit.

"Go, then, Gordianus! Go back to that bitch Terentia's house and tell her what I've just told you. Soon enough, my daughter will put away her mourning garb to put on a bridal stola. Then it shall be Terentia who'll be dressed in mourning! Long ago, Cicero made himself the enemy of this household. He never missed a chance to slander Clodius while Clodius lived, and he slandered him even more viciously after he was dead. He defamed Curio as well, even as he pretended to be his friend—casting aspersions on Curio's love for Marc Antony, telling Pompey that Curio had sided with Caesar because he was a craven opportunist—when the truth is that Curio died a hero's death, loyal to his cause until the very end. But soon enough Cicero shall regret the suffering his words have caused in this house. My daughter shall see to that!"

Her object achieved, Sempronia called for Thraso and ordered him to show us out.

As we were walked down the steps, the great bronze door clanged shut behind us. Davus turned to me wide-eyed and asked, "Father-in-Law, was Cassandra really a witch?"

"I don't know, Davus. But if witches truly exist, I think you may have just met one."

VII

The third time I saw Cassandra was again in the Forum. It was the day the consul Isauricus broke Marcus Caelius's chair of state.

Only a few days before, word had reached Rome that Marc Antony, departing almost three months after Caesar, had successfully made the same sea crossing and was on his way to join his forces with those of Caesar. It could only be a matter of time until Caesar and Pompey met in a grand confrontation. All Rome was abuzz with speculation.

Meanwhile, Marcus Caelius had been setting up his rival tribunal close to that of Trebonius for over a month. The riot that had ensued on the first such occasion had not been repeated, since Caelius, instead of orating and inciting the crowd, was quietly going about the business of taking down the names and recording the situations of the citizens who lined up to see him each day. These citizens were mostly debtors who hoped to take advantage of the legislation Caelius had promised to put before the Senate, imposing a six-year moratorium on debt collection. The fact that such a proposal had no chance of being made into law as long as Caesar controlled the Senate—and the fact that Caelius had no legal authority to set up a tribunal, much less record a registry of debtors—did nothing to deter the long line of desperate men who came to see him each day. Times were hard. Those who came to Caelius were clutching at any hope for relief.

Meanwhile, not far away, Trebonius went about his legitimate business of litigating between the debtors and creditors
who lined up to see him each day. Some of the debtors, once
they finished their business with Trebonius, went directly to
join the queue to see Caelius. In such uncertain times, who
could say whether the agreements struck by Trebonius would
hold? And what debtor would dare to miss out on the relief
that Caelius was promising, however slim the possibility that
it might come to pass?

Since that initial riot, things had been mostly quiet in the
Forum, and the other magistrates, including Trebonius, had
seen fit to let Caelius go about his fictitious business. I imagine
that the official attitude, worked out in private among themselves by Caesar's minions, went something like this: Caelius
was essentially putting on a mime show, a bit of political street
theater; and so long as there was no further violence, the best
thing to do was simply to ignore him.

On this particular day Caelius arrived later than usual, so
that by the time he appeared, escorted by a larger than usual
retinue and proudly carrying his own chair of state, there was
already a large crowd awaiting him, as well as a long queue
at the nearby tribunal of Trebonius. I was there in the Forum
as well, idly passing the time with Davus and Hieronymus and
the usual gang of chin-waggers. Caelius happened to pass very
close to me and caught my eye as he did so. He recognized
me and nodded. Then he raised an eyebrow and smiled faintly,
and I knew that he was about to hatch a new bit of mischief.

The portable tribunal was erected. The milling crowd began
to form a queue. Caelius mounted the tribunal and, with a
flourish, unfolded his chair of state. But instead of sitting, he
remained standing and turned to face the crowd. A thrill shot
through the assembly, felt by everyone there in the same instant, just as a flash of lightning is perceived by all eyes at
once. Farther away, in the queue of men awaiting conference
with Trebonius, heads turned to look toward Caelius. Trebonius himself, hearing the sudden murmur of anticipation, looked
up from the ledger before him and peered toward Caelius. An
expression of mingled exasperation and dread crossed his face.

He summoned one of his clerks and whispered in the man's ear. The clerk nodded and disappeared.

Caelius proceeded to pace this way and that across the small space of the tribunal, his hands on his hips, his eyes scanning the crowd. But he remained silent. The effect was to unsettle the crowd even more. Those at the back pushed forward. Above the general murmur, a few men scattered through the crowd—planted hirelings, most likely—began to shout. "Speak, Marcus Caelius!" they cried, and, "What have you come to tell us, Marcus Caelius?" and, "Silence! Silence! Everyone shut up! Marcus Caelius is about to speak!"

Caelius continued to pace the tribunal in silence. He lifted a fist to his mouth and furrowed his brow, as if debating whether to speak or not. The crowd pressed in closer. More and more men began to shout, until their cries joined in unison and became a chant: "Speak, Caelius, speak! Speak, Caelius, speak! Speak, Caelius, speak!"

At last Caelius stopped pacing, looked out over the crowd, and raised his hands for silence. Some of the rowdier members of the crowd continued to chant for the sheer pleasure of making noise, but they were quickly silenced by elbows in their ribs and swats to their ears.

"Citizens!" said Caelius. "Not long ago, you heard me speak from this platform about the legislation I have introduced before the Senate demanding a six-year moratorium on the repayment of loans. I regret to tell you that, as of today, the Senate has yet to act upon my proposal."

This was greeted by a chorus of catcalls and boos. Caelius raised his hands to quiet the crowd. "In the meantime, my esteemed colleague, the magistrate in charge of the city"—he indicated Trebonius with a sweep of his hand—"has continued to make settlements on behalf of the moneylenders and landlords whose interests he so doggedly represents."

This prompted a considerable uproar. Previously, Caelius had avoided making such a direct attack against Trebonius. Now his rhetorical claws were bared, and the crowd was ready to see blood drawn. He recommenced pacing back and forth, not as before, as if brooding and indecisive, but with his chin up and a swagger in his step. He looked sidelong in the direction of Trebonius, a smirk on his face and a glimmer in his eyes.

"Indeed, the magistrate in charge of the city has taken every possible action to ensure that my proposed legislation is never even considered by the Senate, much less ratified by that obsequious body of sycophants. Not a man among them appears to have a will of his own. They are all, to a man, the tools of a single intelligence—including the magistrate in charge of the city. He is, after all, a soldier first and a public servant second. I presume he was given his orders before the giver of orders left Rome, and now he mindlessly carries them out with no regard to the suffering and distress that surrounds him. Is he blind? Is he deaf?"

Caelius looked toward Trebonius, shaded his brow, and peered across the way, as if Trebonius were miles distant rather than a mere stone's throw away. "Well, I'm fairly certain he isn't blind, because he's looking this way. To be sure, he squints a bit. Scribbling those enormous sums on behalf of the moneylenders has strained his eyes, I suspect." This garnered a huge laugh from a crowd that was eager for any excuse to laugh at Trebonius. Across the way, Trebonius narrowed his eyes even more. The crowd before Caelius's tribunal roared with laughter.

"He's not entirely blind, then—but perhaps he's deaf," suggested Caelius. "Shall we find out? Help me, citizens! Call out his name with me. Like this: 'Trebonius, open your eyes! Trebonius, open your eyes!' "

The crowd enthusiastically took up the chant, raising their voices until the words rang through the Forum, creating a noise like thunder as they echoed off the stone walls of temples and shrines. Such a noise would carry all the way to my house atop the Palatine Hill. I imagined Bethesda and Diana going about their business in the kitchen or the garden and wondered what they would make of it: "Trebonius, open your eyes! Trebonius, open your eyes! Trebonius, open your eyes!"

I looked at the object of this refrain and saw him shift nervously in his chair of state, as if the ivory inlays beneath his buttocks had grown hot to the touch. Even though the words themselves were not directly threatening, it must have been unnerving for Trebonius to hear his name cried aloud by so many hostile voices in unison. As Caelius had said, he was more experienced as a military man than a politician, more accustomed to orderly chains of command than to the volatile dynamics of the Roman mob.

At last Caelius raised his arms. The chanting gradually dwindled to silence.

"Citizens—I think he heard you!" cried Caelius. The response was a tremendous roar of shouting and applause. I looked about and realized that the crowd had grown considerably larger. The chant had served not just to send a message to Trebonius, but as a clarion call to summon others from all over the Forum and the surrounding hills.

Caelius raised his hands for silence. The crowd quieted at once. "Trebonius, Trebonius, Trebonius!" he said, rolling his eyes and feigning utter exasperation. "In you we find that three goods make a single bad!" The crowd, always appreciative of a terrible pun, especially at the expense of a man's name, roared with laughter. Caelius was now pitching his voice to carry as far as possible, and the object of the joke, hearing it clearly, rose red-faced to his feet, clenching his fists at his sides.

"But, citizens," Caelius continued, "I did not come here today to speak ill of my fellow magistrate. He is merely an obedient soldier following orders. Nor did I come today to rail against the sycophants in the Senate, who are too concerned with pleasing their absent master—and enriching themselves— to give a thought to your suffering. No, I came here today for the purpose of delivering good news! Yes, *good news,* if you can believe it, because in the midst of the gloom that hangs over us, there *is* a ray of hope. I have been thinking about the six-year moratorium on debt collection that I have proposed to the Senate—and that the Senate so far has willfully ignored—and I have decided it does not go far enough. No, not nearly far enough! The good people of Rome must have even more relief from the crushing burdens imposed upon them, not just by the moneylenders, but by the landlords, those wealthy tenement owners to whom a man must hand over his lifeblood just to keep a roof over his head.

"Today, citizens, I am putting forward a new proposal. Beginning retroactively from the month of Januarius, all landlords will remit a full year's rent to every tenant! What does this mean? It means that all rents paid since Januarius will be refunded to you, and all rent due for the rest of the year will be forgiven. It means that the renters of Rome shall finally have some money in their pockets—returned to them by rich landlords who won't miss it! It means that you shall have the security of knowing that you cannot be evicted, that you shall have a roof over your head in the uncertain months ahead.

"The moneylenders and the landlords and their minions"— he shot a look at Trebonius—"will tell you that such a measure will utterly destroy the economy of Rome. Don't believe them! They're only looking out for their own narrow interests. A sound economy is based on confidence and mutual trust, and this proposal, as radical as it may sound, is the only possible way to restore the Roman people's confidence in the future and their bond of trust with the property-owning classes. You, the common citizens of Rome, have endured a great deal due to the upheavals of the last year. You have borne the brunt of the suffering. You have suffered enough! We must *all* make sacrifices—not just the common people of Rome, but also the wealthy who look down from their lofty perches and think only of how to make themselves *more* wealthy. Let them feel the pinch for a change!"

This prompted a roar of approval from the crowd. Some resumed the chant of "Trebonius, open your eyes!" The mood seemed more boisterous than angry. Merely by voicing such a radical proposal, no matter how unlikely the chance that it would become a reality, Caelius had given them hope and raised their spirits.

Suddenly the mood changed. The roar died down. The chanting stopped. There were cries of outrage, hisses, and catcalls from the outskirts of the crowd. I rose on tiptoes, trying to see over the heads that blocked my view. Suddenly I was lifted aloft; Davus had clutched me from behind and raised me up as if I weighed no more than a child. Such are the advantages of having a son-in-law with the strength of an ox.

I saw a cordon of bodyguards flanking some important personage—one of the chief magistrates, apparently, because the retinue was headed by lictors, the ceremonial escorts of the superior magistrates. Each lictor bore over his shoulder a bundle of birch rods called fasces, which served as a sheath for an ornately decorated ax. The use of lictors and their ceremonial weapons supposedly dated back to the time when Rome was ruled by kings. Normally, within the city bounds, the lictors would have borne their fasces without axes—but these were not normal times, and I clearly saw the flash of highly polished iron ax heads above the bundled rods.

I also caught a glimpse of the man whom the lictors surrounded and saw that his toga had a broad purple stripe. I counted twelve lictors, and knew that the newcomer could only be Caesar's fellow consul, Publius Servilius Isauricus. In Caesar's absence, Isauricus was the sole head of the state. Thus had Caesar observed the ancient tradition of electing two consuls, one to govern Rome while the other conducted military operations in the field, even though everyone knew that it was Caesar alone who determined the policies of the state. Isauricus was nothing more than a figurehead, a caretaker charged with enacting Caesar's will while Caesar was absent. He and Caesar were very old friends, and it was a sign of Caesar's complete faith in Isauricus that he had contrived to have him elected to serve alongside him as consul for the year.

I remembered seeing Trebonius, before Caelius began his harangue, dispatch one of his clerks with a message; evidently Isauricus had come in response to Trebonius's alarm. Once again Caelius was threatening to spur the mob to a riot, and something would have to be done.

The lictors pushed and shoved their way toward Caelius's tribunal. The churning, raucous crowd might have overwhelmed them by sheer numbers, but in the face of the disciplined lictors the crowd became confused and disorganized. The lictors had another advantage, for the first impulse of a

Roman citizen, no matter how riled, is to show respect to
anyone bearing fasces and to defer to any magistrate accompanied by lictors. Even in that disaffected crowd, a patriotic
respect for Roman authority ran deep.

The lictors reached the tribunal, where Caelius awaited
them with hands on his hips. Isauricus emerged from the cordon of armed men and mounted the tribunal to stand before
Caelius. His face was very nearly the same color as the purple
stripe on his toga. Next to Caelius—a handsome man in his
thirties, worked up by his speech to his highest pitch of charismatic radiance—Isauricus looked like a sputtering, hopelessly out-of-touch old grandfather in a comedy by Plautus.
The weird theatricality of the moment was reinforced by the
fact that the two of them stood on a platform not unlike a
portable stage. All they needed were grotesque masks and a
bit of background music to turn them into comic actors.

Isauricus shook his finger at Caelius and spoke in an angry
voice, keeping his pitch too low for the crowd to hear. Apparently I was not alone in imagining the two as actors, because a wiseacre in the crowd began to shout, "Speak up! We
can't hear you! You're swallowing your lines!" Laughter rip-
pled through the crowd, and someone started a new chant:
"Isauricus, speak up! Isauricus, speak up!"

The consul abruptly looked out at the crowd, furious to hear
his name shouted at him so rudely. Caelius, who had so far
kept a sardonic smirk on his face, appeared to lose his temper
in the same instant. The two commenced shouting at each
other. Whatever they said was drowned out by the swelling
roar of mingled yells and laughter from the crowd, but it was
easy enough to imagine. Isauricus was telling Caelius that he
had no legal authority to set up a tribunal in the first place,
and that by interfering with a fellow magistrate in the commission of his duties he was coming very close to treason.
Caelius was probably resorting to more personal insults; I
could easily imagine him calling Isauricus a finger puppet with
the hand of Caesar up his backside.

Whatever Caelius said to Isauricus, it must have cut to the
quick. The consul, overcome by a burst of fury, abruptly

picked up Caelius's chair of state and lifted it over his head. It looked as if he intended to strike Caelius with it, and even headstrong Caelius quailed a bit, stepping back and raising his arms to protect himself. Instead, Isauricus slammed the chair down in front of him and seized the fasces from the nearest lictor. He extracted the ax from the bundled rods and raised it above his head.

The crowd let out a collective gasp. Davus, unable to see because he still held me aloft, cried, "What is it, Father-in-Law? What's going on?"

"By Hercules," I said, "I think we're about to see a murder!"

Sunlight glinted on the upraised ax. The crowd fell silent except for a few scattered screams. My blood ran cold. The mob had rioted for days and had burned down the Senate House after Clodius was killed on the Appian Way. Now Caelius had taken up Clodius's mantle as champion of the downtrodden. What would they do if they saw him murdered in cold blood by the consul of Rome right before their eyes?

Caelius staggered back, his mouth open in shock, his face as white as a Vestal's stola.

Isauricus brought down the ax—not on Caelius, but on Caelius's chair of state. With a great crash, the seat was shattered. Isauricus raised the ax and brought it down again. There was another crash, and bits of wood went flying in all directions.

For a brief instant a look of relief crossed Caelius's face. Only a moment before he had been staring into the mouth of Hades. Just as quickly, relief was replaced by utter outrage. In a heartbeat his face turned from bloodless white to deepest red. He cried out and rushed toward Isauricus, oblivious of the ax the consul wielded.

At once, lictors swarmed onto the tribunal, unsheathing their axes and interposing themselves between the two magistrates. A moment later, to defend Caelius, men from the crowd jumped onto the tribunal. Isauricus and Caelius were separated, and Caelius was pulled from the tribunal into the crowd. His supporters wanted to protect him, but it seemed to me they were subjecting him to the risk of being trampled to death.

"Enough, Davus!" I said. "I've seen enough. Set me down! We almost got caught in the last riot, and I don't want to make that mistake again."

But it was too late. A vortex of humanity swirled all around us. Men screamed, shouted, laughed. Faces flashed before me: some jubilant, some angry, some terrified. The crowd spun me about until I grew dizzy. I looked for Davus but saw him nowhere. Hieronymus, too, had vanished, along with all the familiar chin-waggers. I gazed about, disoriented and confused, unable to spot a familiar landmark. I saw only a blur of strange faces and, beyond them, a confusion of walls and buildings. The crush of bodies squeezed the breath out of me, lifted me off my feet, carried me along against my will. I saw spots before my eyes—

And then, out of nowhere, incongruous amid so much ugly chaos, I saw the face of the woman called Cassandra. In her eyes I saw no panic, but quite the opposite—a deep serenity, oblivious of the madness around us. Was that a sign of madness, to appear so calm amid such insanity?

I lost consciousness.

∽

When I came to my senses, another face confronted me. For a moment I was confused because he looked so much like Cassandra—the same golden hair, the same blue eyes, the same incongruity of a young, handsome face burned by the sun, smudged with dirt, and surrounded by unkempt hair.

I gave a start and uttered a cry. The young man looming over me gave a start in response and grunted. A figure standing behind him stepped into view. It was Cassandra.

"Don't frighten him, Rupa. He's had a shock."

I rose on my elbows. I was lying on a threadbare pallet in a tiny room with a dirt floor. The only light came from a narrow window set high in one wall, and from the doorway, where a ragged cloth that served as a curtain was pulled back to show a shadowy hallway beyond. From the hallway came a smell compounded of boiled cabbage, urine, and unwashed humanity. From the window came the sounds of a couple arguing, a baby crying, and a dog barking. There was also a peculiar, persistent, not entirely unpleasant sound of metal clinking and clanging against metal somewhere in the distance.

I had been inside enough such buildings over the years to know exactly the sort of place in which I found myself. It was one of the ruder tenements in the city, probably located somewhere in the Subura, where the most wretched of Rome's citizens live tightly packed into close quarters, at the mercy of unscrupulous landlords and each other.

The young man called Rupa looked at me not unkindly, then rose from the pallet and stood. He was a big fellow—as big as Davus, which meant he was big enough to have carried me from the Forum to the Subura over his back. That must have been what happened, for there was no injury to my tunic or my flesh to indicate I had been dragged.

Cassandra stepped forward. "I suppose you'll want to know where you are," she said.

"In the Subura, I imagine. Not far from the Street of Copper Pots."

She raised an eyebrow. "I thought you were unconscious while Rupa carried you here."

"I was. I don't remember a thing since I fainted in the Forum. But I know the smell of an apartment in a Subura tenement, and I suspect that persistent clanking from outside is the sound of copper pots hung up for sale striking against one another. The sound they make is slightly different from the sound made by vessels of iron or brass or bronze. Given the angle of the light from that window and the distance of the sound, I'd say that we're about two blocks to the north of the Street of Copper Pots. Since we're on the ground floor of the tenement—"

"How do you know that?'

"Because the floor is of made of packed dirt. Yet there's a tiny bit of blue sky visible through that window, above the roof of the yellow building next door; therefore, the yellow building can't be more than two stories tall. Rather short for a tenement in the Subura. I think I know the one. Are we in the red building next to it, the one where there's always a barking dog chained next to the entry?"

"Exactly!" She smiled. "And I was thinking you'd wake up and be completely disoriented, like a . . ."

"Like an old man who lost consciousness merely from being spun about a bit? No, my wits are back, or at least such wits as I have left."

She smiled. "I like you," she said, without showing the least awareness of how such a smile and such words, coming from such a beautiful young woman, could suddenly light up the whole world for a man.

Rupa wrinkled his brow and made a signal to her with one hand.

"Rupa says he likes you, too." Her smile wavered. "You see, Rupa is—"

"Mute? Yes, I gathered that. For many years my elder son, Eco, was unable to speak—" I caught myself. Since I had disowned Meto at Massilia, I no longer had an elder and a younger son. Eco was my only son. And Meto—for me, Meto no longer existed. . . .

Cassandra saw the expression on my face. She frowned. "You've lost a child," she said.

I raised an eyebrow, surprised.

She shrugged. "I'm sorry. I shouldn't have said that. But it's true, isn't it?"

I cleared my throat. "Yes, in a way. I've lost a son. Or misplaced him . . ."

She saw that I cared to say no more and changed the subject. "Are you hungry?"

I was, in fact, but I had no intention of taking food from anyone who clearly had as little to spare as Cassandra and her companion. I shook my head. "I should go. My family will be wondering what's become of me." I stood up, feeling unsteady.

"Are you sure you're well enough?"

"When a man reaches my years, he learns to accommodate

small complaints, rather as a rich man learns to accommodate unwanted relatives. It's only a bit of light-headedness. Nothing, I should think, compared to the spells from which you suffer."

She lowered her eyes. "You're talking about that day I fell into your arms. I wasn't sure you'd remember."

"It's not every day a beautiful young woman falls into my arms. Nor am I likely to forget the previous time I saw you."

"A previous time?"

"You were in front of the Temple of Vesta. You did more than faint on that occasion."

"Did I?" She wrinkled her brow. "I suppose I must have. They told me about it later. I don't really remember."

"Have you always suffered such episodes?"

She looked elsewhere. "I'd rather not talk about it."

"Forgive me. I had no right to ask. It's only because . . ."

"What?"

I shrugged. "You fell into my arms. Now I've fallen into your arms . . . more or less. It's enough to make a fellow think the gods must want the two of us to meet."

She raised an eyebrow.

"I'm only joking! You mustn't blame an old fellow for flirting a bit." I glanced at Rupa, who seemed amused. In that moment I suspected he was not her lover. What then? A servant, relative, friend?

She smiled. "You were kind enough to catch me that day. Today in the Forum, when I saw you in distress, I wanted to return the favor."

"Good. That makes us even, then. But I haven't introduced myself, have I? My name is Gordianus."

She nodded. "They call me Cassandra."

"Yes, I know. Don't look surprised. You're not entirely unknown in the Forum. People tend to notice a person . . . such as you. I don't suppose Cassandra is your real name?"

"As real as any other."

"I'm being presumptuous. Forgive me. I should go."

She turned away from me. Had I offended her? Embarrassed her? I hoped for one more exchange of glances before

I left the room, one more look from her troubled blue eyes, but she kept her face averted.

Rupa led me into the hallway, and I passed from the world lit by Cassandra's presence into the world of boiled cabbage and barking dogs. At the front door, where a Molossian mastiff was tethered to a post, Rupa abruptly turned back, giving me no sign at all, not even a nod. I felt a prickle of envy. He was returning to Cassandra.

I walked home alone, feeling a touch of light-headedness, but of a different sort than I had felt before; a similar sensation but curiously pleasant. As I passed down the Street of Copper Pots, the clanking of so much metal seemed to echo the muddle in my own head. An unexpected brush with beauty makes a man feel happy, and carefree, and foolish.

∽

"You will no longer spend your idle hours loitering in the Forum. Too dangerous!"

So declared Bethesda that night in the dining room off the garden. On my safe return, she had met me with an icy stare and spoken hardly a word, but her display of anger was only a show. Hieronymus drew me aside and informed me in a whisper that she had been frantic and close to tears when he and Davus returned to the house without me.

Confronted with Bethesda's decree, I sighed, and unable to think of a rebuttal, picked up my wine cup instead. If I argued that I would always take Davus along to protect me, she would only point out that Davus had failed to do so that very afternoon.

Already outmaneuvered, I soon found myself outnumbered. "Mother's right," said Diana. "Davus does his best to look after you, Papa. . . ." She gave her husband a melting look and patted his hand. He stopped chewing for a moment and actually blushed. Then she turned her stern gaze back to me.— "But even Davus can't be responsible if you're going to start fainting and wandering off in a daze—"

"I didn't wander off! I was carried off by a pair of friendly strangers to a safe place."

"But, Papa, you might as easily have been carried off by strangers who *weren't* so friendly. Those two might have robbed and murdered you and thrown your body in the Tiber, and we'd never have known what became of you."

"Daughter, you tempt the Fates!" Bethesda tore off a bit of flat bread and threw it over her shoulder to distract any malicious (and presumably hungry) spirits who might be listening.

Hieronymus cleared his throat and came to my rescue by changing the subject. "I was quite shocked by that harangue from Marcus Caelius today. Not only what he said—that was radical enough—but how he said it, baiting Trebonius and the Senate in such an open fashion."

"Yes, now that Marc Antony's left Italy to join Caesar, Caelius has grown considerably bolder." I stole a glance at Bethesda, who seemed more interested in the flat bread in her hand. Politics bored her.

"He very nearly spoke ill of Caesar himself," said Hieronymus.

"He never spoke Caesar's name," I pointed out.

"To be sure," admitted Hieronymus, "but his insinuation was clear. Caesar was once the champion of the common people, but now he's their enemy. Once he stood against Pompey and the so-called Best People, but now he's shown himself to be just another politician in the service of the rich."

"Which means that the people need a new champion," I said.

"And Marcus Caelius is offering himself for that role."

I nodded. "For a newcomer to the city, Hieronymus, you're a shrewd judge of Roman politics."

"Politics here are different from politics in Massilia. All this rabble-rousing and rioting would never have been tolerated there. But politicians are the same everywhere. They have a nose for power. They can smell it the way a hungry man can smell bread. When they see an unclaimed loaf, they rush to seize it for their own. That's what Caelius is doing. He looks around and sees that a great many people are greatly unhappy, and he moves to make himself their champion."

"It's been done before," I pointed out, "by Catilina, by Clodius, by Caesar himself. But I don't see how Caelius can accomplish anything except to get himself killed—as Catilina and Clodius did. His problem is simple: he doesn't have an army."

"Perhaps he means to get himself one."

I had been about to take a sip of wine but stopped short. "What an idea, Hieronymus! A third army vying for control of the world?" I shook my head. "Ridiculous, of course. Caelius has a little military experience, but not nearly enough to challenge either Caesar or Pompey."

"Unless those two finish each other off," said Diana. "Who's to say that one or the other must return alive from Greece? Word could reach Rome tomorrow that Caesar and Pompey are *both* dead. Who would take control of Rome then?"

I put down my cup. "By Hercules! Sometimes, Daughter, you see what I can't see, even though it's right before me. You're right. A gambler like Caelius doesn't go through life thinking of all the ways he might fail. He narrows his thoughts until he can perceive the one path by which he might succeed, then bends all his will toward that path, heedless of the odds against him. If he loses, he loses everything. But if he wins . . ."

"He wins the world," said Hieronymus.

VIII

On the day after I called on Terentia and Fulvia, I rose early, taking care not to disturb Bethesda, ate a light breakfast, then called Mopsus and Androcles to come and help me put on my best toga again. The wool was a bit dusty from my outing the previous day. After it was properly draped about me, I stood very still while Mopsus gave it a good brushing.

Androcles stood to one side. "You missed a spot," he said.

"I did not!" said Mopsus.

"Yes, you did. Right there, along the bottom."

"I don't see anything."

"That's because you're blind."

"I am not!"

"Did I say blind? I meant to say stupid."

I clapped my hands. "Boys, stop your squabbling! Mopsus, get back to work."

Mopsus began brushing again.

"You missed another spot," said Androcles.

"Are you deaf? The master told you to shut up. Didn't you hear him?"

"He said no such thing! He told *you* to get back to work."

I took the ivory brush from Mopsus and gave Androcles a sound smack on the head. He gave a cry and reached up to rub the spot. Mopsus clutched his sides and brayed like a donkey. I gave him a smack as well.

Satisfied that I was presentable, I told the boys to wake

Davus if he was not yet up and to dress him. Meanwhile, I looked in on Bethesda. She was still sleeping, but fitfully, tossing and muttering as if in the grip of a fever. I felt her brow, but it was cool. Was she suffering physical discomfort, or simply in the throes of a nightmare? I decided not to wake her. Sleep was her only respite from the malady that had been plaguing her.

Davus was waiting for me in the garden, looking rather cramped in his toga. We left the house and set out on the rim road along the crest of the Palatine Hill.

It was a fine morning, already warm but not yet hot. Golden sunlight slanted through a towering yew tree near my house. Birds sang and flitted amid the branches. A little farther on, I paused to take in a view of the Forum below and the hills beyond. To the right I could see the shallow valley of the Subura, crowded with ugly tenements. More to the center and farther away, atop the Pincian Hill, I saw flashes of sunlight on the tile roof of Pompey's grand house, now deserted and awaiting its master's return. To the left, above the Capitoline Hill, a lone eagle was circling the Temple of Jupiter. Beyond the Capitoline I caught a glimpse of the Tiber, a gold ribbon lit by the sun, with wharves and markets along its banks. In a single, sweeping view I saw a microcosm of the whole world—palaces and slums, the dwellings of prostitutes and Vestal Virgins, temples where the gods were worshipped and markets where slaves were sold.

"What a remarkable city!" I said aloud. Davus responded with a nod. For good or ill, Rome was the center of the world. In spite of all the world's troubles and my own—my crushing debts, my rupture with Meto, Bethesda's mysterious ailment, the murder of Cassandra—such a view on such a morning could still inspire me with that curious sense of hope that young men feel when they rise and greet the world on a sunny summer morning and anything seems possible.

"Where are we going, Father-in-Law?"

"Today, Davus, I intend to pay a visit to Marc Antony's wife—and perhaps to his mistress, as well."

I had never met Antonia and knew her only by reputation. She was Antony's first cousin and his second wife; his first had been Fadia, the daughter of a wealthy freedman. That marriage—for love, people said—had scandalized Antony's family; even though Fadia brought him a handsome dowry, she had been his social inferior. But Fadia died young, and Antony's second marriage had done much to repair his reputation among the Roman aristocracy. Antonia was handsome, well-to-do, and Antony's exact social equal. But she also shared his weakness for adultery. While Antony had scandalized all Italy in the last year by traveling about with his mistress, the actress Cytheris, Antonia had been carrying on with Cicero's dissolute son-in-law Dolabella. According to the chin-waggers in the Forum, the only bond still holding Antony and Antonia together in marriage was their six-year-old daughter.

It was her shrieking I heard from within when a hulking slave opened the door at Antonia's house. A moment later, beyond the slave, a tiny naked figure streaked by, followed by a stooped, hobbling nurse unable keep up with her charge. "I will not! I will not!" the little girl cried, then screamed again. Is there anything so ear-piercing as the scream of a six-year-old girl? I covered my ears. The girl dashed off.

Before the door slave could ask our names or business, Antonia herself appeared, following after the child and the nurse. It was early in the day, so I was not surprised to see her wearing only a simple yellow stola without jewelry, and with her hair undressed, hanging down almost to her waist. With or without adornment, she was a beautiful woman. I thought of poor, plain Tullia, and wondered if the rumors about Dolabella and Antonia were true.

She looked past the door slave at Davus and me, put her hands on her hips, and raised an eyebrow. "Are you from my husband?"

"No. My name—"

She narrowed her eyes. "From Dolabella?"

"No."

"Then what business have you got knocking on my door at such an early hour? No, wait—I know you from somewhere, don't I? Ah, yes, you're the one who buried Cassandra."

"I am."

"Gordianus, isn't it? The so-called Finder? I've heard of you from my husband. You've got the son who goes about with Caesar, taking his dictation. Dictation from the dictator!" She uttered a crude laugh. I winced at this reference to Meto.

Before I could answer, the naked child came racing by in the opposite direction. Antonia stooped down, captured her, and held her wriggling until the nurse arrived. As the screaming child was led off, Antonia shook her head. "She's as willful as her father. The little monster inherited his temperament. And my looks, don't you think? Juno help the man who marries her!" She saw the nonplused expression on my face and laughed. Then her smile faded. "I suppose you're here to talk about Cassandra. Come along, then. There's a nice spot of sun in the garden, and peacocks to amuse us."

There were indeed peacocks in the garden, three of them, all strutting about with their fans in full display. Chairs were brought, along with pitchers of water and wine. Antonia had not yet taken her breakfast; she told the serving slave to bring enough for all three of us. When I saw the plate of delicacies he delivered, I let out a gasp. I had not seen a date stuffed with almond paste in months; the plate was heaped with them. It seemed that the shortages that plagued ordinary citizens did not affect the household of Caesar's right-hand man.

Davus gobbled up a date. He licked his fingertips and was about to reach for another when I stopped him with a look.

Antonia laughed. "Let the big fellow eat his fill. I have more dates and figs and olives than I know what to do with. Before he left to join Caesar, my husband spent months traveling all over Italy—with that strumpet of his, for all the world to gawk at—and he did a very good job of gathering provisions. Rather like a squirrel gathering acorns for the winter. Ostensibly his mission was to cow the locals and impose great Caesar's will, but he was really just extorting everyone. He's

a pirate at heart, you know. A lying, drinking, whoring pirate."
She snapped her fingers and pointed to her empty cup. The
slave poured a measure of wine. Antonia put it to her lips
before he could add an equal measure of water.

"My husband won't last, you know. His days are numbered.
I don't think Caesar much liked the way Antony ran Italy in
his absence, parading about with his whore, bleeding the countryside, getting stinking drunk, and generally making a spectacle of himself. Once Caesar's disposed of Pompey, he'll
come back to run the show himself. If they haven't been disposed of already, he'll deal in short order with this insurrection
that Milo and Marcus Caelius are hatching. He won't need a
drunken bully to do it for him. Antony shall simply be an
embarrassment to him." She narrowed her eyes. "I should have
divorced him before he left Italy. That would have been the
smart thing to do. But perhaps, if I'm lucky, the gods will
make me a widow soon enough and spare me the bother. Anything can happen on a battlefield, they say."

She paused in her tirade to drain her cup, then continued.
"I only married him because my mother wanted me to. 'What
a stroke of fortune!' she said. 'Fadia, that awful creature he
married, is dead; and now's our chance to rehabilitate your
dear cousin, and you're just the one to do it. The whole family
is counting on you. You always got along so well as children.'
Ha! I remember him pulling my hair. And I remember kicking
him in the shins. If only I'd kicked him a bit higher up, hard
enough to crack his eggs, I'd have done everyone a favor.
What's the matter, big fellow? Don't you care for the pickled
figs?"

Davus, caught with his mouth full, finished chewing and
swallowed. "I prefer the dates," he said.

"As you wish. More dates!" she called to the slave. "And
a bit more wine for me. To the brim! That's better. Where
was I?" She looked at me crossly. "You're all alike, you men.
Worthless. I'd divorce my cousin and marry Dolabella, but
he's no better. I'd only be spoiling my own amusement. 'Good
lovers make bad husbands,' as the saying goes. Poor Tullia!
That stupid girl worships him. She has no idea; she must be

blind and deaf. Dolabella treats her with utter contempt. I'd say she deserves it, the little fool, but didn't the gods curse her enough already by giving her that lout Cicero for a father? And Dolabella's no more promising than Antony in the long run. He's made a complete mess of the naval command Caesar gave him. He's likely to end up like wretched Curio, with his head on a stick—of no use to me whatsoever if that happens. Ah, well . . . but you didn't come here to talk about me, did you?"

She gave me a sidelong, heavy-lidded look. I began to suspect she had taken her first cup of wine even before we arrived. I had found her rather good-looking earlier, and her candor refreshing; but with every word she spoke and with each sip of wine she became more and more unattractive, until her vivacity seemed merely vulgar. A weakness for wine was her cousin's vice. Perhaps it ran in the family.

"I came here to talk about Cassandra," I said quietly.

"Ah, yes, Cassandra. Well, she never fooled me. Not for an instant."

I felt a prickling across the back of my neck, a premonition of something unpleasant. But I had come to seek the truth, after all, or at least Antonia's version of it. "What do you mean?"

"All that folderol, swooning and sputtering and rolling her eyes back in her head. Oh, she was very convincing, I'll grant her that."

"You're talking about her fits of prophecy?"

Antonia made a rude exhalation. "Prophecy! That's what she wanted everyone to believe. Well, I didn't fall for it. Oh, perhaps a little, at first. I'll admit I was curious. Who wasn't? Everyone was talking about her and how she'd been invited into some of the best homes in Rome because of her 'gift.' My dear husband himself was convinced of it. After Caesar, he was the first man in Rome to know about Curio's death; yet when he went to Fulvia to give her the bad news, Fulvia already knew because Cassandra had told her. Now that was a bit uncanny, I confess." She suddenly looked thoughtful, as if reconsidering her earlier judgment. Then she shook her head. "But no, the woman was mostly a fake. Perhaps not entirely. Perhaps there was a tiny bit of truth to this notion that she had a gift for prophecy. I'll say that she was nine parts a fake and one part genuine. What do you say to that?"

"I'm not sure."

"Didn't you know the truth about her, Finder? You buried her."

"If I knew everything about Cassandra already, believe me, I wouldn't be sitting here now."

Antonia perceived an insult and bristled, then smiled. "It's all coming back to me now, the things my husband told me about you and your dictation-loving son. You're awfully impertinent, aren't you? My husband admires that in common people." She sighed. "It's a holdover from his younger days when he was married to that daughter of a freedman, Fadia. He comes from one of the best families in Rome, yet he's always had a taste for mucking in the dirt. I suppose it gives him a certain advantage when it comes to endearing himself to the soldiers under his command. They appreciate the common touch. And no one is more common than my husband when he's in his cups, belching and farting and fondling that actress. Cytheris! Do you know where he first saw her? Performing some lewd mime after dinner one night at the house of Volumnius the banker. From that moment on, the two of them commenced to make fools of themselves from one end of Italy to the other. He even wanted to take her along with him when he left Italy to join Caesar. Can you imagine? I told him not to be an idiot. 'Caesar's locked in a life-or-death struggle to make himself master of the world, and you're going to show up at his headquarters with your plaything in tow, both of you reeking of wine and perfume? Do you know what Caesar's going to tell you? "For Jupiter's sake, Antony, put away your sword for once in your life, and get rid of that whore!"' "

She had strayed a long way from the subject of Cassandra. I cleared my throat.

"Ah! But you came here to talk about that *other* actress, didn't you?"

"Actress?"

"Cassandra, I mean. I'd sooner call her that than a seeress. Come to think of it, perhaps she *was* an actress. Like Cytheris, I mean. A trained professional. That would explain . . ."

"Explain what?"

She looked at me glumly. "All right, I'll tell you. I'll tell you everything. Hades, where is that slave? Ah, there you are! I see you skulking behind that pillar. Get over here and pour me more wine. Mind the peacocks don't bite you. And bring more stuffed dates for the big fellow. It amuses me to watch him eat." She poured another cupful of wine down her throat. "There now, that's better. Back to Cassandra. Cassandra the fake! Cassandra the actress? Maybe. I kept hearing so much about her that finally I went looking for her one day—"

"When was this?"

She shrugged. "Late in the month of Martius, not long after Antony left Italy. I still hadn't received word about the crossing, whether he'd made it safely or not. That was my excuse to seek her out, with that particular question in mind. Anyway, I found her near the marketplace by the river, sitting on a wharf with her feet dangling over the edge, mumbling to herself. Pretty, I suppose, in a common sort of way, but awfully scruffy." Antonia wrinkled her nose. "Ordinarily I can't stand being near such people, but I forced myself to make an exception in her case. I sent a slave to ask her to join me in my litter, but the slave came back and said that Cassandra wouldn't respond. 'She's in some sort of trance,' the stupid slave told me. So I actually climbed out of the litter and went to her myself. 'On your feet,' I said. 'You're coming with me. I'll have you washed and fed, and then we'll see what you're good for.' Cassandra looked up at me and didn't say a word. I was about to speak more sternly to her, but then she slowly got to her feet and followed me back to the litter. She didn't say a word all the way back to my house; she just sat there and stared at me and let me chatter on and on like a fool."

"Imagine that," I muttered under my breath.

"As I said, I sought her out especially to ask about Antony and whether he'd made the sea crossing successfully. I thought

I'd test her, you see. When a messenger did arrive with the news, I'd see whether she'd been right or wrong. But she was more slippery than I expected."

"How so?"

Antonia's face darkened. "When we arrived here at the house, I offered her food. She took nothing. That surprised me; I'd heard she was a beggar. Aren't beggars always hungry? Was my food not good enough for her? I offered her clean clothes. She ignored me. I offered her money. She wouldn't take it. I began to think she truly was mad. I asked her what she wanted. She looked at me and said, 'Nothing. You're the one who brought me here. You're the one who wants something.'

"I very nearly struck her, the impertinent bitch! But I decided to test her. 'They say you have second sight,' I said, 'so why should I need to speak to you at all? Can't you tell what I want from you simply by using your gift?' She said, 'It doesn't work like that.' 'Then how *does* it work?' I asked.

"She explained that over time she'd discovered a way to induce her fits by staring into a flame. So I had a lamp brought. She sat on one side; I sat on the other. And that was when she put on her little performance."

"A performance?"

"What else shall I call it? She suddenly pitched forward, knocking the lamp aside, and gripped my forearm with both hands. 'How dare you touch me?' I said. But she wouldn't let go. She only squeezed me harder, until I gave a cry. Some of the slaves came running; but when they arrived, they kept their distance. They were afraid of her, you see—more afraid of her than of me! I could hardly blame them. Her back was arched, and her head was thrown back. Her eyes were wide open but showed only white. She trembled and shuddered and pitched her head about as if her neck had snapped, but she never loosened her grip on my arm."

"Did she speak?"

"Oh, yes. She babbled nonsense for a while . . ."

"What sort of nonsense?"

Antonia raised an eyebrow. "Why are you so keen to know,

Finder? And how is it that you don't know already? You buried her. Weren't you in league with her?"

"In league with her? How do you mean?"

"Surely you know more about her than I do. Why do you think I've allowed you into my house? Because I thought *you* could tell *me* what Cassandra was really up to. Did she put on those performances merely to ingratiate herself, to obtain a bit of food when she was hungry, perhaps a few coins or some cast-off clothing? Did she think she might find a permanent patron, someone who would keep her indefinitely, so long as she kept uttering that mindless drivel? Or was it more sinister than that? Was she deliberately worming her way into this household and that, looking for things to steal? You always have to watch that sort; I knew better than to leave her alone even for a moment! Or perhaps she was looking for information she could use to her advantage. I can imagine her more credulous victims—Cicero's wife comes immediately to mind—opening up to her and spilling all sorts of embarrassing secrets, secrets that could be used against others later. Was that it? Was Cassandra a blackmailer?"

I thought about this. "I don't know. Did she try to blackmail you?"

"No. But I wasn't so foolish as to tell her anything I didn't want her to know."

"How are you so certain that she was merely putting on a performance?"

Antonia sighed. "You really don't know? Then I suppose I'll tell you. After she finished her 'prophesying'—after I threw her out—I decided to have her followed. I have a fellow who's very good at that. I didn't expect him to discover anything useful. I thought she'd simply go back to the wharf where I'd found her or to some hovel in the Subura, or wherever such creatures come from. But instead she headed for the neighborhood past the Circus Maximus. You know the sort of riffraff who live around there—actors, mimes, chariot racers, acrobats. When Cassandra arrived at her destination, my man recognized the place at once. How many times had he followed my husband to the very same house?"

"Cassandra went directly from your house . . . to the house of Cytheris?"

"Exactly. I'm told it's quite a nice little place. Her former master Volumnius bought it for her when he made her a freed-woman—a sort of parting gift for many services rendered, I have no doubt. You know why he freed her? It was at An-tony's request—a sort of goodwill gesture by which Volum-nius hoped to ingratiate himself with Caesar's chief lieutenant. To save face, Volumnius put it about that he'd had his fill of the little whore and didn't mind passing her on to Antony. But I know he was peeved. Well, if he wasn't yet ready to let go of her, he was a fool to show her off at that party where Antony met her. They say Cytheris learned all sorts of ways to please a man—things no respectable woman would consider doing—back in Alexandria where she comes from. That's where her first master, the one before Volumnius, taught her to be an actress. Oh, I call her an actress, but of course women aren't allowed to perform in legitimate plays, only in mime shows, and that's hardly acting, is it? Just a lot of buffoonery and half-naked dancing and declaiming lewd poems. The sort of vulgar nonsense Antony adores!"

"You were saying that Cassandra went to the house of Cy-theris. . . ."

"Exactly! Now what sort of coincidence could that be? Im-mediately after seeing Antony's wife, Cassandra pays a visit to Antony's mistress. Or should I say, 'reports' to Antony's mistress."

"Perhaps she was calling on someone else in Cytheris's household."

"No. My man managed to climb onto the roof of the neigh-boring house, where he could see down into Cytheris's garden. He'd done *that* before as well, keeping an eye on Antony for me. He saw Cytheris greet Cassandra as if they were old friends. Then they sat and shared wine together and talked for a long time."

"About what?"

"My man wasn't able to hear. They were too far away and kept their voices low. But he heard them laugh occasionally—

at me, I have no doubt! Well, I'd sent the bitch away without paying her a sesterce, and I'd told her nothing she could use to embarrass me, so I'm afraid I spoiled whatever scheme those two were hatching against me."

"You think Cassandra was somehow in league with Cytheris?"

"Of course! Don't you see? They're both actresses! That must be how they know each other. They probably met while performing together in some wretched mime show somewhere between here and Alexandria. Ambitious little ferrets! Cytheris managed to get herself nicely set up, thanks to Volumnius and my husband. Meanwhile, Cassandra got herself invited into the best homes in Rome by putting on a mime show of her own, pretending to utter prophecies while falling under some god's spell, all the while working who knows what sort of mischief. Whoever killed her did the decent people of Rome a great favor. That's why I went to her funeral—to see her burn! If only someone would do the same to that accursed Cytheris so that I could have the pleasure of watching the flames devour *her* carcass!"

In a burst of fury, she threw her cup across the garden. A hapless peacock shrieked and skittered away.

"I understand why you despise Cytheris," I said. "But what did Cassandra do to make you hate her so? What was the prophecy she spoke to you?"

Antonia glared at me. "For the last time, it wasn't a prophecy; it was a performance. But if you must know—very well, I'll tell you. For quite a while she rolled her eyes and jerked and muttered a lot of unintelligible noises. Then, gradually, I could make out words. Oh, Cassandra was very good! She made you listen hard to hear her, all the better to convince you that it must be something very special she was uttering. She said . . ."

Antonia stared into space and hesitated so long that I thought she had decided not to tell me. Finally she cleared her throat and went on. "She said she saw a lion and a lioness and their young cub dwelling in a cave. There was a terrible storm raging, but inside the cave all was warm and dry and safe. Eventually, despite the storm, the lion went off to forage. He found a gazelle, such a beautiful, graceful creature that, instead of attacking the gazelle, he mated with it. To get back at him, the lioness invited another lion into her cave and mated with him. But that lion already had a mate, and he soon left her. And her original mate was so happy gamboling about the countryside with his gazelle that he never returned. So in the end, the lioness was left alone . . . forever. Except for her cub, of course . . ."

At that moment the screaming young girl reappeared, dressed in a tunica now, but in the same bad humor. She ran across the garden to her mother, let out an ear-piercing scream, and threw her hands around Antonia's waist. Antonia tensed every muscle. Such a look of mingled fury and despair crossed her face that for a moment I feared she might strike the child. Instead, she took a deep breath and put her arms around the little girl, squeezing so tightly that the child struggled to pull free and finally did so, running back the way she had come, scattering peacocks in her wake and streaking past the over-whelmed nurse in the doorway.

Antonia stared after the child. Her face hardened. "As long as she was making it all up, why tell me things to confirm my own worst fears? Why not make up lies to please me? For a happy vision of the future, I might have given her a few coins and sent her on her way and forgotten all about her. No, she put on that little performance deliberately to torment me, and afterward she went running to her friend Cytheris, and the two of them had a good laugh at my expense. I'm glad she's dead! If someone else hadn't done it, I might have murdered her myself."

IX

The fourth time I saw Cassandra was on the day Marcus Caelius made his boldest—and last—appearance in the Forum.

Obedient to Bethesda's wishes—and leery myself of the violence that had been erupting—I avoided going to the Forum for almost a month following the riot that broke out after the consul Isauricus broke Caelius's chair of state. I whiled away the month of Aprilis in my garden, worrying over the ever-increasing debts I owed to Volumnius the banker, unable to see a way to continue feeding my family without going even further into debt.

All my life I had avoided becoming a debtor. I had even managed to accumulate a modest amount of savings, which I had deposited for security with Volumnius. He was a banker with an excellent reputation, trusted by everyone from Cicero to Caesar. But with the war had come shortages, and with shortages had come outlandish prices, even for the most basic staples of life. I had seen the savings of a lifetime devoured by butchers and bakers in a matter of months. Volumnius—or rather his agents, for I never dealt with the man directly—saw my deposits dwindle to nothing, then offered to extend credit. What could I do but accept? I fell into the trap and learned what every debtor knows: a debt is like a baby, for it begins small but rapidly grows, and the bigger it gets, the louder it cries out to be fed.

Brooding in my garden, I reluctantly admitted to myself

that I missed the jabbering of the chin-waggers down in the Forum. Opinionated old fools they might be, but at least their complaints took my mind off my own problems; and every now and then one of them actually said something intelligent. I missed reading the *Daily Acts* posted in the Forum, with the latest news of Caesar's movements, even if I knew that nothing in such notices was to be entirely trusted since they were dictated by the consul Isauricus. To be sure, Davus and Hieronymus still made forays down to the Forum and always brought back the latest gossip, but there was something stale and unnourishing about such third-hand information. I was a Roman citizen, and the public life of the Forum was part of the very fabric of my existence.

One afternoon I could no longer stand my idleness and isolation. Bethesda, Diana, and Davus had gone to the markets to spend my latest loan from Volumnius. Hieronymus was in my study perusing a very old volume of *The Punic War* by Naevius that Cicero had given me as a gift many years ago; it was the most valuable scroll I owned, and so far I had resisted selling it, since I couldn't hope to get anything approaching its true value. Bored and restless, on a whim I did something I had not done in a very long time. I left my house unaccompanied, taking not even Mopsus or Androcles with me.

Later I would question my motive for leaving the house alone that day. Did I not know, in some corner of my mind, exactly where my feet were taking me when I set out? I decided to avoid the Forum, so I crossed the Palatine Hill and descended on the east side, wandering past the Senian Baths, wending my way through increasingly narrower streets as I entered the neighborhood of the Subura.

If someone had asked me where I was headed, I couldn't have said. I was simply out for a walk, enjoying the weather, trying for a while to forget my troubles. Yet every step brought me closer. It was the barking of the Molossian mastiff chained beside the front door that startled me to my senses. I stopped and stared dumbly at the beast, then confronted the red-washed facade of the shabby tenement where Cassandra lived.

I stepped toward the doorway. The dog stopped barking.
Did the beast recognize me? Did he remember that I had visited the building a month before, when I was carried in, unconscious, by Rupa, and then a little later was escorted out by
him? The dog made no objection when I stepped through the
doorway. He looked up at me and wagged his tail.

I was at once surrounded by a familiar mix of odors—
boiled cabbage, urine, unwashed humanity. My memory was
poorer than the mastiff's; I wasn't sure which doorway opened
into Cassandra's room. Each doorway was covered by a ragged curtain to afford a degree of privacy. One of the curtains,
a faded blue, looked vaguely familiar. I stood before it for a
long moment, listening, but heard nothing from within. I might
have called her name, but somehow I knew the room was
empty. I lifted the curtain and stepped inside.

It was just as I recalled. The floor was packed earth. A
high, narrow window afforded a view of the yellow building
next door and a bit of sky; from nearby came the sound of
clanging metal from the Street of Copper Pots. The only furnishings were a crudely made folding chair and a threadbare
pallet strewn with equally threadbare pillows. A few thin coverlets were neatly folded on the pallet. Next to the coverlets
was a curious object: a short baton made of leather. I picked
it up. Imbedded in the surface I saw the impression of human
teeth. If I were to give it a name, I would have called the thing
a biting stick. I put it back where I had found it.

The walls were bare. There was no box or pouch for keeping coins or trinkets. There was not even a lamp to light the
room at night. Cassandra had no need to fear leaving the room
unattended. There was nothing here to steal.

I heard a noise and turned to see her standing in the doorway. She stared at me and let the curtain drop behind her.

Her hair was slightly damp. Her cheeks were red from
scrubbing. I realized she must have just returned from a visit
to the public baths. In Rome, even beggars can enjoy the luxury of a hot bath for the price of a few coins.

There was no surprise on her face. She looked almost as if

she had been expecting me. Perhaps, I thought, she *does* possess some sort of second sight.

"Snooping?" she said. "There's not much to see. If you'd like, I can tie back the curtain to let in a bit more light."

"No, that won't be necessary." I stepped away from the pallet to the center of the room. "Forgive me. I didn't mean to snoop. Force of habit, I suppose."

"Did someone send you here?" She didn't sound angry, merely curious.

"No."

"Then why did you come?"

I don't know, I was about to say, but that would have been a lie. "I came to see you."

She nodded slowly. "In that case, I'll leave the curtain over the doorway. That will give us a little privacy. Most of the tenants are out of the building at this hour anyway, scavenging for something to eat." She crossed her arms. "Are you sure you weren't spying on me? Isn't that what people pay you to do? Isn't that why they call you the Finder?"

"I don't recall telling you that."

"No? Someone else must have told me."

"Who?"

She shrugged. "What was it you said to me last time? 'You're not entirely unknown in the Forum.' Neither are you, Gordianus. People know you by sight. They know your reputation. Perhaps I was a little curious about you after having you here in my room. Perhaps I asked a few questions here and there. I know quite a few things about you, Gordianus the Finder. I think that you and I are very much alike."

I laughed. "Are we?" Staring into her blue eyes, acutely aware of her youth and her beauty, I could hardly imagine anyone with whom I had less in common.

"We are. You seek the truth; the truth seeks me out. In the end we both find it, only in different ways. We each have a special gift. That gift wasn't something we chose; it chose us. The gift is ours whether we want it or not, and we must do with it what we can. A gift can also be a curse."

"I'm not sure I understand. People say that you have the gift of prophecy, but what's my gift?"

She smiled. "Something far more valuable, I should think. I'm told that people feel compelled to confide in you, to tell you secrets, even when they shouldn't. Something in you draws the truth out of them. I should think that must be a very powerful gift indeed. Has it not provided all that you've gained in life? Your fortune, your family, the respect of powerful men?"

"My fortune, such as it was, has been swallowed up by a certain greedy banker. My family has been torn apart. As for the respect of powerful men, I'm not sure what that's worth. If you can show me a way to eat it, I'll prepare it for dinner and invite you to take the first portion."

"You sound bitter, Gordianus."

"No. Just weary."

"Perhaps you need to rest." She drew closer. Her freshly washed body smelled slightly of the jasmine perfume used to scent the cold plunge at the women's baths. Bethesda sometimes returned home from the baths carrying the same scent. Cassandra's hand brushed against mine.

"Where is Rupa?" I lowered my voice, for she had drawn very close.

She answered in a whisper. "Out scavenging, like everyone else. I don't expect him back anytime soon."

Many thoughts crossed my mind at once. I thought of the foolishness of men, especially men of my age, when they confront a beautiful young woman. I considered the implications of taking advantage of a woman subject to fits of insanity. I stared into Cassandra's eyes searching for some sign of madness there, but saw only a flame that drew me like a moth.

I put my hands on her shoulders. I bent my face to hers. I touched my lips to hers and slid my arms around her. I pressed the slender warmth of her body firmly against mine. I felt an exhilaration, a thrilling sensation of being alive that I had not felt in many years.

Suddenly she broke from the kiss and slipped out of my arms. I cringed and felt my face turn hot. I had miscalculated the moment, after all. I had made a fool of myself—or had she made a fool of me?

Then, with a start, I realized that Rupa had entered the room.

He hadn't seen the kiss. Cassandra, her ears accustomed to the sound of his footsteps in the hall, had heard him coming and had pulled away from me an instant before he stepped through the curtain. Nevertheless, he was agitated about something and signaling frantically with his hands. Just as I had been able to interpret the signs Eco had used in the years when he was mute, so Cassandra could understand what Rupa was trying to tell her.

"Something's happening in the Forum," she said.

"Isn't there always?" I said.

"No, this is different. Something important. Something big. I think it has to do with that magistrate who's been stirring up trouble."

"Marcus Caelius?" I looked at Rupa, who answered with an exaggerated nod. Then he made the universal sign of a hand drawn like a blade across his throat.

"Caelius is *dead?*" I said, alarmed.

Rupa waved his hand. "Not yet," Cassandra interpreted, "but perhaps very soon."

Rupa seized her hand and led her out. Even then, confused as I was by the sudden turn of events, I wondered why a humble beggar like Cassandra should be so interested in the fortunes of a politician like Caelius. On both of the two previous occasions when Caelius had caused chaos in the Forum, she had been there. Was that due to simple coincidence?

I had no time to wonder, for I was caught up in the rush to the Forum, following after Rupa and Cassandra.

The closer we drew to the Forum, the more crowded the street became. As Rupa had promised, something very big was taking place, stirring excitement and attracting people from all over the city. News spreads quicker than fire in Rome, from rooftop to rooftop and window to window. People came rushing out of buildings and side streets to join the crush, like rivulets flowing into a river.

Where it emptied into the Forum, the street became completely jammed. People continued to rush up behind us, making it impossible to either advance or retreat. I felt a prickle of fear. If violence were to break out anywhere in the crowd, there could be a panic and perhaps a stampede. I cursed my bad fortune. For a month I had stayed away from the Forum, fearing just such a predicament. On the one day I chose to go out, I found myself quite literally in the thick of it.

But along with fear, I felt another kind of thrill, far more pleasant. Partly it came from the simple excitement of being in a crowd, but mostly it came from my proximity to Cassandra. I found myself pressed very close to her, feeling the heat of her body, smelling the scent of jasmine on her skin. She turned to look at me, and in her eyes I saw a mirror of the same fear and excitement I was feeling.

I looked around and saw a narrow alley leading off to one side. A few people were emerging from the alley, trying to join the crowd, but no one was entering it. The north side of the Forum is a warren of winding little streets that take unpredictable turns or lead to dead ends. I wrinkled my brow and tried to remember where that particular alley led.

"Come!" I said. "Follow me."

Rupa hung back, frowning, but Cassandra took his hand and pulled him along. I plowed a course through the crush of people, jostling elbows and stepping on toes, until at last we came to the alley and stepped free of the crowd.

"Are you feeling unwell, Gordianus?" said Cassandra.

I laughed. "Is that why you think I wanted to escape that crush? I don't faint every time I'm in a crowd." *Though it would be worth it,* I thought, *if every time I could wake to see your face above me.*

I led them down the alley, which twisted and turned like a serpent so that it was impossible to see very far ahead, especially when the walls on either side narrowed until I could reach out and touch both at once. The alley branched, and I had to pause to remember which way to take. Rupa grew increasingly dubious, shaking his head and making signs to Cassandra that they should turn back. I could see that she was wavering, no longer sure whether to trust me or not.

The alley came to a dead end. The walls on either side were solid brick. In the wall facing us, a narrow door was recessed in the stonework. Rupa gave a snort and tugged at Cassandra's arm.

"Wait!" I said. I knocked on the door. There was no response. I knocked again, harder. Finally a peephole opened, and a rheumy eye stared out.

"Gordianus!" I heard my name through the thick wood of the door. A moment later it slowly opened on creaking hinges to reveal the stooped figure of an elderly man leaning on a crutch. We had arrived at the back door of the shop owned by my old acquaintance Didius. The shop fronted on the Forum's north side. Didius sold various goods required by the army of clerks who worked in nearby temples and state offices—handles and twine for assembling scrolls, Egyptian parchment and inks, styluses and wax tablets, and other bookmaking and record-keeping paraphernalia. He also specialized in copying documents; the work was performed by a small staff of scribes who labored day and night. Some of the documents that passed through his shop contained sensitive information, and Didius's profession often made him privy to more secrets than many of his customers realized. I had found him a useful man to know over the years.

"Gordianus!" he cried. "I haven't seen you in months. Not since you last came in with that copy of Pindar that had some water damage and needed a bit of repair."

"Has it been that long? Didius, these are—" I hesitated. What should I call them? "Two friends," I finally said, "Cassandra and Rupa. We're looking to pass through your shop into the Forum."

"Oh, no," said Didius. "Too crowded out there. Too crazy! I've shut the doors and barred them. But if you want to watch, you're welcome to come up to the roof, along with everyone else."

"Everyone else?"

"All my staff. They can't possibly work with this madness going on. And from the roof there's an excellent view of Caelius and Trebonius and their tribunals, or so I'm told. My eyes are too weak to see that far. Come, I'll show you. Hurry along! Who knows what may happen in the next few moments?"

He led us through a storage room and into his shop. The doors and windows were barred, casting the room into darkness. A ladder in the corner led to an upper story. Didius put aside his crutch and led the way. He hobbled a bit, but was surprisingly spry. We emerged in the room where the scribes worked; after the dimness below, the bright light from the tall windows hurt my eyes. I breathed in the smell of fresh parchment and ink.

Didius ascended another ladder. I followed, with Cassandra and Rupa behind me. Through the opening above I could see a patch of sky.

One of the slaves on the rooftop saw Didius hobbling up the ladder and reached down to help him. As we emerged onto the roof, the scribes crowded along the low parapet made way for their master and his guests. As Didius had promised, we had an excellent view of the rival tribunals in the Forum below.

"I see Caelius," I said, "but where's Trebonius? His tribunal's completely empty—no lictors, no clerks . . . no Trebonius."

"Must have run off," quipped Didius. "I'm not surprised. Caelius's rhetoric against him was scalding hot. He was practically daring the crowd to pull Trebonius off his tribunal and tear him limb from limb. Probably Trebonius had the good sense to beat a hasty retreat while he still could."

I looked down at the massive, seething crowd that surrounded Caelius, who was orating and gesticulating wildly. Above the noise of the mob, I couldn't make out what he was saying.

"What's he going on about?" I asked Didius.

"He's gone the distance."

"What do you mean?"

"Caelius has made his ultimate gambit, or so I should think. It's hard to imagine how he could go any further to pander to the mob. It's because he's about to be arrested. Why hold back?"

"Arrested? How do you know that?"

"I know because yesterday the consul Isauricus came here and asked me to draw up several copies of the Ultimate Decree. That would normally be done by scribes attached to the Senate House, but I suppose Isauricus wanted so many copies drawn up in so short a time that he brought part of the job to me."

"A sensitive commission."

"So Isauricus warned me. I named a steep price and told him I'd keep my mouth shut."

The Ultimate Decree had been invoked by the Senate on only a handful of occasions in my lifetime. It declared a state of emergency and empowered the consuls to use any means necessary to protect the state from immediate danger. Cicero had convinced the Senate to invoke it against Catilina and his so-called conspirators and had used it to justify the execution of unarmed prisoners (one of them being Marc Antony's stepfather—yet another reason for Antony's long-standing hatred of Cicero). More recently Pompey and his faction had invoked the Ultimate Decree against Caesar, goading him to cross the Rubicon. Why would Isauricus want copies of the Ultimate Decree drawn up unless he planned to invoke it? And against whom might he wish to declare it, except Marcus Caelius?

I looked at Didius. "And did you?"

"Did I what?"

"Did you keep your mouth shut?"

Didius cast a glance at Cassandra and Rupa. They were both staring raptly at the spectacle below, but he lowered his voice nonetheless. He shrugged and pointed toward Caelius. "What can I say? I've always liked Caelius. He's commissioned a lot of books from me over the years! Likes to give them to friends as gifts. Slim scrolls of erotic poetry, that sort of thing; impeccable taste. I don't always like his politics, but I like him. This latest campaign of his, carrying on against the bankers and landlords—it's all so much wind, if you ask me. Nothing will come of it, but I still admire his spirit. So I decided to do him a favor. Whispered a discreet word in the right ear. Caelius got the message. I thought we'd all wake today to the news that he had fled the city, but there you see him. I suppose he thinks he can somehow use the moment to his advantage. Maybe he's being clever; but if you ask me, he's cutting it awfully close. You can't say he lacks nerve! But we shall see if he's still alive come nightfall."

"A moment ago you said Caelius had gone the distance. What did you mean?"

"He's talking about new legislation again. No more half measures, he says. The time has come for immediate and complete abolition of all debts. Wipe the ledgers clean! Start over fresh! Can you imagine the chaos that would cause? But there's no shortage of people who like the idea. Look at them out there, swirling around Caelius and chanting his name so loudly you can't even hear him speak. The mob loves him—the way they used to love Clodius and, before him, Catilina."

"And Caesar, not so long ago," I said.

Didius shook his head. "People fear Caesar. But does anyone really love him except his soldiers? Mind you, I don't fault Caesar for refusing to pander to the rabble. A demagogue like Caelius can promise everyone the moon, but if he suddenly found himself really in charge of things, with a treasury to fill and a war to wage and a grain dole to hand out, he'd change his tune overnight."

I nodded toward the crowd below. "What are we seeing down there, Didius? Has Isauricus announced the Ultimate Decree against Caelius?"

"Not yet. The Senate's debating it now. There may be an announcement at any moment. I think Isauricus hoped it would be a surprise so they could take Caelius with no trouble. But now the word's out, and it's too late for that."

"Why today? What prompted Isauricus to take action? Did he know that Caelius was about to announce this plan to abolish debts?"

"Who knows which player blinked first and made the other jump? Something like this was bound to happen; the struggle between Caelius and the other magistrates has been building for months. If you ask me, I think Isauricus is acting now because he happens to have some troops available to him. They arrived outside Rome a few days ago on their way to join Caesar. Isauricus persuaded them to stay for a while. With those troops on hand, he has the muscle to use against Caelius if he needs it, so now's the time for Isauricus to bite a stick and pull out the thorn in his side. If the Senate passes the Ultimate Decree—and who can doubt they will?—Caelius has only a few more hours of freedom, maybe only a few more minutes, so he's cast his final throw of the dice. He's counting on this wild promise of debt abolition to be his Venus Throw, the one play that could turn the game in his favor."

Listening to Didius, I felt the little thrill a man gets when he lets himself imagine that the impossible might actually take place. What if Caelius *did* succeed in sparking a revolution against Isauricus and Trebonius and the other magistrates left in place by Caesar? What if he upset everyone's expectations by making himself—not Pompey, not Caesar—the new master of Rome? What if a single man, channeling the fury of the Roman mob, could abruptly turn the world upside down, sweeping the rich out of their houses and lifting the poor up in their stead? To do that, eventually Caelius would have to win some legions to his side. It *could* happen. If Caesar were to be killed and his troops left leaderless, they might be drawn to a charismatic leader with bold ideas, a man like Caelius. . . .

It was all a fantasy, of course, frightening and fascinating to imagine, but ultimately unthinkable. Then I reminded myself that hardly more than a year ago, it had been unthinkable that Caesar would dare to cross the Rubicon and march on Rome like an invading barbarian.

"Look there!" said Didius. "My eyes are weak, Gordianus, but don't I see men coming from the direction of the Senate House?"

"You do indeed, Didius. Armed men, a whole troop of them, scattering the mob before them. And farther back I believe I see a cordon of lictors with Isauricus in their midst." I couldn't tell whether there had been any bloodshed, but the men scattering before the armed troops were screaming and yelling, making such a noise that it carried above the raucous chanting and cheering of the mob around Marcus Caelius. Caelius himself appeared to hear the noise, for I saw him raise his hands for silence. A moment later, all heads turned in the direction of the Senate House. The cries of the fleeing mob echoed about the Forum, along with another noise, for not all those who fled did so passively; some were casting stones at the soldiers, who responded by drawing into tortoise formation with shields locked around them and above their heads. The flying stones pelting the shields made a racket like heavy hail against a roof. The noise heartened the mob around Caelius. They began to chant: "Abolish all debts! Bankrupt the bankers! Abolish all debts! Bankrupt the bankers!"

I looked on, aghast. In Massilia, during the worst of the siege, I had witnessed something similar—citizens casting stones at their own soldiers. For any city to reach such a level of disorder was a terrifying thing. To see it happen in Rome was appalling.

Suddenly I heard a roar of laughter from the crowd around Caelius. He was strutting across the raised platform holding up his chair of state. I squinted, trying to see what they were laughing at. It was the same deliberately plain, modestly ornamented chair Caelius had used before, the one that Isauricus had broken in a rage. The seat had been mended, not with wood, but with leather straps. In a flash I caught Caelius's little joke, which was typically convoluted, cruel, and vulgar. The one anecdote everybody knew about Isauricus had to do with his father's temper, and the fact that Isauricus had received regular beatings with a leather strap when he was a boy. When others needled him about it, Isauricus tried to make a virtue of his father's abuse, saying such discipline had toughened him up. *Gave him a tough bottom,* people would say behind Isauricus's back. For breaking his chair, Caelius had taken revenge on Isauricus by mending the chair with leather straps—a reminder to everyone of the legendary abuse of Isauricus's father and of the consul's own uncontrolled fit of temper. With Isauricus and a company of armed troops quickly approaching, Caelius, defiant to the last possible moment, was holding up the chair for the crowd's amusement—his way of tweaking his nose at the Ultimate Decree.

Above the roaring laughter and the hail of stones on shields—still distant, but drawing closer by the moment—I heard Caelius's stentorian parting words: "Shame on Caesar's lackeys who dare to call themselves elected magistrates! I give up my office! I give up my chair of state! But I *shall* return!" With that he hurled his chair of state high in the air. It landed in the midst of the crowd. Men swarmed to claim pieces as a souvenir. They tore the chair apart and snapped leather straps over their heads.

When I looked back at the tribunal, Caelius had vanished.

"But where . . . ?" I whispered.

"Into thin air," said Didius, "like a sorcerer!"

A few moments later the armed troops pushed their way into the crowd around the tribunal. Isauricus arrived, surrounded by his lictors, looking furious.

"Abolish all debts! Bankrupt the bankers!" cried the mob.

Caelius was nowhere to be seen.

I glanced at Cassandra, who was watching the spectacle below as raptly as the rest of us. It seemed to me that I saw a faint, elusive smile on her lips.

A few more stones were thrown, but with Caelius gone, the adoring mob had no reason to stay, and neither did the soldiers who had come to arrest him. The crowd dispersed.

When I looked again for Cassandra, she and Rupa had vanished, leaving as little trace as Marcus Caelius.

I talked for a while longer with Didius, then took my leave. I felt an urge to return to Cassandra's apartment, but for what purpose? By now my family must have noticed my absence and would know about the disruption in the Forum. Bethesda would be worried.

I hurried home, bracing myself for her reception. But when I arrived, a little out of breath from hurrying up the Palatine Hill, it was Diana who greeted me. Her brow was furrowed with worry as I had so often seen her mother's.

"I suppose I'm in a bit of trouble," I said sheepishly. "Your mother—"

"Mother's gone to bed," said Diana, quietly.

"In the middle of the day?"

"She became dizzy while we were in the market. She felt so poorly, she had to come home at once." Diana frowned. "I hope it's nothing serious."

That was the first appearance of Bethesda's lingering illness, which was to cast such a deep shadow over my household in the months to come.

X

"I suppose you ate your fill of those stuffed dates at Antonia's house, and we needn't go looking for anything more to eat before our next stop?" I said to Davus.

"They were very good," he said.

"I'll have to take your word for it. I'm afraid our hostess spoiled my appetite."

"She seemed like a very unhappy woman."

"Typically, Davus, you understate. I suppose we should try to be sympathetic. It can't be easy being married to a fellow like Marc Antony."

"Unhappy," he repeated thoughtfully, "and bitter. She spoke very harshly of Cassandra. She said she'd have killed Cassandra herself if someone else hadn't already done so."

"Yes, Davus, I heard what she said."

"So where are we off to now, Father-in-Law?"

"I'm thinking it's time I paid a call on a certain famous actress who keeps a house near the Circus Maximus."

Davus nodded, then reached inside his toga. He produced a stuffed date and popped it into his mouth.

He saw me staring. "I'm sorry, Father-in-Law. Would you like one? I have plenty more."

"Davus! What did you do, slip a handful into your toga while I wasn't watching?"

"Antonia said to take as many I wanted," he said defensively.

"So she did. You should have been an advocate, Davus. Cicero himself couldn't split a hair more finely."

⟡

It wasn't hard to find the house we were seeking. Everyone in Rome knew who Cytheris was, and everyone in the neighborhood of the Circus Maximus knew where she lived. An old woman selling plums from a basket—they should have been made of gold for what she was asking—pointed us in the general direction, down the wide avenue that runs along the south wall of the circus. We passed a troupe of acrobats practicing in the street, much to the delight of a crowd of children. A team of chariot racers all dressed in green came walking by. They were covered with dust, with whips wrapped tightly around their forearms and snug leather caps on their heads. I asked their leader for more specific directions.

He was straightforward enough when he gave them, but as we were walking off, he yelled after us, "Mind you don't let Antony catch you!"

"Or the fat old banker, for that matter!" added one of his companions, cracking his whip in the air to a chorus of raucous laughter.

As Antonia had said, it was a very respectable-looking house, tucked away on a narrow, quiet side street. I noted the fig tree her slave must have used to climb onto the roof of the neighboring house so as to look down into Cytheris's garden, spying on the actress and Cassandra.

Davus knocked. We waited. I told him to knock again. The sun was well up. Apparently Cytheris and her household kept late hours. I was not surprised.

Finally a puffy-eyed young woman opened the door. She was strikingly beautiful and strikingly unkempt, with her auburn hair hanging unpinned and tangled and her sleeping tunica pulled off one shoulder. Her informality revealed much about the household. Women like Cytheris were rare: a slave from a foreign land who had managed, by cunning and beauty, to become an independent, successful freedwoman. Finding herself in Rome without blood relations, it was natural that she should surround herself with slaves who were almost as much friends as servants, companions whom she could trust and confide in and to whom she gave a far greater latitude than a haughty mistress like Antonia (or Fulvia or Terentia) would ever allow. Such slaves would share to some degree in their mistress's notorious debauchery; they would stay up late with her and likewise sleep late, and think nothing of answering the door in dishabille.

The woman who answered the door looked Davus up and down, eyeing him rather as he had eyed the stuffed dates at Antonia's house. Though her hazel eyes eventually settled on me, acknowledging that the senior of the callers was more likely the one in charge, she seemed not really to see me, and certainly not with the riveting attention she had devoted to Davus, as if I were not a man but the shadow of one. Thus do we become more and more invisible as we grow older, until people fail to see us even when they look straight at us.

And yet . . . Cassandra had seen me. To her, I had not been invisible; to her I was still a vivid presence, a man of flesh and blood, vital, robust, existing in the moment, teeming with life and sensation. No wonder I had been so vulnerable to her; no wonder I had fallen so completely under her spell. . . .

My thoughts, wandering, were drawn back to the moment by the young woman's laughter, which was sharp but not cruel. "You look like you could use a drink!" she said, evidence that I was visible to her after all—a gray, glum-looking man in a toga.

"I'll leave it to your mistress to decide whether she'll offer me one," I snapped.

"My mistress?" She raised an eyebrow. Suddenly I knew that I was talking to Cytheris herself. She saw the moment of realization on my face and laughed again. Then her expression became more serious. "You're Gordianus, aren't you? I saw you at the funeral. I saw this one, too. . . ."

"This is Davus, my son-in-law."

"Married, then?" She said the word as if it were a challenge, not a disappointment. "You'd both better come inside.

My neighbors are endlessly fascinated by everyone who comes to this door; they've probably already seen you and run off to spread more gossip about me. Their own lives must be frightfully boring, don't you think, for them to be so fascinated by a simple girl from Alexandria?"

She swept us inside, slammed the door shut behind her, then led us through a small atrium and down a short hallway. The rooms we passed were small but exquisitely furnished. Dominating the little garden at the center of the house was a statue of Venus on a pedestal, only slightly smaller than life-size. At each of the garden's four corners were statues of satyrs in states of rampant excitement, partially concealed amid shrubbery as if they were lurking and stalking the goddess of love. Was this how Cytheris viewed herself and her suitors?

"You're wondering why I answered the door myself," she said breezily. "You Romans, always so strict about that sort of thing, so insistent on decorum! But really, if you knew what I've put the poor slaves through over the last two nights! It's only fair to let them sleep a bit late this morning. Or is it still morning?" She stopped beside the Venus and squinted up at the sun.

I looked around the garden and saw the aftermath of a drunken party. Chairs and little tripod tables were scattered about, some lying on their sides. Wine cups were abandoned here and there; flies buzzed above the crimson dregs. Various musical instruments—tambourines, rattles, flutes, and lyres—were piled helter-skelter against a wall. On the ground beneath one of the lurking satyrs, half-hidden amid the shrubbery, lay a handsome young slave, snoring softly.

"It's this one's job to answer the door," said Cytheris, walking up to him. I thought she was going to give him a kick, but instead she looked down at him with a doting smile. "Such a sweet little faun. Even his snore is sweet, don't you think?" Then she did give him a kick, but gently, prodding him with her foot until he finally stirred and rose groggily to his feet, brushing leaves from his curly black hair. He saw that his mistress had company and without being told gathered three chairs and set them in the shade, then disappeared into the house, blinking and rubbing his eyes.

"Bring the best Falernian, Chrysippus!" Cytheris called after him. "Not the cheap swill I served to that rowdy gang of actors and mimes who were here last night."

She smiled and indicated that we should sit, then finally took a good look at me. I felt a bit uncomfortable under her scrutiny. "Yes," she said, "now I see what it was that Cassandra saw in you. 'It's his eyes, Cytheris,' she said to me once. 'He has the most extraordinary eyes—like a wise old king in a legend.' "

Did I stiffen? Did my face turn red? Cytheris looked from me to Davus and back and pursed her lips. "Oh, dear, was that indiscreet of me?" she said. "You must tell me right away whether I can speak to you candidly or not. I'm not the sort to hold my tongue unless I'm asked to. Perhaps you should send your frowning son-in-law out of earshot for a while— though that would be a pity."

"No, Davus can stay. There's no point in concealing anything about Cassandra . . . now that she's dead. That's why I've come to you. You must have known her quite well if she told you about herself . . . and me."

She looked at me sidelong. "As you say, now that she's dead, there's no point in hiding anything, is there? To whom else have you spoken about her?"

"I've been calling on the women who came to her funeral: Terentia, Fulvia, Antonia. . . ."

"Ha! You're not likely to discover anything important about Cassandra from any of those hens, unless it was one of them who murdered her." A frown pulled at her lips, but she brightened when Chrysippus reappeared bearing a pitcher and three cups. I had no craving for wine, but only a fool would pass up an offer of good Falernian, especially in such hard times. The dark flavor played upon my tongue and filled my head like a warm, comforting mist.

"Terentia and Fulvia think Cassandra was a true seeress. They were both quite in awe of her," I said.

"But not Antonia?"

"Antonia has a very different opinion. She thinks Cassandra was an impostor."

"And Cassandra's spells of prophecy?"

"Merely part of an act."

Cytheris smiled. "Antonia is no fool, no matter what her dear husband says."

"Antonia was right about Cassandra?"

Cytheris considered her answer before she spoke. "Up to a point."

I frowned. Cytheris smiled. She seemed to enjoy my puzzlement. Her smile widened into a yawn, and she stretched her arms above her head. The movement caused her torso to shift in a most intriguing way beneath the loose tunica. Even her most casual movements were marked by a dancer's gracefulness. I would have cursed her condescending smile except that it made her even more remarkably beautiful. I looked at the stone satyrs lurking in the corners, gazing with lust upon the goddess they would never touch, and felt a stab of sympathy for them.

"Shall I explain?" she said.

"I'd be grateful if you would."

"Where to begin? Back in Alexandria, I suppose. That's where I met her, when we were both hardly more than children. I was born to a slave mother; but early on someone saw in me a talent for dancing, and I was sold to the master of a mime troupe—not just any troupe, but the oldest and most famous in Alexandria. The master liked to say that his ancestors had entertained Alexander the Great. People in Alexandria are always making claims like that. Still, the troupe could trace its history back for generations. I was taught to dance and mime and recite by some of the finest performers in Alexandria, and that means the finest in the world."

"And Cassandra?"

"The master acquired her and brought her into the troupe shortly after me. I was terribly jealous of her. Do you know, I think this is the first time I've ever admitted that to anyone."

"Jealous? Why?"

"Because she was so much more talented that I was—at

everything! Her gifts were extraordinary. She could recite Homer and make men weep, or make them weep with laughter by enacting a fable by Aesop. She could dance like a veil floating on the breeze. She could sing like a bird, and do so in whatever language you pleased—because she picked up languages the way the rest of us picked up bits of jewelry from admirers in the audience. And she did all this without apparent effort. Beside her, I felt like a clumsy, sweating, squawking fool."

"I find that hard to believe, Cytheris."

"Only because you never saw the two of us perform side by side."

"You must have hated her."

"Hated her?" Cytheris sighed. "Quite the opposite. We were very, very close back in those days, Cassandra and I. Those lovely days in Alexandria . . ."

"You call her Cassandra, yet that can't have been her real name."

She smiled. "The curious thing is, that *was* what we called her, even then. But you're right. When she first arrived, she had another name. But do you know, I've completely forgotten it. Some totally unpronounceable Sarmatian name; she'd come from somewhere on the far side of the Euxine Sea. But very early on she played Cassandra in a new mime show the master had written. Just a vulgar little skit, really; can you imagine, a comic Cassandra? But she was hilarious, staggering around, harassing the other characters, making rude prophecies and double entendres about the city officials and King Ptolemy. People loved it so much they demanded that mime every time we performed. She made such an impression with the role that the name stuck, and Cassandra was what we called her from then on."

Cytheris gazed thoughtfully into her cup, swirling the Falernian into a vortex. "We begin as we continue in this life. That's especially true of us performers. If we're lucky, we find a role that fits, and we play it to the hilt. I always specialized in playing the wanton woman, the seductress. Look where that role's taken me! Cassandra played . . . Cassandra. I imagine it must be the same for you, Gordianus. To some extent isn't the Finder a role you fell into early on, that you gradually perfected, that you'll keep playing until the end?"

"Perhaps. But if I'm playing a role, where's the playwright? And if there is a playwright, I'd like to complain to him about the nasty surprises he keeps throwing at me."

"Complain? You should be thankful for a life that keeps giving you surprises! Surprises keep you on your toes. You wouldn't want to grow stale in your part, would you?" She laughed, then sighed. "But we were talking about Cassandra. It's such a pity that women aren't allowed to be real actors, performing in the Greek tragedies or even in silly Roman comedies. Instead, only men can go on the legitimate stage. It doesn't matter if the role is a swaggering general or a virgin goddess, it's a man who performs it behind a mask. Women are allowed only to be dancers or to perform mime comedies in the street. It's criminal, really. When I think of what our Cassandra could have achieved performing the great female parts—the Antigone of Sophocles or Euripides' Medea. Or the Clytaemnestra of Aeschylus—imagine that! She'd have made your blood run cold. She'd have made strong men run whimpering from the theater! Perhaps *that's* why women aren't allowed to play women on the stage—the result might be too disturbing for you men in the audience, and too inspiring for the women.

"Even so, we actresses sometimes manage to find the role that takes us where we want to go. We simply have to create it ourselves and live it day by day, instead of performing it on a stage. That's what I did. And that's what our Cassandra did."

"Until the role killed her," I said. "You say you met her in Alexandria. What then?"

"Dear old Volumnius came along. Fat, sweet, incredibly rich Volumnius. This was five years ago—yes, almost exactly five years to the day. Volumnius was in Alexandria on some sort of business trip. He just happened to be passing through the Rhakotis district with his entourage one day when we were performing near the Temple of Serapis. I spotted him in the audience right away, fiddling with his gold rings and his gold necklaces and biting his lips and watching me dance the way a cat watches a sparrow flit through the trees. I put on the performance of my life that day. I was doing the dance of seven veils, taking them off one by one—a bit of naughtiness to spice up the show in between all the clowning. You're supposed to take off only six veils, of course; that's the point, to tease the crowd and make them hang around for more, hoping you'll come back for an encore. But that day I didn't stop at six; I took off the seventh as well."

Cytheris laughed. "Volumnius's eyes almost popped out of his head! As for the poor master, I thought he was going to have a heart attack. Even in Alexandria, women can't dance naked in the street, and the city authorities were always looking for some excuse to shut us down. But I took off that final veil as a gambit, and the gambit worked. The next day I had a new master. When Volumnius headed back to Rome on his private ship, I was with him. And I've never looked back."

"Now you're a freedwoman."

"Yes. Antony helped with that. I still have certain . . . contractual obligations . . . to Volumnius, but this house and everything and everyone in it are mine." She snorted. "No wonder a woman like Antonia hates me so much. What has she ever accomplished on her own merit? Everything comes to her because of her family and her name. She couldn't even find a husband outside her family! I should feel desperately trapped, living such a cramped little life. I've made my own way in the world, using what the gods gave me."

"What about Cassandra?"

"That was the hardest thing about leaving Alexandria—saying good-bye to Cassandra. I wept. So did she. I was sure I'd never see her again. When you're young, the world seems such a big place, so easy to get lost in. But it's not so big after all, is it? All roads lead to Rome. I came by one road. Cassandra came by another. Earlier this year I began to hear the rumors about a madwoman down in the Forum who had the gift of prophecy. People said she was called Cassandra. I thought, *Could it possibly be* my *Cassandra?* I piled into that gaudy litter Antony gave me and went to have a look. And of course it *was* her, standing in front of the Temple of Vesta wearing a ragged tunica, muttering to herself and begging for alms. *What in Hades is she up to?* I asked myself. Then I began to worry. What if she really had gone mad? What if she had taken it into her head that she really *was* her namesake? Perhaps the gods had punished her—had looked down and seen her making a mockery of the Trojan princess whom Apollo tormented, and for her hubris they had driven her mad. Half the lunatics and religious fanatics in the world make their way to Rome; why not Cassandra, if she had gone crazy? You see . . ."

Cytheris hesitated. I gave her a questioning look.

"Even now, all these years later, this isn't easy to talk about," she said. "When we were young, I promised her I would tell no one. She was always so frightened that it would happen while she was performing, that her secret affliction would be exposed. . . ."

"She has no need of secrets now," I said.

Cytheris nodded. "You're right; I'll tell you. Cassandra was subject to spells of falling sickness. In the time I knew her in Alexandria, it happened only twice that I knew of. But it was frightening to watch. I'll never forget the first time. We were alone in the room we shared at the master's house. We were talking, laughing—then suddenly she was thrown to the floor. It was uncanny, bizarre, as if a giant, invisible hand had cast her down and was holding her there while she thrashed and writhed. Her eyes rolled up in her head. She foamed at the mouth. She muttered something incomprehensible. I had the presence of mind to put something in her mouth to keep her from swallowing her tongue, and I did my best to hold her down so that she wouldn't hurt herself.

"When it was over, she gradually came to her senses. She remembered nothing. I told her what had happened. She said it had happened to her before, and she begged me to tell no one. I told her the master would have to know, that he'd find out sooner or later. But she made me promise not to tell him. She said perhaps it would never happen again. But it did, at least once more before I left Alexandria. That time, too, it was in our room, and no one but me saw it."

Cytheris studied my face. "This is familiar to you, isn't it, Finder? Did something similar happen to Cassandra on one of your visits to her? She told me about your visits. I know that you called on her more than once."

I took a deep breath and evaded the question. "I was thinking of something my son—" I stopped myself from speaking Meto's name. "I was thinking of something I once was told about Caesar. For a period of time, during his youth, he suffered from such seizures. He, too, tried to keep them secret. Gradually they stopped, and they've never recurred. A priest once told him his seizures were a sign of the gods' favor. Caesar himself believes they were the result of a blow to his head when he was kidnapped by pirates as a young man."

Cytheris considered this. "I don't know how Cassandra accounted for her spells. But when I saw her again, here in Rome, I remembered them, and I began to wonder. What if everything I'd heard about this madwoman in the Forum was true—that she didn't merely pretend to see the future or imagine such a thing, but that she really *was* subject to divine visions? Why not? Perhaps her seizures in Alexandria had merely been precursors to the full-blown gift of prophecy she had since acquired.

"So which was it? Was Cassandra putting on a deliberate performance? Had she gone mad, imagining herself to be the Trojan princess she'd played in the mime shows? Or in the years since I had last seen her, had she truly become a seeress and somehow ended up here in Rome, a beggar in the streets? I remembered the Cassandra I had known and loved in Alexandria, and I had to know the truth.

"I told the litter bearers to draw alongside her. I could see her through the gauze curtains, close enough to touch, but I didn't think she could see me—you know how such curtains work. And yet, even as I was reaching to draw back the curtains, she turned straight toward me and spoke my name. That gave me a start! Such an uncanny sensation shot through me, for a moment I hesitated to draw back the curtain. When I finally did, my hand was trembling. But when I saw her, all my trepidation melted away. She was smiling, trying not to laugh. Even with her unkempt hair and the smudges of dirt on her cheeks, she was the same Cassandra I had known in Alexandria.

"I burst out laughing and drew her into the litter. I closed the curtains and told the bearers to take me home. That night we drank Falernian and talked until dawn."

"And what did she tell you?" I said. "Which of your hopes or worries for Cassandra turned out to be true? Was she mad? Deluded? Pretending? Or something else?"

Cytheris smiled and at the same time wrinkled her brow. She shook her head. "I wish I knew!"

"But if she was the same Cassandra you had known . . . and if the two of you talked for hours . . ."

"We talked about old times in Egypt. We talked about my fortunes since I came to Rome. We talked about Antony and Antonia, about Caesar and Pompey, about the state of the world. But when it came to talking about Cassandra—how she had come to Rome and why—she drew a veil of secrecy."

"You allowed that?"

"I respected it. Clearly she wasn't mad, not in the sense of having lost the spark of her old self; I could see that at once. But had she been touched by a god, given the gift of prophecy? Or was she acting a part? Had she come to Rome on her own initiative? Or had she been brought here by someone, for some purpose? I can't tell you the answers, because I never knew. Not for certain, anyway. I asked Cassandra—cajoled her, teased her, even begged her a bit—but she wouldn't tell me. She would only say that in the fullness of time I might know everything; and until then it was best if I knew nothing about her comings and goings, and told no one what I knew about her past.

"I finally agreed to stop badgering her. A woman must be allowed to keep secrets; I have a few myself, so why shouldn't Cassandra? Secrecy is sometimes the only power a woman has in this world."

I nodded slowly. "And after that night, after your long visit when you reminisced about the past, did you see her again?"

Cytheris hesitated. "Perhaps I did . . ."

"I know that you saw her at least one more time, late in the month of Martius. She came here immediately after leaving Antonia's house."

"And how do you know that, Finder? No, don't tell me. Antonia had Cassandra followed, didn't she? Suspicious harpy!"

I cleared my throat. "You might ask your neighbor to trim the branches of that fig tree in front of his house. An agile man could climb onto the roof next door and look down into this very garden." I gazed up at the line of the roof, and saw that a tiny bit of the neighbor's higher roof could indeed be seen above the scalloped row of red tiles.

Cytheris nodded. "I see. And might such a watcher be able to hear every word that was spoken?"

"Apparently not."

"Thank Venus for that, at least!"

"What *did* the two of you talk about during that visit?"

Cytheris clicked a long fingernail against her cup, a signal to Chrysippus, who stood at the far corner of the garden, to come and pour her more Falernian wine. She took a sip and for a long moment made no answer. At last she smiled. "Very well, here's the story. But you must swear to me by Venus that you'll never divulge this to Antonia. Gaze at her statue and swear it, both of you!"

Davus looked at me and raised an eyebrow. "I swear by Venus," I said quietly, and Davus did likewise.

Cytheris laughed. "Actually, I've been dying to tell someone. It might as well be you, Finder. You see, even though Cassandra wouldn't tell me exactly what she was up to, I had my suspicions that it might be something—well, a bit devious. So I made a deal with her."

"A deal?"

"I agreed to press her with no more questions and to tell no one of her origins, on the condition that she would do a small favor for me. *Perform* a favor, I suppose I should say."

"And what was that?"

"Antonia is the type who can never be left out of any activity she presumes to be fashionable among her sort, whether it's wearing one's hair in a bun or worshipping some new goddess from the East. I knew that sooner or later she would seek out Cassandra, looking to have her fortune told. I'm afraid I couldn't resist the opportunity to stir up a bit of mischief."

I nodded. "You suborned Cassandra to deliver a false prophecy to Antonia?"

"I'm afraid so. Was that terribly wicked of me? I told Cassandra: Make it grim. Tell her that not only will Antony abandon her in the end, but so will Dolabella, and she'll grow old and toothless with no companion but that harpy brat of hers. That's why Cassandra came here at once after she left Antonia's house, to tell me that Antonia had finally consulted her and that she'd done as I'd asked. We shared a good laugh about that."

"I see. Unfortunately, Antonia had Cassandra followed, and she made the connection to you and to your mime training. Antonia's not stupid, Cytheris. I'm afraid she saw through your little scheme to upset her."

"Too bad. Even so, I think we managed to give her a nasty shock, while it lasted."

"Perhaps. But once Antonia made the assumption that Cassandra was an actress and a fraud, she made another assumption: that Cassandra was a professional blackmailer."

Cytheris pursed her lips. "Perhaps. I considered that possibility myself, but I don't think so. The Cassandra I knew in Alexandria didn't have the temperament to be a blackmailer. She didn't possess that kind of cruelty."

"People change."

"No, Gordianus, people never change; only their roles change. And Cassandra would have been miscast as a blackmailer. Still, I can't entirely rule it out."

"And if Antonia thought she was a blackmailer, then so might someone else. True or not, that might have provided the motive for someone to kill her. What do you know about her death, Cytheris?"

"Only what everyone seems to know, that she collapsed in the market and died in your arms. When I learned the news, I wept. Poor Cassandra! The gossips say that she was poisoned. Was she? Knowing what I did about her past, I had to wonder if one of her seizures had finally proved too much for her. Was it the falling sickness that killed her?"

I shook my head. "No, she was poisoned. Someone murdered Cassandra. Do you have any idea who might have done that, Cytheris?"

"Other than Antonia? No."

I nodded. "What about Rupa? What can you tell me about him?"

Antonia smiled. "Dear, sweet Rupa. I expected to see him at Cassandra's funeral, but he wasn't there, was he?"

"No. Nor did he ever come to my house to see her body. He seems to have disappeared entirely since Cassandra died."

"I certainly haven't seen him," said Cytheris. "He must be in hiding, fearful of sharing Cassandra's fate. Poor thing. It's hard to imagine how he could get along without her. They loved each other so very much."

I frowned. "What was he to Cassandra?"

"She never told you?"

I shook my head.

"Rupa was her younger brother, of course! Couldn't you see the resemblance between them? He was with her when Cassandra joined the mime troupe in Alexandria; the master saw fit to purchase them together rather than separate them. A wise move on his part, as Cassandra would have been devastated to lose her little brother. Rupa earned his keep; he even did a bit of acting himself. Nothing that required much talent, or any spoken lines, of course. He was always big, even from an early age, so he played silent guards and hulking gladiators and grunting monsters. He made a very convincing Cyclops in a skit we did about Ulysses. I played Circe. Cassandra played Calypso. . . ."

I sighed. "I always thought of Rupa as her bodyguard."

"Which he was. But mostly *she* protected *him*. It was always so. Rupa may be big and strong, but the ways of the

world overwhelm him, and his muteness is a great handicap.
From childhood Cassandra was always looking out for him,
taking care of him. I wasn't at all surprised when she told me
she had brought Rupa with her to Rome. It's hard to imagine
how he could have survived alone in Alexandria. It's hard to
imagine how he's surviving now without her. Or do you
think—"

"What?"

"Perhaps Rupa is dead, too," she said quietly.

From the foyer there came the sound of a knock on the
door. Chrysippus went to answer it, then returned. "Volumnius, mistress," he said.

Cytheris gave a sigh of mingled indulgence and exasperation. "Tell him to leave his army of bodyguards outside, and
show him in."

A few moments later, a corpulent figure came shuffling into
the garden. Famous for wearing showy jewelry, on this occasion the banker Volumnius was notably bereft of ornament—
no bracelets, no necklaces, no ring except a plain iron ring of
citizenship. In such turbulent times, even a man as notoriously
ostentatious as Volumnius knew better than to flaunt his
wealth in the streets.

"Cytheris, my rosebud!" he cried. She stood to greet him
and submitted to a kiss on her cheek from his fleshy lips.

"But I see you have guests." Volumnius looked askance at
Davus and me. I stood and gestured to Davus to do likewise.

"Gordianus and his son-in-law were just about to leave,"
said Cytheris.

"Gordianus? I know the name. Have we met?"

"No," I said, "but I've dealt with your agents."

"Ah, yes. You're another of the fine citizens to whom I've
extended a helping hand in recent months. I'm only too happy,
in such trying times, to find that I can be of assistance to so
many of my fellow Romans."

My loans from Volumnius, as crushing as they were to me,
were surely so insignificant in his account books that I was
surprised he knew of them. Did he stay apprised of every loan
authorized by his agents, no matter how small? Perhaps. Peo-

ple said there was an invisible thread attached to every sesterce that left his greedy fist.

"I'm grateful for your assistance, Volumnius," I said. "And even more grateful for your patience. Times are such that even men of goodwill may not be able to meet all their obligations, at least for a while."

"Indeed, citizen, patience is a virtue—to a point. And mine will extend exactly as long as this damnable business with Caelius and Milo remains unresolved. After that, once things are back to normal . . ." He shrugged, which made his shoulders jiggle. "Eventually, obligations must be met. Order must be maintained. Property rights must be respected and loans repaid. Wise Caesar says so." He smiled and took Cytheris's much smaller hand in his and kissed it. In that instant I understood why he had agreed to make Cytheris a freedwoman at the request of the love-struck Antony. To please Caesar's lieutenant was to please Caesar. Her manumission was nothing more or less than a business decision.

"As Cytheris says, Davus and I were just leaving. Goodbye, Cytheris. Good day, Volumnius."

"And good day to you, citizen. Be wise and prosper—so that you may meet your obligations when the day of reckoning arrives."

XI

The fifth time I saw Cassandra was late in the month of Maius. Almost a month had passed since the attempted arrest of Marcus Caelius and his hairbreadth escape, but all Rome was still in an uproar.

Rumors abounded. Some said Caelius had gone off to join Caesar, but it was hard to imagine how he could do so after the insinuations he had made against Caesar in his speeches; was he so rash as to think he could win Caesar's forgiveness by charm alone? Some said that Caelius had not escaped after all but had been arrested, and was being held at a secret location while Isauricus decided what to do with him. Others said that Caelius had indeed escaped but was still in the city, hiding with a band of conspirators who were plotting to assassinate all the magistrates and most of the Senate.

Some said Caelius had gone south to set free a school of gladiators in the vicinity of Mount Vesuvius, with the intention of returning to Rome and staging a massacre. Others said Caelius had gone north to try to rally various cities to his cause, hoping to win them over one by one until he felt confident of marching on Rome with an army of volunteers. From the Forum, Hieronymus reported this remark by Volcatius, leader of the Pompeian chin-waggers: "If Caelius has his way, the rabble of Rome will soon be kicking the heads of their landlords and moneylenders through the streets!"

Yet another rumor said that Caelius was planning to rendezvous with his old friend Milo, and that the two of them were going to sweep across Italy together. To my ears this was the wildest speculation of all. In his days as Cicero's protégé, Caelius had indeed been friends with Milo, but in recent years their politics had drifted so far apart that it seemed impossible that the two could ever reunite in a common cause.

Before his forced departure from Rome, Titus Annius Milo had been the man upon whom the self-styled Best People relied to do their dirty business. As Clodius had ruled the street gangs on the left, so Milo had ruled the street gangs on the right. When a conservative magistrate wanted to break up a demonstration by the opposition, or needed demonstrators of his own to agitate in the Forum, Milo was the man who could produce angry crowds, bloody fists, and a few cracked skulls.

Pompey, who liked to hold himself aloof from the gritty political reality of street brawls, had looked to Milo to act as his henchman. Cicero had doted upon Milo, and saw him as his brutish alter ego; Cicero had the brains, while Milo wielded the brawn. For his efforts Milo was well rewarded by the Best People. He was admitted into their inner circle; he was a man headed for great things. With his marriage to Fausta, the daughter of the late dictator Sulla, his ascent into the highest ranks of Rome's ruling class seemed assured.

And then it all came crashing down. After a skirmish with Milo's entourage on the Appian Way a few miles outside Rome, Clodius was murdered. Milo and Fausta were at the scene, and whether Milo literally bloodied his hands or not, he was blamed for the murder of his enemy. Angry rioters burned down the Senate House and demanded Milo's head. Pompey, called upon to keep order, put Milo on trial and did nothing to help him. The Best People washed their hands of him. Loyal to the end, Cicero took on Milo's defense, but his efforts were to no avail; attempting to give his oration, he was shouted down by the mob. Accompanied by a large band of hardened gladiators, Milo fled from Rome before the guilty verdict was announced and headed for the Greek city-state of Massilia, the destination of so many Roman political exiles.

He left behind a fortune in property that was confiscated

by the state, a bitterly disappointed wife who by all accounts was glad to see the last of him, and a hopelessly divided city. Looking back, it seemed to me that the murder of Clodius and the trial of Milo marked the last gasp of the dying Republic and the beginning of the end of the Roman Constitution. Certainly it had marked the end of Milo; even amid the turmoil of civil war, no one could doubt that Milo's career was over for good. When Caesar conquered Massilia, he had declared amnesty for all the Roman political exiles in the city, with the conspicuous exclusion of only one: Milo.

Abandoned by Pompey, rebuffed by Caesar, beyond the help of Cicero, Milo had become the forgotten man of Roman politics.

Now rumors were reaching the city that Milo had managed to escape from Massilia, despite the garrison of Caesar's soldiers, who had instructions to keep him there. Not only had he escaped, but he had managed to do so with the large band of gladiators who had accompanied him into exile.

Even more bizarre than these rumors was the further assertion that Milo was somehow involved in a conspiracy with Marcus Caelius. Milo's entire career had been based on pandering to the interests of the most rigidly conservative clique among the Roman elite. The idea that he would join forces with Caelius, who had made himself the champion of wholesale revolution, was ludicrous. Or was it? In such times, old friendships and bonds of trust might count for more than differing political philosophies, and men as desperate as Milo and Caelius might take whatever allies they could get. What, after all, did Milo owe to the Best People or to Pompey? In the crisis that followed Clodius's murder, they had cast him aside like a hot coal.

༄

In my own household, all else was overshadowed by Bethesda's illness. Its prognosis and cure were as elusive as the whereabouts and future plans of Marcus Caelius. To pay for physicians, I borrowed more money from Volumnius. They examined Bethesda's tongue. They studied her stools. They poked and prodded her various parts. They prescribed this treatment and that, all of which cost money. I went further into debt. Nothing seemed to help. Bethesda had good days and bad days, but more and more often she kept to her bed.

Her symptoms were obscure. There were no sharp pains, no visible rashes, no vomiting or foul excreta. She felt weak and out of sorts—"uncomfortable in my skin," she said. She was sometimes dizzy, sometimes short of breath. She had no faith in the physicians or their treatments. When she bit one of them for pinching her tongue too hard, I told the quack he was lucky to leave my house with all his fingers, and I decided to send for no more physicians.

A household is not unlike a human body, with a head and a heart and a sense of well-being that depends on the harmony of its various parts. The disposition of my household changed from day to day, depending on Bethesda. Her bad days were bad days for everyone, full of gloom and foreboding. On her good days the household stirred with a cautious sense of hope. As time passed and bad days outnumbered good, hope receded, so that even the best days were tempered by a deep anxiety.

To please Bethesda, I kept to the house as much as possible. For long hours I did little more than sit beside her in the garden, holding her hand while we reminisced. It was in Alexandria that I had found her. I had been a young man, footloose in the world. She had been a slave, hardly more than a child. At the first sight of her I was hopelessly smitten, as only a young man can be. I was determined to purchase her and make her my own, and I did. When I returned to Rome, I brought Bethesda with me. It was not until she became pregnant with Diana that I made her a free woman and married her so that my child would be born free. Why had I waited so long? Partly because I feared that such a drastic change in Bethesda's status would also throw our relationship out of balance; she already wielded quite enough power over me as my slave! But our marriage and the birth of our daughter had only strengthened the bond between us, and freedom had strengthened Bethesda's character in every way. Where before she had seemed willful, she became strong willed; where before she had seemed petulant, I came to see her as fiercely determined. Did these changes take place in Bethesda or merely in my perceptions of her? I couldn't say, and Bethesda was the last person to ask. Paradox and irony held no fascination for her.

When we reminisced, it was not to remark about subtle states of mind or the way things changed but stayed the same. Our conversations served to remind one another of a vast, shared catalogue of people, places, and things. The mere summoning up of these memories brought us a shared pleasure.

"Do you remember the beacon atop the Pharos lighthouse," she would ask, "and how we sat on the deck of the ship the night we sailed from Alexandria and watched it dwindle to nothing?"

"Of course I remember. It was a warm night. Even so, you shivered, so I held you next to me."

"I shivered because I was afraid to leave Alexandria. I thought that Rome would swallow me up."

I laughed. "Do you remember how awful the food was, on that ship? Bread like bricks, salty dried figs—"

"Nothing like our last meal in Alexandria. Do you remember—"

"—the little shop on the corner that sold sesame cakes soaked with honey and wine? The memory makes my mouth water even now."

"And the funny little woman who ran the shop? All those cats! Every cat in Alexandria came to her shop!"

"Because she encouraged them," I said. "She put out bowls of milk. The day before we left, she showed us some kittens, and *you* insisted on smuggling one of those kittens on board the ship with you, even though I expressly forbade it."

"I had to bring something of Alexandria with me. The Romans should have thanked me for bringing them a new deity! Imagine my surprise when we arrived and I saw not a single statue of a proper god anywhere in the whole city, no falcon-headed Horus or dog-headed Anubis—only images of ordinary men and women. I knew then that you had brought me to a very strange place indeed. . . ."

At some point we would both realize that we had had this exact conversation before, not once but many times over the years; it was like a ritual that once begun had to be pursued to its conclusion; and like most rituals its mere observance brought us a curious comfort. One memory would lead to another and another, like links in a chain that wound around and around us both, cinching us together at the very center of the time and space that encompassed our two lives.

And then . . . the shadow of her illness would pass over Bethesda. The corners of her mouth would constrict. Her brow would furrow. Her hand would tighten, then loosen, in mine, and she would say that she was suddenly weary and light-headed and needed to lie down. I would draw a deep breath, and it would seem to me that the very air was thick with worry and repining.

‮ઍ‬

I began to feel like a prisoner in my own house. Small irritations grew into unbearable torments.

Androcles and Mopsus drove me to distraction with their constant bickering. One day I yelled at them so sharply that little Androcles began to cry, whereupon Mopsus began to tease him, which drove me into such a fury that I barely restrained myself from striking him. Afterward I felt so ill that I had to lie down, and found myself wondering if I had fallen victim to Bethesda's complaint.

Hieronymus, whose mordant wit had always amused me, began to strike me as a pretentious buffoon, always prattling on about Roman politics, a subject about which he knew next to nothing. One night, losing my temper over some particularly sarcastic observation of his, I remarked on the prodigious quantities he was able to consume at every meal, at my expense. He turned pale, put down his bowl, and said that from that point onward he would take all his meals alone, after the family ate, dining upon our scraps. He left the room, and nothing I could say would persuade him to return. This was the man who had taken me into his home in Massilia, sharing everything he had with me.

Davus, who had saved my life in Massilia, earned my wrath one day by knocking over a tripod lamp. Trying to pick it up, he tripped and stepped on it and damaged it even more. When he was done, all three of the bronze griffin heads were dented and the pole was bent. It was—or rather, had been—one of the most valuable objects remaining in the house, something I had counted on being able to sell if the direst need arose. I told him that his clumsiness had robbed the household of a month's worth of food.

Even with Diana, I became short-tempered. When little Aulus was noisy, I blamed her, and I found myself arguing with her about her mother's illness and what to do about it. Our disagreements were over small things—whether Bethesda should drink hot beverages or cold ones, whether or not she should be kept awake during the day (so that she might sleep more soundly at night, I argued), whether to heed the advice of a physician who had told us that the blood of a sparrow would be beneficial to her—but the words we exchanged were sharp and bitter. I accused Diana of having inherited her mother's worst traits of stubbornness and wrongheadedness. In a cruel moment she accused me of caring less about her mother than she did. I was cut to the quick, and for several days would hardly speak to her.

I looked to my son Eco for relief. Like Meto, he was my child by adoption. Unlike Meto, we had never had a falling-out of any sort, yet over the years we had grown apart. This was only natural; Eco had his own household. He also had his own livelihood, following in my footsteps, and although we had occasionally consulted one another professionally over the years, Eco had grown increasingly independent and kept his business and financial affairs to himself. Increasingly, he also kept his family to himself. Eco had married up, into an old but faded family desperate for fresh blood, the Menenii. His wife and Bethesda had never really gotten along.

The afternoon I invited Eco and his brood to my house turned into a disaster. Menenia said something to offend Bethesda—some nonsense about the women of her family "staring down" illness rather then submitting to it—and Bethesda promptly retired to her bed. Eco's golden-haired, eleven-year-old twins, who took after their mother, took shameless advantage of Mopsus and Androcles, ordering them to fetch this and that. When Androcles muttered a remark about "losing their heads someday"—a bit of inflammatory rhetoric he had picked up in the Forum, no doubt—Eco was appalled and insisted that I punish the boy like the slave he was; and when I refused, he took his family home. Goaded by his brother, Androcles gloated about his escape, whereupon I finally did deliver a few sound thwacks to his backside. Everyone in the household went to bed miserable that night.

In the past, there had always been someone to whom I could turn in troubled times, even though he was seldom present. Confused, unhappy, seeking solace, I would have locked myself away in my study, taken up my stylus, unlatched the cover of a spare wax tablet and rubbed it blank, and set about writing a letter to Meto. Knowing he might not read my words for many days—secretly fearing he might never read them, for he was a soldier and often in danger—I would nonetheless have set down my thoughts and feelings to share with my beloved son; and having done so, I would have felt a great relief and a lightening of my spirit. But now, by my own decree, that avenue was closed to me. In those dismal days, how bitterly I missed that source of solace!

Oppressed by the uncertain state of the world, anxious about my debts, worried by Bethesda's illness and the discord in my household, aching from the loss of the son I had disowned—such was the state of my mind when I decided to escape the safe confines of my house and go off wandering one day.

I had done much the same thing almost a month before, on the day I found myself at Cassandra's apartment and later witnessed Caelius's disappearing act in the Forum. But whereas on the previous occasion my feet had taken me

straight to Cassandra's door, unwittingly or not, on this day I
found myself taking a much longer walk as I trod a meander-
ing course through the city. Having lived so long in Rome,
knowing it so intimately, it was probably impossible for me
literally to lose myself in the city. Nonetheless, I fell into a
certain musing state of mind, forgetful of my bearings and
direction and alert only to my immediate surroundings and the
sensations they produced.

It was a fine day for such a walk, typical of late Maius,
sunny but not too hot. The charm of Rome was everywhere.
At a quaint neighborhood fountain, water poured from the
mouth of a gorgon into a deep trough from which women
scooped brimming buckets. (Water, if nothing else, was still
plentiful and free in Rome.) Just around the corner, a huge
bronze phallus projecting from the lintel of a doorway proclaimed the presence of a neighborhood brothel. The sun happened to catch the phallus at such an angle that it cast a
shadow onto the street so absurdly enormous that I laughed
out loud. On the doorstep an uncommonly plump prostitute
sat sunning herself like a cat. As I walked by, she opened her
eyes to slits, and I believe I heard her literally purring. A little
farther on, I came to a long alley fronted by continuous walls
on either side; both walls were overgrown with blooming jasmine, and the smell was so heady that once I reached the end
of the alley, I turned around and retraced my steps, just to see
if the scent was as sweet going in the opposite direction.

Every time I turned a corner, I was confronted by memories, sweet and bitter. I had lived so long in Rome that sometimes it seemed to me the city was a map of my own mind,
its streets and buildings manifestations of my deepest memories.

In this austere little house, now painted yellow but bright
blue when I last entered the door, I had once comforted a
grieving widow who summoned me to solve the murder of her
husband—and it turned out that she herself was the murderer. . . .

Down that street a band of thieves, intent on cutting our
throats, had once chased me and my slave Belbo—how I

missed that faithful bodyguard! The two of us had escaped by ducking into a fountain and holding our breaths. . . .

I crested a hill and saw in the distance the terraces and wings of Pompey's vast mansion atop the Pincian Hill outside the city walls; an intervening haze of heat and dust imbued the place with a slightly unreal, floating quality, like a palace seen afar in a dream. When Pompey slept at night, so far from home, was this how he saw the house he had left behind? The last time I had seen Pompey—making his escape by ship from Italy—he had tried to strangle me with his bare hands. The memory made my throat constrict. At that very moment, was the so-called Great One alive or dead? Was he standing over the slain body of Caesar, listening to his soldiers declare him Master of the World—or was he just another mortal turned to ashes like so many before him, whose ferocious ambitions counted for nothing when the jaws of Hades opened to claim them?

At the craggy base of the Capitoline Hill, I passed the gate of the private family cemetery where years ago I had met in secret with Clodia on the eve of Marcus Caelius's trial for murder. How I had been smitten by that mysterious, aloof, treacherous beauty! In all my life, Clodia had been the only woman who had ever tempted me to stray from Bethesda. Until now . . .

No matter how circuitous the route, no matter how distracting or amusing or arousing or appalling the memories summoned up by each turning of a corner, my feet knew where they were leading me.

When I arrived at the doorstep of her tenement, guarded by the dog who did not bark at my approach, was I surprised? A little. The part of me that desired her—totally, without question, beyond reason—had outfoxed the part of me that knew such a thing was impossible, improper, absurd. Absurdity, more than anything else, might have stayed me. A much older man hankering after a beautiful young woman inevitably presents a preposterous scene. I thought of every lecherous old fool I had ever seen on the stage and cringed at the idea of making a comic spectacle of myself. Even assuming that my advances were welcomed and mutually desired, there were complications—not least the fact that the object of my desire might be as mad as everyone said, in which case, was I not equally mad to be pursuing her?

As to the greatest complication of all—my companion and wife of many years, ailing and alone in her bed at home—I could not even bear to think of that. In the end, I was hardly thinking at all as I found myself propelled forward by some mechanism of the body far removed from conscious thought.

If she had not been in her room, or if Rupa had been there, perhaps things might have turned out very differently. But she was there, and she was alone. I pulled back the curtain, unannounced and without warning, expecting to give her a start. Instead, she slowly turned her face in my direction, sat up on the pallet, and rose to her feet. As she slowly walked toward me, her eyes never left mine. She parted her lips and opened her arms. I let the curtain drop behind me. I think I let out a little cry, like a child overwhelmed by an unfamiliar emotion, as her lips met mine and covered them.

XII

The morning after my visits to Antonia and Cytheris, I again rose early. Bethesda stirred and spoke a little, but remained in bed. She had almost entirely stopped eating, and this, even more than her lethargy, was beginning to worry me. Her face had become gaunt, her eyes vacant. The powerful will that had ruled my household for so many years seemed to be seeping out of her little by little, leaving only a shell behind.

The day was already warm, but a chill passed through me. For the very first time—always before I had managed to avoid the thought—I had an inkling of what the world would be like without her. I had experienced life before Bethesda, but so long ago I could hardly remember such a thing. To imagine a life after Bethesda was almost impossible. I reminded myself that in such matters we mortals seldom have a choice, physicians and radish soup and prayers to the gods notwithstanding.

I ate a little. I summoned Androcles and Mopsus to help put on my toga, then sent them to do the same for Davus. Thus my day began as had the previous two, and I realized, with a twinge of mingled pleasure and guilt, that I had begun to enjoy this routine. It gave me something to take my mind off Bethesda, and my debts, and the discord in my household. In a curious way, even though it was all about her, it even took my mind off Cassandra, or at least gave me something to think about besides the obsessive longing she had stirred in me—and the consequent guilt—and the grief I had felt when she died in my arms.

I realized, as I made plans and preparations for the day, that I was *working* again—not for another, and not for money (alas), but working nonetheless at the curious trade that had sustained me throughout my life. In recent years I had gradually retired from that trade, leaving it to Eco. I had become Gordianus the husband, Gordianus the father, Gordianus the chin-wagger in the Forum, and even, against all expectations, Gordianus the illicit lover—but no longer Gordianus the Finder. Now I once again found myself doing what I had always done best, looking for the truth of a matter that no one else cared, or dared, to pursue. I had found my bearings and settled like a wagon wheel into a familiar groove. In spite of all my reasons to feel miserable, at least I could say with certainty who and what I was. I was Gordianus the Finder again, pursuing the course the gods had laid down for me.

Davus stepped into the garden. From the satisfied, slightly stupid look on his face, I suspected that he and my daughter had found their own release from the strains of life at some point during the night. And why not? I tried to suppress a twinge of envy.

"How is—?" Davus's question was cut off with a yawn as he stretched his arms above his head, disarranging the folds of his toga.

"Bethesda is no better . . . but no worse," I said, hoping I spoke the truth.

"And where are we off to this morning, Father-in-Law?"

～

At the height of Milo's power, when he ruled a veritable army of street gangs in competition with Clodius, he and his wife, Fausta, had lived in one of the city's more imposing houses, a worthy habitation for the daughter of the dictator Sulla and the husband from whom she expected great things.

That house and its contents had been confiscated by the state and sold at auction not long after Milo's exile from

Rome. Fausta, though she remained married to Milo, refused to accompany him to Massilia. Without a house, where was she to live and by what means? As it turned out, the law included a provision for an abandoned wife to reclaim her dowry from the first proceeds of confiscated property. Fausta's dowry had been considerable, and after the auction she managed to get much of it back. With that money she had moved into a smaller, more humble dwelling on the far side of the Palatine Hill from my own. She was not exactly poor, but she had fallen a great distance in the world.

"What will this one be like?" asked Davus, as we headed out.

"What do you mean?"

"So far, I haven't known quite what to make of all these women."

I laughed. "What can I tell you about Fausta? On the one occasion when I met her, which was shortly before Milo went into exile, she was taking a bath with two of his gladiators—and she invited me to join them. That sort of behavior was what ended her first marriage, before Milo. She was seeing two lovers on the side—so goes the story—and being rather blatant about it. One was a fuller who owned a wool-washing operation. The other was a fellow called Macula, on account of a birthmark on his cheek that looked like a stain. Her twin brother, Faustus, made a crack about it: 'Seeing that she has the personal services of a fuller, I don't see why she doesn't get rid of that "Stain"! My sister's behavior is less than immaculate.' "

"Im*macula*te," Davus repeated slowly, grasping the pun.

"Exactly. But Fausta's husband didn't find the situation quite so amusing. He divorced her for adultery. Then she married Milo. Several steps up socially, for him. For her, he must have seemed a good prospect. Perhaps Milo's ruthlessness appealed to her; maybe it reminded her of her father. Who knew his career would end in murder and exile just a few years later?

"The scandals started the very day after their wedding, when Milo came home and caught her in the act with a fellow named Sallust. Milo gave Sallust a sound thrashing, which was of course his legal right—indeed, Milo could have killed him, and it wouldn't have been murder—and confiscated his moneybag for a fine.

"But Fausta was incorrigible. Not long after the incident with Sallust, she invited not one but two lovers to come over one afternoon. Then Milo showed up. One of the fellows managed to hide in a wardrobe, but Milo caught the other, dragged him out of the bedroom, and proceeded to beat him to a pulp. Meanwhile, the first fellow slipped back into Fausta's bed, and the two of them made mad, passionate love to the sound of the other fellow screaming and begging Milo for mercy. Before you point out the obvious, Davus, I will: Fausta enjoys being caught."

He frowned. "And perhaps Milo enjoyed catching her. Otherwise, why didn't he divorce her?"

"Because Fausta's connections were too valuable to him, politically and socially. Her dowry was valuable, too. Not all marriages are like yours with my daughter, Davus, based on" —I almost said *blind lust,* but that would have been unfair— "based on mutual love, desire, and respect. Some marriages are based on other considerations—power, money, prestige. Especially marriages among the Best People or those aspiring to join their ranks. Which isn't to say that Milo and Fausta didn't find one another attractive. I think there was a definite spark between them—her, all ginger hair and voluptuous curves; him, all hot tempered and hairy chested.

"Eventually things settled down between the two of them. Maybe Milo finally scared off all her lovers! He tended to his political career. She appeared beside him as his dutiful wife. Who could doubt that one day he would be elected consul, and she would be a consul's wife? Then came the murder of Clodius, and Milo's career went up in smoke."

"Why didn't Fausta divorce him? Especially if she didn't want to go into exile with him, and he was never coming back?"

"I don't know, Davus. Shall we ask her?"

∽

The slave who opened the door had the overfed, oversexed look of a grizzled gladiator gone to seed. That made him a walking contradiction; how many gladiators live long enough to go to seed? Two smoldering eyes peered at us from beneath a single bristling eyebrow, but he was probably cleverer than he looked. How else had he survived long enough to acquire a few gray hairs, not to mention the plum job of waiting on a highborn lady with a special appreciation for gladiators? I wondered how many men he had killed in his life to arrive at this particular perch. He crossed his arms while I gave him my name and requested a few moments of his mistress's time. His forearms were the size of my thighs and covered with ugly scars.

With a jolt, I suddenly recognized him: Birria, one of Milo's most prized gladiators. He had been directly involved in the skirmish with Clodius that day on the Appian Way. He was also one of the gladiators who had been lounging with Fausta in her bath on the occasion when I met her. I was surprised Milo had not taken Birria with him, knowing the slave's reputation as a trained killer. Perhaps Birria had been part of Fausta's dowry settlement and so had remained with her. He had gained a great deal of weight since I last saw him, and not much of it was muscle.

Birria left us in the foyer while he went to announce us. The house was even gloomier and more bereft of ornaments than I had expected. One feature did catch my eye, however. It gave me quite a start.

It is the custom of Roman nobles to display busts of their illustrious ancestors in niches in the foyers of their homes. In Fausta's foyer, there were only one niche and one bust. Pacing the little room, turning on my heel, I abruptly found myself face-to-face with the image of Lucius Cornelius Sulla, the dictator.

I had met him once. Like so many others, I had been charmed—and a little terrified. An appetite for pleasure and for cruelty had radiated from him like the heat of the sun at midsummer; men averted their faces in Sulla's presence, fearful of being scorched. His example—winning a bloody civil war, attaining absolute power and using it to behead his enemies, reforming the state in his image and then turning his back on it—had haunted Rome for two generations. Depending on one's political point of view, his legacy had either broken the Constitution, or else failed to shore it up enough—and in either case had generated a series of disasters that led directly across the decades to the present moment, with the Republic paralyzed and Rome holding its breath for the arrival of a second Sulla. He had been dead now for over thirty years, but the eyes that peered from the marble image in Fausta's foyer still had the power to chill my blood.

From somewhere deeper in the house I heard the sound of a man shouting. The words were indistinct, but the tone was angry and demeaning. Who was shouting? Who was being shouted at?

A little later Birria returned. Was he more sullen than when he'd left? With such an ugly face, it was hard to tell. "The mistress can't see you today," he said.

"No? Perhaps—"

"I gave her your name. She knows who you are. She doesn't have time to see you."

"Perhaps you could go back and mention another name."

He scowled. "What would that be?"

"Cassandra. Tell her that I want to talk about Cassandra."

"Won't make a difference. You'd better go now." He walked up to me, squaring his massive shoulders to block my way. He didn't stop, but strode right into me, forcing me to take tripping, backward steps. Behind me, Davus emitted a threatening grunt. I looked over my shoulder and saw a scowl on his face to match the gladiator's. I felt like a man caught between two snorting bulls.

From behind Birria, I heard a woman's shrill voice. "No! Birria, stop this! No fighting before Papa's image! I've decided to see the Finder after all. I . . . I *want* to see him." Her voice had an oddly plaintive tone, as if she were asking for permission.

Birria stopped and stared down at me, then over my head at Davus. I smelled garlic on his breath—gladiators eat it for strength—and wrinkled my nose. At last he stepped back and out of the way.

"As you wish, mistress," he said, glaring at me.

Davus and I stepped past him toward Fausta. Instead of waiting, she turned away while we were still several paces distant and began to lead us down a dim hallway. "This way. Follow me. Where shall we . . . ? Not the garden, I think. No, definitely *not* the garden. We'll talk . . . in the Baiae room. Yes, that will do."

She kept several paces ahead of me. I found myself staring at the mass of ginger hair pinned atop her head and the jiggling of her ample backside beneath her orange stola. I noticed with a start—for until then she had managed to hide it—that one of her arms was in a sling, and that she was walking with a slight limp. Had she suffered an accident?

The chamber she called the Baiae room was a narrow alcove off a hall. The only light came from the doorway. Lamps were hung from the ceiling, but none were lit, and so the room was dim and shadowy. Even so, I could see how the room came to have its name. The floor was a mosaic in many shades of green and blue, touched with flashes of gold, depicting various creatures of the deep—octopi, whales, dolphins, fish—and bordered with images of seashells. The walls of the room were painted with scenes of villas perched above the sea cliffs of Baiae. I stepped closer, losing myself in the picture, until the voice of Fausta called me back.

"Why don't the two of you sit over there, in those chairs at the far end of the room?" she said. "I'll sit here close by the doorway."

"This must be a very beautiful room when it's well lit," I said, taking a seat and gesturing to Davus to do the same.

"Oh, yes. My brother Faustus used to own this house. He didn't actually live here; he only kept it as a sort of guest house, a place to lend out to visitors and friends. Faustus was awfully flush with money at the time. He spent a great deal on fixtures and stonework and such. He doted on this little room more than any other. The mosaics and the wall paintings are meant to be viewed by lamplight at night. It's quite a

magical place when you see it that way. By day it's rather
dim in here, isn't it? And it could use a bit of restoration. I
don't think the painters quite knew what they were doing. In
places there's an awful lot of peeling and flaking. Of course I
can't afford to have it properly redone, and neither could Faustus these days. But once the war is over, his fortunes will
change for the better. Caesar's rich supporters will lose their
heads along with their estates, and men like Faustus will get
what's due to them. That's how my father rewarded his partisans, giving them the best of the booty seized from his enemies. Pompey will do the same, if he has any sense. What
do you think, Gordianus? Is Pompey half the man my father
was?"

Twice the man, but half the monster, I wanted to say, but
bit my tongue. I had the feeling she was teasing me, but it
was hard to read her expression. She sat with her back to the
door, so the light came from behind her and cast her face in
shadow.

"You think it will be Pompey who triumphs, then?" I said.
"I might have thought, in light of recent events . . ."

"You mean this business with my husband and Caelius?" I
couldn't see her face, but I could hear the disgust in her voice.
"As soon as word reached Rome that Milo had slipped out of
Massilia, Isauricus himself came here to question me. He assumed, since I'm still married to Milo, that I would be able
to tell him exactly what my husband was up to, even though
I hadn't seen Milo in years or exchanged a letter in months.
'Do you think I can read Milo's mind at a distance of several
hundred miles?' I asked him. 'Do you think that I can predict
what the fool will do next?' I ran Isauricus out of the house,
and he hasn't come back."

I nodded. Considering the state of Fausta's household, the
consul had probably decided that she posed no threat and
wasn't worth keeping an eye on. I shifted uneasily in my chair,
frustrated at being unable to see her face clearly.

Fausta sighed. "Fortune was cruel to Milo. Cruel to us both.
To be perfectly candid—and I'll be more candid with you than
I was with Isauricus—I wasn't the least bit surprised when I

heard about Milo escaping from Massilia and coming back to Italy. Nor was I surprised to learn that he had taken up with Marcus Caelius. Each chose to follow a different leader. Both of those leaders cruelly let them down; Pompey abandoned Milo, and Caesar shunted Caelius aside. Milo and Caelius are like two orphans, taking up with each other so they won't be alone. There must be many more like them, big men and little men, all feeling abandoned by whichever leader they chose, all feeling angry and cheated at the prospect of either of those leaders winning. Why not turn away from Caesar and Pompey both, and find a third way to the future? It makes perfect sense—*if* they can pull it off."

"Can they?"

"How should I know. Do I look like Cassandra?"

I drew a breath. "How well did you know her?"

"Did anyone *really* know Cassandra? That's why you've come, of course. Not to ask after Milo, or me, but because I came to Cassandra's funeral, and you want to talk about her. Am I right?"

"Yes."

She nodded. "I sought her out one day in the market. I invited her here. She stared at a flame and had a fit. I listened to what she had to say, gave her a few coins, and sent her on her way. Why not? Every woman in Rome was desperate to hear what Cassandra had to tell them."

"And what did she tell you?"

Fausta laughed. "A bunch of garbled nonsense. Truthfully, I couldn't make sense of it. I suppose I'm too literal minded for that sort of thing. Why do oracles and portents always have to be so obscure? Call a truffle a truffle, that's what I say! I never much liked plays or poetry for the same reason. I've no patience for metaphors and similes."

"Cassandra didn't foretell Milo's return and his alliance with Caelius?"

Fausta shrugged and winced a bit—I heard her hiss—as she rearranged her arm in the sling. "Oh, there was something about a bear and a snake, I think. And two eagles. Was the bear Milo? Was the snake Caelius? Were the eagles Pompey and Caesar? Or was it all the other way around? Your guess is as good as mine." She sighed. "Milo was always so much more interested in that sort of thing than I was."

"Really?"

"Oh, yes. He always took omens very seriously. More now than ever, I should think."

"Why do you say that?"

"Because"—she sighed heavily—"on that fateful day when Clodius died, Milo saw all sorts of bad omens before we ever set out on the Appian Way. He saw a vulture flying upside down, and then a duck with three feet crossed our path, or so he claimed. Later, when everything started going wrong that day, Milo kept muttering, 'I should have paid attention to the signs; I should have known there would be trouble; we should never have set out; we should have stayed home.' You probably never saw that side of him. He didn't talk much about premonitions and such, except to me, because Cicero would make such fun of him for being so superstitious. But Milo was always on the lookout for portents. A lot of good it ever did him! What's the use of seeing a falling star if it's careening straight toward you?"

I nodded. "You say that I came only to ask after Cassandra, not you and Milo, but that's not entirely true. Would you take it amiss if I asked you a personal question?"

"Ask and find out."

"Why are you still married to Milo? You didn't go with him to Massilia; you stayed here, with no prospect of his ever returning to you. Why not divorce him so that you might remarry?"

She snorted, and for a moment I thought I had offended her. But her exasperation was with her fate, not with me. Like many people burdened with regrets, she was not averse to voicing her bitterness to a relative stranger. "One divorce has pretty much become the standard these days, hasn't it? Among the fashionable set, I mean. But *two* divorces—well, that begins to look a bit careless, don't you think? My first husband divorced me as a sort of punishment for cuckolding him. That wasn't a problem with Milo. Milo rather liked being cuckolded, I think. It gave him an excuse to vent his rage. It . . . *stimulated* him. He was never such a tiger in bed as he was right after catching me with another man. So strong. So . . . violent. I'm afraid I rather developed a taste for that sort of thing."

She readjusted her sling, and hissed. "But I digress. I stayed married to Milo because it was the respectable thing to do. Believe it or not, that still matters to me. I *am* Sulla's daughter. I won't have people saying I abandoned my husband simply because he ran into a bit of trouble."

A murder conviction and lifelong exile hardly seemed to me to be a "bit of trouble," but my standards differed from those of Fausta in many matters. "Or could it be," I said, "that in the long run you had faith in Milo? That you could foresee a time when he might return to Rome in triumph, beheading his enemies as your father beheaded his, making himself the first man in Rome and yourself the first among women?" Such a thing might actually come to pass, I realized with a chill. Whether Caesar or Pompey eventually returned, in the meantime Milo and Caelius might pull off their mad scheme and make themselves masters of Rome. Such a thing would never happen without the spilling of much blood.

She made a derisive sound deep in her throat. "Don't compare Milo to my father! *He* knew how to make this town come to heel, instead of letting the she-wolf bite him in the ass. We shall never see his like again—not in Caesar, not in Pompey, certainly not in Milo. The best I can hope for"—she hesitated, but a sudden burst of emotion was too much for her to contain—"the best I can hope for is to become Milo's widow. People shall pity me then. And respect me! They shall say, 'Poor Fausta! She suffered greatly from her second marriage. But she stood by that fool to the very end, didn't she? She proved her mettle. She was truly Sulla's daughter!' "

I considered this for a long moment, wishing I could see her face more clearly. But the light from outside was growing stronger as the morning drew on, casting her features even deeper into shadow. "I don't quite understand," I confessed.

"I wouldn't expect you to. You're not one of those who count—not one of us."

"Not a noble, you mean?"

She shook her head. "Not a woman!" She stood, indicating that the interview was at an end.

In the hallway, she drew back into a shadowy corner. Again I noticed her slight limp. Birria appeared, to show us out. He curled his lip and from under his bristling brow gave her a look that seemed to border on madness, until I realized it was lasciviousness I saw in his eyes. I looked at Fausta. Despite the shadows, I saw what she had been deliberately concealing by sitting against the light—a bruised, black crescent beneath one of her eyes.

I looked back at Birria and matched his glare with my own. "Fausta," I said, "do you need our help?"

"What do you mean?"

"You limp. Your arm is in a sling."

She shrugged. "It's nothing, really. Certainly nothing to concern *you*. A small accident. I'm a bit clumsy sometimes."

"I find that hard to believe of Sulla's daughter."

"What you believe is of no consequence, Finder. Go now. And, Birria, after you've shown these two out . . . come straight back to me."

He gave her a snarling grin, but it was the crooked smile she flashed back at him that made my blood run cold. I turned and walked quickly to the front door, not waiting for Birria to lead the way. In the foyer I paused for a moment to gaze at the marble bust of Sulla and to wonder at the curious events it must have witnessed in that house.

XIII

The sixth time I saw Cassandra—and the seventh and eighth and ninth and all the other times before her death—are jumbled in my mind. Even the exact number of times eludes me. My memories of those meetings blur together, as the heated flesh of two lovers becomes blurred in the act of love, so that the lover cannot tell where his own body ends and that of the beloved begins.

After the first time we made love, we arranged to meet again in her room in the Subura, at a specific time, on a specific day. Thus our pattern was set. These arrangements were determined by Cassandra, partly, I think, to coincide with her mornings at the public baths, for I always found her fresh and clean, but also, I assumed, to make sure that Rupa would not be there when I came. Was he her lover? Her slave? A relative? I didn't know. She never told me. I never asked.

What *did* we talk about in the spells between lovemaking? Nothing remotely to do with our complicated circumstances; nothing that might impinge upon the special world the two of us created in that room. I think I did speak sometimes of Diana and Davus and little Aulus, and Hieronymus, and Androcles and Mopsus, especially if one of them had just done something to frustrate me or to make me laugh. And I told her about Meto and the heartbreak I felt at losing him. But I never spoke of Bethesda or Bethesda's illness. And Cassandra never spoke of Rupa or about her visits to the houses of the highborn and well-to-do women of Rome, nor did she tell me where she came from.

I didn't care; I didn't want her history, and I had no thought of the future. I wanted from her the thing that she gave me in that room, the joining of two bodies that filled the present moment to miraculous perfection. I expected nothing else from her. She seemed to expect nothing else from me.

She stirred in me sensations of youth almost forgotten. In flashes I imagined myself a young wanderer in Alexandria again. I *was* the young man I once had been, in love with the power of his own body; in love for the first time with the body of another; in awe of the extraordinary pleasures those two bodies could share and naive enough to think that no one else on earth had ever experienced sensations so exquisite. In Cassandra's room, time and space lost all meaning. Together we conjured a kind of sorcery.

What did Cassandra see in me? Long ago I had accepted that the attractions of women would always be a puzzle to me; best to accept the inexplicable without question when it worked in my favor. Still, looking at my face one day in a mirror of polished silver—the last time I looked in that mirror, for soon after I sold it to get a few sesterces to feed the household—I saw a gray-bearded man whose face was lined with worries, and I wondered what Cassandra could find attractive in that weathered countenance. I gazed for a long time in that mirror. I squinted, I blurred my eyes, I looked sidelong, but I couldn't catch even a fleeting glimpse of the man I became when I was with her.

There was some advantage in appearing so unlikely a lover. No one in my household suspected. When I reappeared after being gone for hours at a time, Diana, if she noticed, might chide me for going out without Davus to protect me. Hieronymus might ask what news I brought from the chin-waggers in the Forum. Bethesda, calling from her bed, might ask why I had failed to bring her the latest impossible-to-find item she had decided might cure her. They were scolding, or curious, or complaining, but not suspicious.

Nonetheless, they all noticed a change in me. I was more

patient, less truculent. I no longer snapped at Hieronymus; once again his wit delighted me, and eventually I convinced him to again take dinner with the family. The antics of Mopsus and Androcles amused rather than rankled. When Davus seemed most slow-witted, I found him most charming and thought to myself, *No wonder my daughter fell in love with such a fine fellow!* Diana was more beautiful and intelligent than ever, and little Aulus, no matter how noisy, was the best of all grandsons. And Bethesda . . .

Bethesda remained unwell. Her malady had settled into her body like a spiteful vagrant lurking in a house, careful never to be seen but leaving unnerving signs of his presence everywhere. At first, her illness had made her snappish and demanding. Then she became increasingly withdrawn and quiet, which was much worse because it was so out of character for her. Her spirits darkened even as mine became lighter.

In her presence I was torn with guilt, not so much because I had been with another woman—the physical act of sex conjured no shame in me—but because I had stumbled into something singular, wonderful, and wholly unexpected, even while Bethesda fell prey to something awful, uncertain, and lingering. All our lives, Bethesda and I had shared everything, as much as any two people could. Now we each had ventured to a place where the other could not follow—and in opposite directions. My experience was magical, hers miserable. I felt the guilt of the well-fed man watching his loved one choke on sawdust and bones.

❧

In the meantime, news of the war continued to arrive from Greece. One heard all sorts of contradictory reports—that Caesar had outmaneuvered Pompey; that Pompey had outmaneuvered Caesar. For a while, from Aprilis to mid-Quinctilis, the two made their camps and built fortifications in the region of Dyrrachium, the principal seaport on the eastern side of the Adriatic Sea. Both sides seemed set to make the rugged, maze-like hills and gorges around Dyrrachium the arena for a decisive battle. But after an engagement in which Pompey very nearly overran his forces, Caesar saw himself at a disadvantage and moved inland, toward the region of Thessaly. The decisive battle was yet to come.

∽

My visits to Cassandra blur together in my memory, but two incidents stand out.

Just as she never spoke of her visits to highborn women, so she never spoke of the reason for those visits: her spells of prophecy. I did begin once to ask her about them, but she replied by placing her forefinger perpendicular to my lips and then distracting me in other ways. Why did I not press her for details? I can see reasons, but only in retrospect. If she were a fraud, I didn't want to know it. If she were genuine, and gazing into a flame could induce her to utter prophecies, I didn't want to hear them. Why seek a glimpse of the future when the future could hold only darkness? In Cassandra I had found a way to live in the present.

Nevertheless, on one occasion I saw the god pass through her.

We were lying naked side by side on her pallet, sweat lubricating our flesh where our bodies were pressed close together. I was watching the progress of a fly on the wall, its wings made iridescent by sunlight from the high window. Cassandra was humming softly, her eyes closed. For a moment I thought I recognized the tune—an Alexandrian lullaby Bethesda had sung to Diana—then decided I must be mistaken. The melody was close, but not quite the same. . . .

The humming stopped. I heard only the buzzing of the fly across the room.

Cassandra gave a lurch so violent that I almost fell from the narrow bed. She struck my nose with her elbow.

I rolled away, covering my face. I jumped to my feet and looked back. Cassandra remained on the bed, her head rolling, her trunk twisting, her limbs flailing. The effect was uncanny, as if every part of her had become a separate animal with a will of its own. Her eyes rolled upward, showing only white.

Suddenly, she sat bolt upright. I thought the spell was over. Then she fell back on the bed, arching her spine and convulsing. I had never seen anything like it. The fit she had suffered outside the Temple of Vesta had been nothing like this.

Something Meto had once said came back to me: *He was always afraid he might swallow his tongue. He's told me I must be prepared to put something in his mouth if his fits should ever recur. . . .*

Meto had been talking about Caesar. I seemed to hear his voice in my ear: "Put something in her mouth!" I jumped and looked over my shoulder, thinking for a moment that Meto was actually in the room. Anything seemed possible. A god was passing through Cassandra. The very air around me seemed to shudder and spark with intimations of the supernatural.

I remembered the leather baton I had noticed once before, the first time I came to see her. I reached under the mattress and found it almost at once, as if an invisible hand guided me to it.

I clambered atop Cassandra, holding her down with my weight. I tried to pin her wrists with one hand so that I could force the biting stick between her teeth, but she was too strong. As soon as I managed to contain one part of her, another part broke free. The bed itself seemed to come alive, pitching up and down and banging against the wall. From down the hall I heard someone shout, "For Venus's sake, you two, keep it down in there!"

As suddenly as it had begun, the seizure ended. Beneath me, her body went limp. The change was so abrupt that for a moment I thought she might be dead. I pushed myself up and looked down at her, my heart in my throat. Then I saw her chest rise as she drew a deep breath. Her eyelids flickered. It seemed to me that the passage of the god had forced her spirit out of her, and for a moment, after the god passed through, there was no animation in her at all. Gradually reentering her body, her spirit seemed confused, uncertain it had returned to the right place.

She blinked and opened her eyes. She seemed not to recognize me.

"Cassandra," I whispered, reaching out to wipe flecks of foam from her lips. I brushed my fingers against her cheek. She reached up to cover my hand with hers. Her grip was as weak as a child's.

"Gordianus?" she said.

"I'm here, Cassandra. Are you all right? Do you need anything?"

She closed her eyes. I felt a stab of fear, but she was only resting. She reached up and pulled me against her, embracing me, humming the lullaby she had been humming before, rocking me gently as if I were the one who needed comforting.

Where had she been? What had she seen? After that day, I understood the fascination she inspired in the rich and powerful women who thought they could harness for their own ends the power that coursed through Cassandra.

Later that day, when I returned to my house, everyone noticed my split lip, including Bethesda, who at dinner was in better spirits than she had been in for quite a while and in a mood to gently scold me.

"Run afoul of some ruffians in the Forum, Husband?" she asked.

"No, Wife."

"A brawl in some shady tavern, then?"

"Of course not."

She raised an eyebrow. "Perhaps a beautiful woman gave you a slap for getting fresh with her?"

My face grew hot. "Something like that."

Bethesda smiled and told Mopsus to bring her more stewed leeks, the latest cure in which she had vested her hopes. She seemed satisfied to allow the cause of my swollen lip to remain a mystery, but I noticed that Diana, reclining on one elbow beside Davus on their dining couch, had fixed me with a darkly questioning gaze.

❧

Among those meetings with Cassandra that blur together in my memory, another incident stands out, not least because it occurred on the last day we met in her room in the Subura. It was the last day we would be alone together; the last time we would make love.

I had no way of knowing that at the time. Had I known, would I have held her more tightly, made love to her more passionately? That hardly seems possible. I fear I might have done the opposite, become remote and drawn away from her—doing as many men do when they realize they must lose the thing they love, looking for a shortcut around their suffering. They push away the thing they love before it can be snatched from them.

I never had to confront that dilemma; I never saw what was coming.

It was a warm early afternoon, the day before the Nones of Sextilis. Not a breeze stirred in all of Rome. A stifling haze had settled over the city. Cassandra's room in the Subura was like a heated cubicle at the baths. Warmth radiated from the walls. A shaft of sunlight entered through the high window and struck the opposite wall, so thick with motes of dust that it seemed a solid thing, a strangely glowing beam lodged above our heads.

I had thought the heat would stifle our lovemaking, but it had the opposite effect, acting on us like a drug. The normal limitations on my body melted away. I transcended myself. I entered a state of rapture so complete I no longer knew where or who I was. Afterward, I felt as light and insubstantial as one of those motes of dust riding the sunbeam above our heads.

A delicious lethargy overcame me. I felt heavy, solid, inert. My limbs turned to lead. Even a finger was too heavy to lift. I seemed to dream, yet the images conjured by Somnus slipped away before I could apprehend them, like shadows glimpsed from the corner of one's eye. I neither slept nor woke.

Slowly, gradually, I heard voices.

They seemed to come from somewhere above me, muffled by distance. Two men were speaking. Their words were indistinct, but I could tell that their discussion was heated. "Keep your voice down!" one of them said, loud enough for me to hear.

I knew that voice.

I stirred. I seemed to be waking from a dream. For a long moment, I thought the voices had been part of that dream. Then I heard them again. They came from the room above. Partly I heard them through the floor, but mostly from the high window, which must have been directly below a window of the room above.

I sensed that Cassandra was gone even before I reached for her and found the place beside me empty. The spot was still warm from her body.

The speakers in the room above lowered their voices. I heard them now only as a murmur. Surely I had only imagined that I recognized one of those voices. . . .

I got out of bed, reached for my loincloth and stepped into it, then put on my tunic. I stepped past the curtain that covered Cassandra's doorway, into the hallway beyond. Around a bend, past other curtained doorways, I came to a flight of wooden steps. I took them slowly, trying to make no noise. Even so, the very last step before I arrived at the next floor made a loud creak. The murmur of voices that came from the room at the end of the hall abruptly ceased.

I took another step. The floorboard creaked. From the room at the end of the hall there came only silence. I stood motionless for a long time. Then I heard a voice, the one I had recognized before, say quite distinctly, "Do you think that's him?"

"It must be," said the other man. With a start, I recognized his voice as well.

I had to be mistaken. My imagination was running away with me. To prove it I walked steadily down the hallway, heedless of creaking floorboards. I confronted a curtain much like the curtain that covered Cassandra's doorway.

I stared at the curtain. From beyond came only silence— or rather, not quite silence, but the sound of men breathing. Did I only imagine that, or could they hear me breathing as well?

I raised my hand to grip the curtain's edge and imagined someone on the other side doing the same. Would he be holding a dagger in his other hand?

I yanked the curtain aside, hardening my nerves to confront a face staring back at me, nose-to-nose. But I was alone at the threshold. The occupants—just the two of them, without a bodyguard in sight—were seated in the middle of the small room. At the sight of me they rose from their chairs. After the dim hallway, the light from the window dazzled me for a moment. I saw them only as two very different silhouettes, one broad and stocky, the other tall and elegantly slender. Gradually their faces came into focus.

"You see," said Marcus Caelius to his companion, "it's Gordianus, just as I said."

"So it is," said Milo, crossing his brawny arms. "Well, don't just stand there, Finder. Drop the curtain and come inside. And keep your voice down!"

XIV

My interview with Fausta left me in a foul mood. I almost
decided to leave off for the day and return home. But what
would I do there except brood? There was plenty to brood
about—Cassandra dead and my investigations leading me no
nearer to the reason; Bethesda ill and growing weaker, with
no cure in sight; Rome tottering on a narrow precipice with a
chasm on either side, one called Pompey and the other Caesar,
and two mastiffs called Milo and Caelius biting at her
heels. . . .

The day was in direct counterpoint to my mood. The sun
shone bright and warm, its intensity relieved by a succession
of magnificent clouds that advanced slowly across the azure
sky, spaced apart as evenly as if some parade master had arrayed them like elephants in an imperator's triumphal procession.

"That one looks like a tragedy mask. You can even see the
holes for the eyes and mouth," said Davus.

"What?"

"That cloud up there. Isn't that what you're staring at?"

We sat on a stone bench in a little square not far from
Fausta's house. I had told Davus that I needed to rest for a
moment. In fact, it was my mind that was weary and needed
to come to a complete stop. I had been staring at the parade
of clouds and emptying my head of every thought.

"Yes, Davus, a tragedy mask."

"Only now it's changing. See how the mouth is bending. You might almost say it was a comedy mask."

"I see what you mean. But the whole shape is changing, isn't it? It's not really like a mask anymore. More like—nothing, really. Just a cloud . . ." *Rather like my pursuit of the truth about Cassandra,* I thought. My interviews had yielded a continual series of impressions that flowed one into another, all slightly different, all somehow askew, none of them quite recognizable as the Cassandra I had known. The truth about her was as elusive as a cloud, holding its shape only until the next interview changed it into something else.

"Only two more to go," I said.

"Clouds?" said Davus.

"No! Only two more women to talk to, of those who came to watch Cassandra's funeral pyre: Calpurnia and Clodia."

"Shall we go see one of them now, Father-in-Law?"

"Why not? On such a beautiful day, I think I know where Clodia will be."

❧

We crossed the bridge to the far side of the Tiber and turned to the right, keeping as close to the river as we could. Here, away from the bustle of the city's center, the wealthiest families of Rome kept little garden estates, called horti, along the waterfront. Clodia's horti had been in her family for generations. It was there I had first met her eight years ago when she summoned me to investigate the murder of the Egyptian philosopher Dio. Marcus Caelius had been her lover, but they had fallen out, and Clodia had been determined to exact her revenge by prosecuting him for Dio's murder.

Clodia's horti were also the last place I had seen her, when I came to her after her beloved brother's murder on the Appian Way. Fulvia had been Clodius's wife, but there were those who said Clodia was the true widow, no matter that she was the dead man's sister.

As Davus and I walked along the road, I caught only occasional glimpses of the river to our right. More often, high walls blocked our view. Once, access to the horti along the Tiber had been relatively open, but in recent years many owners had built high fences and walls to keep out strangers. When we did pass by an unwalled estate, I saw patches of woodland and tall grass interspersed with meticulously cultivated gardens. Through the foliage I caught glimpses of rustic sheds and charming little guest houses, shade-dappled fishponds and splashing fountains, stone-paved walkways adorned with statuary, and boat ramps projecting into the glimmering Tiber.

Clodia's horti were far enough from the city's center to feel secluded, yet close enough to reach by foot—an enviable location for a piece of riverfront property in the capital of the world. Cicero, who had done a thorough job of destroying Clodia's reputation in the process of defending Caelius, had had the gall to try to buy her horti from Clodia only a few years later. Clodia had refused even to speak to his agent.

Unlike many of her neighbors, Clodia had resisted the trend of encircling her horti with high walls. Coming upon the narrow lane that led off the main road into her grounds, I had the feeling of being somewhere far away from the city with all its crimes and riots. The lane was bordered by sprawling berry bushes that met overhead, shading the way. This tunnel-like path opened onto a broad swath of high grass. Once, I remembered, that grass had been kept closely mown by a pair of goats. The goats were gone. What had once been a lawn had become a wild meadow.

Facing the meadow and perpendicular to the river, which was almost entirely obscured by an intervening stand of dense trees, was a long, narrow house with a portico running along the front. The house was not as I remembered. Tiles were missing from the roof. Some of the shutters were askew, hanging from broken hinges. The shrubbery along the portico, perfectly trimmed in my memory, was overgrown and choked with weeds.

I remembered Clodia's horti echoing with music and the laughter of naked bathers on the riverbank. All I heard on this day was the buzzing of cicadas in the high grass. The place seemed utterly deserted, with not even a groundskeeper to look after it.

"Doesn't look like anyone's here," said Davus.

"Perhaps not. On such a beautiful day, it's hard to imagine she wouldn't be here. She used to love this place so much! But times change. People change. The world grows older." I sighed. "Still, let's take a look down by the river."

Avoiding the high grass, we walked along the portico that fronted the house. Where the shutters hung off their hinges, I peeked inside the windows. The rooms were dark, but I could see that some had been stripped entirely of their furnishings. The place smelled of dust and mildew.

We came to the end of the portico. Here a little path wound among magnificent yew trees and cypresses, leading down to the water's edge. I had given up on finding Clodia, but for nostalgia's sake I wanted to stand for a moment at the place where I had first met her. She had been lounging on a high couch in her red-and-white-striped pavilion wearing a gown of sheerest gossamer, while she watched a band of young men, including her brother, Clodius, frolic naked in the water for her amusement.

We made our way through the trees. To my surprise, a lone figure sat in a folding chair on the riverbank facing the water. It was a woman wearing a stola better suited for winter days; the wool was dark gray and the sleeves covered her arms. Her dark hair was streaked with gray and pulled back in a bun. What was she doing here? She hardly looked like the sort of woman to be a friend of Clodia's.

She must have heard us, for she turned about in the chair and peered up at us, shading her brow against the sun so that her face was obscured.

"Does Clodia know you're here?" I asked.

The woman laughed. It was her laugh I recognized—sly, indulgent, intimating unspoken secrets. "Have I really changed that much, Gordianus? You haven't changed a bit."

"Clodia!" I whispered.

She lowered her hand. I saw her face. Her eyes were the same—emerald green, as bright as sunlight on the green Ti-

ber—but time had caught up with the rest of her. It had been
only four years since I had last seen her. How could she have
aged so much in that time?

To be sure, she had taken no pains to look her best. That
in itself marked a change; Clodia had always been vain about
her appearance. But on this day she wore no makeup to ac-
centuate her eyes and lips, no jewelry to adorn her ears and
throat, and a drab stola that did nothing to flatter her. Her hair,
usually elaborately dressed and colored with henna, was pulled
back in a simple bun and showed an abundance of gray. The
most subtle difference, and yet the most telling, was the fact
that she seemed to be wearing no scent. Clodia's perfume, a
heady blend of spikenard and crocus oil, had haunted me for
years. It was impossible to think of her without recalling that
scent. Yet on this day, standing near her, I smelled only the
rank green smell of the riverbank on a summer day.

She smiled. "Whom did you expect to find here?"

"No one. The house appears deserted."

"So it is."

"There's no one else here?" I said. "No one at all?" Clodia
had always surrounded herself with admiring sycophants who
spouted poetry, beautiful slaves of both genders, and a veritable army of lovers—cast-off lovers, current lovers, would-
be lovers awaiting their turn.

"No one but me," she said. "I came by litter early this
morning, then sent the bearers back to my house on the Palatine. I come here very seldom nowadays, but when I do, I
prefer to be alone. Slaves can be so tiresome, standing about
waiting for instructions. And there's no one left in Rome worth
inviting to a bathing party. All the beautiful young men are
off getting themselves killed somewhere. Or they're dead already. . . ." She looked past me, at Davus. "Except for this
one. Who is he, Gordianus?"

I smiled, despite a twinge of jealously. "Davus is my son-
in-law."

"Can your little girl really be old enough to be married?
And to such a mountain of muscles! Lucky little Diana. Maybe
he'd like to take a swim in the river." She stared at Davus like

a hungry tigress. Perhaps she had not changed so very much after all.

I raised an eyebrow. "I think not."

Davus gazed at the sparkling water. "Actually, Father-in-Law, it's such a hot day. . . ."

"By all means, go jump in the water," said Clodia. "I insist! Slip out of that silly toga . . . and whatever you're wearing underneath. You can hang your things on that tree branch there. Just as all the young men used to do; I remember that branch piled high with cast-off garments. . . ."

Davus looked at me. His brow glistened with sweat. "Oh, very well," I said.

Clodia laughed softly. "Stop glowering, Gordianus. Unless you'd like to take a swim as well, you'll find another folding chair in that little lean-to over there. There's also a box with a bit of food and some wine."

When I returned with the chair and the box, Davus was striding toward the river's edge, barefoot and wearing only his loincloth.

"Young man!" called Clodia.

Davus looked over his shoulder.

"Come back here, young man."

Davus headed back, a questioning look on his face. As soon as he was within range, Clodia reached out, gripped his loincloth, and deftly pulled it off. She sat back in her chair and spun the loincloth on her forefinger for a moment before tossing it with perfect aim atop the toga draped over the tree branch. "There, that's better. A fellow as handsome as you should go into the river just as the gods made you."

I expected Davus to blush and stammer, but instead he grinned stupidly, let out a whoop, and ran splashing into the water.

I sighed. "You still have the power to make grown men into little boys, I see."

"Every man except you, Gordianus. By Hercules, look at the thighs on that fellow—and what's between them. He's a veritable stallion! Are you sure he's not too much for little Diana to handle?"

I cleared my throat. "Perhaps we could speak of something else."

"Must we? On such a day, how pleasant it would be to speak only of youth and beauty and love. But knowing you, Gordianus, I suppose you've come to talk about misery and murder and death."

"One death, in particular."

"The seeress?"

"She was called Cassandra."

"Yes, I know."

"You were there to see her burn."

Clodia was silent for a moment, watching Davus splash in the water. "I thought perhaps you had come to bring me . . . other news."

"About what?"

"That monster Milo . . . and Marcus Caelius. This silly, doomed revolt of theirs."

"What do you care about that?"

"They shall both get themselves killed."

"Probably."

"Caelius . . ." She stared at the water, lost in thought. "Long ago when we were lovers, Caelius used to swim out there while I watched. Just the two of us, alone on this stretch of the riverbank; we needed no one else. I remember him standing just where your son-in-law is standing now, naked, with his back to me—Caelius had a delicious backside—then slowly turning around to show me his grin . . . and the fact that he was rampant and ready for love."

"You must have seen many men since then, bathing naked out there."

"None like Caelius."

"Yet you came to hate him."

"He deserted me."

"You tried to destroy him."

"But I didn't succeed, did I? I only did harm to myself. And now, without any assistance from me, Caelius seems determined to destroy himself." She closed her eyes. "Gone," she whispered, "all gone: my dear, sweet brother; Fulvia's beloved Curio; so many of the beautiful young men who used to come here, cavorting in the water without a care. Even that pest Catullus with his wretched poems. Whom shall the Fates take next? Marcus Caelius, I suppose. After so many years of laughing in their faces, the Fates shall snatch him up and send him straight to Hades."

"You'll be revenged on him at last."

She nodded. "That's one way of looking at it."

"I came to talk about Cassandra, not Caelius."

"Ah, yes. The seeress."

"You say that with irony in your voice. Did she prophesy for you?"

"Why do you ask, Gordianus?"

"She was murdered. I want to find out why she died, and who killed her."

"Why? It won't bring her back." She tilted her head and looked at me keenly, then made a face. "Oh, dear. Is that it? Now I see. Well, well. Cassandra succeeded where Clodia failed."

"If you mean—"

"You were in love with her, weren't you?"

I had never said that word aloud, not even to Cassandra herself. "Perhaps."

"At any rate, you made love to her."

"Yes."

She released a sigh of mingled exasperation and amusement. "Fortune's wheel spins round and round! Now Clodia finds herself celibate—and the ever-faithful Gordianus is an adulterer! Who would ever have thought it? The gods must be laughing at us."

"So I have long suspected."

She stared abstractedly at the glinting sunlight on the water and bit her thumbnail. "That was rude of me, to speak so glibly. You must be quite devastated."

"Cassandra's death was a blow to me, yes, among many other blows of late."

"Gordianus the stoic! You should learn to vent your emotions. Drink yourself into a stupor. Destroy some irreplaceable object in a rage. Spend an hour or two torturing one of your slaves. You'll feel better."

"I'd rather find out who killed Cassandra, and why."

"And then what? I saw the other women who came to watch Cassandra's funeral pyre. If it was one of them, what action could you possibly take? The courts are a shambles. No magistrate will show any interest in the murder of a nobody like Cassandra. And every one of those women is too powerful for you to take on by yourself. You'll never find justice."

"Then I'll settle for finding the truth."

"How strange you are, Gordianus! They say each mortal has a guiding passion. Seeking pleasure seems endlessly more sensible to me, but if finding truth is yours, so be it." Clodia shrugged. Even though the gesture was almost swallowed by her voluminous stola, even though age and suffering had changed her outwardly, in that eloquent rise and fall of her shoulders I caught a glimpse of the essential Clodia. That shrug summed up everything about her in an instant. She had lived a life larger than most men dreamed of, had devoured every sensation flesh could offer, had followed every emotion to its utmost extremity—and in the end, Clodia shrugged.

I knew in that moment why I had succumbed to my desire for Cassandra, yet had never quite succumbed to Clodia. It was impossible to imagine Cassandra shrugging like that. The intensity with which she lived in the moment made such a gesture unthinkable. Once Clodia had seemed to me the most vital woman alive, but only because I mistook a raging appetite for a love of life, and I had no one to show me the difference until I met Cassandra.

"You can't tell me anything that might be of use to me?" I said.

"About Cassandra? Tell me what you know about her already."

It seemed to me that Clodia was intentionally avoiding my question. "I know that she was invited into the houses of some of the most powerful women in Rome," I said. "Some of those women think she was a genuine seeress. Others think she was a fraud. I know she came from Alexandria, where she acted in the mimes. But her seizures—at least some of them—were entirely real."

"What else do you know?"

I took a breath. "I think she may have been involved in some way—how, I'm not sure—in this business with Milo and Caelius."

Clodia raised an eyebrow. "I see. And why is that?"

"I have my reasons."

Clodia turned her gaze to Davus, who had swum a considerable distance up the river and was now swimming back. "What a pair of shoulders," she murmured. "I hope your daughter appreciates them."

"I think she does."

"He's going to be hungry when he climbs out. A good thing my pantry slave always packs more food into that box than I could possibly eat by myself. What else do you know about Cassandra? I think, Gordianus, that you're leaving something out."

"I don't know what you mean."

"Don't you? The most important thing of all. You were in love with her. Hopelessly in love, from the look on your face. But did *she* love *you?* Ah! Really, you should go take a look at yourself in the water, Gordianus. You'd see the face of a man who's just been poked where he can least stand to be touched. That's what this is really about. Not, 'Who killed Cassandra?' but, 'Who *was* Cassandra?' What was she really up to? And most important of all, what did she really want— not just from those lofty Roman matrons, but from a humble fellow called the Finder. But if you don't already know the answer to that question, you'll never find it now."

Davus emerged from the water, glistening wet and shaking the water from his hair. "Magnificent arms," whispered Clodia, growling like a tigress. "The war has turned Rome into a city of old men and boys. I thought Pompey and Caesar had snatched up all the worthy specimens to feed to Mars, but they somehow overlooked this one."

Davus fetched his loincloth and covered himself, moving with a natural, unself-conscious grace that did him credit, given that he must have felt Clodia's eyes following his every move. Clodia sent him to fetch a third folding chair, then offered him the contents of her box. She gazed at him, enthralled, as if no better amusement could exist than watching a hungry young man devour a roasted chicken and suck the juice from his fingers.

I sensed that I would learn no more about Cassandra from her, at least not on this occasion. I decided not to press her. Only later would I realize how deftly she had avoided telling me anything of importance, and how completely she had disarmed me with the charms she still exerted over me.

"So," I said, "you think that Milo and Caelius are doomed to fail?"

A shadow crossed her face. "It seems impossible that they could succeed."

"Your brother's old nemesis and the man you hate most in the world, both destroyed once and for all. I should think that prospect would make you very happy."

Clodia made no reply. She continued to watch Davus eat, but the enjoyment I had seen on her face drained away, replaced by another emotion I could not decipher.

XV

They met under a rose.

I looked from face to face, hardly believing what I saw: the two most dangerous men in Italy, their whereabouts and intentions the subject of every conversation, in a bare room in a shabby tenement in the heart of Rome. Bare, that is, except for the two chairs in which they had been sitting, a cupboard against one wall, and the room's single ornament, a pocket vase made of terra-cotta hung on the wall above their heads, and in that vase a single blood-red rose.

They were meeting *sub rosa,* invoking the ancient custom that all who meet under the rose are bound to silence. Following my gaze, Marcus Caelius glanced up at the rose.

"Milo's idea," he said. "He takes that sort of thing very seriously, you know—signs, portents, vows, omens. Thus, a rose to ensure discretion—as if either one of us could possibly benefit by betraying the other. Of course, it obliges *you* to keep silent as well, Gordianus. What's the matter? You look as if you'd seen Medusa. Come in! I'm afraid we have only the two chairs, so I suppose we should all remain standing."

I let the curtain fall behind me and stepped into the room, overwhelmed by the strangeness of the moment. What were they doing here in the Subura? More to the point, what were they doing in the room directly above Cassandra's, and on a day when Cassandra knew I would be coming?

They were dressed to suit the room and the neighborhood,

in shabby tunics and worn shoes. Milo's hair was longer than I had ever seen it, pushed back from his face in a shaggy mane, and his beard was untrimmed. Caelius had a smudge of dirt on his cheek, like some common laborer. It was not the first time I had seen them in disguise. During one of the bloody riots following the murder of Clodius, Milo and Caelius had escaped together from an angry mob by taking off their togas and their citizenship rings and passing as slaves. On this occasion Caelius was wearing his ring, but Milo's finger was bare. He had been stripped of his citizenship and the right to wear a citizen's ring when he was exiled from Rome.

"Are these the disguises you use to go about Rome incognito?" I asked. "You pose as the poor master, Caelius? And you pose as his slave, Milo?"

Caelius smiled. "I told you he was clever, Milo. There's not much the Finder misses."

Milo grunted and peered at me with barely concealed hostility. He was no longer fat and dissipated, as when I had last seen him in Massilia, enduring his exile in a drunken stupor. The danger and difficulty of his escape and his return to Rome were written on his weathered features. His stocky wrestler's physique was back in fighting trim. There was a hard, desperate glint in his eyes.

"You said the Finder would be glad to see us, Caelius," said Milo. "He doesn't look glad to me. He looks rather distressed."

"Only because we've taken him by surprise," said Caelius. "But how else could we approach you, Gordianus? We could hardly have come calling at your house, could we? That would have put your dear family in danger. As it is, you've taken *us* a bit by surprise. We were thinking we would send someone down to fetch you in a bit, after your nap. But here you are of your own accord."

"I heard the two of you talking," I said. "I recognized Milo's voice."

"Ha! And he was the one telling *me* to keep quiet," said Caelius. "But that's our Milo. He's never known his own strength, whether cracking two heads together or shouting at me to keep my voice down."

I shook my head. "I don't understand. What are you doing here?"

Caelius raised an eyebrow. "Plotting a revolution, of course."

"No, I mean—here, in Rome. Everyone thinks you're long gone."

"So I was. So I shall be again. I come and go like a puff of smoke! But just now I happen to be back in Rome. Plotting a revolution is complicated business, Gordianus. Tedious, as well—and you know I've never liked hard work. You wouldn't believe the logistics it entails. I have to be everywhere at once, encouraging my partisans, whispering comfort in the ears of the doubtful, holding the hands of the fearful, pressing coins in the palms of the greedy. And not least, approaching old friends and acquaintances to ask for their support." He fixed me with a penetrating gaze.

"And you, Milo?" I said. "I can't believe you've dared to set foot in Rome. Caesar showed mercy when he let you keep your head and stay in Massilia. He'll never forgive this. Does your wife know you're here?"

"Leave Fausta out of this!" snapped Milo.

I shook my head. "You're both mad, meeting like this in the Subura. You're bound to be recognized or overheard. If Isauricus and Trebonius find you—"

"They won't," said Caelius. "They haven't so far. I come and go as I please in the city. I have many, many supporters, Gordianus. More than you realize, I imagine."

"Enough to stage a successful uprising, here and now?"

His smile wavered. "Not quite. The tender shoots still require cultivation. Milo and I have determined that our best course is to raise an armed force in the countryside in order to take the city by force."

"Raise an army? How? From where? Every available fighting man is already enlisted to serve either Caesar or Pompey."

"But not all those men are happy. There are soldiers garrisoned all over Italy who were forced into Caesar's service.

They're bored and discontented and ripe for sedition. They're jealous of their comrades who crossed the water with Caesar and Antony, because those are the soldiers who'll share in the spoils of victory, not the ones left behind; all they get to do is bully a few cowering townspeople and plant babies in the local girls."

"But you'll promise them something better? An attack on Rome itself—complete with plunder for the victors? Will you let them sack the city, Caelius? Is this your revenge on Rome, Milo?"

Caelius shook his head. "There'll be plenty of plunder to reward the soldiers, but it won't be taken from ordinary citizens like you, Gordianus. It will come from the greedy landlords and moneylenders who've made themselves rich as Croesus in the last year. The wealth they've stolen and hoarded will be reclaimed and redistributed, beginning with the soldiers loyal to the revolution."

"Loyal to *you,* you mean."

Caelius shrugged. "Someone has to lead the fight."

"You're deluding yourself, Caelius. If you take Rome by force, you won't be able to control what happens next. You say you'll only plunder the landlords and moneylenders, but you can't guarantee that. Even Caesar's men have slipped out of his control from time to time over the years, looting and burning when he gave them express orders not to—and you're not Caesar, Caelius."

"Rome is sick, Gordianus. She requires a drastic cure."

"Even if it kills her?"

"Perhaps, to be reborn, Rome first must die. A better city will rise from the ashes, like the phoenix."

I shook my head. "This whole argument proceeds from a fallacy. You're presuming you can subvert enough of Caesar's garrisons to storm the city. I simply don't believe it. A few soldiers are that unhappy, perhaps—but the rest will remain loyal to Caesar. They'll band together and destroy you before you ever reach Rome."

"You underestimate the discontent throughout Italy, Gordianus. I've seen it. Antony did Caesar no favors when he crisscrossed Italy before leaving for Greece. He alienated one city after another with his arrogant blustering—traveling like an Eastern potentate with a retinue of sycophants, lounging in his gilded litter with that whore of his, Cytheris. The soldiers liked what they saw no better than the city fathers. To Caesar they might have remained loyal, but not if he intends to leave the likes of Antony in charge when he's absent."

Milo spoke up. "And we needn't rely just on the garrisons. There are plenty of *other* trained fighters to call on." Caelius raised his hand and gave him a withering look, but Milo blustered on. "I'm talking about the gladiator training camps down south! The biggest, strongest, most vicious slaves in all of Italy end up in those camps, and they're trained to kill without mercy. When it comes to killing, one gladiator is worth a century of common soldiers. The slaves in those camps are desperate—they're all headed for an early, painful death, and neither Pompey nor Caesar offers them any hope for the future. After we set them free, they'll be loyal to us alone!"

For years, Milo had been attended by his own private army of gladiators; he had left Rome with them, they had protected him in Massilia and had helped to defend the city against Caesar's siege, and now they had returned with Milo to Italy. He had grown so used to the company of his gladiators that he didn't realize how shocking it was to suggest that such men be recruited to overthrow the Senate and the magistrates of Rome. To be sure, Caesar himself had set the precedent of freeing gladiators whom he owned and turning them into soldiers, but he had been careful to disperse them among different legions and to use them outside Italy. But Milo was hinting at something very different—setting free whole bands of gladiators and letting them lay siege to Rome itself. Such men were the lowest of the low—desperate, mistreated slaves trained only to kill, lacking any soldierly discipline, without families or any vested interest in Rome's future or her institutions. If soldiers could not be trusted to refrain from looting and burning, what would happen if Rome were overrun with gladiators?

"Do you see yourself as a second Spartacus, Milo? Is that

the legacy you intend to leave behind? Milo, who made his reputation as watchdog for the Best People, then ended by setting bloodthirsty slaves loose on Rome? The Fates have led you on a strange path, Milo."

"Milo speaks prematurely," said Caelius, wincing. "We'll use gladiators only as a last resort."

"A cure certain to kill the patient! Gladiators are trained to kill, not to take orders. You're playing Pandora if you set them loose."

Neither Caelius nor Milo answered. They stared at me for a long moment, then exchanged a glance—Milo looking vindicated, Caelius disappointed. I had reacted just as Milo expected, but Caelius had hoped for a different reaction.

"What do you want from me?" I asked.

Caelius sighed. "Merely for you to act in your own best interests, Gordianus. You've poisoned your relationship with Pompey. I don't know exactly what happened between you, but I do know he tried to strangle you with his bare hands when he was fleeing by ship from Brundisium. You barely escaped alive! What will you do if Pompey returns to Rome in triumph? And your relationship with Caesar seems hardly better. Your adopted son Meto is still close to Caesar—but you've disowned Meto and offended Caesar in the process. Where will you stand if Caesar wins and makes himself king of Rome? I was as loyal to Caesar as any man—I fled Rome with Curio to join him at the Rubicon; I fought beside him in Spain—and you see how he rewarded me, with crumbs! What reward can *you* expect from Caesar?

"But forget Pompey, forget Caesar and the darkness that will fall over this city if either of them triumphs. I should think, Gordianus, that my recent speeches in the Forum would have touched a nerve with you. I happen to know a bit about your finances. You're up to your ears in debt to that cannibal Volumnius. He never forgives a debt. He's insatiable! He shall suck the life from you as a man sucks marrow from a bone. Your family will be reduced to beggars, perhaps even slaves. Pompey will do nothing to stop him. Neither will Caesar; it's Caesar's fault that men like Volumnius are having their day, growing fat off of other men's misery. Only I can save you from Volumnius, Gordianus. Only I can promise you justice. Cast your lot with me. It's your only choice."

"Why me, Caelius? I have no power. I have no money. I have no family connections. Why do you care whether I join your cause or not?"

"Ah, but you have something far more important to us than any of those things, Gordianus." Caelius tapped his skull. "You're clever! You see the world as it is. You know the ways of men. Great men and small men, you've moved among them all. Most importantly, you care about truth, and you long for justice. 'The last honest man in Rome,' as Cicero once called you. You're exactly the sort of man who will matter after everything has been turned upside down. Your day shall finally come; there's no limit to the heights to which you might aspire. You need us, Gordianus. But we need you, as well."

He spoke so earnestly—looking me in the eye, pitching his voice just so—that I felt compelled to listen. I recognized an orator's trick he had learned from Cicero—first incite fear (of Pompey, of Caesar, of Volumnius), then promise hope (freedom from debt, justice for all, my own virtues finally recognized and rewarded). He stared at me, waiting for an answer.

I took a deep breath. "We can't possibly be safe, meeting like this. At any moment, Isauricus might send men to storm this building. The two of you wouldn't stand a chance."

Milo emitted a harsh, barking noise that passed for a laugh. "Ha! Do you suppose we haven't taken precautions? This building is thoroughly guarded. You didn't notice the armed men outside and on the rooftop? Good. That means they're doing their job and staying out of sight. But I need merely to snap my fingers and in the blink of an eye you'd be twitching on the floor with your throat cut." A gleam lit his eyes.

"What about the tenants? If I overheard you, then others—"

"A friend of Caelius's owns this building. He's gradually cleared out every tenant who can't be trusted and replaced them with die-hard partisans."

"*Every* occupant of the building is a partisan of Caelius's?"

I thought of Cassandra, trying to imagine how she fit into their scheme.

"Including the occupant standing in front of me, I hope." Caelius smiled. "What do you say, Gordianus? Are you with us? The way is hard, but the rewards will be great beyond imagining."

"What do you want from me?"

"Nothing yet. But the time will come when I shall call on your craftiness, your cunning, your honesty and wisdom—and when I do, I want to be able to rely on your loyalty without question."

"You'd trust me to simply give you my word?"

"No." He went to the cupboard against the wall and returned with a piece of parchment. "I want you to sign this."

I held it at arm's length, for the letters were small, and read:

ON THIS DATE, ONE DAY BEFORE THE NONES OF SEXTILIS IN THE YEAR OF ROME DCCVI, I PLEDGE MY LIFE AND MY FORTUNE TO THE CAUSE OF MARCUS CAELIUS RUFUS AND TITUS ANNIUS MILO. I ACCEPT THEIR AUTHORITY AND I WILL OBEY THEIR ORDERS. I REJECT THE LEGITIMACY OF THE SENATE AND THE MAGISTRATES OF ROME ELECTED UNDER ORDERS OF GAIUS JULIUS CAESAR. LIKEWISE I REJECT THE LEGITIMACY OF THOSE SENATORS AND MAGISTRATES WHO FLED FROM ROME AND FIGHT UNDER THE BANNER OF GNAEUS POMPEY MAGNUS. ALL ARE IMPOSTORS WHO BY THEIR ACTIONS HAVE CEDED ANY CLAIM TO CONSTITUTE THE LEGITIMATE GOVERNMENT OF ROME. UNDER GUIDANCE OF MARCUS CAELIUS RUFUS AND TITUS ANNIUS MILO, THE ROMAN STATE SHALL BE RECONSTITUTED IN ACCORDANCE WITH THE WILL OF THE ROMAN PEOPLE. ONLY THE GOVERNMENT ESTABLISHED BY THEM, AND NO OTHER, SHALL HAVE LEGITIMACY TO CONDUCT THE AFFAIRS OF STATE. BY MY NAME BELOW, SIGNED BESIDE THOSE OF MARCUS CAELIUS RUFUS AND TITUS ANNIUS MILO, AND BY THE IMPRESSION OF THE DEVICE ON MY CITIZEN'S RING IN

THE WAX SEAL ON THIS DOCUMENT, I FREELY PLEDGE
MYSELF TO THIS CAUSE AND FORSAKE ALL OTHERS.

I looked up. "You must be joking. A contract to conspire
against the state? I'm not Cicero, but even I know this isn't
legally binding."

"Not under the present regime, perhaps," said Caelius.

"The only possible use for such an incriminating document
is blackmail," I said.

"You call it blackmail. We call it insurance," said Milo
dryly. "If you want to leave this room, you'll sign."

"And if I refuse?"

Caelius sighed. "I'd hoped you'd sign it readily, even eagerly. Pompey wants you dead. Caesar has corrupted your son.
Volumnius will make a beggar of you. Why should you *not*
sign?"

I stared at the parchment. Would they kill me if I refused
to sign? Looking at Milo, who was glaring at me balefully, I
had no doubt of it. To sign meant escaping with my life. But
what would happen when Caelius and Milo were destroyed
and Caesar or Pompey returned to Rome? My name on such
a pledge could mean the destruction, not only of myself, but
of everyone close to me. Of course, in the vagaries of war,
the parchment might be destroyed or lost and never seen again.
And—what if . . . ?

For a brief moment I allowed myself to think the unthinkable. What if Caelius and Milo ultimately won? In such an
unlikely circumstance, by signing such a pledge I might stand
to achieve a status I had never dreamed possible. From standing always on the sidelines, watching the great game at a distance, the Gordiani might find themselves at the very center
of a new republic. Senator Gordianus? If that meant nothing
to me, then what about my family and their future? Why
should Diana not be elevated by a stroke of fortune to the rank
of a Fausta or a Clodia or a Fulvia? Why should Eco's children
not have the opportunity to shape the world to their liking
rather than submit to the schemes of others? How else are

great fortunes and great families established except by a single act of wild daring, a mad gamble?

Caelius and Milo promised wholesale revolution. Revolution inspired men without hope to think the unthinkable.

But what would it matter that Volumnius were forced to forgive my debts, if all Rome, my house included, were burned down in a wholesale conflagration? What would it matter that the Senate was emptied and its seats promised to new men like myself, if rampaging gladiators were set loose to do what they wanted with our daughters? Caelius promised a world reborn in justice, but in the end he cared only about power. His alliance with Milo and his willingness to attack Rome with gladiators proved that.

I crumpled the parchment in my fist and threw it across the room.

"I told you!" snapped Milo. "I told you he'd never sign."

Caelius sighed. He clapped his hands. I heard a noise behind me and turned to see two burly men step through the doorway. They must have been waiting just outside the room. They had the look of hired assassins.

"A couple of my fellow future senators?" I said.

Caelius stepped to the cupboard. A few moments later he returned with a cup and held it out to me. "Take it," he said.

I looked in the cup. "Wine?"

"Cheap stuff. Sorry it's not a better vintage, but the likes of Volumnius have sucked up all the good stuff. Drink, Gordianus. Swallow every drop."

I stared in the cup. "Wine . . . and what else?"

"Drink it!" said Milo.

Behind me the two henchmen stepped so close I could hear them breathing, one in each ear. I heard the slither of daggers drawn from scabbards. "Do what he says," one of them whispered. "Drink!"

"Either that," said the other, "or else—" I felt the prick of a dagger against my ribs, then the prick of its twin from the other direction.

Why poison me? Because a man of my years found dead without a mark on him would raise no suspicions, prompt no questions. They could leave my body in the street, and anyone would think I had died of natural causes.

Or would they carry me down the stairs and leave me in Cassandra's bed? Did she play some role in their scheme—or was she, too, a victim? What if they killed her as well, and left our bodies to be discovered together with the poison beside us? I imagined my family's shame and consternation. The cup trembled in my hand.

"Cassandra—" I said.

"Shut up and drink!" yelled Caelius. In a flash, as if he'd dropped a mask, his face changed completely. One moment he was the charming, unflappable orator, and the next, a vicious, desperate fugitive easily capable of murder or of crimes much worse. I had been afraid of Milo; it was Caelius I should have feared more.

The daggers pressed harder against my flesh. Caelius and Milo stepped closer.

"You don't want to die by daggers," growled Milo. "Think of it! The metal slicing into your flesh, pulling out, cutting into you again. The blood spurting out of you. The cold seeping into your limbs. The long, agonizing wait to die. Drink, you fool!"

He gripped my wrist and forced me to raise the cup. Wine sloshed against my lips, but I kept my mouth shut.

"Never mind the daggers. Grab his arms!" shouted Milo, taking the cup from me. The men behind me twisted my arms behind my back. Caelius pinched my jaw and forced it open. Wine poured into my mouth and down my throat. The taste was bitter. I swallowed to keep from sucking it into my lungs.

"All of it!" whispered Milo. "Every drop!" I coughed and sputtered. Wine trickled over my chin and cheeks, but most of it went into my belly. He poured until the cup was empty.

Caelius and Milo stepped back. Their henchmen released me. I staggered forward, feeling dizzy. I dropped to my knees. Caelius and Milo spun above me, going in and out of focus each time I blinked. The room became dark, as if night fell.

Their voices echoed strangely and seemed to come from a great distance. "We should have put hemlock in the wine instead of that other stuff," said Milo. "We should lop his head off, here and now."

"No!" said Caelius. "I gave her my word. I promised, and you agreed—"

"A promise made to a witch!"

"Call her that if you want, since you're not worthy to utter her name! I gave her my word, and my word still means something, Milo. Does yours?"

"Don't bait me, Caelius."

"Then don't speak of killing him!"

"It was your crazy idea to try to win him over."

"For a moment, I thought I had. The fool! No matter. By the time he wakes . . ."

Caelius's voice faded away. The floor rushed up to my face. The room turned black.

As if in a dream, I saw Cassandra standing on a distant horizon. Her lips formed words I could not hear. She stretched out her arms, beckoning to me even as she receded farther and farther beyond my grasp, until she vanished altogether.

∾

I opened my eyes.

My head pounded. My body was stiff. The least movement caused me to groan. My mouth had a strange, unpleasant taste. My bladder was uncomfortably full. My stomach growled.

I lay on the hard, bare floor. I stirred and managed to sit upright. Judging from the angle of the sunlight that entered the window, no time at all had passed since I fell to the floor. Indeed, the light seemed to indicate that time had regressed by an hour or two. I blinked in befuddlement.

One of the chairs had been pushed against the wall. The other lay on its side on the floor. The cupboard doors stood open. From where I sat, I could see that its shelves had been emptied.

I stared at the pocket vase on the wall. The rose drooped. Half its petals had fallen to the floor below.

I had been unconscious for almost twenty-four hours.

I managed to stand. For a moment I thought I was all right, then I felt light-headed. I staggered and clutched the cupboard to stay upright. Oily spots swam before my eyes. The dizziness slowly passed.

I turned toward the doorway and gave a start. I was not alone in the room.

A man was lying face down on the floor just inside the doorway, before the curtain that was closed for privacy. He was a large fellow, with massive limbs and a neck like a tree trunk. From the way he was lying, with his neck unnaturally bent, I was almost certain he was dead.

Even so, I approached him cautiously, taking unsteady steps. I reached down and lifted his head by a handful of hair. I heard a sickening crack. His neck was broken.

I looked at his face. He wasn't one of the men who had held me while Caelius and Milo forced the drugged wine down my throat.

Who was he? Who had killed him and left me alive?

I stepped over the body and pushed aside the curtain. The hallway was empty. I made my way to the head of the stairs and carefully descended, taking unsteady steps. I reached the bottom, negotiated the hallway, and came to the curtain that hung over Cassandra's doorway.

I whispered her name. My voice was hoarse and feeble. I spoke her name again, louder. There was no answer.

I pushed aside the curtain. The room was completely bare. Not even the pallet remained.

I stood for a long time, feeling nothing, waiting for my head to clear. Suddenly I was desperately thirsty. I moved to the doorway. As I was stepping through, my foot struck something concealed amid the folds of the curtain. I stopped to pick it up. It was Cassandra's leather biting stick.

Had she left in great haste? Or had someone else cleared out the room? Cassandra had so few possessions, it seemed hardly possible she could have forgotten such a personal object. If she had overlooked it somehow, surely she would have missed it and come back for it.

Where was Cassandra?

I left the building and walked down the street, shielding my eyes against the sunshine. I felt that sense of unreality that comes from having slept a very long time and waking at an odd hour of the day. I walked down the Street of Copper Pots, wincing at the clanging of metal against metal. I found a public toilet and emptied my bladder. I found a public fountain and splashed my face, then drank until my thirst was quenched. I was famished, but that could wait.

I took the shortest route toward my house, cutting across the Forum. Amid the formal squares and ornate temples, my sense of unreality only deepened. I seemed to be walking in a dream.

"Gordianus!"

I turned around and confronted one-armed Canininus. The rest of the chin-waggers stood in a group nearby. One by one they looked up from some heated discussion to stare at me.

"So you *are* alive," said Canininus, "even if you look half-dead."

Mild-mannered Manlius stepped closer, followed by the others. "Gordianus! Your family is worried sick about you. Your son-in-law and that crazy Massilian have been scouring the city for you. They say you went off somewhere on your own yesterday and never showed up for dinner. They were here not an hour ago, along with those two little mischief makers, asking if anyone's seen you. Where *have* you been?"

Volcatius, the old Pompeian, flashed a lecherous grin. "I'll bet I can guess. You know the old Etruscan proverb: when a man's gone missing, it's because of a miss. Am I right, Gordianus? Was she worth the trouble you'll face when you get back home?" He tittered.

"Meanwhile, you've missed the best gossip in ages," said Canininus. "Milo and Caelius were both spotted right here in the city, together, only this morning."

"It's a fact!" said Manlius. "Someone saw them heading from the Subura toward the Capena Gate with an entourage of very rough-looking fellows—some of Milo's notorious gladiators, most likely. They were posing as master and slave—"

"Caelius playing the master, of course, since he's the one with the brains," said Canininus. "As soon as they were outside the gate, they mounted horses that were waiting for them and sped like lightning toward the south. What do you make of that?"

I shrugged. "Another wild rumor?" I managed to say. Despite the water I had drunk, my mouth was as dry as chalk.

"Never mind Caelius and Milo," said Volcatius. "Gordianus never answered my question. Who was she, Gordianus? Some cheap whore in the Subura? Or one of those great ladies you occasionally call upon in your line of work? She must have put you through quite a marathon if you're just now staggering home."

I pushed past him and hurried on. I tripped on an uneven paving stone and heard laughter behind me.

"She's crippled him!" cried Volcatius. "I want to meet this Amazon."

"You needn't be rude," Manlius called after me.

"Gordianus thinks he's too good for the likes of us," said Canininus. "He never comes around anymore. When we do see him, he goes stalking off in a huff like a . . ."

His voice receded behind me. I walked as fast as I could, heading for the steep pathway at the far side of the Forum that would take me home. Inside the folds of my tunic, I clutched Cassandra's biting stick.

❧

"Where in Hades have you been?"

The tone—frantic, furious, and relieved all at once, implicitly warning me never to do such a thing again—reminded me of Bethesda. How many times over the years had I heard that precise tone when I returned home from some scrape I had gotten myself into? But it wasn't Bethesda who rushed up to me in the foyer, looking fit to be tied. It was Diana.

I told my daughter the truth—or part of it. That I had met unexpectedly (for me, if not for them) with Milo and Caelius in the Subura on the previous day, that they had put forward a proposition that I refused, that they had forced me to swallow a soporific of some sort, that I had only just awakened and had made my way straight home.

"What were you doing in the Subura in the first place?" asked Diana, frowning. "How is it that Milo and Caelius were able to find you? Did they have you followed, or did they just happen to come upon you? What sort of drug did they give you?" Diana had inherited my own inquisitive nature, but she had yet to master the rules of a successful interrogation. Ask too many questions at once and you invite the overwhelmed subject to shrug helplessly and give no answer. That was exactly what I did.

"Everyone in the household is out looking for you," she said. "Davus is down at the fish market. Hieronymus is at the Senian Baths. I sent Mopsus and Androcles over to Eco's house to find out if he'd turned up anything. We've all been mad with worry."

"What about your mother? This must have been especially hard on her."

Diana sighed. "I managed to keep it from her. She didn't come out of her room even once yesterday, so she didn't see the rest of us all flustered and in a panic when you didn't show up for dinner. But she did ask for you later, and I had to make up something on the spot—a lie about you spending the night away from the city because an old client needed to tap your memory about a trial from years ago. I don't think I could have fooled her if she wasn't so unwell. As it was, she just nodded and turned her face away and pulled the coverlet around her neck. How can she be cold when the weather's so hot? But at least she didn't realize you were missing, so she didn't have that worry to add to her illness."

"How is she today?"

"Better, I suppose, because she's determined to go out. A little while ago she sent for one of the slave girls to come help her dress. She says she wants to go to the market. She says she's thought of something that might make her better—radishes. She says she must have radishes."

A few moments later, Davus arrived home. He was so glad

to see me, he let out a roar and lifted me high in the air, squeezing the breath out of me. Diana shushed him and told him to put me down at once because Bethesda was coming and mustn't see him making such a fuss. Davus obediently put me down, but couldn't stop grinning at me.

Bethesda stepped into the room. Dressed in a freshly laundered stola, with her hair combed and pinned, she looked slightly pale but better than I had seen her in quite some time. She gave Davus a sidelong look but said nothing and shook her head ruefully, no doubt wondering once again how her daughter had come to marry such a grinning simpleton.

"Radishes!" she announced. Her voice was hoarse, but surprisingly strong.

And so we made our way—slowly, to accommodate Bethesda—down to the market, in search of the latest commodity Bethesda imagined might provide a cure for her malaise.

We walked from vendor to vendor, searching in vain for a radish that would satisfy Bethesda's discriminating gaze. I suggested that Bethesda might look for carrots instead. She insisted that the soup she had in mind would allow no substitutions.

At last Bethesda cried, "Eureka!" Sure enough, she held in her hands a truly admirable bunch of radishes—firm and red, with crisp, green leaves and long, trailing roots.

The price the vendor named was exorbitant.

"Perhaps I could manage with just two radishes," said Bethesda. "Or perhaps only one. Yes, one would do, I'm sure. I imagine we can afford one, can't we, Husband?"

I looked into her brown eyes and felt a pang of guilt, thinking of Bethesda's suffering, thinking of Cassandra. . . .

"I shall buy you more than one radish, Wife. I shall buy you the whole bunch of them. Davus, you're carrying the money bag. Hand it to Diana so that she can pay the man."

"Papa, are you sure?" said Diana. "It's so much."

"Of course I'm sure. Pay the scoundrel!"

The vendor was ecstatic. Bethesda, clutching the radishes to her breast, gave me a look to melt my heart. Then a shadow crossed her face, and I knew that she suddenly felt unwell. I touched her arm. "Shall we go home now, Wife?"

Just then, there was a commotion from another part of the market. A man yelled. A woman shrieked: "It's her! The mad-woman!"

I turned about to see Cassandra staggering toward me. Her blue tunica was torn at the neck and pulled awry, her golden hair wild and unkempt. There was a crazed expression on her face, and in her eyes, a look of utter panic.

She ran to me, reaching forward, her gait uneven. "Gordi-anus, help me!" She fell into my arms and dropped to her knees, pulling me down with her.

"Cassandra!" I gasped. I lowered my voice to a whisper. "If this is some pretense—"

She clutched my arms and cried out. Her body convulsed.

Diana knelt beside me. "Papa, what's wrong with her?"

"I don't know."

"It's the god in her," said Bethesda. "The same god that compels her prophecies must be tearing her apart inside."

A crowd gathered. "Draw back, all of you!" I shouted. Cassandra clutched at me again, but her grip was weakening. Her eyelids flickered and drooped.

"Cassandra, what's wrong? What's happened?" I whispered.

"Poison," she said. "She's poisoned me!"

"Who? What did she give you?" Our faces were so close that I felt her shallow breath on my lips. Her eyes seemed huge, her blue irises eclipsed by the enormous blackness of her pupils.

"Something—in the drink . . ." Cassandra said.

A moment later, she was dead.

XVI

Davus and I left Clodia on the banks of the Tiber, gazing at the sunlight on the water, alone with her memories. We retraced our steps past the riverside gardens of the rich and back into the city.

Davus was refreshed from his swim, but the heat of the day oppressed me. I was weary in mind and body. By the time we made our way up the slope of the Palatine to my house, I wanted nothing more than a few quiet hours of rest in a shady corner of my garden.

I had spoken to them all now—all the women who'd come to see Cassandra end in flames—except one.

Would Caesar's wife deign to see me? The more I thought about it, the less likely it seemed. Calpurnia would be surrounded by an army of advisors and attendants and bodyguards to protect her both from those who sought her husband's favors and those who sought his destruction. There was the complication that she might consider me an enemy since I had turned my back on Caesar along with Meto in Massilia.

From what I knew of Calpurnia, she was not the sort to act on a sudden whim or a sentimental impulse or out of prurient interest. She was sensible, discreet, and utterly respectable—precisely the qualities that had convinced Caesar to marry her. Everyone knew his famous quip about his previous wife, whom he had summarily divorced after she became the subject of gossip: "Caesar's wife must be above suspicion." Calpurnia was said to be so devoid of even petty vices that no scandal could ever be attached to her; not the sort of woman, I thought, to admit the likes of myself into her presence, even for a formal audience. People might talk.

And yet, she had come to see Cassandra burn.

I sat on my folding chair in the shade and leaned back against a pillar. I narrowed my eyes and watched a bee flit from flower to flower. I shut my eyes and listened to the buzzing of his wings as he circled the garden and flew over my head. I must have dozed, for the next thing I knew, Androcles had hold of my arm and was shaking me awake.

"Master, there's a man at the door asking for you, and a great litter out in the street, and bodyguards, lots and lots of bodyguards, and—"

"What? What are you talking about?"

"A visitor for you, Master."

I blinked, cleared my throat, and brushed my fingers through my hair. "Very well, send him in."

"No, he says that *you* must come to the door."

I felt a sudden chill. A great litter, an army of bodyguards, a high-handed summons to come to my own front door—who could it be? Only one person would be so presumptuous, I thought: the man who would own this house himself soon enough, once all my debts came due and I was found to be penniless. Why had Volumnius come to harass me now on this particular day?

"Where's Davus?" I asked.

"With Diana, in their room," said Androcles.

"Napping?"

"I don't think so. The door's shut, but I'm pretty sure they're not asleep."

"How can you tell?"

"All that noise they make! I'm surprised you can't hear them out here. He grunts and squeals like a boar with a spear in his side, and then she—"

"Enough, Androcles! Never mind fetching Davus. Surely even Volumnius won't dare to have a Roman citizen beaten on his own doorstep," I declared; but as I rose, unbending my stiff knees, I had my doubts.

I made my way across the garden and through the atrium, with Androcles scurrying after me. The man in the foyer didn't have the look of a debt collector; he was too old and too small. He had the self-assured, sophisticated air one associates with slaves who act as personal secretaries to citizens of wealth and taste. With relief, I knew that it was not Volumnius who had come calling on me. Who, then? Something in the slave's manner suggested that he waited upon a mistress, not a master. A woman in a sumptuous litter, attended by many body-guards . . .

In my experience, the gods in their whimsy so fashion the world that sometimes the thing that seems most unlikely is precisely the thing that occurs. I knew at once, and with absolute certainty, whom the slave represented.

"Will your mistress do me the honor of stepping inside?" I said.

The slave raised an eyebrow. "Alas, much as it would please her to grace your household with her presence, her schedule today will not permit it. But she very much wants to speak to you. If you'll follow me, there's a litter waiting. We think it best if you come alone."

"Of course. Androcles, when Davus and Diana . . . reappear . . . let them know that I've left in the company of Caesar's wife. And I shall be returning . . . ?" I looked at the slave.

"You should be gone for no more than an hour or so," he assured me. "That's all the mistress can spare. May I?" He extended his open hands, almost touching me, and I realized he intended to search my person. I nodded and allowed him to run his hands over my tunic. Satisfied that I carried no weapons, he stepped back and allowed me to walk out the door ahead of him.

Two identical litters were waiting in the street, each fitted with a resplendent canopy made of ivory poles and white draperies that shimmered with golden threads, hemmed with a purple stripe. The drapes of the first litter were closed, concealing its occupant. I was ushered into the litter behind it. The slave joined me, closed the drapes, and settled back into the pile of cushions opposite me.

With a steady gracefulness that did credit to the bearers, the litter rose and began to move forward.

"Where are we going?" I said.

The slave smiled. "We'll be there very shortly."

I felt the motion of the litter each time we took a sharp turn, but we never seemed to go downhill. That meant we were still somewhere on the Palatine Hill when the litter came to a stop. I heard the sound of a heavy bar being lifted on a hinge and gates swinging open. We moved forward into a graveled courtyard; I could hear the stones crunching under the bearers' feet. The litter stopped. The gates swung shut, and the bar dropped back into place. The slave parted the drapes with his forefinger and peered out, awaiting a signal. At last he pushed back the drape and gestured for me to exit the litter.

As soon as my feet touched the gravel, I was flanked by two bodyguards who escorted me across the narrow courtyard, up a short flight of steps, and into a small but elegantly appointed foyer. The white walls were trimmed with blue and gold. A small bronze statue of Venus occupied a scalloped niche. The floor was decorated with a mosaic of Venus emerging naked from the sea. I was reminded that Caesar claimed Venus as his ancestress. It was Venus his soldiers called upon for victory.

The guards escorted me through an atrium where goldfish darted across the sunken pool. Ahead I caught a glimpse of sunlit greenery, a garden surrounded by a portico, but the guards led me to one side, down a short hallway, and into a small library. The far wall was lined with a tall bookcase, its pigeonholes filled with scrolls. Paintings depicting a battle covered the walls on either side. Arrayed across the wall to the right was the army of the ancient Greeks led by Alexander the Great, instantly recognizable by his chiseled features and his golden mane of hair. On the opposite wall was the army of the Persian king Darius, whom Alexander had defeated to become master of the world.

Seated before the bookcase, dominating the room despite

the massive, dramatic pictures, was Calpurnia. She was handsome enough, though not a great beauty. She seemed oblivious of the latest fashions, with their Eastern and Egyptian influences; from her clothing, jewelry, and hairstyle, she might have been an austere Roman matron of a century ago. Her countenance was as severe as her costume; she looked like a mistress about to rebuke a wayward slave, and I reflexively braced myself. But before she spoke, she smiled, just enough to put me at ease—or to put me off my guard?—and I saw that she possessed a certain charm not unlike her husband's. Had she possessed it before Caesar met her, or had she learned it from him?

"Sit," she said. I turned my head to see that a chair had been placed behind me. The guards had discreetly withdrawn to a post just outside the door.

She waited until I was seated, then paused for several heartbeats before she spoke again. That, too, was a technique of Caesar's, never to seem rushed. "We've never met, Gordianus, but I know of your reputation and of my husband's high regard for you. You've had a long and interesting career in this city. I had thought that you were retired, but I understand that for the last few days you've been rather busy, crisscrossing Rome with that burly son-in-law of yours."

"You've had someone following us?"

The brusqueness of the question left her unfazed. "Let us say that you have been observed. One by one, you've been visiting each of the women who came to Cassandra's funeral. I was there, too. You must have seen my litter. Yet you haven't yet called on me."

"I intended to do so."

"Why didn't you come to me first?"

I cleared my throat. "Out of deference, I suppose. Great Caesar's wife must be a very busy woman, with little time to answer the queries of a humble citizen like myself. Or so I thought. May I ask where we are?"

"In a house tucked away on a little cul-de-sac on the Palatine Hill. You needn't know the exact location. My husband has owned this place for years, but only a very select few have ever stepped inside it. Even some of his closest advisors are unaware of its existence. It seemed an appropriate place for you and I to meet, since this was where Cassandra resided."

I frowned. "Here? But I thought—"

"That shabby room in the Subura? Her residence there was a pretense, part of the role she played. This was the house where she kept her possessions. It was to this house that she retreated whenever she felt she might be in danger, or whenever she grew too sick of her role as a pauper and needed a taste of luxury. I imagine she would have liked to bring you to this house, Gordianus, but that wasn't possible. Her room was just across the garden. It was in this room that I came to meet with her. I would sit here, and she would sit where you're sitting, in that very chair."

"You met with Cassandra?"

"On a regular basis, so that I could give her instructions, and so that she could deliver any valuable information she had uncovered since our last meeting."

I took this in. "Cassandra was your spy?"

"My husband's spy, to be more precise. It was Caesar who recruited her, Caesar who briefed her on what he expected from her, and Caesar who trained her—as a spy, I mean. Cassandra was already an accomplished actress, of course, but the arts of the spy are somewhat more specialized." She peered at me intently. "Are you grinding your teeth, Finder?"

"Always Caesar!" I said, staring up at the image of Alexander, then across to the image of Darius. Which would Caesar resemble more when the story of his life came to an end? The conqueror beloved by gods and storytellers, or the arrogant emperor who owned the world but lost it? On his journey to his destiny, Caesar had swept the whole world along in his wake. He loomed over everything, casting his shadow not just over armies and kings but over every thing and every person I loved. Now I found his shadow had covered Cassandra as well.

Calpurnia looked at me coolly. "I understand that you harbor some sort of grudge against my husband for having claimed the loyalty and affection of your son—"

"Meto is no longer my son!"

She nodded. "Even so, Caesar harbors no resentment against you, Gordianus. In time, he hopes that he may once again be able to count you among his friends." That was always Caesar's way, to mend breaches, to convert enemies, to draw everyone into his circle, even if later the need arose to destroy them.

"But we were talking of Cassandra," she said. "I know that her death has caused you great distress. I think Caesar would want me to reveal to you who Cassandra was, and how and why she came to Rome. What do you already know about her?"

That she was beautiful and tragic and doomed, I thought. *That I fell in love with her, or thought I did, knowing nothing about her.*

"That she came from Alexandria," I said. "That she performed in the mime shows there and knew Cytheris. That she suffered from seizures and falling sickness—unless that was a pretense. That she may or may not have possessed the gift of prophecy. That she used her reputation as a seeress to play a cruel joke on Antonia, at Cytheris's behest. That she may have done the same thing to a number of other powerful women in Rome who sought her out—unless she was blackmailing them. Or spying on them."

Calpurnia nodded. "If I tell you that my husband has a number of agents who gather intelligence for him, I presume that will come as no surprise to you. Agents of all sorts, high and low—from street urchins and tavern keepers to centurions and senators. You never know who might overhear something of importance. It takes skill, patience, and experience to make sense of all the information that comes in, to scrutinize the sources, to disregard lies planted by the enemy, to decide between conflicting accounts. All those bits of information are like tiles in a mosaic; separately they signify nothing, but together, from the right perspective, they form a sort of picture.

"It's an intricate business, all the more complicated because it takes place in the shadows. That's what my husband calls it—the shadow war between himself and his enemies. The battles that everyone knows about take place in broad daylight between soldiers who fight with swords and spears. There are other battles that take place in the shadows, which no one sees or even knows about—but people die in those battles, nonetheless. I suppose one could think of Cassandra as a kind of Amazon, a woman warrior. It's the only way a woman *can* be a warrior, I suppose, fighting in the shadow war."

"Why did she fight for Caesar?"

"Why does any soldier fight for him? Because he paid her, of course. As part of the arrangement, she became a free woman, and she was very handsomely paid in regular installments that I held in trust for her. The work Cassandra did was dangerous, but she was well rewarded. She would have returned to Alexandria a wealthy woman . . . had she survived."

"How did Caesar recruit her?"

"As soon as Pompey was driven from Italy, Caesar set about reorganizing the Senate here in Rome and deciding whom to place in charge in his absence—Marc Antony, as it turned out. Everyone became a Caesarian overnight once Pompey was gone—but whom could Caesar really trust, and what sort of plots were being hatched against him? It was imperative that he should organize a network of agents to gather information. Some of those agents were already in place. Others had to be recruited. It was I who pointed out to him that his greatest weakness would be in obtaining information from the women of Rome—the wives and mothers and daughters and sisters who had been left behind by both allies and enemies. Such women always know more than they're given credit for, often more than they themselves realize. They know the most secret longings and most fervent loyalties of their men. A casual remark in a letter from a husband could lead to a secret hiding place or a cache of arms or a buried store of gold. But what sort of person could obtain access to so many diverse women and extract whatever valuable information they might possess?

"It was Caesar who hit upon the idea of recruiting an actress to play the part of a mad seeress. I told him that no Roman matron was that gullible and no actress that skillful.

He proved me wrong on both counts. He dispatched an agent to Alexandria to find the right actress. Why Alexandria? Because the mime masters there are famous for training their players to perfection, and because it's far enough from Rome that the agent might find a suitable performer who would be unknown here. It was several months before the agent returned from Alexandria, bringing Cassandra with him. They entered the city in a covered litter, and the agent installed her, secretly, in this house.

"Only a few days later, Caesar returned to Rome after securing Spain and Massilia. As soon as he was able to take time from overseeing elections, he met with Cassandra. It was in this very room. I was with him. He said he wanted my opinion of her, but I'm sure he made up his mind before I could say a word."

"She auditioned for Caesar, like an actress auditioning for a mime show?"

"If you wish to put it that way. She was certainly beautiful; I could see that Caesar was duly impressed, but beauty was not the quality we were looking for. She spoke excellent Latin with only the faintest accent; she was quite a polyglot, you know. But she seemed rather nervous. That was understandable, perhaps, for a young woman meeting Caesar for the first time, but it worried me; this was the person we were counting on to keep a cool head even as she deceived some of the shrewdest women in Rome. Caesar commenced to explain what he wanted from her. She seemed distracted, and increasingly agitated. Suddenly she collapsed to the floor, writhing and foaming at the mouth. The agent had warned us that she suffered from the falling sickness. Caesar at once went to her assistance. He found a leather biting stick on her person and put it between her teeth, then held her until the spell subsided. I could see that he was moved by her suffering—Caesar himself has experienced such fits in the past—but I wondered if such a condition might rob her of her wits and cause her to fail in her mission. I was about to say as much when Cassandra suddenly sprang to her feet, laughing out loud.

"She had been acting, you see. It was all a performance—

the nervousness, the fidgeting, the fit. I was furious, at first. Caesar was delighted. She won him over on the spot. If she could fool both of us, then surely she could fool anyone."

"I don't understand. Did she truly suffer from the falling sickness or not?"

"Oh, yes, she was subject to fits. She suffered more than one, staying in this house. But she had also learned to mimic those fits so convincingly that no one could tell the difference. That skill, among her others—not least her intelligence, for I don't think I've ever met a woman more intelligent than Cassandra—made her ideal for the role Caesar had in mind.

"Before he left for Greece, Caesar briefed her very closely, taking more time with her than with any of his other agents. She learned the name and family history of every important woman in Rome. More than that, she learned everything we could glean about those women's personal habits, their eccentricities and superstitions, their dreams and fears. She took copious notes on wax tablets, but kept them only long enough to memorize every detail. Then she would rub the tablets clean. She kept everything in her head.

"When Caesar was satisfied, she left this house and made her first appearances in the city. It wasn't long before people were talking about the madwoman in the Forum. I remember being at a dinner party and trying not to smile the first time I heard her mentioned. Overnight, everyone seemed to know about the mysterious woman who could see the future, even though no one had any idea who she was or where she came from. It was said that if she stared into a flame, she could induce such visions at will.

"Her method was simple. She would wait until a woman invited her home, or in some cases, practically kidnapped her. Inducements would be offered—money, food, shelter. Soon the lamp would be produced. Cassandra would oblige by staring at the flame, suffering a fit and going into a trance, then uttering cryptic but transparent prophecies based on what she knew about her hostess. Cassandra would tell each woman what that woman *wanted* to hear. There's no surer way to gain a person's confidence. With Cassandra, they let down their guard. They became naked before her—vulnerable, frightened, ambitious, boastful. They said things they would never have said to anyone else. Many more women consulted her than the handful who came to see her burn. Half the senators' wives in Rome have had Cassandra in their houses."

I thought of the women I had spoken to. Terentia, Tullia, and the Vestal Fabia had all accepted Cassandra's prophetic powers without question. What bits of information about Cicero and Dolabella, not to mention the inner workings of the Vestal Virgins, had they inadvertently let slip while Cassandra was in their presence?

"What about Fulvia?" I said. "Cassandra gave Fulvia specific details about Curio's death—the battle in the desert, the fact that he was beheaded. This was before anyone in Rome even knew that Curio was dead."

"Anyone but Caesar."

"What do you mean?"

"When the messenger from Africa arrived in Rome, he went directly to Caesar and to no one else. Caesar was distraught, of course. Curio was like a son to him. Caesar had had such great hopes for Curio; that was why he gave him the African command. But as Caesar says, information is like gold: one must spend it wisely. Secretly he met with Cassandra in this room and told her the details. The next morning, from informants in Fulvia's household, we learned that Fulvia intended to call on friends that day, and we determined the route she would take. Cassandra waited along that route. When Fulvia passed by in her litter, Cassandra pitched her voice to sound like a whisper, just loud enough to reach Fulvia's ears. She said—"

I remembered the words that Fulvia had quoted to me, and spoke them back to Calpurnia: " 'He's dead now. He died fighting. It was a brave death.' "

Calpurnia nodded. "Exactly. Those were the very words Caesar told her to say. Fulvia stopped, of course. She took Cassandra home with her. And when Cassandra revealed the specific details of Curio's end, which were later confirmed, it seemed like a true vision from the gods. Thus Cassandra won

Fulvia's unquestioning trust, along with that of her mother, Sempronia."

"And meanwhile Caesar kept the news of Curio's death to himself?"

"He swore the messenger to secrecy and told no one, not even Marc Antony—not even me—for two days. Information is gold. By spending that particular nugget of information with the utmost discipline, Caesar bought Fulvia's faith in Cassandra."

"But Curio died fighting for Caesar. Why send a spy into his widow's house?"

"Why not? We wanted to know the temper of that household and anything those two women might be secretly planning. Don't let her grieving fool you, Gordianus. Fulvia is still madly ambitious. So is Sempronia. Many a time I've told Caesar, 'We have to watch those two, especially the daughter. No matter that she's married to Curio, no matter that Marc Antony's married to his cousin—mark my words, Fulvia has her eye on our Antony, and if those two should ever join forces . . . beware!' "

I shook my head. "But for now, Antony remains married to Antonia. *She* saw through Cassandra's pretense."

"Yes. With Antonia, Cassandra made a grave miscalculation. She acted on her own initiative, outside her mission for Caesar."

"Not entirely her own initiative. It was Cytheris who put her up to making a distressing prophecy to Antonia."

"I know. Cassandra confessed as much to me when I pressed her. She said that Cytheris had known her in Alexandria, and threatened to expose her if she didn't do a favor for her. Cassandra argued that her prophecy to Antonia was only a small matter. I disagreed, and I chastised her quite severely for destroying any chance to build a bond of trust with Antonia. That was stupid of Cassandra, and certainly not a part of Caesar's plan. It was also my first indication that Cassandra seemed to be slipping out of my control."

"Only the first indication?"

"Her affair with you was another. That should never have

happened. She knew from the beginning that she was not to form any such bond with any man while she was in Caesar's employ."

"Her time with me was *not* a part of Caesar's plan?"

Calpurnia looked at me shrewdly. "You're worried that it might have been otherwise? That perhaps Cassandra sought you out and seduced you merely to gain your confidence? No. Not in her role as Caesar's agent. She was acting on her own initiative when she formed whatever bond grew between you."

"How is it that you know about it, then?"

She smiled. "Purely by surmise. Why else would you have shown such an interest in Cassandra after her death, unless you were her lover?"

I made no reply.

She shrugged. "Who can explain the mysteries of Venus? Cassandra managed to keep your affair a secret even from me; that's why she could never bring you here, where the two of you would have been much more comfortable than in that hovel in the Subura. You were her little secret, just as she was yours." Calpurnia looked at me thoughtfully. "To be sure, even before Cassandra met you, she knew who you were from the very thorough briefings Caesar gave her. And of course, she was acquainted with your son—with Meto, I mean. Meto was present at some of those briefings. That young man has a flair for this sort of thing—playacting, secret codes, hatching plots under the rose."

"Cassandra knew Meto? She never told me."

"How could she, without giving away the fact that she was Caesar's agent? To have told you would have exposed you to the same dangers she faced. You might have shared her fate."

"Her fate." I tasted the word like wormwood on my tongue. "Do you know who killed her?" I asked, half suspecting now that it must have been Calpurnia herself.

She read the look on my face. "I had nothing to do with her death. I don't know who killed her or why. It might have been any of those women who came to see her burn. It might have been someone else. But . . ."

"Yes?"

She rose from her chair, strode to the painting of Alexander, and peered at it intently, though she must have seen it many times before. "When he was briefing Cassandra about various women in Rome, Caesar himself suggested specific prophecies or visions that she might use in order to gain a particular woman's confidence or frighten her or otherwise get her to speak what was on her mind. He did so in the case of Fulvia, as I've told you. But Caesar couldn't foresee every eventuality. After he left Rome, when a woman sought out Cassandra for her gift, in most cases Cassandra had to improvise, using her own skills and whatever she already knew about that woman.

"But circumstances change. Cassandra needed to be kept abreast of developments. That job fell to me whenever I met with her in this house. One such development was this business with Marcus Caelius and Milo. Even Caesar didn't foresee that Caelius would turn against him or that Milo would dare to return to Italy—and no one imagined that the two of them might join forces. Trebonius and Isauricus—what a pair of bunglers! They should have put a stop to Caelius the moment he set up his chair of state in the Forum and began to agitate the mob. Now the situation is out of control." She looked at me sharply. "Did you know that Caelius and Milo were both in the city as recently as the day Cassandra died?"

I answered carefully. "I heard a rumor in the Forum that the two of them were seen riding out together that morning, heading south."

"That rumor was true. That day was our last chance to stop Caelius and Milo from trying to raise a revolution in the south. I had hoped to do so using Cassandra."

"How could Cassandra have stopped them?"

"By using her gift, of course."

"Why would either of them have listened to Cassandra?"

"Caelius might not have taken her seriously, but according to my sources, Milo might very well have heeded her. I'm told that he's grown increasingly superstitious in recent years. He looks for omens and portents everywhere. If Milo could have been convinced by Cassandra to abandon this mad enterprise, Caelius might well have abandoned it as well."

"But even if Caelius and Milo were secretly in the city for a while, how could Cassandra possibly have gained access to either of them?"

"The building in the Subura where she stayed was one of Caelius's strongholds in the city. That's why I placed her there, thinking it might eventually lead to some way for her to spy on Caelius. Certainly it made her accessible to him should he ever wish to call on her. And Cassandra might also have reached either Milo or Caelius through the two women closest to them—Fausta and Clodia."

I shook my head. "Fausta may still be Milo's wife, but she despises him. She wishes him dead. She told me so. Would Milo even bother to contact Fausta while he was in the city? As for Clodia, surely there's no one she hates more than Caelius—unless it's Milo! Clodia and Caelius may once have been lovers, but I can't imagine that she's even spoken to him since the prosecution she mounted against him."

"You might think these things, Gordianus, but you would be wrong. According to my sources, Milo almost certainly contacted Fausta while he was in Rome. As for Clodia, she's been receiving Caelius at her house on the Palatine and at her horti on the Tiber for months, ever since he returned from Spain with Caesar."

"I don't believe it!"

"Do believe it, Gordianus. My sources for that fact are quite reliable."

"Are you suggesting that Clodia and Caelius renewed their love affair, after all these years, despite the bitterness between them? Impossible!"

"Is it? It seems to me exactly what one might expect from a woman as weak as Clodia, who allows herself to be dominated by whims and emotions. We Romans believe that a man must be the master of his appetites or he's no man at all, but we forgive such a defect in a woman. It wasn't so in the days of our ancestors. A woman like Clodia, enslaved by her neediness, would have been despised by everyone. Nowadays people call such a creature fascinating, and men as weak as she is make poems about her." She made an expression of disgust.

It occurred to me that no one would ever make a poem about Calpurnia.

"As for Caelius," she said, "perhaps he never stopped loving Clodia, despite their falling out and her attempt to destroy him. Or perhaps, always the pragmatist, he simply saw some use for her in this scheme of his to win over the rabble and seize power. Who knows what drives such a man? The fellow's like quicksilver."

I shook my head, trying to make sense of this. "If Cassandra, at your bidding, was supposed to dissuade Caelius and Milo from staging an armed insurrection, then she obviously failed," I said.

"I'm not sure what happened. The last time I spoke to Cassandra, which was several days before her death, she told me that she had made the acquaintance of both Clodia and Fausta. Fausta had told her that Milo was aware of her existence—it wasn't clear whether he was in Rome at the time or not—and that he wanted to seek her out for a prophecy. As I said, Cassandra was living in a building that I knew to be one of Caelius's strongholds in the city. I told her to stay there, where Caelius and Milo could find her if they wished. If that should happen, she was to stall the two of them as best she could. 'Put them off, keep them in the city, and send Rupa to me at once;' I told her. 'If you must give them a prophecy, then tell them that their plans for a revolution are doomed and their only hope is to give themselves up and throw themselves upon the bountiful mercy of Caesar.' That was the last time I saw Cassandra. Several days later, I learned that Caelius and Milo had come and gone, and Cassandra was dead. So far as I can reconstruct the sequence of events, she died only a few hours after they rode out of Rome together."

"And Rupa?"

"He was here with Cassandra when I last spoke to her. After that, I never saw him again. I don't know whether he's alive or dead."

"But you believe there was some connection between Caelius and Milo, and Cassandra's death?"

"It seems very likely. Exactly what that connection may

have been, I don't know. Right now, all my efforts are bent
toward containing this insurrection Milo and Caelius are trying
to raise in the south, and making sure that the next time they
arrive in Rome, it's with their heads on sticks. Cassandra's
dead. She's of no further use to me. I don't have time to be
concerned with who killed her or why. I leave that to you. I
understand you have a nose for that sort of thing. If you do
manage to sniff out the truth, come tell me. If she died in
Caesar's service, then whoever killed her shall answer to Caesar's justice."

XVII

That night, Bethesda was delirious with fever. She shivered beneath her woolen coverlet and murmured incoherently. Diana prepared a concoction of brewed willow bark and a mild soporific that seemed to help; the fever lessened, and Bethesda fell into a fitful sleep. I stayed by her side, holding her hand, mopping her brow, and hardly slept at all.

Fever had not been a symptom of her malady before. I feared that it marked a new stage in her illness. I felt stupid and helpless.

Diana fell ill that day as well. I came upon her bent over in the garden, throwing up her breakfast. Afterwards, she insisted that she felt perfectly well, but with a chill I wondered if her sickness was somehow connected to her mother's. What if both were to fall victim to the same lingering illness? I had no more money for physicians. Physicians had proved to be useless, anyway.

What would become of the household if both Bethesda and Diana were bedridden? What would happen when the banker Volumnius began pressing me for repayment of my loans? The first installment would fall due in a matter of days.

I fell into a black mood and did not stir from the house.

❧

Days passed. After that first miserable night, Bethesda's fever lessened and receded. Diana seemed well, but there was something furtive in her manner. I sensed she was hiding something from me.

I might have kept pursuing my quest for the truth about Cassandra, but a kind of stasis of the will settled over me. Rome itself seemed gripped by a trancelike paralysis, awaiting news from Greece about Caesar and Pompey, awaiting news from the south about Caelius and Milo's insurrection. A sense of impending catastrophe loomed over the city, over my house, over my spirit. It clouded every moment, poisoned every breath.

Another thing stopped me from taking any further steps to find Cassandra's killer. By telling me what she knew, by charging me with the task of finding the truth, and by promising Caesar's justice, Calpurnia had effectively enlisted me to become yet another of her informants in the city. I had deliberately severed every tie to Caesar, even disowning Meto. Yet if I wished to see the search for Cassandra's killer through to the end, how could I do so without becoming a spy for Caesar?

∽

It was Hieronymus who brought me the news.

One morning while I brooded in the garden, he came striding in, eyes flashing, slightly out of breath. I knew at once that something terrible had happened—terrible for someone, if not for Hieronymus. Mayhem and the suffering of others excited him.

"It's all over!" he announced.

"What's over?"

"They're dead. Both dead, and all their followers with them."

For a brief moment I thought he meant Caesar and Pompey, and I tried to imagine the immensity of the debacle that could wipe them both from the face of the earth along with their armies. Had Jupiter himself sent down lightning bolts, had Neptune flooded the mountains, and Hades opened chasms beneath them? I felt a cold spot in my heart in the place where my love of Meto had once resided.

Then I knew what he meant.

"Where?" I said. "How?"

"One hears conflicting details, but according to the best sources down in the Forum—"

Davus rushed in. "Milo and Caelius are dead!" he cried. "Both of them, dead! A huge crowd is gathering in the Forum. Some are celebrating. Some are weeping and tearing their hair. They say it's all over. The insurrection is over before it even began."

Hieronymus gave Davus a sour look. "As I was saying . . . it seems to have happened like this: Milo and Caelius headed south from Rome, but they split up to carry out separate actions. Milo started by going from town to town claiming he was acting on orders from Pompey, making wild promises and trying to get the town leaders to join him. But that got him nowhere. So he used his gladiators to set free a great number of field slaves, the type made to work under a whip and kept in pens along with animals or in barracks no better than cages—the most desperate of the desperate. Milo's ragtag army went on a rampage, plundering temples and shrines and farmhouses all around. Raising a war chest, Milo called it. He must have gathered a great number of slaves—hundreds, maybe thousands—because he dared to lay siege to a town called Compsa, garrisoned by a whole legion. But it all went wrong when Milo was struck down by a stone hurled from the ramparts. The rock hit him square in the forehead, shattered his skull, and killed him instantly. With no one to lead them, the slaves panicked and fled."

"And Caelius?"

"Caelius started by trying to raise a revolt among the gladiators in Neapolis. But the city magistrates got wind of the plot and put the ringleaders among the gladiators in chains before they could rally the rest. The magistrates tried to arrest Caelius as well, but he managed to slip through their trap. Word that he was an outlaw traveled ahead of him. No city would open its gates to him. He headed toward Compsa to join up with Milo, and learned of Milo's death from slaves who were fleeing the battle. Caelius tried to rally the slaves, but they wouldn't listen and ran off in all directions. How did one-armed Canininus put it? 'All those years bending to the lash and buggering sheep rendered them immune to Caelius's rhetoric.' Caelius headed farther south, practically alone—they say he had only a handful of supporters still with him, no more than five or six men. He pressed on until he came to the coast. Apparently there's a town called Thurii situated in the instep of Italy. That was where Caelius made his last stand."

Poor Caelius, I thought, *Vain, ambitious, restless, quicksilver Caelius!* With Milo dead, every city closed to him, and no army—not even an army of field slaves—he must have known there was no hope, that he was doomed. Thurii was the end of the line, the end of the world, the final terminus in the cometlike career of the young orator who had been Cicero's scintillating protégé, Milo's staunch defender, Caesar's brash lieutenant, Clodia's faithless lover, and the last desperate hope of the disgruntled, dispossessed masses of Rome.

"What happened to him?" I asked.

"Well, as I heard it . . ." Hieronymus lowered his voice. His eyes glittered with excitement at being able to deliver the details to a virgin ear, but Davus, too agitated to hold his tongue, interrupted him.

"They cut him down!" said Davus. "When Caelius arrived at Thurii, he strode right through the open gates of the city—word hadn't yet reached them to be on their guard against him. He walked through the market, into the forum, and up the steps to the porch of the town senate building. He clapped his hands and called to a group of soldiers to go and fetch their companions because he wanted to address them. A crowd gathered. Caelius started speaking. They say his voice was too big for the little forum at Thurii. People could hear him all over the city and even outside the walls and in fishing boats out on the water. More townspeople and soldiers gathered until the little forum was packed.

"Apparently, most of the soldiers stationed at Thurii are Spaniards and Gauls from Caesar's cavalry. Caelius tried to get them excited by reminding them of all the slaughter and destruction Caesar had brought to their native lands. But the soldiers would have none of it. They refused to hear a word against Caesar. They started booing and hissing and stamping their feet, but Caelius only raised his voice. He told them that Caesar had betrayed the people of Rome, and it was only a matter of time before he would betray them as well. The soldiers pelted Caelius with stones, but he kept talking, even with blood running down his face. Finally they rushed up the steps. They tore Caelius limb from limb. He screamed at the soldiers, calling them fools and lackeys. He never stopped talking until they threw him to the ground and crushed his windpipe by stamping on his throat."

Milo's skull had been crushed. Caelius had been torn apart. What had become of their heads, which Calpurnia had so fervently desired to have brought to her? Only their heads could provide her with incontrovertible proof that the menace was over; only then could she write to Caesar with the good news without fear that her informants might be wrong. Would she gloat over those heads just a little, indulging her emotions in a manner unbecoming to a Roman matron?

". . . were crucified," I heard Davus say, jarring me back to the moment.

"What?"

"The gladiators at Neapolis and the field slaves who fought with Milo: they were crucified. The gladiators were already in custody. As for the field slaves, the soldiers from the garrison at Compsa hunted them down. Some died fighting, but most of them were rounded up and crucified alongside the roadways. They say so many slaves haven't been crucified at one time since the days of Spartacus, when Crassus put down the great slave revolt and lined the whole length of the Appian Way with crucified slaves."

A silence fell over the garden. Hieronymus, sensing an opening, flashed a sardonic expression and began to say something, but I held up my hand. "I've heard enough," I said. "I want to be alone for a while. Davus, go to Diana. She's with her mother, I think. Hieronymus, I heard a commotion in the kitchen a moment ago. Androcles and Mopsus are probably behind it. Would you go and have a look?"

They departed the garden in separate directions and left me alone with my thoughts.

I was surprised at how powerfully the news affected me. Milo had been a hotheaded brute and no friend of mine. Caelius had been either a mad visionary or a crass opportunist. Did it matter which, in the end? Together they had tried to bully me into joining their cause. When I refused, they had allowed me to escape with my life—but only, so far as I could make out, because Cassandra somehow compelled them to do so. What had been her connection to the two of them? Now that Milo and Caelius were both dead, in retrospect it seemed more impossible than ever that their mad scheme could have possibly succeeded.

Cassandra had been murdered. Why? By whom?

An idea came to me. How could it not have occurred to me already? It was so obvious, yet I had somehow tricked myself into overlooking it. The instant of revelation was so acute as to be palpable, almost painful, as if a spring inside my head suddenly uncoiled. I must have actually cried out, for Davus reappeared in the garden, quickly followed by Hieronymus and the boys.

"Father-in-Law," said Davus, "you're weeping!"

"I had no idea he would take the news so hard," whispered Hieronymus.

Androcles and Mopsus looked at me aghast. They had never seen me so shaken, even at Cassandra's funeral.

"Fetch my toga," I told them. "I must pay a formal visit."

"Where are you going, Father-in-Law? I'll put on my toga, too—"

"No, Davus, I shall go alone."

"Surely not on such a day," insisted Davus. "You don't know what it's like down in the Forum."

"The young man is right," said Hieronymus. "The streets aren't safe. If Caelius's supporters riot, and Isauricus calls on his own ruffians to keep order—"

"I shall go alone," I insisted. "I won't be going far."

❧

She would not be at her horti, not on a day such as this, with so much uncertainty and the potential for violence in the city.

She would be safely locked up in her house on the Palatine, only a short walk from my own. I kept to the smaller streets and saw hardly anyone afoot. Every now and then I heard echoes from the Forum—shouts of jubilation, as far as I could tell. Isauricus must have called up every partisan he could muster to make a show of celebrating the news from the south.

Her house was situated at the end of a quiet lane. In recent years the trend among the wealthy and powerful had been to erect massive, ostentatious houses that brazenly proclaimed their owners' status, but hers was a very old house and had been in her family for generations; it followed the old-fashioned custom of houses of the great patrician families by presenting an unassuming face to the street. The front was windowless and stained with a muted yellow wash. The door-step was paved with glazed red and black tiles. The wash needed redoing, I noticed, and some of the tiles were cracked or missing. Framing the rustic oak door were two towering cypress trees. They, too, had an unkempt look; they were shot through with pockets of dead, brown foliage and masses of spiderwebs. Those trees were visible from the balcony at the back of my house. I never noticed them without thinking of Clodia.

I expected a handsome young man or a beautiful girl to answer the door—Clodia had always surrounded herself with beautiful things—but it was an old retainer who greeted me. He disappeared for a few moments to announce me, then returned and escorted me deeper into the house. Once it had been among the most sumptuously appointed homes in Rome, but now I saw pedestals without statues, places on the walls where paintings should have been, cold floors that lacked rugs. Like so many others in Rome whose place in the world had once seemed unshakable, Clodia had fallen on hard times.

She was in her garden, reclining on a couch beside a little fishpond, dropping bits of meal into the water and watching the fish dart about, their scales flashing in the watery sunlight. This was the garden where years ago I had attended one of her infamous parties; Catullus had declaimed a poem of passion and grief while couples made love in the shadows. Now it was silent and empty except for Clodia and her fish.

She looked up from the pond. The sunlight reflected from the surface of the water had a flattering effect; I caught a glimpse of Clodia as she had appeared when I had first met her years ago, when her beauty had been at the very end of its bloom.

"Another visit, so soon?" she said. "For years you forget me, then you come calling at my horti, and now at my house. So much attention is likely to spoil me, Gordianus." She seemed to produce this banter by rote; her voice had the proper lilt, but there was no spark in her eyes.

"You've heard the news?" I said.

"Of course. Rome has been saved once again, and all good Romans must assemble in the Forum to shout, 'Hurrah!' The Senate will pass a resolution to congratulate the consul. The consul will issue a proclamation to congratulate the Senate. The commander of the garrison at Compsa will receive a promotion. The soldiers at Thurii—" Abruptly she stopped. She gazed down at the hungry fish, who crowded together and gazed back at her.

"For months you've been seeing Marcus Caelius," I said, "ever since he came back from Spain with Caesar. All spring and summer, while he was stirring up trouble in the Forum, he was also coming here to your house."

"How do you know that, Gordianus?"

"Calpurnia told me. She has spies all over the city."

"Does she think I was in league with Caelius?"

"Were you?"

Clodia's face drew taut. The flattering moment passed; she looked her age. "For people like Calpurnia, the world must seem such a simple place. Others are in league or not in league; allies or enemies; to be trusted or not. She has the mind of a man. She might as well not be a woman."

"Curious," I said.

"What?"

"Calpurnia has an equally low opinion of you, but for opposite reasons. She says you're driven by whims and emotions. She says you're weak and have no control."

Clodia laughed without mirth. "We'll see how long a woman like Calpurnia can hold Caesar's interest, if and when he makes himself master of the world. Can you imagine making love to such a block of wood?"

"You've changed the subject. Were you in league with Caelius?"

"In *league* with him? No. In *love* with him . . ." Her voice broke. She shut her eyes. "Yes."

I shook my head. "I don't believe you. You were lovers once, but that was years ago. You prosecuted him for a murder. You did your best to destroy him, to have him driven out of Rome. Instead, he humiliated you in the court. He stood up for Milo after your brother was murdered. After all that, you can't possibly—"

"How would you know what I'm capable of, Gordianus?"

I felt a sudden, cold fury in my chest. "I'm afraid I may know exactly what you're capable of."

"What do you mean by that?"

"I don't think you fell in love with Caelius all over again. That would make you as flighty and foolish as Calpurnia paints you. And you're not a fool. You're hard and shrewd and endlessly calculating. I think you hated Marcus Caelius more than ever when he came back to Rome with Caesar. There he was, the man you despised most in the world, standing proudly at Caesar's side, rewarded with a magistracy, still a player in the great game despite all your efforts to destroy him—while you languished in obscurity, your fortune squandered, your reputation a joke, your beloved brother dead and gone. Vengeance must never be far from your thoughts. What else is there for you to think about now that everything that once brought you pleasure is gone, including your beauty?"

She stared at me blankly. "You needn't speak so cruelly, Gordianus."

"You dare to call *me* cruel when it was you who deliberately snared Marcus Caelius a second time in your net, all the while plotting how finally to destroy him? I said your beauty was gone, and it's true. But Caelius knew you when you still possessed it. He was under its spell once, and he never forgot. He remembered you as you were—as I remember you. You sought him out. You seduced him a second time; you managed to make him fall in love with you all over again. You made him trust you. And then what? How did you plant the seeds of discontent in his heart? Very subtly, I imagine, with a well-placed word here and there. You cast aspersions on Caesar—mild at first, then more and more caustic. You reminded him of the power of the Roman mob and the fact that no one since your brother had successfully harnessed their power. I can hear you: 'Caesar doesn't know your value, Marcus. He's wasting your talents! Why does he reward mediocrities like Trebonius above you? Because he's jealous of you, that's why! Because he secretly fears you! If only my dear brother were still alive. What an opportunity he could make of this situation! The people are miserable, they've lost their faith in Caesar, they despise him—all they need is a man who can harness their anger, a man with the gift of speech and the nerve to pit himself against the lapdogs Caesar has left in charge of the city. Such a man could make himself ruler of Rome!' "

Clodia stared at me, her eyes flashing, but she said nothing.

"Shall I go on? Very well. You encouraged him to make wilder and wilder promises to the mob, to bait his fellow magistrates, to insult the Senate, to speak words of sedition against Caesar himself. When he finally went too far and Isauricus tried to arrest him, how that must have delighted you! But Caelius slipped the net. He went into hiding. Then he made common cause with Milo—the convicted killer of your brother—and how that must have galled you! Meanwhile, you never ceased plotting Caelius's destruction. I think you were still in touch with him, still guiding him toward his ruin. Perhaps he balked, seeing the hopelessness of the prospect before him. Did you goad him on, telling him the gods were on his side? Did you cast aspersions on his manhood? Did you tell him only a coward would stop in midcourse? And when Milo—superstitious, omen-fearing Milo—sought out a seeress to show him the future, what did you do about that, Clodia?"

I waited for her to answer, wanting to hear the truth from her own lips, but she only continued to stare at me with a wild look in her eyes.

"Cassandra was Calpurnia's spy," I said. "Did you know that?"

She wrinkled her brow and spoke at last. "No. But I'm not surprised."

"Milo wanted to seek her out for a prophecy. Did you know that?"

"Yes."

"So you *were* still in touch with Caelius, even after he went into hiding?"

"Yes. After his escape from Isauricus, he came to this house a few times, always in disguise. False beards. False bosoms!" A smile crept over her lips, though she seemed to fight it. "He loved that sort of thing, going about in disguises. He was mad, completely mad, from the first day I knew him to the last. You might have thought he was taking part in some adolescent prank, not trying to bring down the state. He told me that he'd been in contact with Milo, and Milo was almost ready to join forces with him. 'I know how much you hate him,' he said to me, 'but it's the only way. Together we can pull it off!' There was only one catch. Milo had heard of what he called 'this half-mad seeress, this woman called Cassandra'—it was Fausta who told him about her—and he was determined first to hear what Cassandra had to say. Milo had latched onto the idea that Cassandra, and only Cassandra, could tell him the future. He was utterly convinced of it. He refused to take another step until he heard from Cassandra's own lips that the enterprise would succeed."

I shook my head. "But Cassandra had explicit instructions from Calpurnia to tell Milo no such thing. She was to predict only doom for the insurrection. She was to send Milo and Caelius scrambling to throw themselves on Caesar's mercy. From what you've just told me, if Cassandra had succeeded in carrying out Calpurnia's instructions, then Milo would never had ridden south with Caelius that day. Someone must have prevented her from delivering that prophecy, someone who wanted the insurrection to go ahead, knowing that it could end only in the destruction of both Milo and Caelius. And that was what you wanted above all else, wasn't it, Clodia?" I shook my head. "I understand your hatred for both of those men. I don't doubt that you wanted to see them humiliated and dead, their memories disgraced, their heads delivered to Calpurnia as trophies. But why did Cassandra have to die? Was there no other way?"

Clodia's eyes brimmed with tears. "Is that what you think? That I wanted Caelius to die? That I murdered Cassandra? You think you know everything, Gordianus, yet you know nothing!"

XVIII

I had never seen her so completely unguarded, so wracked with emotion. I could never have imagined her so vulnerable. The tears that ran down her cheeks gave her a curious kind of beauty that transcended any she had previously possessed. I gazed at Clodia in wonder.

"Tell me, then. Tell me what I don't know," I said.

She caught her breath. She covered her face for a moment. When she withdrew her hand, the tears had ceased. Her features were composed. She stared at the fish in the pond as she spoke.

"For years I hated Marcus Caelius. A part of me lived for that hatred, the way that one can live for love. I turned to it whenever I saw no other reason to go on existing in a world where everything gold had turned to lead. In a strange way, that hatred nurtured me. What a poem Catullus could have made of that! Catullus knew that passion is passion; whether it's love or hate, it drives the spirit. Hating Caelius gave me a reason to draw my next breath.

"As it turned out, Caelius had never forgotten me, either. Men have more ways than women do to distract themselves from such a passion—building a political career, traveling the world, fighting in battles. But when he returned with Caesar from Spain, something stirred him to come and see me. I think he was suddenly struck by the futility of all his frantic pursuits for money and power. Caesar had turned the world upside down, and for a little while anything seemed possible. Sheer exhilaration drove Caelius forward until he realized that nothing was going to change, except perhaps for the worse. He found himself back in Rome, stuck with a meaningless magistracy, bored out of his wits. He was dispirited, angry, depressed. On a whim, one afternoon he came to see me. I was here in the garden. When the slave announced him, I thought surely the slave was mistaken, or else someone was playing a joke on me. 'Show him in!' I said, and a few moments later, Caelius appeared. A thousand thoughts rushed through my head, not least that I wanted to murder him. I imagined stabbing him and pushing him into this fishpond. That thought filled me with immense pleasure. How it came about that he was sitting beside me on this couch, I can't tell you. Nor can I tell you how it happened that his lips were on mine, and our arms were around each other, and we both were weeping.

"You think that I hatched some insidious plot against him, Gordianus, that I schemed to seduce him. But Caelius came to me, and what happened between us was totally spontaneous and totally mutual. Years ago, before we fell out, I thought I was in love with him. But what I had felt for him then was nothing compared to what I felt when he came to me that day. Both of us had received some very hard blows. We had learned a few lessons about humility and survival and what really matters in the world. The Caelius who came to me that day was neither the Caelius I had loved nor the Caelius I had hated, but another man, larger than either of those others and infinitely more capable of loving me. And I was a different woman from the one who had loved and then hated Caelius, though I didn't know it until that moment when we were reunited."

"Yet I never heard a whisper of gossip about you and Caelius," I said. "Such a tale would have been just the thing to excite the chin-waggers in the Forum."

"We made no show of what happened between us. We were discreet. Others would never have understood. It was no one else's business."

"Yet Calpurnia knew that Caelius was seeing you," I said.

"As you say, she has spies everywhere. Perhaps she intentionally had Caelius followed, or perhaps one of her informants just happened to notice him coming or going. What happened between us may have piqued her curiosity, but surely she had more pressing affairs of state to worry about."

"Caelius eventually gave her plenty to worry about. After Caesar left Rome, when Caelius began to press his radical legislation and to agitate in the Forum—what role did you play in that?"

"You think I planted the idea in his head, encouraged him, spurred him on. Nothing could be further from the truth! Do you think, after seeing what became of my brother, that I wanted to see Caelius meet the same end? 'The Roman mob is fickle,' I told him. 'You can stir them up easily enough, but once there's blood on the ground, they'll scatter like dust. For the moment, the moneylenders and landlords hold Caesar and his Senate in the palms of their hands. Volumnius and his sort have rattled the dice and cast a Venus Throw. There's no beating them at their own game.' But Caelius wouldn't listen to me. Just as he'd found me at last—found the passion he'd been missing for years and desperately searching for—so he thought that he'd finally hit his stride as a politician. He was no longer Cicero's errant flunky, you see. No longer Milo's red-faced apologist. No longer Caesar's underutilized underling, fobbed off with a safe, useless post in the government. Caelius had become his own man, dreaming his own dream. I feared for him. I told him so. I begged him to stop, to make peace with Isauricus and Trebonius, but it did no good. He believed he had discovered his destiny. There was no stopping him.

"At last he went too far. The Senate passed the Ultimate Decree against him. They made Caelius an outlaw, and then he had no choice but to play his final gambit. He had been in communication with Milo for quite some time, encouraging him to break out of Massilia and to bring his troop of gladiators back to Italy. I think it was in Caelius's mind from the beginning to raise an armed revolt. He meant for it to begin in Rome, then spread across the countryside, but even *his* powers of persuasion couldn't incite the rabble to sacrifice themselves in such a hopeless cause.

"Caelius went underground, slipping in and out of Rome like a shadow, often wearing a disguise, rallying his supporters and trying to make alliances—'laying the groundwork for a revolution,' he called it—though I don't think he accomplished much. Eventually he arranged to rendezvous with Milo, secretly, here in Rome. He had the temerity to ask me if he could bring Milo here to my house. Absolutely not, I told him. To even suggest such a thing was an insult to the shade of my brother. So they met in that apartment building in the Subura, the one where Cassandra kept a room. I suppose it was Calpurnia who arranged for Cassandra to rent that room as a way to keep watch on Caelius and his supporters in the building?"

"I think so, yes."

Clodia nodded. "Caelius was suspicious of Cassandra, but he didn't know anything about her for certain—whether she was genuine or not, or a blackmailer, or a spy or nothing more than a petty schemer. I think he was glad to have her in the building for the same reason in reverse, so that he could keep an eye on her and that mute companion of hers, Rupa. That was how I found out about you and Cassandra. Caelius's agents had observed you coming and going in a manner that suggested only one thing: that the two of you were lovers. Imagine my surprise! Gordianus, that pillar of rectitude and restraint, indulging his animal appetites at last! It amused me that you of all people should have been stung by Cupid's arrow. But secretly I was happy for you. I was in love myself. I wished for the whole world to be in love, including you. Why not?

"Caelius met twice with Milo, two days running. I saw him the night after the first meeting. He was very excited, very talkative. I knew it might be the last time I would see him. Let him talk all he wants, I told myself. You may never hear his voice again.

"He told me about Milo's fascination with Cassandra. Fausta had told Milo all about Cassandra, and he was desperate to meet her and receive a prophecy. It hadn't happened that day—Cassandra was out apparently, nowhere to be found. Caelius hoped she would be in the next day, because Milo seemed absolutely determined to hear what she had to say before he fully committed himself to the insurrection. Doesn't that sound just like Milo? Stubborn and stupid and superstitious. Caelius was almost certain Cassandra would be in her room the next day, because his agents had observed a certain pattern in her routine—that would be the day that you would be calling on her. Caelius took it into his head, not only to consult Cassandra, but to try to win you over to the cause. I told him that you'd never agree to such a thing. 'What if you approach Gordianus, and he refuses?' I said. 'Then we shall have no choice but to kill him,' said Caelius. I absolutely forbade him to do that. I made him give me his word that no harm would come to you, no matter how you responded when he and Milo tried to win you over."

I drew a sharp breath. "It was *you* to whom Caelius made that promise! I had thought—" I tried to remember exactly the exchange I had heard between Milo and Caelius as I lost consciousness. . . .

"We should have put hemlock in the wine instead of that other stuff," said Milo. *"We should lop his head off, here and now."*

"No!" said Caelius. *"I gave her my word. I promised, and you agreed—"*

"A promise made to a witch!" said Milo.

"Call her that if you want since you're not worthy to utter her name! I gave her my word, and my word still means something, Milo. Does yours?"

I had thought it was Cassandra who had somehow extracted that promise from Caelius—but it was Clodia.

"What about Cassandra?" I asked. "When I woke the next day, she was gone, and so was Rupa, and her room was empty, as if she'd never been there."

"I'm not sure what happened. I didn't see Caelius again, but I did receive a message from him—a few scribbled words, obviously written in haste. I think he must have handed it to a messenger just as he was leaving Rome. He mentioned Cassandra, though not by name; he was careful to use no actual names, with the intention of protecting me, I suppose, should the message be intercepted. He ended by cautioning me to burn the parchment at once."

"Did you?"

Her smile seemed to arise from some ironic reflex, the only possible response to a question so foolish. Her fingers trembled as she reached into the bosom of her stola and pulled forth a small, rolled piece of parchment. She handed it to me, and I felt it still warm from its contact with her flesh. I unrolled it and read, squinting to make out some of the more hastily scribbled words:

LITTLE SPARROW, I AM OFF. WISH ME THE FAVOR OF THE GODS. DON'T SAY THAT THE CAUSE IS IMPOSSIBLE. A YEAR AGO, WOULD YOU NOT HAVE SAID THE SAME ABOUT ANY CHANCE THAT YOU AND I WOULD REDISCOVER THE JOY WE HAD LOST? MY SKITTISH PARTNER IS NOW BURSTING WITH CONFIDENCE, THANKS TO THE WORDS OF THAT TROJAN PRINCESS. SHE HAS PROMISED US SUCCESS BEYOND OUR WILDEST HOPES! I THINK THAT SHE TRULY IS A SEERESS, AND IT WAS APOLLO HIMSELF WHO SHOWED HER OUR GLORIOUS FUTURE. MAKE A SACRIFICE TO APOLLO IF YOU WISH TO DO SOMETHING USEFUL. BETTER YET, START WORKING ON THAT LIST, AND MAKE IT A LONG ONE. LOOK FOR GOOD NEWS FROM THE SOUTH. WHEN I SEE YOU NEXT, EVERYTHING SHALL BE DIFFERENT!

I handed the message back to her. "He refers to a list," I said.

"A private joke. He used to say, 'Make a list of the people you want beheaded, Little Sparrow, and I shall see to it straightaway when I take over the city.' "

I felt a chill. The joke had been on Caelius. "But I don't understand what he says about Cassandra. He makes it sound as if she gave Milo the encouraging prophecy he was hoping for."

"I presume she did. 'Success beyond our wildest hopes,' he says."

"Yet Calpurnia gave her specific instructions to do quite the opposite. Cassandra was to do all she could to discourage them from mounting an insurrection. Why did Cassandra disobey Calpurnia?"

"Perhaps someone bribed her to do so. If she took money from Calpurnia, why not from someone else, if that person offered her more?"

I wrinkled my brow. Cassandra had disobeyed Calpurnia to placate her old friend Cytheris. She had disobeyed Calpurnia when she chose to see me. But those had been petty infractions. Would she have dared to disobey Calpurnia in a matter such as this, with so many lives at stake? Who would have encouraged or bribed or threatened her to do so? "Who knew how much Milo was depending on that prophecy?" I said. "Who wanted so desperately for Milo to embark on the insurrection? Caelius, of course . . ."

Clodia shook her head. "Caelius didn't bribe Cassandra. You read the note, Gordianus. He himself was persuaded by her. He believed she was a genuine seeress."

"Then it can have been only one person."

⚓

There was a black wreath on her door. I thought of the wreath that so recently had hung on my own door in memory of Cassandra, and the wreath I had seen on Fulvia's door still marking her grief months after Curio's death. This wreath made a mockery of those others. No doubt I would find her wearing black, with her hair undressed. Did it amuse her to put on the trappings of a bereaved widow? Did she think of her widowhood as an honor she had earned?

Even the gone-to-seed gladiator who answered the door was wearing black. "Hello, Birria," I said. "That color flatters you. It hides your fat."

He scowled at me, then saw I was not alone. It was not Davus who stood behind me, but a troop of Calpurnia's bodyguards. From Clodia's house, I had gone straight to Calpurnia's. After a brief audience with Calpurnia, I had come here.

"I'll tell the mistress you're here," Birria said, and skulked off.

A little later he returned and invited me to follow him. The bodyguards remained outside; but when Birria tried to close the door on them, one of them blocked it with his foot. The fellow was every bit as big as Birria and surrounded by ten more like him. After a brief staring contest, Birria relented and stepped back. The door remained open with the bodyguards standing at attention just outside.

Birria led me to the chamber called the Baiae room, then stepped across the hallway into the garden, looking nervous. Fausta stood just inside the room, dressed in black. Her masses of ginger hair were unpinned and hung about her shoulders. Beside her was a little tripod table set with a small pitcher of wine and a single cup. As on the previous occasion when I had called on her, she indicated that I should take a chair at the far end of the room.

"I'd rather stand," I said. "And I'd rather stay here where I can see you in the light. Black suits you, Fausta. It matches that bruise under your eye."

She winced at my rudeness and touched her face self-consciously. "You've come without that handsome son-in-law of yours, Gordianus?"

"I didn't have time to fetch him. I've come here straight from Calpurnia's house. She was very interested to hear what I had to tell her. She sent some of her men with me."

"So Birria told me. Is she trying to frighten me? I can't imagine why. My husband is dead. Poor Milo! He never posed much of a threat to the state, anyway."

"He incited a great many slaves to revolt. Along with Milo's gladiators, they caused considerable havoc in the region around Compsa."

"Yes, that was unfortunate. But all Milo's gladiators are dead now, and so are all those slaves, aren't they?"

"Yes. They either died fighting or else were crucified, thanks to Milo and the false hope he gave them."

"A tremendous waste of manpower, I'm sure."

"A tremendous amount of suffering!"

"Do slaves really suffer like the rest of us? I'm not sure the philosophers are agreed on that subject, Gordianus. But certainly Milo had a lot to answer for—property damage, lives lost, wasted slaves, not to mention the scare he threw into everyone! But he paid the price, didn't he? He cast the dice, and they came up dogs, and now his lemur is wandering about Hades without a head. But what has any of this to do with me? Since when is a wife held liable under Roman law for her husband's actions?"

"You conspired with Milo against the state."

"Nonsense!"

"You encouraged him to raise the insurrection. He might have balked at doing so, but for your meddling."

She looked at me coldly. "You can't prove that."

"Calpurnia didn't require proof. I merely had to convince her. I explained what I knew, and she insisted on sending those men along with me to make sure you don't try to slip away before Isauricus and his lictors come for you. Conspiring against the Roman state is a crime punishable by death."

Fausta laughed shrilly. "Will they put me on trial, then?"

"They won't have to. The Ultimate Decree is still in effect. The consul Isauricus has the authority to take any steps necessary to safeguard the state. That includes the summary execution of traitors."

She looked at me with fear in her eyes. "Damn you, Gordianus! Why are doing this to me?"

"You did it to yourself, Fausta. Why couldn't you leave Milo to his fate without interfering?"

"Because he was a hopeless bungler and a fool and a coward!" she cried. "Left to his own devices, he'd still be hiding in some hole in the Subura waiting for the right omen to come along. He needed a nudge—no, a kick in the backside!—to get him moving."

"And you gave him that kick by arranging for Cassandra

to utter a prophecy of success for the insurrection."

"Yes! And it worked like a charm. What an actress she was! She delivered a performance that convinced even Caelius. It must have been quite magnificent. I only wish I'd been there to see it, but I'd surely have laughed and given her away."

"Where did it happen? When?"

"In her shabby little room in the Subura. She stalled them until nightfall—the visions she described were always more convincing by lamplight, she told me—and then she delivered the last performance of her life. While you were upstairs, sleeping off the drug they gave you, Cassandra was groveling on the dirt floor of her room, foaming at the mouth and uttering the words Milo most wanted to hear. I'd told her just what to say, of course. I knew the images that would appeal most to Milo's brutish imagination. Describe it thus, I told her: An endless triumphal procession with Milo and Caelius at the head, the acclamations of the people like thunder in their ears, Trebonius and Isauricus and all their other enemies in chains behind them, and statues of solid gold in their likenesses installed in the Forum, while somewhere in a gray void we see Pompey and Caesar reduced to the size of dwarves, ripping open each other's bellies with their teeth, devouring one another's entrails in an endless circle, like the worm that eats its own tail. Imagine the dreams that vision put into Milo's head! The next morning he could hardly wait to set out. Caelius was just as eager. They met with their closest supporters, took some with them, left others to manage affairs in their absence, and off they went, convinced that Fortune and the Fates were firmly on their side."

"While I still slept," I whispered, "alone in that room upstairs."

"Not alone. Before he left that morning, Caelius told Cassandra what had become of you. She looked in on you, then left Rupa to look after you."

"Where did she go?"

"She came to this house, of course, to collect her money."

"Money," I said dully. "That was how you persuaded her

to go against Calpurnia's wishes? All it took was a little gold?"

"No. It also required a great deal of persuasion. When I told her what I wanted her to do—to encourage Milo to get on with his hopeless insurrection—she resisted. For a while she kept up her pretense of being a genuine seeress. I told her it was no use trying to fool me, and whatever Calpurnia was paying her—that was an educated guess on my part, that she was Calpurnia's agent—I would pay her more. I kept harrying her and offering more gold, until at last she weakened. Put yourself in her place, Gordianus. Here in Rome, thanks to all the skullduggery surrounding the war, Cassandra found herself in a position to make a great deal of money—probably the only chance in her lifetime for such a woman to make so *much* money. Can you blame her for seizing the opportunity to maximize her fortune? 'Where's the risk?' I asked her. 'If Milo wins, he'll shower you with riches and honors. If he dies, he'll be silent forever. Whatever happens, you'll receive your pay from both of us, with Calpurnia never the wiser.' "

I shook my head. "Then it's just as I said: in the end, all it took was a little gold."

"Not a *little* gold, Gordianus, a great deal of it! That's what I promised her, anyway. And it wasn't entirely for herself. She said she needed the money . . . for you."

"For me?"

"So she said. When she came here to collect her money, she seemed to think she had to justify herself to me—as if I cared about her sense of honor. 'I would never have done it,' she told me, 'except that I need more money. I need it for the man I love. He's in a great deal of trouble. He's accumulated an enormous debt. It's crushing the life out of him. If I can free him of it, I will.' You didn't know, Gordianus? Cassandra was thinking of you."

I felt a fire in my head. "But instead of paying her, you poisoned her. Why, Fausta?"

"Because I had no more money! The partial payment I had given her in advance was all I had. She came here looking for the balance, but I had nothing to give her, not even a token payment. I stalled her for as long as I could; I told her I was sending a slave to fetch the money for her. In fact, I dispatched the fellow to the Subura to finish off Rupa. The slave I sent was a big, burly fellow, a former gladiator like Birria. I thought he'd have no trouble, but it seems that Rupa was more than a match for him."

"That was the dead body I found when I woke! Rupa killed him—there in the room while I lay unconscious. Cassandra left Rupa to watch over me. When your man arrived, there must have been a struggle, and Rupa broke his neck. Then Rupa must have panicked. He gathered up everything in Cassandra's room and ran off." Everything, I thought, except her biting stick, which he must have dropped or overlooked.

"So far as I know, the mute is still in hiding," said Fausta.

"And even as I woke, Cassandra was here, in this house. . . ."

"Waiting with me in the garden. When one of the slaves brought in a cold porridge for the midday meal and served a portion to each of us, Cassandra suspected nothing."

"What poison did you use?"

"How should I know? I bought it from a fellow who's been in that sort of business a long time; Milo used to go to him occasionally. Painful, or painless, he asked me. I told him I didn't care so long as it was guaranteed to work quickly. But it didn't. The poison acted very slowly. We both finished our porridge and put the bowls aside. Nothing happened. I began to think I had misjudged the dose, or perhaps I'd even given her the wrong portion. Had I poisoned myself? I sat there imagining a burning in my gut as I watched her, unable to take my eyes off her, waiting to see the first sign of distress on her face. Finally—finally!—the poison began to take effect. At first she merely felt ill. She said she thought something in the porridge had disagreed with her. Then a look came over her face—shock, panic—as she realized what was happening. She screamed and threw her empty bowl at me and ran from the garden. I tried to stop her. We struggled. I tore her tunica. She escaped and ran from the house. Birria went after her, but she lost him. He didn't know which way she'd gone.

"I was frantic with worry. Who might she see before the

poison finished her? What might she tell them? Finally, later
that day, I heard the report of her death in the marketplace.
She died in your arms, I was told. Had she told you what
happened? Surely not, because hours passed, then days, and
you did nothing about it. Still, I was torn by doubts. That was
why I dared to come to see her funeral pyre. You were there.
So were Calpurnia and some of the other women who had
known Cassandra. Everyone saw me, yet no one reacted. That
was when I knew for certain that no one suspected I had killed
her. I watched her burn, and I was finally satisfied that I had
gotten away with it. At last I could turn my thoughts to Milo
and wait for the delicious news of his destruction."

I shook my head. "I thought it was Clodia! I thought Clodia
would stop at nothing to destroy Marcus Caelius, but in the
end she was desperate to save him—from himself! And I
thought that you would do whatever you could to *stop* Milo
from carrying out such a mad scheme, but your only desire
was to see him destroy himself."

"Paradoxes amuse you, don't they, Finder? I told you, I've
no patience with playwrights' devices, similes, metaphors, and
such. Ironies and enigmas displease me even more. But I do
know when the final act is over." Fausta reached for the
pitcher on the table beside her and filled the cup to the brim.
"You'll forgive me if I don't offer you a cup as well," she
said, lifting it to her lips.

I gave a start and reached for the cup, but too late. She had
swallowed the contents in a single draught.

Fausta put down the cup. Her eyes glittered. She blinked
and swayed slightly. "The poison merchant promised me that
this one would act much more quickly and without . . . too
much . . . pain." She grimaced. "The liar! It hurts like Hades!"
She gripped her belly and staggered out of the room, into the
portico off the garden. "People will say I did it out of grief.
It's an honorable thing for a widow to take her own life . . .
after her husband dies in battle. Sulla's daughter shall bring
no shame to his memory!"

Fausta collapsed to the floor. Birria, who had been pacing
the garden, gave a cry and rushed to her. He knelt and scooped

her up. Her eyes were open, but she was as limp as a sack of grain in his arms, already dead. He threw back his head and let out a howl. Tears streamed down his face. "No!" he cried. He stared up at me. "What have you done to her?"

"She did it to herself," I said, pointing to the doorway and the little tripod table just inside.

Birria spied the pitcher and the cup. For a long moment he stared into Fausta's lifeless eyes. Finally he released her. I heard a slither of metal as he pulled his short sword from its scabbard. I started back, but the blade was not for me. Kneeling over Fausta, he turned the sword against his belly and braced himself. A look came over his features such as one sometimes sees on the face of a gladiator in the arena at the end—a look at once resigned and defiant, contemptuous of life itself.

Birria drew a last breath and fell onto his sword. His eyes rolled back in his head, and he let out a gasp. Blood poured from the wound and trickled from his lips. He pitched and heaved for a moment, then stiffened, then collapsed across the body of his mistress.

XIX

"Egypt!"

Bethesda delivered this pronouncement in much the same fashion that she had announced her previous, sudden insights into a cure for her illness. How she arrived at these revelations, where the knowledge came from, and why she trusted it, I had no idea. I only knew that where once she had uttered, "Radishes!" and the household had gone on an expedition in search of radishes, now she uttered, "Egypt!"

A trip to Egypt would cure her—that, and only that.

"Why Egypt?" I asked.

"Because I came from Egypt. We all came from Egypt. Egypt is where all life began." She said this as if it were a fact that no one could possibly dispute, like saying, "Things fall down, not up," or, "The sun shines during the day, not at night."

I had thought she might say: *Because Egypt is where we met, Husband. Egypt is where you found me and fell in love with me, and Egypt is where I intend to reclaim you and purify you of the transgression you committed with another woman.* But that was not what she said, of course. Did she know about Cassandra? I thought not; she had been too preoccupied with her own illness.

Did Diana know? Not for certain, perhaps, but Diana had to suspect something. So far, she hadn't confronted or questioned me. If she had suspicions, she kept them to herself—

more for her mother's sake, I suspected, than for mine. What was done was done, and the important thing was to keep peace in the household, at least until her mother got better.

"I must return to Alexandria," Bethesda announced at breakfast one morning, and not for the first time. "I must bathe once more in the Nile, the river of life. In Egypt I shall either find a cure, or I shall find eternal rest."

"Mother, don't say that!" Diana put down her bowl of watery farina and gripped her stomach. Had her mother's words upset her digestion—or was Diana, too, falling prey to some malady? She was nauseous as many mornings as not. It seemed to me that a curse had fallen on all the women in my life.

This was the first time that Bethesda had explicitly mentioned the possibility of dying in Egypt. Was that the real point of the journey she insisted on making, and was all her talk of a cure a mere pretense? Did she know that she was dying, and did she wish to end her days in Alexandria, where her life had begun?

"We can't afford it," I said bluntly. "I wish we could, but—"

There was a noise at the front door, not a friendly or respectful knocking, but a loud, insistent banging. Davus frowned, exchanged a guarded look with me, and went to answer it.

A moment later he returned and spoke in my ear. "Trouble," he said.

"Stay here," I said to the others, and followed Davus to the foyer. I looked through the peephole. On my doorstep a pair of hulking giants flanked a small ferret of a man in a toga. The ferret saw my eye at the peephole and spoke up.

"It's no good hiding behind that door, Gordianus the Finder. A man can avoid the day of reckoning for only so long."

"Who are you, and what are you doing on my doorstep?" I asked, though I knew already. Since the annihilation of Caelius and Milo, the moneylenders and landlords of Rome reigned supreme. Any organized resistance to them had evaporated. Trebonius was said to favor creditors quite blatantly now in any negotiation he brokered between them and their debtors; those who had sought relief before the stillborn insurrection had received much better deals than those who were seeking relief now.

"I represent Volumnius," said the ferret, "to whom you owe the sum of—"

"I know exactly how much I owe Volumnius," I said.

"Do you? Most people have difficulty calculating the interest that accumulates. They almost always underestimate the amount. They don't understand that if they miss making even a single payment—"

"I haven't missed a payment. According to the agreement I made with Volumnius, the first installment isn't due—"

"—until tomorrow. Yes, this is merely a courtesy call to remind you. I presume you *will* have the first installment ready for me, first thing in the morning?"

I peered out the peephole at the faces of the ferret's two henchmen. Both had hands the size of small hams and small, beady eyes. They looked too slow and stupid to be gladiators. Their sort was good for only one thing, overpowering and intimidating victims smaller and weaker than themselves. The sum of their brainpower combined was probably below that of the average mule, but they could probably follow simple orders from the ferret—"Break this fellow's finger," say, or, "Break his arm," or, "Break both arms."

"Go away," I said. "Payment isn't due until tomorrow. You've no right to come harassing me today."

"Harassing you?" said the ferret, flashing a wicked smile. "If you call this harassment, citizen, then just wait until—"

I slammed shut the little hatch over the peephole. The noise it made was as feeble as I felt at that moment. "Go to Hades!" I shouted through the door.

I heard the ferret laugh, then bark an order at his henchmen to move on, then the sound of their footsteps receding.

Davus frowned. "What are we going to do if they come back tomorrow?"

"*If* they come back, Davus? I don't think there's any doubt about that."

We returned to the dining room. Bethesda looked at me expectantly. Diana, I noticed, looked first to Davus to ascertain his expression, and only then at me; further proof, if any was needed, that she was now more his wife than my daughter. That was only proper, but still it irked me. Hieronymus was eating the last of his farina very slowly and looking glum. Androcles and Mopsus, having risen and eaten before anyone else, were in the garden, where I had assigned them some tasks to work off their morning burst of energy. Through the window I could see them squabbling and pelting each other with pulled weeds, oblivious to the crisis in the household.

I opened my mouth to speak, but what was there to say? False words of reassurance? An abrupt change of subject? Or perhaps a resumption of the previous subject, namely the hopelessness of Bethesda's demand for a journey to Egypt? At that moment, nothing would have pleased me more than the prospect of a trip to Alexandria, or to any other place, as long as it was as far from Rome as possible.

I was spared from having to speak by an abrupt knock at the door. "Not again!" I muttered, stalking back to the foyer. I didn't bother with the peephole but threw back the bar and pulled open the door. Even the ferret and his henchmen wouldn't dare to attack a Roman citizen on his doorstep on the day before a loan came due. Or would they? I wondered if I could gouge out the ferret's eyes before the two giants had time to disable me. . . .

"What are you doing back here?" I shouted. "I told you—"

The man on my doorstep stared at me blankly. I stared back at him just as blankly, until I recognized him. He was the personal secretary to Calpurnia who had called at my door previously.

"What are you doing here?" I asked, in a very different tone of voice.

"My mistress sent me. She wants to see you."

"Now?"

"As soon as possible. Before—"

"Before what?"

"Please, follow me and ask no questions."

I looked down at the old tunic I was wearing. "I shall have to change."

"No need for that. Please, come at once. And you might want to bring a bodyguard with you, for later."

"Later?"

"To walk you home safely. The streets are likely to be—well, you'll see." He smiled, and I had a glimmer of what he was trying to tell me, or more precisely, what he was trying not to tell me.

"Come along, Davus," I called over my shoulder. "We've been summoned by the first woman in Rome."

∾

The slave led us across the Palatine Hill to the large house where Calpurnia was residing in her husband's absence. Even before we reached the house, I could see that the surrounding streets were busier than normal. Messengers were fanning outward from the house while men in togas were converging upon it. There was a sense of excitement, of a charge like lightning in the air. It intensified in the forecourt of the house, where men in small groups talked in hushed voices while slaves scurried to and fro. I recognized several senators and magistrates. Trebonius and Isauricus stood together off to one side, surrounded by their lictors. Something important had happened. The eyes and ears of all Rome were becoming trained upon this house.

The slave ushered us through the forecourt, up the steps, and into the house. The guards recognized him and allowed us to pass without question.

From the buzz of excitement outside, I expected the inside of the house to be a veritable beehive, but the hall down which the slave led us was surprisingly empty and quiet. We emerged in a sunlit garden where Calpurnia, seated in a backless chair, was dictating in a low voice to a scribe. At our approach she looked up and made a sign for the scribe to withdraw. At another sign, the slave who had escorted us also vanished.

"Gordianus, you came very quickly." With a raised eyebrow she took note of my shabby tunic, and I knew I should have taken time to put on my toga, no matter what the slave had said.

"Your man indicated that the summons was urgent."

"Only because, in a few moments, all Rome shall know. Once the word is out, there's no telling how people will react. I assume that most people will be as overjoyed as I am—or will pretend to be."

"You've received good news, Calpurnia?"

She drew a breath and closed her eyes for a moment. She had not yet repeated the news often enough to have become inured to it. When she opened her eyes, they glittered with tears. Her voice trembled.

"Caesar has triumphed! There was a great battle in Thessaly, near a place called Pharsalus. Pompey's front lines gave way; then his cavalry broke and fled. It was a complete rout. Caesar himself led the charge to overrun the enemy's camp. Some of their leaders escaped, but the engagement was decisive. Almost fifteen thousand of the enemy were slain that day, and more than twenty-four thousand surrendered. Caesar's forces lost scarcely two hundred men. Victory is ours!"

"And Pompey?"

Her face darkened. "Even as Caesar was leading his men over the ramparts into the enemy's camp, Pompey fled from his tent, threw off his scarlet cape to make himself less conspicuous, mounted the first horse he could find, and escaped through the rear gate. He made his way to the coast and boarded a ship. He appears to have headed for Egypt. Caesar pursues him. That's the only bad news, that Caesar can't yet return to Rome. But that was to be expected. Caesar will have to settle Rome's affairs in Egypt and elsewhere before he can at last come home to rest."

For a long moment, I took in the momentous nature of what Calpurnia had just told me. Waves of emotion passed through me. Like her, I experienced a trembling in my throat, and tears came to my eyes. Then doubts and questions intruded on my thoughts.

Could it *really* be over? With a single battle, was the war truly ended? What of Pompey's naval fleet, which had always been superior to Caesar's and which was still presumably intact? Who else besides Pompey had survived, and how easily would they give up the fight? What of Rome's other enemies, such as King Juba, who had annihilated Curio and his expedition in Africa? What of Egypt, which was engaged in its own dynastic civil war? Calpurnia spoke of settling affairs there as if the job involved tools no more complicated than a broom and a dustpan, but when had anything to do with Egypt ever been that simple? Would it really be such a trivial task to track down Pompey, as if he were an escaped slave? If and when Caesar trapped him, did he intend to murder Pompey in cold blood? Or would he bring him back to Rome as a prisoner, parading him in chains behind his chariot in a triumphal procession, as he had done to Vercingetorix the Gaul? Doubts shadowed the news Calpurnia had given me, but I said nothing of them. How many of the men in her forecourt were entertaining the same questions, and how many would feign jubilation and leave their doubts unspoken—for the time being?

"Remarkable news," I finally managed to say.

"Is there nothing you wish to ask? No one you wish to ask after?"

I thought for a moment. "What of Domitius Ahenobarbus?" He was one of Caesar's fiercest enemies. At the outset of the war, he had lost the Italian city of Corfinium to Caesar, botched a suicide attempt, and been captured. Humiliated by Caesar's pardon, he made his way to Massilia—where his path crossed mine—and took command of the forces resisting Caesar's siege. When Caesar and Trebonius took Massilia, Domitius Ahenobarbus had escaped once more, to join Pompey.

"Redbeard is no more," said Calpurnia, with a glint of satisfaction in her eyes. "When the camp was overrun, Domitius fled on foot and headed up a mountainside. Antony's cavalry hunted him down like a stag in the woods. He collapsed from fear and exhaustion. His body was still warm when Antony found him. He died without a wound on him."

"Faustus Sulla?"

"Fausta's brother apparently escaped. There was a rumor he might head for Africa."

"Cato?"

"He, too, eluded capture. He may be on the way to Africa as well."

"Cicero?"

"Cicero lives. He missed the battle entirely, on account of an upset stomach. Rumor has it he's headed back to Rome. My husband is notorious for his clemency. Who knows? He may yet forgive Cicero for siding with Pompey." She stared at me for a long moment. "Why not ask what you most want to ask, Finder?"

Why not, indeed? I bowed my head and sighed. I tried to control the trembling in my voice. "What news of Meto?"

She nodded and smiled, a bit more smugly than was warranted. "Meto is well. According to my husband, he distinguished himself admirably throughout the campaign and most especially in the battle at Pharsalus. He remains at Caesar's side, traveling with him to Egypt."

I shut my eyes and held them shut, to hold back tears. "When did this battle take place?"

"Four days after the Nones of Sextilis."

I drew a breath. "The day Cassandra was buried!"

"So it was. I hadn't realized that."

On the very day Cassandra turned to ashes upon her funeral pyre, the fate of Rome was decided. I thought of all that had transpired and all I had discovered in the time it took the news from Pharsalus to reach Rome. I thought of the women who had shared with me their secrets, none of us knowing that even as we raked over the past and agonized over the future, the battle between the titans was already decided.

"Why did you summon me here, Calpurnia, and bid me come so quickly? I should think that every man out there, shuffling nervously about your forecourt, is more deserving to be kept abreast of the latest news from Caesar."

She laughed. "Let those senators and magistrates grind their teeth and swap rumors and stand on pins awhile longer. I intended to call you here today, anyway, because of a certain other event. Rupa, step forward."

He had been standing in the shadows. When he stepped into sight, the look I saw on his face was closer to chagrin than anything else. He put his hands on my shoulders and gave me a rather stiff embrace.

"So you're alive, after all," I said. "Where have you been all this time?"

He covered one hand with the other. *In hiding.* Who could blame him? Fausta had sent a slave to kill him. When he learned about Cassandra's death, he must have been as baffled as I was, not knowing whom to blame or whom to fear.

"He should have come straight to me, of course," said Calpurnia. "But I suppose he was afraid of me, thinking I might have had something to do with Cassandra's death. But ever since Fausta died, all sorts of rumors have been circulating about her death and her role in the insurrection, including a rumor about her poisoning Cassandra. Rupa heard it and decided to risk coming here to find out the truth. I told him of all your efforts to find his sister's killer, not to mention the care you took to see that she was properly cremated."

Rupa looked in my eyes and embraced me again, less stiffly. At that moment he looked very much like Cassandra.

"He also came here to collect Cassandra's earnings, which I kept in trust for her. It's a considerable sum. But there's a slight problem. It has to do with you, Finder."

"Please explain."

"At some point, Cassandra gave Rupa a letter addressed to me, to be delivered only in the event of her disappearance or death. Rupa can't read, and of course he didn't dare to show the letter to anyone besides me, so he's had no idea what's in the letter until today, when he delivered it to me. I've read it to him and discussed what it means. He's agreed to its terms, but I can't be certain that you will."

"I don't understand. The letter mentions me?"

"Yes. Shall I read it to you?" Without waiting for an answer she produced a scrap of parchment and read aloud:

To Calpurnia, wife of Gaius Julius Caesar:

In recent days, I have found myself thinking a great deal about my death. Were I truly gifted with the power of prophecy, I might almost say that I have experienced a premonition of death. Perhaps I am only suffering a normal measure of trepidation, given the inherent danger of my work for you.

But if you are reading these words, then I must indeed be dead, for my instructions to Rupa are to deliver this letter to you only in the event of my death, or if I should disappear under circumstances such that my death can almost certainly be presumed.

In such an event, this is my desire regarding the disposition of the money I have earned from you and which you are holding for me. Because Rupa himself would be ill-disposed to handle such a large amount of money, I wish for the entire sum to be given to Gordianus, called the Finder, a man who is known to you and to your husband, upon this condition: that he shall take Rupa into his household and shall adopt him as his son. In return for assuming a father's responsibility for Rupa's well-being, Gordianus may dispose of the money as he sees fit. I know he has great need of it. I hope it will come as a boon to him and to his family.

This is the wish of your loyal agent, Cassandra.

Calpurnia put down the letter. "I'm not sure about that last bit—her loyalty, I mean. She did conspire with Fausta to induce Milo to raise arms against the state. One might argue that she was a traitor in the end, and that I would be entirely justified to seize all her assets—including the money I was holding in trust for her. But I ask myself: *What would Caesar do?* And the answer is obvious, for no leader of the Roman state has ever shown as great an inclination to clemency as Caesar. Cassandra cannot be made to suffer any more for her collusion with Fausta; she paid for that mistake with her life. I see no reason why Rupa should also suffer, and I have no wish to take from you, Gordianus, the money that Cassandra wished for you to have. You did me a great favor when you uncovered Fausta's perfidy, and while I suspect you don't wish to be paid for that effort—that would make you my agent, wouldn't it?— I do hope that this audience and its outcome may mark the first step toward a complete reconciliation between you and my husband, as well as those who serve my husband . . . including young Meto."

I stared at her, not sure how to answer. "What is the sum you hold in trust for Cassandra?" I asked.

She named it. The amount so surprised me that I asked her to repeat it.

I looked at Rupa warily. "Do you understand the amount of money that your sister earned?"

He nodded.

"Yet you accept the terms she laid out in her letter? That you should receive none of that money, and instead should become my son by adoption?"

He nodded again and would have embraced me a third time had I not stepped back. I looked at Calpurnia. "Perhaps it would be fairer if Rupa and I were to split the amount," I suggested.

She shrugged. "Once you receive the money from me, Gordianus, you can do with it whatever you wish. But you'll receive it only if you agree to adopt Rupa, as Cassandra requested. You appear to be a bit taken aback by her generosity, but I think she showed great wisdom in making such an arrangement. Rupa is a strong young man, probably an excellent bodyguard, and able to take care of himself in a fight— he certainly got the better of that gladiator Fausta sent to kill him. But in many ways he's not fit to look after himself. Cassandra was the one who always took care of him. Now that she's gone, it was her wish that you should do so. And why not? Haven't you a propensity for taking strays into your house—the two sons you adopted and that pair of rowdy slave boys you acquired from Fulvia? It was also Cassandra's wish that the money she earned should buy you out of the hole you've dug yourself into. I understand your debts are considerable. Even so, given the amount she's left you, there should be a tidy sum left over—enough to look after Rupa and the rest of your family for quite a while."

I thought about this and took a deep breath. I looked over my shoulder at Davus, who had followed the entire exchange in silence. He looked back at me with a furrowed brow, and I realized that I would face no easy task when it came to explaining to Bethesda and Diana how I had come into such a fortune, and why I was coming home with a new mouth to feed.

But why should I worry about explaining myself? Was I not a Roman paterfamilias, the supreme head of my own household, granted by law the power of life and death over everyone in that household? A paterfamilias had no need to justify himself. So tradition dictated, although real life never seemed to adhere very strictly to the model. If my wife or daughter pestered me with uncomfortable questions about Cassandra or Rupa or my sudden windfall or the abrupt vanishing of my debts, I could always fall back on my privileges as paterfamilias and simply refuse to answer them . . . for a while, anyway.

"Do you accept Cassandra's terms?" asked Calpurnia, suddenly impatient for the audience to end.

"Yes."

"Good. I'll have the money delivered to you this afternoon. Take Rupa with you as you go. Stay in the forecourt for a while if you wish to hear the formal announcement." She made a wave of dismissal. Guards appeared from the shadows to see us out.

We lingered for only a few moments in the forecourt before Calpurnia appeared on the steps. Every voice fell silent as all eyes looked to her.

"Citizens, I stand before you with wonderful news. Caesar

has triumphed! There was a great battle in Thessaly, near a place called Pharsalus. . . ."

She repeated the news just as she had given it to me, word for word. When she was done, the forecourt was oddly silent as those present absorbed the enormity of the news. Isauricus and Trebonius were the first to cheer. Others joined them, until the forecourt rang with acclamations for Caesar and cries of "Venus for victory!"

And so I made my way home with not one but two stout young men to act as my bodyguards—and a good thing that was, for the streets of the Palatine were suddenly thronged with people cheering and weeping and kissing one another and madly jumping up and down. Some appeared quietly pleased, some genuinely ecstatic. How many were simply experiencing a rush of emotion at the tremendous release of the tension that had been building in everyone for months? And how many were not happy at all, but were doing their best to laugh and shout and blend in with the rest?

As we slowly made our way through the crowd, I was startled to see, some distance off, a familiar face amid the throng. It was old Volcatius, Pompey's most vociferous partisan among the chin-waggers. His hands were in the air; his head was thrown back, his mouth open. Amid the din I could hear his reedy voice, shouting, "Hurrah for Caesar! Venus for victory! Hurrah for Caesar!"

"We are all Caesarians now," I muttered under my breath.

XX

"What about this?" asked Diana, holding up one of my better garments, a green tunic with a Greek-key border in yellow along the hem.

"Surely I've packed enough clothing already," I said. "The shipmaster charges passengers by the trunk, so we should take only what we need for the journey. It will be cheaper to buy what we need when we get there."

"Mother will like that. A shopping trip!" Diana forced a smile. She was not happy about her mother's trip to Alexandria; she had done all she could to dissuade her. That part of the world was already unsettled and dangerous, she pointed out, and likely to become more so if Pompey had fled there with Caesar chasing after him. Besides that, a sea journey was always dangerous, and autumn was coming; if we stayed in Egypt past the sailing season, we might be stranded there for months, unable to find a ship willing to risk stormy waters. But Bethesda would not relent: to be cured of her malady, she must return to Egypt and bathe in the Nile.

Diana's greatest worry she left unspoken: that she would never see her mother again if the rigors of travel proved too much for her, or if Bethesda's true purpose in returning to Egypt was to die.

"Perhaps—perhaps I *should* come along," she said.

"Absolutely not, Diana! We've already discussed this."

"But—"

"No! You have Aulus to look after—and his little brother or sister, as well. It's unthinkable that a young woman in your condition should take off on such a long and uncertain journey."

"I shouldn't have told you."

"That you're with child? You couldn't have hidden it much longer. You don't know how relieved I was to find out that your morning sickness was due to pregnancy and not something else. No, you will remain in Rome to oversee the household, and Davus will remain by your side. And don't worry— your mother and I will be back in plenty of time to see the birth of our grandchild. Do you think Bethesda would miss that?"

Diana forced another smile and busied herself checking the contents of my trunk. "What's this?" she asked, holding up a sealed bronze urn.

I took it from her and returned it to the trunk. "Ashes," I said.

"Ah. *Her* ashes."

"You can say her name: Cassandra."

"But why are you taking them to Egypt?"

"It was Rupa's idea. Cassandra lived most of her life in Alexandria. He wants to scatter her ashes in the Nile."

"I don't see why *she* should go along on Mother's trip."

"Don't forget that it's *her* legacy that's paying for the trip."

"Ironic, isn't it?" said Diana sharply. "If this trip *does* cure Mother's condition, it shall have been paid for by the woman who—" She saw the look on my face and left the thought unfinished. "I suppose it *is* a good thing that you're taking Rupa with you, since Davus isn't going along to protect you. Rupa will know his way around the city."

"You forget that I lived in Alexandria myself for a while."

"But, Papa, that was years and years ago. Surely it's changed since then."

The Alexandria of my youth was fixed in my memory, encircled by nostalgia as a city is encircled by walls to keep it safe. It seemed unthinkable that it could have changed, but why not? Everything else in the world had changed, and seldom for the better.

Diana clicked her tongue. "But I'm not sure about the advisability of taking Mopsus and Androcles."

"I'm an old man, Diana. I'll need quick feet to run my errands."

"So will I, once my belly begins to grow."

"I suppose I could take only one of the boys with me, and leave you the other. . . ."

"No, it would be unthinkable to separate them. But they're likely to get themselves thrown overboard if they behave on the ship the way they behave in this house. They're such a handful, those two little . . ." Something caught in her throat. She cleared it with a cough and a sniffle and lowered her voice. "A shame you're not taking Hieronymus. He keeps hinting that he'd like to go. Having lived all his life in Massilia, he's eager to see the world."

"At my expense! No, Hieronymus can stay here. Surely he hasn't exhausted all the discoveries that Rome has to offer."

I sat on the bed. Diana sat beside me. She took my hand in hers. "There's something we haven't yet talked about," she said.

"Your mother? I think she truly believes this trip will cure her. You shouldn't worry that—"

"No, not that."

I sighed. "If you wish to finish what you were saying earlier . . . about Cassandra . . ."

Diana shook her head. "No. I think it was the Fates who guided your course, and hers, toward an end that neither of you foresaw."

"What, then?"

She hesitated. "We've talked before about the danger in that part of the world. . . ."

"Surely it's no more dangerous than Rome!"

"Isn't it? Ever since old King Ptolemy died, the Egyptians have been as torn apart as we Romans. Young Ptolemy is at war with his sister—what's she called?"

"I believe her name is Cleopatra. Marc Antony once mentioned to me that he had met her. He said the oddest thing. . . ."

"What was that?"

"He said that she reminded him of Caesar. Imagine that! Cleopatra couldn't have been more than fourteen when Antony met her. She must be about twenty-two now—yes, exactly the same age as you, Diana."

"Wonderful! You shall find yourself in Alexandria with Pompey at his most desperate, a royal civil war going on, and a young female Caesar to contend with—if one can imagine such a creature!"

I laughed. "At least it shouldn't be boring."

"But still—this wasn't what I meant to talk about."

"What then?"

She sighed. "Caesar will be there, too, won't he?"

"Very likely."

"And if Caesar is there . . ."

"Ah, I see where you're going."

"You'll already have so much to deal with—and I don't mean Pompey and Cleopatra and all that. I mean Mother, whether she gets well . . . or not. And the ashes in that urn, and what you'll feel when you scatter them in the Nile. And I know you'll be worried about me and the child I'm carrying, back here in Rome. And on top of all that, if you should happen to confront Meto again . . ."

"Daughter, Daughter! Do you imagine that I haven't thought of all this myself? I've been lying awake at night, pondering this journey and all the places it may lead. But looking ahead serves no purpose. It's as you say: the Fates lead us to unseen ends. So far, on balance, the Fates have been kind to me."

There was a noise at the door. Both of us looked up to see Bethesda. She looked pale and delicate, but in her eyes I saw a steady flame that signaled hope. The journey to Egypt had come to mean everything to her.

"Are you done packing, Husband?"

"Yes."

"Good. We leave at dawn. Diana, if you've finished helping your father, come help me sort my things."

"Of course." Diana rose and followed her mother. In the doorway she paused and looked back. Her eyes glittered with tears. "Can it really be tomorrow that you're leaving, Papa? I suddenly feel like Hieronymus; I envy you! You shall see the Nile, and the pyramids, and the giant Sphinx. . . ."

"And the great library," I said, "and the famous lighthouse at Pharos . . ."

"And perhaps you shall even meet . . ."

We laughed, knowing we shared the same thought without speaking.

"Cleopatra!" I said, finishing her sentence.

"Cleopatra!" she echoed, as if that odd, foreign-sounding name were a code for all that was understood between us, spoken or unspoken.

After she left the room, I rose from the bed and stepped to the trunk. I reached down and picked up the bronze urn. I held it for a long time, feeling the metal's cold rigidity, sensing the heaviness of its contents. Finally I returned the urn to the trunk and slowly, gently closed the lid.

Author's Note

After two novels recounting political maneuverings and military operations at the outset of the Roman Civil War—*Rubicon* and *Last Seen in Massilia*—it was my wish to return to the city of Rome and to see what its beleaguered citizens, especially its women, were up to.

While Caesar and Pompey conducted an overt war in northern Greece, who can doubt that covert operations continued at an equally furious pace back in Rome? We can easily imagine that espionage, bribery, betrayals, profiteering, and all sorts of other skullduggery were rife, but when it comes to eyewitness or even secondhand accounts, our sources for this particular time and place—Rome in the year 48 B.C.—are scattered and obscure.

The challenge to the status quo posed by Marcus Caelius, and its outcome, are recounted in several ancient sources, including Velleius Paterculus, Livy, Cassius Dio, and Caesar's *The Civil War*. Unfortunately, these authors offer contradictory and fragmentary details and do little to establish even an approximate timetable. But the same chronological uncertainty and paucity of detail that constrain the historian offer a certain elasticity to the novelist, of which I have taken considerable advantage.

In trying to make sense of the political milieu and the mood of Rome in 48 B.C., I found myself returning again and again to a book by Jack Lindsay, *Marc Antony: His World and His*

Contemporaries (London: George Routledge & Sons Ltd., 1936). Lindsay offers a far more complex ideological interpretation of the aims of Marcus Caelius than do most historians, who tend to dismiss Caelius as a mere opportunist. For details of the conflict between Pompey and Caesar, T. Rice Holmes's closely argued, exhaustively annotated *The Roman Republic and the Founder of the Empire* (Oxford: The Clarendon Press, 1923) provides a vivid reconstruction. The letters of Cicero also yield much information on the chain of events; I have spent many hours appreciating the labors of Evelyn S. Shuckburgh of Emmannel College, Cambridge, who not only translated but arranged and indexed the entire correspondence in chronological order in *The Letters of Cicero* (London: George Bell and Sons, 1909).

What of Titus Annius Milo and his fate? Did even his old champion Cicero mourn him? Perhaps not. Consider that Titus Annius may have added the "Milo" to his name because he wished to equate himself with the legendary Olympic athlete Milo of Crotona; consider that Cicero probably felt guilty to the end of his days for botching Milo's defense at his trial for murdering Clodius; consider that, in the dying Republic, Milo must have become the epitome of the has-been who wouldn't stay gone; and then read the following rather catty passage by Cicero in his treatise "On Old Age," written in 44 B.C., four years after Milo's death. This is Michael Grant's translation, from Cicero's *Selected Works* (Penguin Books, 1960):

> A man should use what he has, and in all doings accommodate himself to his strength. There is a story about Milo of Crotona, in his later years, watching the athletes train on the race-course. With tears in his eyes he looked at his own muscles, and said a pitiable thing: "And these are now dead." But you are the one who is now dead, not they, you stupid fellow, because your fame never came from yourself, it came from brute physical force. . . . Milo is said to have walked from end to end of the race-course at Olympia with an ox on his back; well, which would you prefer to be given, Milo's physical

vigour, or the intellectual might of [Milo's friend] Pythagoras? In short, enjoy the blessing of strength while you have it, and have no regrets when it has gone . . . nature has one path only, and you cannot travel along it more than once.

Was this Cicero's way of declaring to the world that *his* Milo had no one to blame but himself?

What of the women of Rome who populate these pages? Terentia, Tullia, Fabia, Fulvia, Sempronia, Antonia, Cytheris, Fausta, Clodia, and Calpurnia all existed. Gordianus has encountered some of them previously in the *Roma Sub Rosa* series—Clodia in *The Venus Throw* and *A Murder on the Appian Way*; Fulvia, Sempronia, and Fausta in *A Murder on the Appian Way*; and Fabia in the eponymous short story in *The House of the Vestals*.

Terentia's marriage to Cicero ended when he divorced her and married a much younger woman, probably late in 46 B.C. At about the same time, Tullia and Dolabella also divorced. Tullia's death the next year caused her father much grief, but according to Pliny, Terentia went on to reach the remarkable age of 103.

Probably Fulvia made the greatest impact on history, especially after her marriage to Marc Antony in 47 B.C., following Antony's divorce from Antonia; Antony even gave up Cytheris for her. But neither Fulvia nor any of these other women speaks to us across the ages in her own voice. We have letters written by Pompey and Antony and Caelius, we have whole books by Caesar and Cicero, but for these women we have only secondhand sources, and mostly hostile sources at that. (Unable to account for Fulvia's ruthlessness and ambition, Velleius Paterculus called her "a woman only on account of her gender.")

As remarkable as these women must have been, no ancient historian saw fit to leave us a biography of any of them; to write the life story of a woman was beyond Plutarch's imagination. The reader who wishes to know more about them will find only scattered crumbs, not the rich banquet afforded to anyone with an appetite for Pompey, Caesar, or any number of other men of antiquity. For the modern historian working from such sources, the task of bringing these women to life is problematic to the point of being insurmountable; so it seems fitting that they should find a prominent place in the *Roma Sub Rosa,* a secret history of Rome, or a history of Rome's secrets, as seen through the eyes of Gordianus.

Thanks are due to my editor at St. Martin's Press, Keith Kahla, for his attentiveness and patience; to my agent, Alan Nevins, for keeping me too busy to get into any trouble; to Penni Kimmel and Rick Solomon for their comments on the first draft; and to my good neighbors at the Berkeley Repertory Theatre, whose splendid production in the spring of 2001 of the complete *Oresteia* by Aeschylus inspired the creation of Gordianus's Cassandra.